SPIRAL

Roderick Gordon

From The Chicken House

OK. This is really quite frightening. When I got the manuscript I wasn't sure *Tunnels* fans were ready for the rather gut-churning secret of the Styx. But when Rod started laughing in, frankly, rather a deranged way, I knew he was committed to delivering the most thrilling book yet in a truly awesome series. Just watch out, that's all I'm saying.

Barry Cunningham
Publisher

SPIRAL

Roderick Gordon

BOOK FIVE
OF
THE TUNNELS SERIES

Chicken House

2 Palmer Street, Frome, Somerset BA11 1DS

Text © Roderick Gordon 2011
www.tunnelsthebook.com
www.roderickgordon.com
Cover illustration © David Wyatt
Inside illustrations: Humvee, Pylons, Chinook, Geiger Counter, Lizard Boy,
Thermonuclear Device, Booster Rocket, chapter headers and paragraph
spacer © Roderick Gordon; Drake and Eddie, Rebecca Twins and Captain Franz,
Sweeney, BT Tower and Old Styx © Kirill Barybin.

First published in Great Britain in 2011
The Chicken House
2 Palmer Street
Frome, Somerset BA11 1DS
United Kingdom
www.doublecluck.com

Cover design by Steve Wells
Designed and typeset by Dorchester Typesetting Ltd
Printed in the UK by CPI Bookmarque, Croydon, CR0 4TD

The paper used in this Chicken House book is made from wood
grown in sustainable forests.

1 3 5 7 9 10 8 6 4 2

British Library Cataloguing in Publication data available

ISBN 978-1-906427-84-9

The freezing fog in mid-November
Downhill all the way, downhill all the way
How I wish the roads were straighter
Let's panic later, let's panic later

Let's Panic Later, by Wire, from *154,* 1979.

There is a point at which there is no point at which.

The Book of Proliferation, fifteenth century.
Translated from the original Romanian.

PART ONE

The Phase

Chapter One

*B*oom.

Apart from the noise and the gut-wrenching fear of physical injury, the most terrifying thing about an explosion is the millisecond in which the whole world fractures. It's as though the very fabric of time and space has been split asunder, and you're falling through it with no idea what lies on the other side.

When Colonel Bismarck came to, he was spreadeagled on a marble floor. For a moment he was unable to move, as if his body forbade it. As if it knew better than he did.

Although there was utter silence, the Colonel didn't question it. He felt no alarm, no urgency. He was staring up at the shattered ceiling where snowy chunks of plaster rocked gently. He became captivated by their movement – backwards and forwards, forwards and backwards – as if they were caught in a breeze. He was even more bewitched by the spectacle as some of the pieces broke loose, falling in slow motion to the floor around him.

His hearing began to return.

He made out a sound that reminded him of woodpeckers.

'*Vater,*' he said, recalling the hunting trips in the jungle around New Germania with his father. Sometimes they'd be gone for as much as a week, sleeping in a tent and shooting game together.

It was a comforting memory. Lying in amongst the blast debris the Colonel sighed, as if he didn't have a care in the world. He heard the rattling sound again, still so remote. He didn't associate it with the rapid fire of automatic weapons.

Then the Royal Mint building was rocked by a second blast. The Colonel shut his eyes at the blinding flash of light, every bit as bright as the sun in his world at the centre of the Earth.

The percussive wave swept brutally over him, sucking the air from his lungs.

'*Was ist . . . ?*' the Colonel gasped, still on his back as shards of glass flew across the room like driving sleet and tinkled on the polished marble around him.

He knew then that something was wrong. Not only was everything quickly becoming hazed by a choking black smoke, but his mind seemed to be full of it too.

'*Wie komme ich hierher?*' he said, groping for comprehension.

How he'd come to be there he had absolutely no idea. The last memory that felt substantial enough to rely on was of being ambushed in New Germania. He remembered being captured by the Styx, but after that – and he found this strange – he could only remember purple light. No, purple *lights*, many of them, burning with such intensity that his memories were dim by comparison.

He vaguely recalled the long journey to the outer crust, and then not much else until he found himself in a lorry with a squad of his New Germanian troops. They'd been taken to a large building – a factory. And associated with this factory, and still in the forefront of his mind, was something he'd had to do. A task so vitally important that it overrode all other considerations, even his own survival.

But, right now, he couldn't put his finger on what this task had been. And he didn't have time to dwell on it further as a burst of gunfire from close by galvanised him into action. He sat up, wincing from the sharp pain in his head where it had struck the floor. Coughing and choking as the acrid smoke caught in his throat, he knew his first priority was to get himself to cover.

He crawled through a doorway where the smoke was less dense and found that he was in an office, with a high ceiling and a desk with a vase of flowers on it. Kicking the door shut, he lay behind it while he checked himself over. His hair was sodden from an injury at the back of his head, but he couldn't tell how serious it was – the skin around it was numb and he knew from experience that head wounds always bled profusely. He ran his hands over the rest of his body, finding no further injuries. He wasn't in uniform but wearing a coat and civilian clothes, none of which he recognised. But at least he had his military-issue belt around his waist, and his pistol was still in its holster. He took it out, its weight reassuring in his hand. Something he knew. He waited, listening for sounds on the other side of the door.

He didn't have to wait for long. After a brief lull, he caught English voices and the sound of boots crunching on debris in the hallway where he'd been. Someone shouldered the door of the room open and stormed in. The man was dressed in black, with POLICE emblazoned across his chest. He wore a gas mask and helmet, and was armed with an automatic weapon the likes of which Colonel Bismarck had never seen before.

Catching the policeman by surprise, the Colonel wrapped an arm around his neck and rendered him unconscious. While the man's radio buzzed, the Colonel quickly removed his uniform and dressed himself in it. As he slipped on the gas mask, he realised that even more blood had seeped from his head injury, but he couldn't worry about that now.

He familiarised himself with the assault rifle, which he found was pretty straightforward. Then he emerged from the office and took a couple of steps into the black smoke, only to come face to face with another policeman dressed in identical siege gear. As their gaze met through the lenses of their masks, the other man gave a hand signal, but the Colonel didn't know how he was meant to respond. A question formed in the other man's eyes. Thinking that his disguise had been blown, the Colonel began to raise the H&K assault rifle in his hands.

He was saved by another explosion that ripped through the hallway and swiped him off his feet. In a daze, the Colonel picked himself up and staggered through the main entrance where the doors hung crookedly on broken hinges. Almost losing his balance as he missed the step, he found himself reeling on the pavement outside the building.

He stopped dead.

He was confronted by a cordon of armed men – too many for him to take on. They were all behind discarded vehicles or riot shields, their laser sights clustered on him.

He wasn't prepared for what happened next. With his head still spinning and his senses dulled, he didn't react when his rifle was snatched from his grip. At the same time, he was hoisted off his feet by two policemen and carried away in double-quick time.

'It's all right, old mate, don't you worry. We'll get you some help,' the man on his left told him sympathetically. The second policeman said something, but the Colonel didn't take it in.

His escorts removed his helmet and gas mask. 'You're not one of our guys,' the policeman said, as he saw the Colonel's bloodied face.

'Must be from E Team – a country boy,' the other said. But the Colonel wasn't listening. Not twenty feet away a body was stretched out in the gutter. Around it a circle of policemen laughed and joked as one of them nudged it with his toecap. The Colonel recognised the dead man instantly. It was a New Germanian from his own regiment. He knew the soldier and his wife well – they'd recently had a daughter born to them. The Colonel tried to pull against the two policemen supporting him, but it was taken as a show of anger.

'Yeah – the rest of them'll be bagged and tagged within the hour,' the largest of the two policemen promised in a growl. 'Whoever these bastards are, we've already slotted four of 'em.'

As the Colonel continued to try to free himself, the other policeman spoke, his words staccato as if he was about to explode with fury. 'Take it easy, officer. Leave it to us to finish the job.'

The Colonel grunted a 'Yes', realising he had to play along if he didn't want to be identified as one of the protagonists. He allowed the two policemen to help him to the end of Threadneedle Street and then into a side road where ambulances were waiting.

'See to him, will you? He got caught up in the last explosion,' one of the policemen ordered a medic. They left him there and sped back to the Bank of England.

In the ambulance the medic began to examine the Colonel. 'That's a very fine moustache,' he told him. From the way his hands were shaking, the young medic had clearly never seen action like this before. He cleaned the wound on the Colonel's head and was putting the finishing touches to a field dressing when shouts came from the top of the street. Several new casualties were being carried in on stretchers. The medic went to their aid, giving the Colonel the opportunity he'd been looking for. Although he was still a little groggy, he eased himself down from the back of the ambulance and stole away.

With so many uniformed personnel flooding the area – both police and increasing numbers of military – no one took any notice of the Colonel. Sticking to the back streets, he only stopped when an entrance at the rear of one of the large office buildings caught his eye. Beyond a pair of open doors, he could see a ramp leading down to an underground car park. The Colonel descended into it, and was trying the vehicles to find one that was unlocked when a man wearing a pinstripe suit appeared. The man went straight to a large four-by-four, and just as he was stowing two briefcases in its boot the Colonel knocked him out cold. Swapping the police jacket for the unconscious man's, the Colonel then heaved him in beside his briefcases and slammed the boot shut.

Although he had only driven left-hand-drive cars before, the Colonel had no difficulty in manoeuvring the vehicle up the ramp and through the streets. As he joined a line of traffic waiting to get away from the trouble in the City, he rummaged through the pockets of the man's jacket. He came across a wallet from which he extracted the credit cards, flipping them onto the passenger seat as he examined them. Then he found a driving licence with what he assumed was the man's home address on it, and began to scan the road signs around him. Although he had no idea how he was going to find his way to the man's home, now he was out of immediate danger he could take his time.

He touched a control on the console beside his seat, and the blue and white BMW emblem flashed on a small display in the dash. He smiled. Within a few clicks he'd navigated to the onboard GPS system. He immediately typed in the post-code from the driving licence. As an authoritative female voice began to reel off directions, the Colonel nodded, allowing himself an even broader smile.

'*Bayerische Motoren Werke,*' he exhaled, running his hands appreciatively around the luxurious leather rim of the steering wheel. '*Ausgezeichnet.*' The Colonel knew this marque well because his father had flown aircraft manufactured by them in the Great War.

Aspects of this outer world that the Colonel now found himself in were so familiar he could almost pretend he was still in New Germania. But other aspects would take some getting used to. For starters, the gravity was so strong here that every movement was an effort, as if his limbs were weighed down with lead.

And the sun . . .

He peered through the tinted windscreen, marvelling at the fiery globe hanging in the heavens, which was smaller and weaker than the ever-burning and omnipresent one he'd known all his life. Even now it wasn't directly overhead, and it was a revelation to him that it would dip below the horizon with the onset of night, the onset of *darkness*.

And the people in the streets. People of all races. He watched as an elderly black man tripped and took a bad fall.

A white woman instantly went to help him.

Not out of choice, but because of its origins, New Germania had been monoracial, and Colonel Bismarck knew only too well what atrocities had gone on in wartime Germany. As he surveyed the mix of people making the exodus from the City, he smiled. He truly was in an enlightened civilisation.

Continue for three hundred metres to Old Street roundabout, then take the second exit, the GPS dictated mechanically.

The Colonel might have been plucked from his motherland by the Styx and thrust into this new and alien environment, but he wasn't about to throw in the towel. He was a resourceful man, a survivor.

And besides, he had a score to settle.

Chapter Two

'Dammit!' A low voice seeped through the treacly gloom inside the small crofter's cottage on Parry's estate. If anybody had been there to witness the speed at which the man crossed to the cobwebbed window, they would have doubted their eyes. As he hooked a ragged curtain aside, the rain-filtered light fell on his face – the face of a man in his sixties.

But it wasn't any normal face; the skin was slightly raised in a series of concentric circles radiating out from each of his eyes. And there was a grid of lines across his forehead that extended down his temples and under his ears. It was as if worms had threaded through his flesh and left their tracks behind.

'Who in the blazes is that?' the man said, grimacing as he pressed the flaps of his cap hard against his ears, the metal-foil lining inside them crackling as he did so. Repeating the question, he backed slowly away from the window.

'Stop!' rasped Chester, as Will tore towards the gate across the track in front of them.

Will pulled up and consulted his digital watch, unaware of

the discomfort the innocuous electronic device was causing the man in the darkness. 'Why? We've only been running for about thirty minutes,' he told Chester. It was only then that he caught sight of the moss-covered roof of the crofter's cottage through the trees, but he made no comment about it to his friend.

'Half an hour?' Chester puffed, blinking as the drizzle fell into his eyes.

'Yep. Why don't we see where this leads?' Will said, glancing along the track. 'Or maybe you've had enough? We could call it a day and go back to the house,' he offered.

'No way. Not me,' Chester said with some indignation. He pointed at the sign on the gate. 'But this says, *Danger – Keep Out.*'

'Danger? When did that ever stop us?' Will said, immediately climbing over the gate. Chester followed him reluctantly.

'I'm just getting my second wind,' he lied.

'Okay then, race you over to that wood,' Will challenged, putting on a turn of speed as the rain grew even heavier.

Chester struggled to keep up with his friend in the downpour. 'I thought we *were* racing,' he grumbled.

Drake had been away for almost a month and in his absence Parry had been putting the boys through their paces, sending them off on runs and teaching them to use the weights in his antiquated gym in the basement. Parry's idea of physical training harked back to his army days and he pushed them hard, but they didn't complain because they wouldn't have dared refuse the old man, and because it filled the hours as they hid from the Styx.

Their feet slipping in the mud, they continued along the track until Chester gasped, 'Time out. Weather stops play!'

They took refuge under an old elm tree, its branches affording them some protection from the rain.

'We look like a couple of escaped convicts in these,' Will chuckled as he examined the thick grey tracksuits that Parry had produced for them.

'Too right,' Chester agreed. 'And these trainers are like something from the Stone Age.' He stamped his feet to try to remove the mud from his heavy black plimsolls, then looked around at the leaves on the trees, which were beginning to show the first signs of autumn. 'Funny – all the time I was underground I didn't have the foggiest idea where I was. But now I'm Topsoil again, I'm just as much in the dark.'

'Well . . .' Will began thoughtfully, 'the rainfall seems to be above average here – maybe because the wind is coming in over water, or even the sea.' He wiped the moisture from his face with a sleeve. 'Yes, I think we might be close to the coast. Could be Wales or Scotland.'

Chester was impressed. 'Really? You can tell that?'

Will laughed. 'No,' he admitted.

'You dipstick,' Chester said.

'Maybe, but I'm a faster dipstick than you,' Will replied, breaking into a run again.

'We'll see about that!' Chester shouted at Will's back. He was hard on Will's heels as they thundered around a bend in the muddy path, only to come face to face with a man holding a shotgun.

'Good afternoon,' the man said as Will slid to an abrupt halt, Chester bumping into him. The shotgun was broken over the man's arm – the correct way to carry the weapon when not in use – so neither of the boys felt any particular alarm. To their eyes, the man looked ancient, his wrinkled skin burnt a dark brown by the sun, and his sparse hair almost as white as Will's.

'You must be the Commander's guests?' the man said. He was referring to Drake's father, and Will realised right away that this had to be Old Wilkie, the groundsman employed on the estate.

Will nodded slowly, not quite sure how he should respond. 'And you must be . . . er . . . Mr Wilkie?'

'That's the one, but please call me Old Wilkie. Everyone does,' the man said. 'And this is my granddaughter, Stephanie.'

'Steph,' a girl's voice corrected him as she stepped into view. She was around fifteen or sixteen, and had striking red hair and a pale complexion dusted with freckles. She looked both boys up and down with a somewhat disdainful glance, but said nothing more, adjusting the brace of dead pheasants hanging from her arm as if they were more interesting to her.

Old Wilkie was regarding the girl with a look of pride. 'Stephanie comes to stay for the odd weekend. She goes to school at Benenden, you know. The Commander is a real gentleman – he's always taken care of the school fees—'

'Gramps!' Stephanie said sharply, spinning around on her slim legs and strolling away in the opposite direction.

Old Wilkie leant towards the boys conspiratorially. 'Now she's a teenager, she says life in the country is dull, and just wants to be in London, shopping and seeing her friends. She wasn't always that way – she used to love it here when she was little. Anyway, by all accounts, London and the south are in such a mess she's better off up here until it all blows—'

Out of sight, Stephanie shouted, 'Gramps, you coming or what?'

Old Wilkie straightened up. 'Are you and the rest of the party staying with the Commander for long?'

Will and Chester exchanged glances. Drake had specifically warned them not to give the man any information about themselves.

'We're not sure yet,' Will replied.

'Well, if you're serious about doing some training – commando style – you might be interested in the Tree Walk,' Old Wilkie said.

'What's that?' Will asked.

'Starts there.' Old Wilkie pointed at a ladder on a metal frame built around the trunk of a massive pine, then raised his finger to the branches up above, where the boys could see something running between the trees.

'It's an assault course I built for the Commander way back,' Old Wilkie said. '10 Para down in Aldershot copied my idea, but mine's bigger and better. I keep it in working order even though the Commander hasn't used it in years.' Old Wilkie smiled at the boys. 'Stephanie can get around it like greased lightning. You should challenge her – see if you can beat her time.'

'Sounds fun,' Will said.

'Yes, we should do that,' Chester chimed in unconvincingly, as his eyes followed the metal track, which zigzagged through the tree canopies.

'Well, gentlemen, I'd better be getting on. I hope that we come across each other again,' Old Wilkie said. He began to whistle to himself as he strolled off after Stephanie.

'You're not getting me up there,' Chester said, then smiled. 'Not unless Steph wants a race. She's really nice, isn't she?' He pursed his lips as he thought of something. 'Have to say I'm not too keen on redheads after what Martha did to me, but I'm prepared to make exceptions.' He had a dreamy look on his face.

'So you like her more than Elliott?' Will teased.

'I . . . er . . .' Chester stalled in embarrassment.

Will was looking at his friend with surprise. He hadn't meant the comment to be taken seriously.

'Well, it's not as if we see much of Elliott these days, is it?' Chester blustered. 'She's always in her room, taking endless baths and doing her nails and all that girl stuff.'

Will nodded. 'She told me her back was hurting her . . . that her shoulders ached all the time.'

'Maybe it's that, then, and she's just under the weather,' Chester surmised. 'But she's not at all like she used to be. It's like she's gone soft or something.'

'True,' Will agreed. 'Since we've been here she's changed so much. I'm really quite worried about her.'

As the rain continued to hammer down and they jogged the last mile to the house, Will and Chester were joined by Bartleby and Colly, the two huge Hunters.

'Got ourselves a big cat escort,' Chester laughed as the animals positioned themselves either side of him and Will. Their heads held high, the Hunters were loping along with steady, easy strides, as if showing off that the pace was nothing to them. In response Will and Chester sped up, but the Hunters did likewise.

'We'll never beat them,' Will chuckled, out of breath, as the four of them reached the house. They thundered up the steps of the main entrance and crashed through the doors into the hall. Parry appeared almost immediately.

'Shoes off, boys, eh . . .' he urged them, seeing that they had already tracked mud across the black and white marble floor. 'And look at the state of those two mangy animals.' He glowered at the cats, their bald skin streaked with dirt. 'They're polishing off all the grouse on the estate. Soon there won't be a single blessed bird left,' Parry added resentfully. The tough old man with his wayward hair and shaggy beard was wearing a kitchen apron over his tweed suit trousers, and in his hand was a sheaf of papers – it was a print-out of some kind. 'You've both been gone longer than I expected,' he noted, glancing at the grandfather clock.

The boys stood there mutely, wondering if they should say something about the encounter with Old Wilkie and his granddaughter. But they didn't and Parry spoke again, 'Well, I'm pleased you're taking your training seriously. I expect you could do with some food now?'

Both Will and Chester nodded eagerly.

'Thought so. I've left some soup on the hob and there's a fresh loaf to go with it. Sorry there isn't more, but I'm rather busy at the moment. There's something going on.'

Opening the door to his study, Parry hurried inside. But before the door slammed shut, the boys caught their first glimpse of the interior.

'Was that your dad in there?' Will asked. Before the door closed, the boys had spotted Mr Rawls standing over what appeared to be an old-fashioned printer from the loud clattering it was making.

'Yes, I saw him too. I thought the study was off limits to all of us,' Chester replied. He shrugged, then knelt down to remove his plimsolls. 'Come to think of it, I haven't seen much of Dad lately – maybe he's been in there all the time?'

'And I wonder what Parry was talking about. Do you think it's you-know-who up to their tricks again?' Will posed. It had been several months since the attack on the financial district in the City of London and the explosions in the West End, but then the Styx seemed not to have continued with their offensive against Topsoilers.

'If there's anything going on, it'll be on the news. Let's grab our food and eat it in front of the TV,' Chester suggested.

'Sounds like a plan,' Will said.

Due to the security precautions there were long queues to get into the special performance of *La Bohème* at the Palais Garnier in the 9th arrondissement of Paris. The additional precautions had been laid on because the French President and his wife were attending that night.

As the gendarme used handheld scanners to check each member of the audience before they entered the foyer, a woman stood patiently in line.

'*Bonsoir, Madame*,' a gendarme said as her turn came, and she handed him her clutch bag to inspect.

'*Bonsoir*,' she replied, while his partner ran the scanner over the full length of her body, back and front.

'*Anglaise*,' the gendarme observed casually as he made sure her ticket was valid. 'I 'ope you enjoy the performance.'

'Thank you,' Jenny replied, then the gendarme waved her through. As she went in search of her seat, she walked like someone who was wading through thick fog and couldn't see the ground in front of them. She eventually found her place and sat there quietly, waiting for the curtain to go up.

The woman, Jenny Grainger, had raised no red flags as she

passed through the scanner and the security checks at St Pancras International before boarding the Eurostar to Paris. And neither did she do anything to arouse suspicion during the rest of the journey, although her face was drawn and perhaps a little jaundiced, and most of the time she seemed to stare straight ahead with unblinking eyes. But if anyone had paid her any attention, they would most likely have assumed that she was suffering from fatigue.

But now in the Palais Garnier, as everyone rose to their feet while the French President and his attractive wife were shown to their seats, Jenny began to fidget with her bag. The lights dimmed and the curtain was raised.

In the seat next to her, Jenny's neighbour became annoyed as she continued to fidget, whispering frantically to herself. As the man watched her more closely, he saw that she appeared to be in some difficulty. She had her hand on her abdomen and was pressing it hard. As he was a doctor, it was natural for him to enquire if she needed help. But when he spoke to her, she didn't reply, her whispered ramblings only becoming louder.

Jenny suddenly jumped to her feet. Disturbing everyone in the row, she made her way hastily to the central aisle. However, instead of turning right in the direction of the exit, she dropped her clutch bag and began to run towards the stage. Towards the French President.

She never reached him, but the explosion killed over twenty members of the audience.

A number of witnesses stated that one second she'd been there, and the next there'd been a flash of blinding light and a massive bang. But while some thought she'd tripped on the carpet, others swore that a member of the President's staff had intercepted her. This couldn't be substantiated because the man had been killed outright. Whatever had stopped her, Jenny never reached her target, and the President and the First Lady were rushed out of the theatre by their protection officers.

Although the records showed that Jenny had no known terrorist affiliations or political interests, other than having once been a member of the Young Conservatives, it was assumed she'd somehow smuggled a device into the theatre. But this conflicted with all the CCTV and forensic evidence, which pointed to something extremely bizarre.

It appeared that the explosion had come from within her, and the detailed analytical work supported this because much of her body mass was missing from the blast scene.

The theory quickly emerged that Jenny's internal organs had been removed to make room for a two-part explosive, which, when mixed, became a potent weapon.

This very ordinary housewife from London, who would most likely have died anyway within a few days from the horrific mutilation of her body, had been a walking bomb.

On his way home after work, the man emerged from the Tube station and turned right into Camden High Street. With his glasses and neat appearance, he had a studious air about him as he surveyed the disparate groups of people in the area.

In the last decade, the market at Camden Lock had become a popular destination for black-clad teenagers who hung around the various boutiques and covered markets. But in amongst them, even at this hour in the evening, there was still a smattering of tourists hoping to catch the last boat tour down to Little Venice, or to see the sequence of working locks on the canal itself.

In his sober suit, the man was rather at odds with the meretricious displays in the shop windows of brightly coloured boots, and leather belts with large brass buckles of screaming skulls or crossed bullets.

He came to a sudden stop just before the bridge over the canal, then stepped back from the edge of the pavement to allow a phalanx of Australian tourists to pass. Taking a mobile phone from his jacket, the man appeared to start speaking on it, chuckling as he did so.

'Call that a disguise?' he said. 'You're far too old to pull off the goth look.'

Several feet away, in a shadowy bay between two buildings, Drake laughed. 'Maybe, but you know they're called emos these days. Anyway I'm still a big fan of The Cure,' he said.

Drake pulled further back into the shadows, pressing himself against the pitted Victorian brickwork. Decked out in a loose-fitting black combat jacket and trousers, he had a pair of Doc Martens on his feet. But this wasn't what the man had found so amusing; Drake had completely shaved his head, and sported a moustache and goatee. He'd topped this off with a pair of small round sunglasses, the lenses mirrored.

'Thought you might be in touch,' the man said, as his expression became serious. 'I followed up on the three Dominion specimens we lodged—'

'But they've vanished from the pathogen banks,' Drake interrupted. 'And there'll be no trace of them on the main database any more.'

'How . . . ?' the man exclaimed. 'How do you know that?' He began to turn towards Drake.

'No!' Drake warned. 'They might be watching.'

The man turned towards the road again, nodding as if he was agreeing with the person on the other end of his phone conversation.

'And that's why I badly need your help,' Drake went on. 'I need you, Charlie, my favourite immunologist, to cook up some more Dominion vaccine for me, then I'll figure out another way to distribute it. And I've got some other stuff I want you to look at for me.'

'Your *favourite* immunologist?' Charlie repeated with mock indignation. 'Bet I'm the *only* immunologist you can call on, and certainly the only one stupid enough to risk their life for you.' Taking a breath, he asked, 'So how do we go about it, this time?'

'When you get home, you'll find a package hidden behind your bin – I've left some more blood samples in it, and also some viral specimens I grabbed from the Colony.' Drake paused as a woman passed Charlie on the pavement, then he resumed. 'There's a really nasty strain in there – a killer – so watch how you handle it.'

'We treat every pathogen as if it's the Great Plague,' Charlie said.

'That's uncannily near the truth,' Drake whispered, his voice grim. 'Now you'd better not hang around here any longer. I'll swing by your place in a few days.'

'Okay,' Charlie said, pretending to press the button to end the nonexistent conversation before he went on his way again. After a moment, Drake stepped out behind two aged rocka-billies, schlepping along in their suede shoes and with large quiffs of hair dyed an unfeasibly black black. He kept behind them as they headed towards Camden Tube station, where numerous police vans abruptly pulled up.

London Transport employees were ushering people out of the station and the trellis gates were pulled across its entrances. More than a dozen police in full riot gear had disembarked from their vehicles with some urgency, only to stand around and look rather confused as to what they were doing there. One was tapping his baton on his riot shield as an announcement came over the Tannoy that the Tube station was closed so a suspicious package could be investigated.

Drake blended into the crowd collecting outside the station, and listened to the resentful comments of the commuters. This type of occurrence had become increasingly commonplace in London following the first wave of attacks by the Styx or, more accurately, their Darklit New Germanians.

In the months after the bombings in the City and the West End, the country – already in a precarious financial position – had been tipped into a bleak and spiralling recession. The assassination of the head of the Bank of England had rattled people badly. And while these outbreaks of terrorism by unidentified perpetrators seemed to have petered out, the general unrest continued. The populace had called for a change of government, and an early election had been held. The resulting hung parliament led to a power-sharing arrangement, and a climate of indecision and confusion in which industrial action was rife.

Ideal conditions for the Styx as they forged ahead with their plans. As Drake knew only too well.

'Move along now, people,' a policeman directed the crowd. 'Station's closed. You'll have to take alternative forms of transport.'

'What d'y'mean?' one of the rockabillies demanded.

'Y'mean take the bus? Did y'forget they're all on strike again this week?'

As people in the crowd began to shout in agreement and surge forward, Drake decided he'd better extricate himself before it got out of hand. He strolled casually away. Following the attacks in the City he was a wanted man – the Styx had made sure of that. And although he was confident his disguise would help him to avoid light scrutiny, the police might begin to make arbitrary arrests to disperse the mob, and he didn't want to tempt fate. Not while he had so much to do.

Chester woke up earlier than normal the next morning, racked by cramp in his leg.

'I've overdone it,' he moaned to himself, massaging his calf and remembering how far he and Will had run the day before. All of a sudden he stopped kneading the locked-up muscle and stared into the middle distance. 'Growing pains,' he said, recalling what his mother would say when his aching legs made him shout with pain in the middle of the night. Mrs Rawls would rush to his room and sit beside him on the bed, talking to him in her soothing voice until the pains had subsided. They never seemed to be so bad with her there, and now he had no idea where she was, or even if she was still alive. He tried not to think about what the Styx might have done with her, because that felt worse than any physical pain. He still harboured the hope that she was safe and hiding out somewhere.

Once he was dressed, Chester left his bedroom and went along the hall, taking long paces in an effort to loosen up his legs. He rapped twice on Will's door as he passed, to let his friend know he was up, but didn't wait for a response. Downstairs there was no sign that anyone else had surfaced yet, and as usual the door to Parry's study was firmly shut. Chester lingered outside it for a moment; for once the printer was silent, and he couldn't hear any other sounds from inside. He pushed open the door into the drawing room and entered.

The air was warm from the fire in the hearth, in front of which, sitting cross-legged on a tartan travelling rug, was Mrs Burrows.

Her eyes were closed and her face blank, and although she must have heard Chester come in, she said nothing. The boy didn't know what to do; should he announce himself and risk disturbing her, or should he simply slip out of the room and leave her to it?

A thump behind him made him start as Will jumped down the last flight of stairs.

'You're up early,' he announced to Chester in a loud voice. 'Bet you're—'

He trailed off as Chester pressed a finger to his lips and then pointed at Mrs Burrows.

'It's all right,' Will said. 'She's just meditating. She does it every morning.'

'Can she hear us?' Chester asked, still speaking softly.

Will shrugged. 'I think so, although she can choose to stay in a trance if she wants.'

Although Mrs Burrows' eyes remained shut and she was so still that she seemed not even to be breathing, her jaw suddenly dropped open. What appeared to be freezing cold air seeped from her mouth. Condensation hung before her expressionless face for an instant, despite the raised temperature in the room.

'How does she do that?' Chester whispered.

'Dunno,' Will replied distantly, more preoccupied with the rumbling sounds coming from his stomach. He glanced over his shoulder into the hallway. 'I can't smell anything cooking in the kitchen. I'm starving. I could murder one of Parry's fry-ups.'

Chester shook his head dourly. 'Think we're out of luck on that front. He's too busy to cook. Something's definitely going on.'

'Not according to the news,' Will said. They'd searched the channels the evening before and drawn a blank. He gestured at the blackboard in the corner of the drawing room. 'Maybe we won't be having *commando school* today, either.'

In addition to encouraging the boys to get fit, Parry had also done his best to keep their minds active by giving them lectures every morning. To do this, he drew on what he knew best, so somewhat bizarrely they were treated to lessons on map reading, military tactics and combat fieldcraft.

'Choke points and interlocking fields of fire,' Chester said, recalling what Parry had told them about ambush theory.

'My favourite was combat driving techniques.' Will smiled. 'Now that was something they didn't teach at our school back in Highfield.'

Chester became thoughtful for a moment. 'Just think how many lessons we've missed in the last year. It all seems like a lifetime ago. I hardly remember anything about it . . . except putting that little squit Speed in his place.'

'I'm still amazed that Parry trusted us with his beloved Land Rover,' Will continued, not really listening to his friend. 'I really thought it was going to tip over when I powered down those slopes.'

Chester came back to the present with a chuckle. 'Yeah.

26

And he wasn't too happy when I took the wing mirror off on a tree, was he?'

'Not particularly,' Parry declared from the doorway. Chester looked sheepish as the old man continued, 'Afraid you'll have to look after yourselves this morning, lads. I've been up all night, monitoring the situation.'

'So it is the Styx?' Will asked.

'It has all their hallmarks. If I'm right, they've just entered the second phase of their initiative.' Parry frowned. 'Still can't quite figure out why there was a two-month hiatus after they stoked things up in the City with those full-frontal attacks.'

'But is this latest stuff serious?' Will asked.

Parry nodded. 'And damnably clever.'

The boys exchanged glances, waiting for Parry to elaborate, but he was staring absently at the fire. He appeared to be exhausted, leaning with both hands on his walking stick.

'Is Drake dealing with it?' Will finally said, hoping this might elicit some further information.

'No, he's gone dark.'

'Gone dark?' Will asked.

'He's operating on his own, probably in London. I've left messages for him to come back here if he ever deigns to listen to them,' Parry replied, beginning to turn from the doorway.

'And my dad – is he helping you now?' Chester enquired hesitantly.

'I'll give a briefing later on – when I know more,' Parry mumbled as he crossed the hall to his study.

Chapter Three

'Does anyone actually *live* in a grot hole like this?' After the car left the motorway, Rebecca One had sat up and begun to take notice of the succession of sprawling commercial areas they were driving through at some speed. 'Even the name of the place sounds ugly. *Slough. Sluff. Sloff.* Who thought of that?' She was thrown to the side as the car took a corner. 'Oh, look, yet another roundabout. What a drag.'

Rebecca Two didn't reply. She was peering through the tinted car window beside her, lost in thought as the streetlights strobed her face.

Irritated by the lack of response from her sister, Rebecca One gave a small snort. She began to scrape her sharp little nails on the stretch of seat between them, marking the luxurious hide. 'This crush of yours is becoming a little too in-your-face. Don't think it's gone unnoticed,' she announced. She had her reaction now, as her sister immediately swivelled round to her.

'What are you on about?' Rebecca Two asked.

'This thing you've got for your toy soldier there,' Rebecca One replied spitefully, tipping her head at the man behind the wheel of the Mercedes. It was Captain Franz, the young New Germanian officer that Rebecca Two had taken a shine to while they were in the inner world. 'We should have one of our own driving us, not your blue-eyed boy all decked out in a chi-chi chauffeur's uniform. You don't even make him wear the cap because then you wouldn't be able to see his lovely blond locks.'

Rebecca One's eyes burned into the back of Captain Franz's handsome head as he continued to drive, seemingly oblivious to the exchange behind him.

'You do talk a load of rubbish!' Rebecca Two fumed. 'It's not like that.'

'Oh, sure. I'm your sister . . . you can't kid me,' Rebecca One retorted, shaking her head. 'And I just don't get it.'

Rebecca Two noticed the look in her twin sister's eyes – she was genuinely troubled. 'Don't get what?' she asked.

'Well, for starters, what's so special about him? He's just another human, same as any of these worthless Topsoiler slugs up here. But, worse than that, he's been so Darklit he's a zombie.' With her tongue lolling from her mouth, Rebecca One went cross-eyed to emphasise the point. 'He's like some broken, empty doll you drag around for kicks, and it's not healthy.'

Captain Franz brought the Mercedes to a stop before a pair of factory gates. Rebecca One ceased her tirade as she saw where they were. 'It's massive,' she said, taking in the hangar-sized buildings.

'Yes,' Rebecca Two agreed, relieved her sister had other things on her mind now.

A pair of Limiters in Topsoil clothes opened the gates. Having checked who was in the car, they waved Captain Franz on.

Rebecca One leant forward and prodded the New Germanian roughly in the shoulder. 'Hey, lap dog, go around the side. I want to see the warehouses first.'

Captain Franz immediately did as he'd been ordered, steering the car past the small office building, but then he began to slow. 'Keep going, dumb dumb! Take us into that opening!' Rebecca One shouted, then slapped him on the head with such force that he swerved the car. 'And watch your driving!'

Rebecca Two clenched her jaw but said nothing as the Mercedes entered the warehouse.

'Stop here,' Rebecca One said brusquely. Captain Franz slammed on the brakes, the tyres squealing on the painted concrete floor. As the Rebecca twins stepped from the car, the Old Styx and his assistant, their stark white collars visible under their long black coats, were already hurrying over.

'Some place,' Rebecca Two complimented the Old Styx as she looked around.

'A total of forty thousand square feet split over three warehouses. Through there,' he pointed to a set of doors in the far corner of the spacious building, 'is the field hospital where we carry out the mass Darklighting and the bomb implant procedures,' he said. 'Like so many businesses round here, this factory had gone bust, so we picked up the premises for a song. It's ideal for what we want, and who'd think of looking for us here?'

'And how secure is it?' Rebecca One enquired.

'From yesterday we doubled up on all the entry points. We've got both our men and New Germanians on round-the-clock sentry duty,' the Old Styx replied. 'We'll also be putting roadblocks on all the approach roads to the estate.'

Rebecca One nodded. 'So when will everything be ready for our guests?'

The Old Styx smiled, his black eyes flashing with excitement. 'This first warehouse will be fully prepped by nightfall.' He fell silent as he and the twins watched a procession of New Germanian troops wheeling hospital beds out across the floor, which they then began to arrange in rows. 'With all the NHS hospital closures, we had no trouble obtaining as many beds as we needed,' the Old Styx said. 'We should comfortably fit around a hundred and fifty in this area, and at least the same number again in the adjoining warehouses. Then we'll bring in the humidifiers and fine-tune the atmosphere. We want everything to be perfect.' Putting his head back, he sniffed the air, then clapped his gloved hands together. 'Our moment is fast approaching. It's finally coming.'

'Oh, I can feel it, I can feel it,' Rebecca One whispered. While the Old Styx had been talking, she'd slid her fingers down the nape of her neck and had been kneading her back between her shoulder blades. As she withdrew her hand, Rebecca Two saw there were tiny spots of blood on it.

And she herself was only too aware of the dull ache at the top of her spine, and the irresistible pull of nature.

Styx nature.

Although she and her sister hadn't yet passed through puberty and couldn't take part in what was to happen here, the longing was intense. And intoxicating. It was as if some strange electricity rippled through her body, fizzing in her veins. The ancient force was calling her, forcing her, to participate in a cycle that took hundreds if not thousands of years to manifest itself.

Rebecca Two wiped the sweat from her brow. She realised

with a start that she was trying to fight the impulse. She was alarmed by this, because why should she want to resist?

That wasn't natural.

She turned away from her sister and the Old Styx in case they were able to somehow sense her internal struggle.

There was a screech and the pipes rattled, then a message arrived with a final clunk. Clutching his stomach, the First Officer lumbered as fast as he could from his office. He located the correct pipe and opened a hatch in it, through which he prised out a bullet-shaped vessel, the size of a small rolling pin.

'What's up, sir?' the Second Officer asked, as he came through from the Hold and into the reception area.

'Give me a chance,' the First Officer replied sharply. 'I haven't read it yet, have I?' With all the recent turmoil in the Colony, neither of them had had a proper night's sleep in weeks, and tempers were seriously frayed.

'I was just asking,' the Second Officer mumbled under his breath.

The First Officer unscrewed the cap from the end of the cylinder and fished out the small scroll from inside. Due to his fatigue, he dropped it and, with a few choice swear words, bent to retrieve it from the floor. As he stood up, he complained, 'Oooh, me guts,' and held still for a moment, his hand pressed against his stomach and his face a little green.

'Still bad?' the Second Officer asked.

As he thought the question was completely unnecessary, the First Officer gave him a sour glance. He finally straightened out the scrap of paper and held it at arm's length as he tried to focus on the tiny lettering. 'Trouble in the North . . . fighting . . . the Styx are asking for all available officers to attend.'

The Second Officer didn't respond right away, but it came as no surprise that there was unrest in the North Cavern. There'd been numerous incidents concerning Colonists turning on each other, and he didn't blame them for it. Many had been moved out of their homes, which were being commandeered as billets for the massive influx of New Germanian troops. And all the Styx offered these poor evictees was temporary accommodation in the mushroom fields, where a shanty town of hastily erected huts had been built on the damp earth.

Then there was the severe rationing; a huge proportion of the Colony's food was being diverted to the troops as they underwent their training by the Styx.

And thrown into this already explosive mix were outbreaks of a disease causing severe diarrhoea, most likely as a result of the current chronic overcrowding in the caverns. The First Officer was still suffering from the effects of this.

So, no, the Second Officer wasn't surprised there was more trouble, nor that the Styx were calling on the Colony police to sort it out.

The First Officer was staring at him, drumming his fingers on the counter.

'I can deal with it if you want,' the Second Officer said.

'I do want you to,' the First Officer replied curtly.

'Righty-ho. If you're happy to hold the fort.'

Despite the fact that the cells were full to bursting with malcontent Colonists, the First Officer humphed at the suggestion that he might not be able to manage on his own. As

he crumpled up the message from the Styx, there was an inde-
scribable sound from his stomach. 'Got to go,' he groaned,
rushing back into his office and slamming the door.

'Keep your pants on, will you?' the Second Officer murmured. 'Or maybe that's not such a good idea,' he said,
allowing himself a small chuckle. His merriment evaporated
as, shaking his head, he reached over the counter to retrieve
his helmet from where it hung on a peg. He put it on, then
reached over the counter a second time for his baton. He
might need it where he was headed – the riots were becoming
increasingly violent.

Swinging his baton, he pushed through the doors and
stepped outside the station, pausing a moment at the top of
the steps as he surveyed the houses across the way. By the light
of the ever-glowing luminescent orb lampposts, he saw movement in an upper window, as if someone was watching the
station. It was probably nothing, but the Second Officer was
jumpy. He had never known such a mood of rebellion in the
Colony, or such strong antipathy towards the Styx, the ruling
class. But the Styx seemed to be so intent on their Topsoil
operations that they no longer cared what the Colonists
thought, or did – their only priority was to proceed with their
plans unhindered.

The Second Officer walked unhurriedly down the flight of
steps and, as he reached the bottom, he heard a whimpering
noise. He still harboured a vague hope that his Hunter, Colly,
would one day come back to him. She'd bolted after the explosion in the Laboratories, an incident for which the Second
Officer had received a commendation because he'd valiantly
pursued the attackers. At least that was what he'd told the Styx,
and they seemed to have accepted his version of events.

But when the Second Officer looked down, he didn't see his cat, but a small albino dog. It was a young greyhound with a coat of the purest white. The dog was standing there, its tail quivering between its legs as it peered up at the large man though its pink eyes. It was obviously hungry, but what unsettled the Second Officer more than anything was that only the well-to-do families in the Colony kept purebreds like this one. Someone must have been so hard pressed for food that they'd simply abandoned it.

'Poor little chap,' the Second Officer said, offering a hand with the dimensions of a bunch of bananas to the dog. It whined and sniffed his fingers, then came nearer so he could stroke its head.

And when he began to walk down the street, the dog followed right beside him.

Before long the Second Officer reached the Skull Gate. A Styx, wearing the distinct grey-green camouflage of a soldier from the Division, immediately stepped from the gatehouse. The Second Officer used this route to and from the Colony several times a day, not only to go to work but also for his official duties. Nevertheless, the Styx soldier scrutinised his warrant card, from time to time glancing suspiciously at the greyhound as if the Second Officer was attempting to smuggle contraband past him.

Finally the soldier returned the warrant card and raised his lantern as a sign for the gate to be opened. It trundled into the huge skull carved into the rock above as if the monstrous apparition was retracting its teeth. The Second Officer continued on his way, stepping into the mouth of the skull. As he began down the dark passageway which was the main thoroughfare between the Quarter and the Colony, he welcomed the company of the little dog trotting along beside him.

A thrumming sound filled his ears as he walked through a last turn of the passage and the Colony opened up before him. From this elevated position he could survey the South Cavern with its endless ranks of houses, all covered in a gauze-like mist of warm air and smoke.

'How goes it?' someone shouted.

The Second Officer stopped as he traced the multiple flights of cast-iron steps up the rock wall and located the Fourth Officer right at the very top. The man was on duty at the entrance to the control room for the Fan Stations, from where the low thrumming was emanating. Like many in the Colony police force, the Fourth Officer was a stocky man with a prickle length of white hair. And he was stationed there because the security had been tightened ever since Drake and Chester had used the air system to spread a mild nerve reagent through the Colony.

'How goes it?' the Fourth Officer repeated, more loudly this time in case the fans had drowned him out.

'The usual,' the Second Officer shouted back. 'A rumpus in the North.'

The Fourth Officer nodded, then spotted the greyhound. 'See you've made a friend.'

The Second Officer looked at his new companion and gave a shrug in response before continuing down the rest of the slope.

As soon as he came to the level ground at the bottom, he heard the sound of many feet striking the cobblestones in unison. A group of New Germanians – around fifty of them – were running in formation, as a Division soldier on horseback set the pace.

The greyhound hid behind the Second Officer's legs as the group thundered past. The men were like automatons, staring straight ahead as they moved in perfect synchronisation. He knew why their expressions were so vacant – they had all been heavily Darklit.

Manoeuvres like this were a common sight in the Colony these days – and just as common was the sight of these men collapsing from exhaustion during their training, some even dying from heart failure. The Second Officer had heard on the grapevine that the Styx were pushing the soldiers so hard because they wanted to acclimatise them to higher levels of gravity than they were used to in their world.

'C'mon boy. It's nothing to be frightened of,' the Second Officer assured the dog as the soldiers retreated into the distance. He entered one of the outlying streets of the Colony. But rather than heading directly towards the North Cavern, he instead made a detour to his house.

As he walked in, Eliza emerged from the sitting room. 'What are you doing back so early?' his sister demanded. 'Do you kn—' she began, then her eyes fell on the little greyhound. 'Oh no! You haven't!' she exclaimed.

'I couldn't just leave the little fella out in the cold,' the Second Officer said. He knelt down, his knee joints cracking like rifle shots, and stroked the dog. The greyhound's nervous eyes met his briefly. 'I'm expected in the North now, but I'll find out where he lives when I come back.'

Eliza crossed her arms disapprovingly. 'The patron saint of waifs, strays and Topsoilers,' she fumed at him. 'I would've thought you'd learnt your lesson by now.'

The Second Officer grunted and straightened up. 'Where's Mother?' he asked.

'She's upstairs, rest—' Eliza began, then interrupted herself as she remembered what she'd been wanting to tell her brother. 'You'll never guess what happened today. The Smiths were moved out.'

The Second Officer nodded. The Smiths were neighbours two doors along and they'd lived there as long as anyone could remember – certainly for several decades before he was born.

'Mother's taken it very badly. There are hardly any of us left in the street now.' Eliza frowned. 'We're being pushed out for all these New German soldiers, and they never so much as answer if you speak to them. They act as if you're not there. It's not right what's going on.' Her voice was wavering she was so distraught, but she now lowered it in case someone overheard her. 'I don't even know if our people are actually being taken to the North or not – there are rumours down the market that whole families are disappearing, lock, stock and barrel.' She put her hand on her brother's arm. 'Can't you do something? Can't you talk to the Styx?'

'You are joking? Me?' the Second Officer asked.

'Yes, you. The only reason *we* haven't been uprooted yet is because the Styx believe you're a hero, taking on those Topsoilers all on your own when they came to rescue your lady love.' The Second Officer found it hard to bear the withering look Eliza gave him. He may have been able to deceive the Styx, with his old friend the watchman from the Laboratories to corroborate his story, but his sister knew him too well. 'And if they think you're so *bloody* marvellous, perhaps they'll listen to what you have to say.'

The Second Officer wasn't sure if he was more shocked by his sister's swearing, or by her outlandish suggestion that he somehow tackle the Styx over what they were doing in the Colony.

He shook his head as he crossed to the front door, careful to shut it behind him because he didn't want the dog to follow. He left the fuggy warmth of the house with huge reluctance, uneasy about what he would be expected to do in the North Cavern, and generally very unhappy with his lot in life.

Parry waited until they had all gathered in the hall. Elliott was the last to arrive as she floated down the stairs, wearing a red dress and her glossy black hair done up in a chignon. She'd grown considerably since she'd arrived Topsoil, putting on several inches of height and even adding a little weight to her boyish figure. This may have been as a result of Parry's over-generous helpings at mealtimes and his insistence that they all eat well, or perhaps it was because of her age. Whatever the reason, to Will and Chester she'd never looked so feminine before, and they were now doing their best not to gawp at her. For her part, she didn't look at anyone in particular, least of all either of the boys.

'Right. Come along,' Parry announced, swinging open the heavy oak door to his study. They filed in without speaking, glancing around the room they'd been forbidden to enter until now. It was larger than Will had expected, with a row of safes along the panelled walls – one of these was open and Will could see files stacked inside.

'Hi, Dad,' Chester said, and Mr Rawls, in his crumpled clothes and a day's growth of stubble on his chin, rose from a chair beside the ancient printer. It was still rattling away, accompanied by a grinding sound as a roll of paper with perforated edges fed its seemingly endless appetite.

Will saw some computer displays on a bench beside the printer, but they were all dark. There was another screen on a desk in front of the far wall, but it was pointing away so Will couldn't tell if it was turned on or not. And on the far wall itself was a large map of Scotland, with the highland and lowland areas depicted in pastel shades. With the exception of Mrs Burrows, everyone's gaze had come to rest on it.

'Yes, you're in Scotland,' Parry said, raising his voice to be heard over the printer. 'Sixty miles due north of Glasgow to be precise.' He aimed his walking stick at the point on the map. 'Just about there.' The hairs pricked up on the back of Will's neck; it obviously no longer mattered that they'd be able to identify the location of the estate, and that was a little ominous. Parry opened his mouth to talk, but then clucked. He swung to Mr Rawls. 'Put that bloody thing on pause, will you? Can't hear myself speak.'

Mr Rawls swiped a switch on the printer as Parry perched on the edge of the desk and continued. 'You'll doubtless be wondering why Jeff and I have locked ourselves away in here for the last twenty-four hours.' He glanced at Mr Rawls, who gave a small nod, then Parry tapped the floor twice with his stick. 'I asked him to help because I needed someone to man the telex. I'm still on the distribution list for the COBRA bulletins.' Parry smiled, but it wasn't out of amusement. 'The powers that be keep me in the picture. In my former line of work, you never really retire.'

Mr Rawls saw that his son was frowning. 'COBRA is a government committee convened whenever there's a security risk to the country,' he explained.

'Wouldn't it be quicker to get the information over the net?' Will asked, looking from the aged printer beside Mr Rawls to the computer screen.

'The web is never secure,' Parry said. 'The only way to trace this telex would be to dig up the miles of dedicated trunk line it's connected to.' He took a deep breath. 'So where do I start . . . ? My son – who you know by the preposterous moniker of Drake – has always steadfastly refused to allow me into his struggle against the Styx. He's even been going round telling everyone I've popped my clogs just to protect me.' Parry raised his eyebrows. 'But my safety isn't an issue any more because the game's changed. Would you take them through the latest COBRA bulletins?' he said to Mr Rawls.

'Of course. Just over a day ago reports began to surface of incidents all over Europe – multiple assassination attempts on heads of state and key political figures. In France, the President and his wife escaped death by the skin of their teeth, but two further attacks on the Spanish and Italian parliaments killed several dozen politicians. And in Brussels a room full of assorted MEPs were taken out.'

'But there wasn't anything about this on TV last night,' Will said.

'And we couldn't even get the news this morning – most of the channels had this notice up that they're not available,' Chester added.

'I'm not surprised,' Parry said. 'But first things first. Please go on, Jeff.'

'Sure,' Mr Rawls said. 'The news of these assassination attempts has been suppressed because of the sensitivity sur-rounding them – they all originated from here.'

'From Britain,' Parry clarified. 'Ordinary English people

have become suicide bombers . . . they've turned into walking bombs. The nature of the explosives inside them – no ferrous components – means that conventional detection equipment is useless.'

'Walking bombs? How does that work?' Mrs Burrows asked, frowning.

'A bodged attempt at the German parliament in Berlin resulted in the capture of a live bomber,' Mr Rawls said. 'The woman was found to have had major body organs removed from her thorax and abdominal cavities.'

Parry reached over to the other side of his desk to retrieve a print out from the telex, then put on his glasses to read from it. '*Lobectomy of the right lung.*' He looked up as he explained, 'The medical inspection revealed that an entire lung had been surgically removed from the woman.' Parry consulted the print out again. 'And a *cystectomy, splenectomy, cholecystectomy* – that's removal of the bladder, spleen and gall bladder respectively. Lastly, and this is the really grisly part, just about all of her upper and lower colon were missing, and replaced with a makeshift bypass. Her intestines had been whipped out.'

Will noticed that Chester was grimacing and looking a little pale.

'She would have died anyway?' Mrs Burrows asked.

'Yes, in a matter of days,' Mr Rawls answered. 'She was still able to drink and take in fluids, but she couldn't digest any solids. But even before the lack of nutrition finished her off, without specialist medical care, infection or the massive trauma she'd suffered would have probably killed her.'

'Like a fish that's been gutted, she was eviscerated . . . emptied . . .' Parry said, removing his glasses and rubbing his brow. 'Instead, inside her were a pair of plastic containers filled with chemicals. When mixed by means of a mechanical pull at the waist, the chemicals would've detonated with considerable force. And ceramic shot was packed around the explosive mixture to widen the kill radius.'

Mrs Burrows was shaking her head. 'So the Styx did this – they Darklit innocent people, and then butchered them to turn them into these body bombs. But why?'

'Why?' Parry boomed with such ferocity that everyone in the room was taken aback. 'So the British government can't offer the world any explanation as to why its supposedly non-radical, run-of-the-mill citizens are embarking on these wanton acts of terrorism,' he growled. 'Because of our lax border policies in the past, the US and many other nations have always regarded our country as a melting pot for dissident groups, anyway. The Styx are just fulfilling a prophesy.'

He regained his composure as he went on. 'Accordingly, all UK borders are to be closed at 1 p.m. today – and all flights suspended. And it's very likely that the country will be put under martial law.'

There was a chiming sound and Parry slipped something from his pocket. The size of a pack of cards, it looked more like a paging device than a mobile phone as he glanced at its small LED display. 'Won't keep you a moment,' he said, as he leant over his desk to glance at the computer monitor on it. Chester took the opportunity to speak. 'But what does all that mean?' he asked.

'It means that the shutters will come down on our small island, and we'll be completely isolated from the rest of the world . . . and under military control,' Parry said, replacing the device in his pocket. 'The army will take charge of the streets.'

'Then the Styx will make their move,' Elliott said in a low voice. It was the first time she'd spoken a word and she had their full attention. 'I know how the White Necks think. They're going to invade your country using all the New Germanians they've brought up with them. And your own soldiers too, once they've been Darklit.'

'But even if they did command significant land forces, they've got one hell of a job on their hands.' Parry looked mystified. 'No, it can't be just that. There must be another ingredient in their plan that I'm missing. And it's driving me bloody mad trying to figure out what it is.' Parry pushed himself upright from his desk and stood before them. He appeared to be extremely weary and not at all the bastion of strength that Will had known up until then.

'Whatever they're up to, they can't be allowed to get away with it,' Mrs Burrows said.

'Precisely,' the old man replied. 'And if not us, who's going to stop them?' He twisted towards the open door of the study. 'You made it up here in good time.'

As a black-clad figure wheeled into sight, both Will and Chester thought the worst – that it was a Styx – and they both began to react. But Mrs Burrows caught her son's arm to still him.

'Whoa!' Chester exhaled as he and Will recognised the man with the completely bald head and goatee.

'Who's going to stop them?' Drake said, repeating his father's words. '*We* damned well are.'

Elliott rushed forward and flung her arms around him, then she stepped back, a huge grin on her face. It was a flash of the old Elliott – the Elliott that Will and Chester had been missing so much. 'You look like a real renegade now,' she chuckled. 'A mean and nasty one at that.'

'Hah! But look at you,' he replied, admiring her dress and the way she'd done her hair. 'Quite the young lady.' Drake moved into the room, greeting the boys, Mrs Burrows and Mr Rawls, and then took his place next to Parry.

'So you've been allowed into the inner sanctum.' Drake flicked his eyes around the room before addressing them again. 'Some late-breaking news for you,' he said. 'Just before dawn there were simultaneous strikes on television transmission centres, internet hubs and several of the main phone exchanges.'

'That's why we couldn't get anything on TV,' Chester realised.

'Quite so – it's denial of service – the Styx are targeting our comms and information hubs. And it's really bad down there in London, I can tell you. People are running scared – there's panic buying in the shops, which aren't being restocked. And public services are erratic to say the least – streets are piled high with rubbish, schools have been shut, and hospitals are being run by skeleton staff. And there've even been a couple of power-outs – whole areas of London have had intermittent electrical supplies for the last week. Yes, it's really rough down there. And there's also the odd rumour or two knocking around that a number of cabinet ministers have gone missing.'

'Decapitation. Textbook stuff,' Parry put in. Will and Chester glanced towards each other as they both wondered if he was referring to his favourite tome on insurgency by Frank Kitson. Parry drew his hand across his throat. 'You remove those at the top – *the head* – and the rest of the country – *the body* – hasn't got any idea how to organise itself.'

'Except that in all likelihood the head will be put back on,'

Drake said, 'but it'll be a Styx head.'

'I don't understand. With what's happening, can't we just go to the authorities and tell them who's behind it?' Chester suggested.

'That would be a very quick way to get us all killed,' Drake answered him. 'The problem is you can't tell who's been got at already. You don't know who you can trust.'

Parry clapped his hands together. 'I do,' he said. 'It's time to wake up some old ghosts.'

Drake met eyes with his father as if he knew what he was referring to, then held a finger up as he remembered something. 'Talking of old ghosts, I'm forgetting my manners,' he said, as he strode back to the doorway. He was gone for a second, reappearing with a man with a hood over his head. Everyone in the room knew what that felt like – Drake had insisted they wear them when he'd driven them to his father's estate.

The man's hands were bound together with a plastic tie, which Drake sliced through with his knife. Then, with a dramatic flourish, he whipped the hood off.

There was a sharp intake of breath from Will and Elliott.

'Colonel!' the girl exclaimed, immediately recognising who it was even though he was dressed in an expensively tailored but rather ill-fitting double-breasted City suit.

'That's the New Germanian who helped you?' Chester said to Will, who didn't respond as he stared at the man distrustfully. Although Colonel Bismarck had delivered him and Elliott from the clutches of the Styx in one of his helicopters, Will knew the only reason he was now Topsoil was that he must have been part of the attacks in the City.

The Colonel blinked in the unaccustomed light as he

stepped fully into the room. With a formal bow and a click of his heels, he took Elliott's hand. 'An honour to see you again,' he said, then acknowledged Will, who made no move to shake hands with him as he continued to eye the man with undisguised suspicion.

'It could be a set-up – a Styx trap,' Will said. 'You should never have brought him here. He's been Darklit.'

On the contrary, Drake appeared to be completely relaxed about his presence. 'Yes, although he must have been heavily programmed, it seems that a blow to the head snapped him out of it. He saw what the Styx were doing to his men – using them to do their dirty work – and for that he wants revenge.'

Colonel Bismarck nodded as Drake went on, 'And, yes, you're right, Will. The Colonel's aware he could be a risk to us. He's agreed that he's going to be kept under lock and key while he's here.' Drake glanced at the map on the wall. 'Particularly now he's got an idea where we are.'

Parry was regarding the Colonel with interest. '*Willkommen,*' he said. It was apparent that he recognised another military man like himself.

'*Danke,*' Colonel Bismarck replied.

'And how did you come across the Colonel?' Parry asked his son.

'Someone here was a bit free and easy with the emergency number to my secret server.' Drake smiled. 'Luckily, the Colonel had it on a scrap of paper tucked in his belt kit, and the Styx didn't find it.'

'You hope,' Will said under his breath.

Drake ignored the comment. 'And the Colonel left a message for the certain someone in this room.'

Everyone glanced at each other with bemusement until

Elliott spoke up. On the receiving end of a sharp look from Will, she mumbled, 'I was hoping he'd never need to use it. But I had a hunch that he and his men would show up here on the surface before too long.'

Will was about to say something but Drake got in first. 'Well, I'm just glad you did, Elliott. The Colonel gives us another card in our forthcoming fight with the Styx. And we've got a pretty lousy hand at the moment.'

A mile away, Bartleby was scaling an ancient oak, his long claws gouging into the bark as he went higher and higher. He finally reached a cleft in the trunk, then meowed down to Colly, who meowed back and immediately began to climb after him. When she too had reached the cleft, Bartleby edged along a bough that overhung the perimeter wall to Parry's estate. The humans might have understood how important it was that they didn't wander too far, but this was meaningless to the Hunters, with their voracious appetite for fresh prey.

Left largely to their own devices since being let loose in the grounds, they'd had the time of their lives mopping up Parry's grouse, which he bred specially for the shooting season. In fact, the rather dopey birds had had very little idea what had hit them as the two cats stalked and ate their way through almost the whole population. And now the grouse were rather thin on the ground, it was the Hunters' natural instinct to hunt further afield.

Once he was over the top of the wall, Bartleby continued a little further, the bough bending under his and Colly's combined weight. He flicked his broad head, indicating to Colly that she should jump first. She'd have smiled if she'd been able. Bartleby was such a considerate mate – he didn't want her to harm herself by leaping from too great a height, particularly not in her condition.

She landed safely, but her departure caused the branch to spring up. Caught on the hop, Bartleby was forced to jump before he was ready. His tail spinning wildly to try to control the fall, he touched down with an ungainly thump. Right away Colly scampered over to him to rub her cheek affectionately on his.

Bartleby let out a small whine and, like any male, milked the moment for all the sympathy he could get from his partner. He made a big show of licking the pad on his forepaw where it had been hurt by a sharp stone. After a few seconds of this, Colly had had enough, and cuffed him gently on the head.

That did it – Bartleby concentrated on the business in hand. First thing first; he chose a suitable spot to cock his leg and sprayed it with copious amounts of urine. After the new territory was well and truly marked, he began to advance with his nose to the ground as he relied on his highly developed sense of smell to locate their next meal.

But it wasn't easy – they were on the fringes of a dense pine forest that extended up the hill before them, and the aromatic tang given off by the decaying needles on its floor made it tricky for him to pick up a trail. But this didn't deter him in the slightest. Although the Hunters had only trapped a single roe deer that had made the fatal error of taking a short cut across Parry's estate, they'd caught glimpses of a herd of them grazing in this forest. Saliva hung in necklaces from the Hunters' maws at the prospect of more of the delicious venison. But, for Bartleby, the ultimate prize would be the stag he'd heard at nightfall as it made its distinctive roaring sound to keep its harem of females together.

Bartleby ascended the hill, crossing back and forth over the ground as he attempted to pick up a scent trail. Colly followed, but made sure she maintained a gap of twenty feet between herself and Bartleby. Every so often, they'd stop to seek each other out through the trunks of the pines.

Parry and Drake would have been proud of their tactical skills; the way the cats worked was to perform a pincer movement on their unsuspecting prey, surrounding it back and front. The one Hunter would charge in, and the prey would panic and bolt straight into the open jaws of the other Hunter.

Somewhere a bird squawked, and the sound of its wings beating against high branches made both Hunters peer above themselves. But then, as a breeze filtered through the trees, Bartleby fixed his eyes on the slope up ahead. He slunk down, his nose twitching as he surveyed the area. A flick of his ears told Colly all she needed to know.

He was on to something.

Bartleby's shoulder blades rose and fell as he began to advance, carefully positioning each paw as he went.

Colly soon lost sight of him in the trees. Still she waited – hunting was all about patience and timing. Then, when she'd decided he must be in position, she began to edge forward, making no sound above the rustle of the branches in the wind.

She froze as she heard a small thud. A cone had dropped to the ground. It was nothing to worry about, so she began to move again.

Unfortunately the trees further up the slope weren't quite

so numerous and didn't provide much cover for her. So she took her time. She didn't want to spook the prey too early – if it didn't bolt back to where Bartleby was waiting, but to the left or right, the game was up. Their quarry would slip the net. But then she saw a felled tree on the ground up ahead. She adjusted her path accordingly, so the prey on the other side wouldn't spot her.

Her chest was brushing the forest floor, she was so low to the ground.

What was odd was that she couldn't get a clear picture of the prey from its scent. Both she and Bartleby were familiar with the smell of deer urine and droppings, and although there was the faintest whiff of these, they weren't as strong as she would have expected.

But maybe it was a lone deer, and not the full herd. She didn't mind; a single animal would provide them with ample meat for the night.

When she judged she must have gone far enough, she dug her feet into the ground in readiness. Then, hissing and growling and making as much noise as she could, she tore ahead at full speed.

Limiters aren't like Topsoil soldiers.

Whatever environment they operate in, they live completely within it – using, eating, *becoming* what's around them. The pair of Limiters smelt like the pine forest because they'd been hiding out in it for weeks. To sustain themselves, they'd eaten not just rabbit and any birds they could catch, but also fungi and the other abundant flora. In comparison to the Deeps, it was a veritable fast food outlet. And, once or twice, they'd dined on the raw meat from a roe deer, the faint traces of which Bartleby had detected.

Colly had left the ground with enough momentum to clear the felled tree when she saw something that didn't fit.

The glint of glass in a telescope. It was mounted on a tripod.

And from behind the telescope appeared the Limiter's skull-like face.

A millisecond later she saw the flash of his scythe.

With a warning meow, she arched her back and flailed her legs in a desperate bid to alter her trajectory.

The felled trunk was in front of her. If only she could bring herself low enough to land on it – rather than go over it – she could use it to spring away.

The Limiter had the scythe raised, ready.

As he began to whip his arm to throw it at her, she heard Bartleby's rasping growl. In order to save his mate, he'd attacked. In a blur of grey skin and bunched muscles, he cannoned straight into the Limiter's back, his claws piercing deep into the man's neck.

But the scythe was already airborne.

With a single rotation, the gleaming blade nicked Colly's flank. Glancing off her, it continued for a few feet until it imbedded itself in a tree.

It was only a superficial wound, but she still howled with shock.

Hearing this, Bartleby became a whirling tornado of limbs. He wrapped himself around the Limiter's head, raking at the soldier's face with his hind legs. The Limiter was wearing some form of woolly hat, and Bartleby was about to bite down on it when the second Limiter thrust his scythe into the Hunter's neck, at the base of his skull. It was a skilful and well-aimed strike, the blade severing the spinal cord.

Bartleby let out a high-pitched wail that ended almost as soon as it had begun.

Ended with a death rattle.

The big cat was dead before he flopped to the ground.

Colly knew what that rattle meant.

She ran and ran, finding the tree they'd used to climb over the wall.

She ran all the way back to the house.

Parry was sitting at the kitchen table, peering through his reading glasses at a cookery book with a tattered and stained cover. '*Baste the joint every . . .*' he was reading, but stopped as Colly shot in through the doorway, crashing against his legs as she hid under the table. 'Bloody hell! Damned moggies are after our food again!' he shouted, leaping up.

Mrs Burrows inclined her head, inhaling sharply through her nose. 'No, that's not it,' she said quickly. She immediately swung around from the work surface, flour sprinkling from her hands. 'Not it at all,' she added, as she crouched down beside the Hunter. 'She's very frightened.'

Wiping her hands on her apron, she gently touched Colly, whose skin was running with sweat. 'What's wrong, girl?' She caught the smell of blood on the Hunter. 'Fetch me a clean tea towel from the cupboard, will you?' she asked Parry, who raised his eyebrows, then went off to do as he'd been requested.

'What happened?' Mrs Burrows asked the cat, who'd lowered her head between her paws. She was still panting from the exertion of the dash home.

'Here you are,' Parry said, passing the towel down to Mrs Burrows, who began to wipe the sweat and blood from the cat.

'Something's definitely wrong,' Mrs Burrows said again, as

Colly rolled onto her side with a whimper.

Parry frowned. 'Why do you say that?'

'I just know it. She's very frightened, and she's been hurt.'

'Badly?' Parry asked, getting down on his knees. 'Let me see.'

'It's not serious – just some grazes, and a small cut on her side,' Mrs Burrows told him. 'But something's not right with her. I can feel it.'

'Such as?' Parry said, as he watched her continue to wipe the animal down.

'Well, where's Bartleby? They've been inseparable since the day they met. When do you *ever* not see the two of them together?'

Parry shrugged. 'These bloody animals come and go as they please. Maybe the other one's got himself trapped somewhere, or had an accident?' He grunted as he got to his feet. 'I'll ask the boys to have a scout round for him.' He was halfway out of the room when he paused. 'Maybe Wilkie's seen him.'

As Mrs Burrows laid a palm on Colly's slightly extended belly, then took it away, a flour print of her hand was left on the cat's smooth skin.

A knowing look came into her sightless eyes, then she frowned. 'I do hope nothing's happened to him,' Mrs Burrows said. 'Not now.'

Chapter Four

The Buttock & File, one of the most popular watering holes in the Colony, stood at the intersection of two main roads. As the Second Officer passed by, it was completely deserted. It had once been a lively tavern – a meeting place for the Colonists after a day's labours – but now the doors were bolted and the place silent.

Several streets later, he turned the corner and immediately stopped. The area was one of the poorer ones and not well lit, and although the front doors of all the terraced houses were wide open, they were completely dark inside. But this wasn't what had brought the Second Officer to a halt. Along the side of the street was a fifty-strong squad of uniformed New Germanians. As though they were shop mannequins, they waited in a single line, their wide, staring eyes to the front.

There didn't seem to be a Styx in attendance, but in the distance the Second Officer could see the Garrison building within the Styx compound. From the windows of the squat building came tiny sparks of purple-tinged light, like faraway stars glinting in an unknown constellation. The Second Officer shook his head – he'd never seen Dark Lights used on this scale before.

A little while later he passed through the short access tunnel which led into the North Cavern. The cluster of huts was visible in the distance, ringed by a number of luminescent orbs on stands set up around the perimeter of the shanty town. The North Cavern was an agricultural area where much of the Colony's produce was grown and, up until recently, the least densely populated of all its caverns. As he came nearer, he saw that even more of these basic dwellings had been built, taking the total number to at least several hundred. But despite the size of the new town, there were very few Colonists out in the open.

The Second Officer had that sixth sense which those in police enforcement develop. If there had been any trouble, it was all over now. A crushed, thick silence hung over the place. As he continued down the track, in a clearing between the hotchpotch accretion of huts, he spotted the Third Officer slumped on the ground. He was holding his head.

'You all right?' the Second Officer said, as he immediately strode over to him.

'Took a couple of punches,' the Third Officer replied shakily. 'Nothing serious.'

As the man raised his head, the Second Officer noticed the blood on his face. 'Who did this to you?' he asked.

The Third Officer pointed at the area beside one of the huts. 'They did,' he said.

Spotting the corpses, the Second Officer unclipped the police lantern from his belt and went to investigate.

There were three of them, sprawled amongst rotting pennybuns, which had been trampled into a grey mush. Not far from the bodies, a collapsible table lay on its side, cards scattered in the mud. 'Cresswell,' the Second Officer said under his breath as he rolled the nearest corpse onto its back. 'The blacksmith. He's been shot in the neck.'

The Third Officer mumbled something. Despite the fact that he was injured, the Second Officer ignored him. He had no time for the man – the Third Officer was a dullard, not at all suited to the job of policeman. An uncle on the Board of Governors had propelled him up the ranks, and for that he was universally disliked by his fellow officers.

The Second Officer was the first to admit that he wasn't the brightest orb in the Colony, but he had what his sister called 'Earth Smarts' – he was streetwise and shrewd enough to get by. And he'd been promoted to his current rank based on his determination and years of sheer hard graft.

The Third Officer was mumbling again.

'Shush a minute,' the Second Officer silenced him, moving on to the next corpse. 'Grayson . . . a stonemason,' he said. As he rolled the body over to inspect the gunshot wound in it, the Ace of Hearts slid from where it had been concealed in the man's sleeve.

Clutching his forehead, the Third Officer had staggered to his feet and was pointing at the last of the bodies. 'And Cresswell's cousin, Walsh,' he said.

'Yes, so I see. Another precise shot to the neck,' the Second Officer observed. It was indeed Heraldo Walsh, a heavily muscled, squat man with a distinctive red scarf tied around his neck. The Second Officer scratched his chin as he pieced the scene together. 'So Cresswell and Grayson were playing cards . . . gambling with these packs of tobacco as the stakes,' he said, inclining his head at the foil packets lying amongst the scattered cards. 'They argued, probably because Grayson was trying to bamboozle him, then Walsh came to his cousin's aid.'

'When I stepped in to break up the fight all three started on me instead,' the Third Officer said. 'And a mob had formed – I thought they were going to lynch me.'

The Second Officer blew through his lips. 'These days people have no respect for the law,' he said, knowing there was a single and rather crucial piece of the puzzle still missing. He thought he knew the answer, but he had to ask the question. 'And who fired the sh—?' He clammed up immediately as he became aware of the Limiter. The soldier had materialised behind him like a ghost, his rifle at his shoulder. This was no great surprise in itself; it was general knowledge that Limiters had been drafted in to stop pilfering from the pennybun fields deeper into the cavern.

And the Limiter's presence explained how the men had been killed with such extreme precision, but the Second Officer was still more than a little bemused by one of the deaths. It was generally known that Heraldo Walsh had been in the pay of the Styx, snooping on Colonists for them and occasionally stirring things up when it suited them. Not exactly a model citizen, Walsh had led a charmed life until this moment, getting away with far more than most Colonists because of the latitude the Styx granted him.

'Took your time getting here,' the Limiter snarled in a low voice. The Second Officer was about to explain that he'd travelled all the way down from the Quarter when the Limiter kicked Heraldo Walsh's head.

The Second Officer didn't have much cause to deal with Limiters and, quite frankly, they terrified the living daylights out of him. He steeled himself to say something, because he would need to know all the facts for his report on the incident.

'Although they assaulted a policeman, I don't see any weapons on these men. Was it necessary to shoot them?'

The Limiter snapped his head towards the Second Officer, bringing the full force of his eyes on him. They were like two points of fire set deep in the man's grizzled and scarred face. The Second Officer was a seasoned policeman, and he'd seen some truly horrible things in his time, but now he shivered. It was as though he was peering through twin windows into hell itself.

'It's up to you to take care of your own,' the Limiter growled. 'You weren't here.'

The Second Officer swallowed a 'Yes,' then looked away from the soldier. He knew he should remain silent, but he continued nervously, 'There'll need to be an inquiry. We'll move the corpses to the m—'

'No inquiry,' the Limiter said in a voice like distant thunder, gripping his long rifle as if he was considering using it again, but this time on the Second Officer. 'And you leave the corpses where they are. As an example to the rest.' In the blink of an eye he'd gone, slipping back into the shadows.

'No inquiry,' the Second Officer muttered. So now the Styx were summarily dishing out the death penalty without any form of judicial process. He and the Third Officer exchanged glances, but said nothing to each other, because it wasn't their place to question the Styx.

'Appalling,' the Second Officer sighed, as he stepped slowly between the bodies in their attitudes of death. Children would wake the next morning to see them covered in slugs – that's if any stray Hunters hadn't chewed pieces off them during the night.

The Second Officer sent the Third Officer home to recover, then spent several hours doing the rounds between the huts. Everyone was keeping well out of sight after the incident, but from behind closed doors he caught sounds of women crying, and also the rumble of angry, dissenting voices. In a couple of the huts where the doors had been left open, eyes flashed resentfully at him as the red bowls of pipes glowed.

The Second Officer was finally relieved by one of his colleagues and, his feet aching from all the patrolling, returned home. Letting himself quietly in lest he wake anyone at that late hour, he heard sounds coming from the kitchen.

'Hello, Mother!' he said as he entered the steamy room, surprised to see her up.

The old lady started, spinning round from the stove. 'Oh, 'ello, son,' she said. 'You must be all done in. Go and put yer feet up by the fire. Me and Eliza 'ad our dinnah, but I've kept yours nice 'n' piping. You can 'ave it on your knees.'

In the sitting room, the Second Officer lowered himself gratefully into his armchair. He glanced wearily across at Will's spade, left in a prominent position on top of the sideboard. After they'd discovered it in the room his mother and sister had intentionally left it on show as a reminder, almost a warning to him, following the episode with Mrs Burrows. But it had quite the opposite effect – he was comforted to see it there. It reminded him of Celia.

''Ere you are, love,' his mother said, plonking the tray, with a massive bowl on it, in the Second Officer's lap. He was ravenous, and eagerly snatched up the spoon and began to shovel the food down with much slurping – the usual abysmal table manners found throughout the Colony.

His mother was gabbling away ten to the dozen as he ate. 'I couldn't believe it when the Styx pitched up at number twenty-three and moved the Smiths out there 'n' then. It was a sorry sight. Mrs S had her dresses under 'er arm – some of the ones I stitched for 'er too. 'Er daughter made a right spectickle of 'erself. She was 'owling and giving it the full waterworks and all that – you should 'ave 'eard 'er. But Mr S just went where they led him, his 'ead down, like 'e was going to the gallows. It was 'eartrending to watch. Bet it was 'orrible too in the North.' She raised a hand up as if she couldn't bear to hear anything about it, then waited expectantly for her son to tell her.

When he didn't, she went on. 'You know I wouldn't blame you if you *'ad* gone above grass with that Topsoiler woman. They don't give a tinker's about us these days, the Styx. This isn't somewhere for a young person to be, though you and Eliza are 'ardly spring chickens no more.'

The Second Officer stopped chewing, his spoon poised in front of his mouth. This was not the way the old lady ever spoke about the Colony or the Styx. One of the most respectful members of their society, she would never normally hear a bad word said about anyone in authority.

'Mother!' the Second Officer exclaimed. 'You don't mean that!'

She bowed her head. She hadn't combed her thinning grey hair after her nap, and it was as dishevelled as a wind-ravaged bird's nest. 'I do, 'fraid to say,' she whispered in a downbeat way. 'I do. I think it's all over for us now.'

'You don't really believe that.' There was a note of reprimand in the Second Officer's voice, even though he was talking with his mouth full. Realising that gravy was dripping from his spoon onto his blue tunic, he sat up so any spillage would instead be caught by the tray. As he did so, he sniffed, catching the aroma coming from the stew. 'This is tasty,' he complimented his mother, in an attempt to lift her spirits. 'You've really outdone yourself.' He frowned. 'But we never normally have rat on weekdays, do we?'

He stirred the watery gravy in the bowl. As he did so, something floated up from the bottom.

Although the heat had turned most of it a dull grey, in one place the greyhound's tiny eyeball still had a pinkish hue to it.

He dropped the spoon in the bowl.

'You didn't!'

His mother was up and out of her chair and beetling rapidly towards the door. 'Times are 'ard. There's not enough food to go r—'

'You monstrous old hag!' the Second Officer shouted, throwing the tray across the room. 'You did! You cooked my bloody dog!'

'I hear my father got you behind the wheel, so why don't you do the honours?' Drake lobbed the car keys at Will. 'And take it slowly because I want to brief you both on the way,' he said, pointing at the track which led to the woods.

He continued to talk as they trundled along. 'I'm going to introduce you to some old friends. They aren't exactly used to having people around, so you have to tread carefully with them.'

'Why? Who are they?' Chester asked from the back seat.

'They're here on the estate because they didn't have anywhere else to go. They've all worked with Parry in the past – even as far back as his tours in Malaya. Many of them are . . . how can I put it . . . ?' Drake ran a hand over his clean-shaven scalp as he chose the right words. '. . . battle weary. And some of them were deemed too much of a liability to be allowed back into the general populace. So Parry under-took to the authorities that he'd give them a home here.'

The boys absorbed this, then Will ventured, 'So are they dangerous?'

'Potentially, yes. These men have served their country in ways you couldn't even *begin* to imagine. They've been to the dark side – a place you don't return from unscathed.'

As Will recognised the gate with the *Danger* sign on it, Drake told him to stop. He slowed the Land Rover to a jud-dering halt and turned off the ignition. Drake made no move to get out, so the boys remained in their seats.

'But how well do you know these people?' Will asked.

'They were around while I was growing up. My mother died young, and they helped Parry to look after me, particu-larly as he went abroad a lot. They were kind of like my extended family.' Drake smiled to himself. 'A bunch of extremely strange, but incredibly interesting uncles.'

'But why are *we* meeting them?' Chester asked. 'Why not my dad and Mrs Burrows?'

Drake swivelled round in his seat so he could speak to Will and Chester at the same time. 'You have no idea how much you've both changed, do you?'

'What do you mean?' Will said, exchanging a glance with Chester.

'When I first took you under my wing in the Deeps, you were a couple of baby-faced kids, with no idea what you were doing. But you have now.' Drake let his words sink in before he went on. 'I know it hasn't been easy for you with the Styx on your tail.'

'You can say that again,' Chester muttered.

'And it shows,' Drake said. 'These men will recognise that in you. They've been there too, in their lives. And I need them to realise that the threat is real, and persuade them to come on board . . . I need them with us if we've got a chance in hell of beating the Styx.'

As they got out of the vehicle, Drake turned to them. 'Make sure you haven't got anything electrical on you. Anything with a current. A torch, for example.'

Will and Chester checked their pockets, then Will remembered his digital watch. 'Just this, but it only has a small batt—'

'Doesn't matter. Take it off,' Drake interrupted. 'If he's not expecting it, you can't take anything like that near him.'

'Who's not expecting it?' Chester enquired, becoming quite unnerved.

'First up we're meeting Captain Sweeney. He's known as Sparks, but you shouldn't call him that – not yet, anyway.'

Will undid the strap on his watch and left it on the car seat. Then Drake unlatched the gate and began down the track, the same track that Chester and Will had run along a few days earlier to reach the woods.

'Through here,' Drake directed as Will spotted the moss-covered roof he'd noticed before. Drake left the path and began down a bank. He pushed into what seemed to be a tangle of impenetrable bracken, but in its midst was a narrow track that took them to the crofter's cottage at the bottom of a small hollow.

It was difficult to believe anyone lived in the building,

which was completely ramshackle. Although the front windows were intact, they were virtually opaque from the bloom of algae on the glass.

'Stay behind me, and it's better if you don't speak. If he does ask you anything, keep your voice low . . . and I mean really low,' Drake said. He knocked once on the door – so gently as to hardly make a noise – and nudged it open on its rusting hinges.

Drake stepped into the darkness with Will and Chester shuffling blindly behind him as they wondered what they were getting themselves into. The only noise in the room came from their boots crunching in the loose dirt on the bare stone floor, and the air smelt fusty and damp. Unable to see anything, the boys kept close to Drake, until Will felt pressure from Drake's hand on his arm, which he took as a sign to stop. 'Hello Sparks,' Drake said softly. 'Hope we've come at a convenient time?'

'Sure, I was expecting you. Your father said you'd be dropping by,' a gruff voice responded from a far corner. Will and Chester listened as Drake advanced towards the voice, but as much as they strained their eyes they were unable to make out who was there in the gloom. A match was struck and an oil lantern began to glow wanly through a carbon-streaked shade.

Beyond Drake's silhouetted body, someone else was just visible. Although it was still difficult to discern much by the light of the hissing lantern, the man was a good six inches taller than Drake and built like a bear. 'Been far too long,' the man added in a rumble, although there was affection evident in his voice.

'Yes, it has,' Drake said.

'You've brought them both with you. I suppose you'd like

me to come outside so they can meet me properly?'

With Drake guiding them, Will and Chester retraced their steps back through the front door. Like a wraith reluctantly showing itself, the man emerged into the daylight. Although his face was far from clean, the boys saw that around each of his eyes was series of concentric circles, suggesting something under the skin. The lines were almost black, and the effect was quite disarming – it was evocative of a face decorated for some tribal ritual.

As Will regarded the man, he couldn't help but think of Uncle Tam, who'd been similarly well built. However, Sweeney looked like he could have given Uncle Tam a run for his money. He had massive shoulders and his wrists, where they emerged from his army woolly pulley, were thick and muscular.

He was also wearing a pair of stained and loose-fitting camouflage trousers, and on his head was an army-issue cold-weather hat with flaps hanging down over both ears. As he removed it from his head, the insides reflected the light as if it was lined with metal foil.

'Does that help?' Drake asked.

'Not much,' Sweeney grumbled in reply.

Now that the man was without his headgear, Will could see that his forehead was also crossed with an intricate lattice of raised lines. Will found it difficult to tell how old Sweeney was because of his strange face, but estimated he had to be at least in his sixties from his thinning grey hair.

Narrowing his bizarre eyes, Sweeney studied Will and Chester in turn. 'Told you anything about me, has he?' he demanded, sticking a thumb in Drake's direction.

The boys shook their heads mutely.

'Thought not,' he said, then cleared his throat. 'Forty years ago, I was in the Marines, the SBS to be precise. But there's a history of progressive myopia in the family, and my eyesight was on the slide. So it was either a discharge on medical grounds, or spend the rest of my career shuffling papers behind a desk, when this boffin chap from an Army research programme showed up at the barracks asking for me. It was as though I was being offered a miracle; he promised he'd fix my eyes so I could go back into active service. The army was my life, and I couldn't imagine doing anything else, so I grabbed the opportunity. But you know what they say . . .'

'Never volunteer for anything,' Drake put in with a smile.

'Damned right. Anyway, it was all to do with perception enhancement for combat applications.' With two fingers Sweeney described a figure of eight around his eyes as if he was administering himself a benediction. 'You see, by surgically implanting some gizmos in my retinas and ears, then boosting nerve conductivity and the synapses in my noddle, my vision and hearing were tuned to way beyond human limits. A side effect is that my reaction times are pretty fast too.' He cleared his throat uneasily. 'I was the third soldier the surgeons got their mitts on, and by the time it was my turn to be opened up and rewired, thank Christ they'd got their act together. More or less. The other guinea pigs weren't so fortunate – one poor sap died on the table, and the other was paralysed from the neck down.'

As Drake had directed them, Will and Chester remained silent. Filled with awe, they simply stared at the man as he continued. 'So . . . I'm fast, and I can see and hear things you can't,' Sweeney said, then peered down at the hat in his hands. 'Which is mighty handy for night ops and deep jungle insertions,' Drake explained.

'Yes, that was how they deployed me – three decades of skulking around in the dark,' Sweeney said, nodding as he looked up. 'Everything is amplified . . . supercharged . . . if I'm not prepared for it, loud noises can be excruciating.' He frowned, the grid on his forehead forming a succession of Vs. 'But, in the end, what gets you is that there's no "off" switch. What they didn't envisage was the 24/7 sensory overload. It can drive you clean off your rocker.'

He pointed loosely at the woods and cocked his head to one side. 'Right now, I can hear insects burrowing under the bark in those trees. They sound like jackhammers.' He swung in the direction that Drake and the boys had come from. 'And the vehicle you left by the gate . . . I can hear the engine block cooling. It's like icebergs exploding in here.' Sweeney raised his hands to his temples but didn't touch them. 'And there's no way to make it stop.'

'You can really hear all that?' Will asked quietly.

'Sure. And as for my eyes, I can put up with sunlight, but only for limited stretches.'

'Me too,' Will muttered.

Sweeney looked at him with incomprehension before continuing. 'The real downside, though, is that anything with a current can play havoc with the circuitry in my bonce. So I've no choice but to live completely without power here in my cottage. I burn oil for the little light I need, and cook on a wood stove. Sometimes I feel like I'm back in the flipping Middle Ages.'

'And don't try playing hide and seek with Sparks – he'll beat you hands down,' Drake advised with a grin as he tried to lighten the mood. 'He can locate you just by your breathing.'

'Come on, I let you win every now and then.' Sweeney let out a low, booming laugh, then swung his huge arm around Drake's shoulders and squeezed him so hard his feet left the ground. Releasing Drake, Sweeney then leant in towards him. 'You and I need to talk,' he said, flicking his outlandish eyes in Will and Chester's direction. 'Very nice to meet you, lads.'

'I'll see you two back at the car,' Drake said, and the boys set off up the incline, leaving him alone with Sweeney.

Once Drake had rejoined them, it was Chester's turn at the wheel. When Will figured they had driven far enough that Sweeney wouldn't be able to eavesdrop, he asked, 'Can't all the stuff in his head be taken out, so he's normal again?'

'Maybe, but he didn't want them tampering with his brain a second time. Yanking out the wires after so long might cause all sorts of problems,' Drake answered, glancing over his shoulder at Will. 'Sparks is pretty highly strung and can get a bit crotchety at times. But he'll be very useful to us if I can persuade him to go operational again.'

Will pulled a face. 'Just as long as he's on our side.'

Drake nodded. 'Know what you mean. And in a way, he's similar to your mother – with both of them on the team, we'll have the next best thing to a Styx radar. All of which is rather apposite, considering who we're seeing next.'

'And who's that?' Will asked.

'Professor Danforth,' Drake replied. 'He worked in defence electronics, in areas like low-level radar and fail-safes for nuclear weaponry. Now he just potters around at home . . . well, sort of. The Prof is the cleverest man I've ever known – an out-and-out genius.' Drake gestured at the last building in the row. 'Stop over there.'

As the Land Rover ground to a halt, Will glanced at the

rather twee cottage with its hanging baskets of red and yellow primulas beside the door and windows.

'Anything we need to know,' Chester asked as they got out and began towards the cottage, 'before we meet him?'

'Not particularly – he's pretty harmless, but he's got a hang-up about being touched. Thinks he might catch something,' Drake said, going to the front door and placing his palm over what appeared to be a glass panel set into its surface. With a series of solid clunks, bolts retracted in the frame, and the door swung open.

As they entered the brightly-lit interior, the boys were at once struck by the contrast with Sweeney's cottage. The interior was warm and dry, and the walls were a dark yellow, and hung with fussy little watercolours of rural scenes. More pictures were arranged on the mantelpiece above the fireplace, and the Georgian furniture in the room was so highly waxed it shone.

A man rose from an armchair. Sporting a pair of thick spectacles, he was neatly turned out in a russet-coloured waistcoat and fawn trousers. He'd been working on something by the light from the window, and placed it on the table beside his chair before he came over. He was birdlike in his movements and his shoulders stooped. He resembled some ancient uncle.

Drake towered over the diminutive man as the two faced each other. 'After all these years, your palm scanner still works like a dream,' Drake said, holding his hand up and spreading his fingers as if it was some form of special greeting between them. 'And you left my imprint in the system.'

'Of course – unlike your father, I never believed anything untoward had befallen you. I knew you'd be back with us one day,' Danforth said, adding with a chuckle, 'The devil looks after his own.' He turned away from Drake. 'And these are the boys he mentioned . . . I mean Parry, not the devil – although I sometimes ask myself if they're one and the same.'

He focused on Will through his pebble-thick spectacles. 'Albinism . . . so you'll be Will Burrows . . . yes . . .' The Professor's gaze became distant as he recited, '*His head and his hairs were white like wool, as white as snow; and his eyes were as a flame of fire.*'

Then the full force of Danforth's scrutiny was back on Will. 'Albinism . . . *aka* achromia, achromasia or achromatosis. Occurrence about one in seventeen thousand, a recessive inherited genetic condition,' he said, the words pouring out in an uninterrupted gush.

'Er . . . hello,' Will mumbled when the Professor finally fell silent, more than a little taken aback by all the attention he was receiving. Will automatically offered the man his hand, but Danforth immediately retreated a step, muttering what sounded like 'Egg . . . breaking my egg.' He cleared his throat at great volume and switched his attention to Chester. 'And you'll be Rawls. Good, good.'

Annoyed with himself that he'd forgotten Drake's advice about the Professor's dislike of physical contact, Will was examining what the man had been working on when they'd entered. Laid out on a small cushion some ten inches square was a piece of lace, with many bobbins dangling from its sides. It was largely unfinished, but in the completed areas Danforth had stitched the most involved and intricate geometric patterns.

'An anachronism, I know, but it assists my mental processes,' the Professor explained, noticing Will's interest. 'I find that cogitation is a largely preconscious activity.'

As Will nodded back at him, Danforth flicked his eyes in Drake's direction. 'I taught this whippersnapper everything he knows. Tutored him in basic electronics when he still couldn't tie his own shoelaces. I took him on as my apprentice.'

'Merlin's apprentice,' Drake said, an affectionate smile on his face. 'How could I forget; we began with a cat's-whisker radio when I was three or four, then quickly progressed to robotics and exploding drones.'

'Exploding drones?' Chester enquired.

'Remote-controlled aeroplanes to military spec, which carried our home-made explosives,' Drake replied. 'Parry put a stop to our test flights on the estate when one crashed into the greenhouse and nearly blew Old Wilkie's head off.'

The Professor twitched impatiently as if all this had begun to bore him. 'Yes, well, I received your package with the components and the drawings. Fascinating stuff, I must say.' He removed his glasses and began to polish them with an obsessive thoroughness. The mannerism was so familiar to Will that he nearly gasped; it struck him that there was much about Danforth that was reminiscent of Dr Burrows, Will's late father. And the similarity wasn't lost on Chester, who seemed to pick up on it at the same time. Catching Will's eye, he gave him a small nod.

Danforth was in full flow, as if he'd launched into a lecture. 'The Styx – by pursuing a parallel evolutionary course to us with their scientific development – have come up with some truly ground-breaking technology. Their accomplishments in both subsonics and mind control are something the US military were frantically trying to develop in the sixties. And, I can tell you, the Americans would pay a pretty penny to get their h—'

'But did *you* get anywhere with the Dark Light?' Drake interrupted.

'Did I get anywhere?' the Professor said as if Drake's question was an affront. 'What do you think? Step this way.' In his strange gait, he hopped towards the rear wall of the room where there was a bookcase and – as Drake had done when he placed his hand on the scanner outside – Danforth now pressed his palm against what appeared to be an ordinary mirror. The middle section of the bookcase clicked and swung open, revealing a hidden room.

'I swear it's Dexter's laboratory,' Chester whispered irreverently to Will as they all followed Danforth into the room which, from floor to ceiling, was filled with electronic equipment. A bewildering array of lights blinked on and off in different sequences on the various units.

But they clearly weren't stopping there as the Professor headed for a set of narrow wooden stairs in the corner, at the top of which Will and Chester found themselves in a long attic. At more than a hundred feet from end to end, it evidently ran the full length of the row of cottages, and again was filled with equipment, although much of this was obscured by dust sheets. Beyond some test benches, at the very end of the attic, was a metal chair bolted to the floor. As Danforth reached it, he wheeled a trolley into view, on which were many boxes of electronics.

The Professor hit a switch, and a green line skittered across a small circular display, settling down into an undulating sine wave. Then he held up what was evidently some form of harness for the head, with two pads to cover the eyes, and numerous wires connecting it to the equipment on the trolley.

'Did I get anywhere?' Danforth said once again with indignation, waving the device in front of Drake. 'Of course I did. Here's what you asked for – an antidote to the Dark Light.' He pressed a switch on the back of the harness, and with a hum the eye pads began to glow an intense purple. As Danforth turned with the harness still in his hands, Will caught sight of the purple light. He felt a prickling behind his eyes, then a rapid swell of pressure as if something – a traction beam – was trying to drag both his eyeballs from their sockets.

He let out an involuntary breath and staggered back. He'd only caught the briefest glimpse of the light, but it was as though the spiked ball of energy had pushed its way inside his cranium again. 'No,' he grunted, overwhelmed by a welter of unwanted memories of the Dark Light sessions that the Styx had put him through when he and Chester had been imprisoned in the Hold.

After he'd recovered, he found Drake was watching him. 'It affected you, too?' Drake asked.

As Will swallowed a 'Yes' in response, Danforth was making a trilling noise. 'Good, good. It's far more potent than the Styx's efforts,' he said, sounding delighted.

Keeping his eyes shielded from the glowing pads on the headset, Drake addressed Danforth. 'So you're saying this apparatus will purge anyone who's been Darklit?'

'Theoretically, yes,' Danforth replied as he turned the headset off again. 'The ancillary sensors take a reading of the subject's normalised alpha brain activity,' he said, glancing at the green wave flowing across the small screen. 'Then I employ a feedback loop to erase anything extraneous – anything extra the Styx might have implanted.'

'And you're sure it works?' Drake asked. 'Without any

unwelcome side effects? No memory loss or mental impairment of any kind?'

The Professor gave an impatient sigh. 'Yes, according to my calculations it'll work. And when have I ever been wrong?'

'I suppose there's only one way to find out,' Drake decided on the spot. Shrugging off his jacket and dropping it on the floor, he immediately climbed into the chair. 'Let's do it.'

Will and Chester were flabbergasted. 'Drake, do you really think this is such a good—?' Chester began.

Drake cut across him. 'How else can we tell if it works? We can hardly test it out on a rabbit, can we?'

'But we could try it on Bartleby first,' Will suggested. 'He was Darklit, too.'

Danforth had no time for such objections. Gingerly proffering the harness at Chester because he didn't want the boy too near him, he inclined his head towards Drake. 'Put this on him. Make sure the sensors are fixed firmly on the temples or the readings won't be reliable,' the man ordered.

'Okay,' Chester agreed reluctantly. He seated the harness on Drake's bald scalp while Danforth made adjustments to the controls on the boxes of electronics.

'Help, will you?' the Professor snapped at Will. 'Strap him in. Make sure he's buckled tight.'

Will looked at Chester with a blank expression, then he did as he'd been told, making sure Drake's arms and legs were secured to the chair by the various straps.

There was a moment of silence as the Professor made the last adjustments. Again it struck Will how much like his dead father the scientist was – it didn't seem to matter to him one jot that there was a person in the chair who, if the process backfired, could be hurt. And, more than this, Danforth had known Drake from the time he was a child, and had evidently had such a huge influence on him. Drake's specialisation in optoelectronics and his time studying it at university must have arisen from Danforth's influence, and yet the Professor was only interested in finding out if his contraption worked. Dr Burrows had been the same, sacrificing anything and anyone around him if it was necessary in his quest for knowledge and discovery.

'All systems go,' Danforth announced, clicking a switch. For several seconds nothing happened. Drake remained still in the chair, his eyes covered by the pads.

Will's anger and resentment grew to the point that he felt like punching Danforth. He wanted to call a stop to the proceedings and free Drake from the chair, but then the birdlike man spoke.

'I've taken the normalised readings,' he announced. 'Now for the purge.' He jabbed a button.

Drake twitched several times. Then he cried out at the top of his lungs, his body arching in the chair and his muscles going into such severe contraction that Will thought he might actually snap the bindings around his wrists and ankles.

The humming of the boxes seemed to resonate through everything in the attic. A small amount of purple light was leaking from around the edges of the eye pads, which meant Will found it difficult to look directly at Drake's face.

Chester muttered, 'Oh, no,' as he saw the sweat coursing down Drake's face and soaking his shirt.

'You can tell that he's had quite a degree of conditioning,' Danforth noted drily as if he was commenting on the weather. 'I'm going to increase the amplitude now, to complete the purge.' He twisted a dial.

Drake's mouth was open but there was no sound any longer, no scream. The tendons in his neck and wrists were stretched so tight that they looked as though they might burst through his skin. Then he began to babble.

'My God, listen . . . that's Styx!' Chester exclaimed. 'He's speaking in Styx!'

Will listened in astonishment as Drake's lips moved and the bizarre sounds came from the back of his throat in short bursts, like the tearing of dry paper. It was so strange to hear a non-Styx speaking in their tongue. 'We should be recording th—'

'We are,' Danforth interrupted, pointing at the apex of the roof directly above the chair, where a mirrored dome was fixed.

'Elliott might be able to tell us what he's saying,' Chester suggested as the Professor waved his hand through the air in a flourish.

'And that should be it,' he announced.

He flicked a switch. The humming reduced and the purple light in the eye pads dimmed as Drake slumped loosely forward.

'Take it all off him now,' Danforth ordered Chester, who quickly did as he was told, removing the harness and the sensors from Drake's dripping skin.

Will undid the straps binding him to the chair, then stood up. 'Drake? Hello?' he said, his voice concerned as he took hold of the man's arm and shook it. 'Are you all right?'

Drake didn't move, his head slumped onto his chest. He appeared to be out for the count. 'What do we do now?' Will asked, stepping back.

'Slap him,' the Professor said, kneading one hand with the

other as if the thought of doing it himself was abhorrent.

'You mean it?' Chester quizzed him.

'Yes,' Danforth confirmed. 'Slap him.'

'Okay then.' Chester propped up Drake's head, then struck him.

Danforth hissed, 'Put your back into it, boy. Hit him harder than that.'

But Chester was spared the task as Drake's head jerked up. 'He's awake,' Chester said gratefully.

'Tell me how many,' the Professor asked as he thrust three fingers in front of Drake's face. 'How many do you see?'

'Four and twenty blackbirds,' Drake answered drunkenly, squinting through his half-lidded eyes.

'Slap him again,' Danforth said.

Chester swallowed and went to do it, but Drake caught his hand before it made contact with his face.

'I was joking, for God's sake,' Drake exclaimed as he sat up straight in the chair and mopped the sweat from his brow. 'I'm perfectly all right.'

Will was looking at Drake with disapproval.

'I know, I know,' Drake said, then drew in a deep breath. 'In normal circumstances I wouldn't have taken the risk. But with what's facing us, I have to do everything I can to improve the odds.'

'Are you sure you don't feel any different?' Will asked, scrutinising him. 'Your voice sounds funny.'

'No, I'm fine. Really. I've bitten my tongue – that's all,' Drake replied. He did sound slightly odd, and perhaps it was because of their relief that he'd come through unharmed but Will and Chester couldn't help themselves – they both began to laugh helplessly. 'Thanks a bunch, you two,' Drake said, feeling the end of his tongue. He smiled, but then his expression became serious. 'I suppose we won't know how well it's worked until we run into the Styx again.'

'Ye of little faith,' Danforth said testily.

Drake groaned as he lifted himself from the chair. It took him a few seconds to find his legs, then he turned to examine the boxes of electronics on the trolley. 'Can you miniaturise this kit? We need it to be portable so we can deprogramme subjects in the field.'

'Already made a start on a handheld version,' the Professor replied. 'Now, who's up next?' he asked, looking at Will with cold detachment.

'Well . . . me . . . I suppose,' Will gulped.

'Shouldn't be too bad,' Drake tried to reassure the boy as he took off his jacket and climbed into the chair. 'Remember, we've already negated the death wish they planted in you.'

'Yes, that's true, Will,' Chester agreed, trying his best to sound upbeat. 'You don't want to throw yourself off buildings any more, do you?' he said as he put the harness on his friend's head and made sure the sensors were in contact with his temples.

'Not until this moment,' Will said under his breath.

Drake finished buckling the restraints on Will's arms and legs, then rolled up a handkerchief and placed it in the boy's mouth. 'Here . . . bite down on this,' he advised. 'I don't want you losing the tip of your tongue.'

'Thanks,' Will said through the handkerchief. He could hear the Professor clicking switches but he couldn't see anything with the eye pads in place. 'I just know this is going to be horrible,' he tried to say.

'Be quiet and keep still,' Danforth scolded him. 'So I've

taken the normalised wave pattern . . . and now I . . .'

As he threw the main switch, the darkness became an intense purple, gushing into Will's head. Then there was severe pain, but not from any particular part of his body – in fact he wasn't aware of his body as he pitched forward into a huge space where there were bursts of white light, precisely as if camera flashes were going off. The flashes came more and more frequently, and between them Will caught fleeting glimpses of dark figures. He realised that he was seeing the two Styx from the Dark Light sessions he been subjected to all those months ago after he'd been captured in the Quarter. But what was most bizarre was that everything seemed to be playing backwards.

There was more pain, as though his head was about to explode. Quite suddenly it stopped, and he found that Drake and Chester were leaning over him.

'Okay?' Drake asked.

'Sure,' Will said, although his mouth felt bone dry and his arms ached.

'I thought you were going to burst my eardrums with all that screaming,' Chester said quietly. 'You spat the handker-chief out and nearly blew the roof off. Thank God you're all right!'

Will noticed how pale his friend was. 'Why? What happened?' he asked. 'And where's the Professor?'

'You've been out cold for about ten minutes,' Drake told him.

The Professor appeared – he'd evidently been downstairs. 'Ah, he's come round. So we won't be needing the smelling salts or the first-aid kit,' he said tetchily.

'You had us worried,' Drake said. 'The Styx must have put

more programming into you than I'd anticipated. We'll probably never know what it was now it's been weeded out.'

Chester curled his lip as if he'd tasted something unpleasant. 'You were speaking Styx – it was so creepy.'

'What? Me too?' Will said. 'Weird. I really don't remember anything.'

Then it was Chester's turn to be treated with *Danforth's Purger*, as they'd begun to refer to the apparatus. At first he hardly broke into a sweat, but then his face was streaming and he too cried out and began to babble away in what sounded like Styx. And he was barely conscious at the end of the treatment.

'Suppose that means they stuck something in my head too while they had us in the Hold,' he said, once he'd drunk some water and had a chance to recover.

'I'm afraid so. They don't miss an opportunity, do they?' Drake said. 'The only consolation is that your reaction was less severe than mine or Will's, so I assume you had less of it than we did.'

'Power down,' Danforth announced, as he turned off the last box on the trolley and the humming faded away to nothing. 'A very satisfactory outcome, I'd say.'

As they were leaving the Professor's house, Drake turned to the peculiar little man. 'And what about Jiggs – is he around?' he asked.

'We're not talking at the moment,' Danforth replied. 'He's probably watching us from those trees over there. He spends the night up in them now, you know, like some baboon. He still can't abide being cooped up after his tenure at Wormwood Scrubs.'

'Right,' Drake said, as if none of this came as a surprise.

'Give him my best if you do happen to bump into him.'

'Not likely,' the Professor replied, closing the front door.

As Will and Chester trailed after Drake on the way back to the Land Rover, they were peering at the area of woodland and wondering what Jiggs had been in prison for, and also what sort of man would sleep in a tree.

'You won't spot him, you know. Not even if he was ten feet away from us,' Drake said, without looking at the boys as he strode over to the car. 'That's what Jiggs does. He hides. And he's very good at it.'

Chapter Five

Bartleby had failed to return for two full days, and Will and Chester went on yet another outing to look for him, this time accompanied by Mrs Burrows.

'He could be anywhere,' Chester said, walking on the muddy path beside the bulrushes at the edge of the lake. He stopped to peer at the water. 'And if he's fallen in and drowned, we'll never find him. He might have been after the fish.'

'He's not that careless – and anyway he can swim. I'm sure he's okay, wherever he is,' Will said hollowly. He was trying his best to remain positive, but Chester was unconvinced.

'If you say so,' he murmured.

Will was nodding slowly to himself. 'I bet he just shows up at the house again, as if nothing's happened.'

'No,' Mrs Burrows said abruptly.

Both boys looked at her as if she was about to deliver some bad news, but she was referring to her new sense, which she'd been using in an attempt to shed some light on the Hunter's whereabouts. 'Maybe a few echoes of where he's been before, where he's marked his territory, but I'm not picking up any-thing fresh.'

Turning to the east, Mrs Burrows held her head high and then moved it slowly around until her unseeing eyes were gazing out at the island in the middle of the lake. She was wearing a long dress of white cotton that Parry had found in a trunk of clothes in one of the spare bedrooms. As the breeze caught it and also ruffled her hair, there was something saintly about her as she stood on the bank.

'So you don't think Bartleby just dumped Colly and ran for the hills?' Chester posed. 'He's a cat, after all, and cats are sort of unreliable.'

'Like husbands,' Mrs Burrows replied distantly, then suddenly turned her head to the west as if she'd heard something.

The boys waited, hoping she'd picked up on the Hunter's scent, but she remained silent.

'Mum, is it him?' Will asked eventually.

'Something else . . . a long way off . . . can't tell . . . maybe deer,' she said quietly.

Chester took hold of one of the bulrushes and broke it off. 'Parry said Old Wilkie's drawn a blank too while he's been doing his rounds.' Chester was thoughtful for a second as he tapped the brown seed head against his open hand. 'Say . . . you don't think *he* might have had something to do with it?'

'There might be insects in that,' Will said mischievously, knowing his friend's almost phobic fear of anything that crawled. 'And what do you mean? Why would Old Wilkie do anything to harm Bart?'

Chester immediately dropped the bulrush and rubbed his palms together, then examined them carefully. 'Well . . . Parry said Old Wilkie's spaniel went missing, and you just know who was to blame for that?'

Will was dismissive of the idea. 'You think he'd lie to Parry?

Old Wilkie's worked for him for years. That's not likely.'

Mrs Burrows was still facing in the same direction, to the west where the pine forest covered a small mountain like a green blanket. Where the Limiters had had their observation post. 'Yes . . . deer . . . must be deer,' she decided. 'I'm going back now,' she announced, turning towards the house and starting up the slope.

'Okay, Mum,' Will said. 'We'll try a few more places.'

Chester waited until Mrs Burrows was out of earshot, then spoke. 'You know this is a total waste of time, Will. We're not going to find him. Why don't we lure him back with a rabbit or a chicken? Or we could tie a live goat up in front of the house and wait for him to sniff it out. That would get him home fast enough.'

'I've got a bad feeling about all this,' Will replied, not giving his friend's suggestions any credence. 'Let's take a quick look up that hill.' He set off along the side of the lake, to where the land rose sharply.

Chester's face on the monitor contorted. As the boy screamed so loudly the soundtrack broke up, Elliott shifted in her chair. She crossed her arms and hugged herself, massaging a shoulder with her fingertips.

'Is this hard for you to watch?' Drake asked, pausing the film.

'No, it's not that,' Elliott answered. 'My back's been a bit uncomfortable recently.'

Elliott had been the last to be treated with Danforth's Purger, although it had produced no reaction in her whatsoever, establishing that the Styx had never used their mind control on her. Everyone else on the estate had been purged, with three exceptions. Drake was concerned that it would be too traumatic for Mrs Burrows after the excessive Darklighting she'd received in the Colony, so he excused her from it. And nothing on Earth would induce Parry to undergo it – he told Drake he'd never let anyone near his brain, not even Danforth whom he trusted implicitly. And Jiggs, because nobody knew where he was.

Drake had brought back copies of the footage taken in the Professor's attic, and he and Elliott were now reviewing them on a monitor he'd set up in the billiards room. Danforth had made two versions of each clip; one was a straight recording, while the other played in reverse, because the more intensely Darklit victims, including Drake and Will, appeared to be speaking backwards.

'It's so weird hearing Styx coming from Chester and all of you,' Elliott said.

They'd already been through the films of Drake's, Will's and Colonel Bismarck's sessions with the Purger, but Elliott hadn't been able to glean much more than a few highly garbled and completely meaningless sentences. Certainly nothing that gave a clue about the nature of their programming.

'Okay if we go on?' Drake asked.

Elliott nodded.

Drake pressed the remote, and they listened to the rasping Styx words emanating from Chester.

'It's just rubbish.' Elliott gave a small shrug. 'Mostly odd words, and even when there's more it still doesn't make any sense,' she said, as she listened carefully. 'It's like someone talking in their sleep.'

Drake took a deep breath. He'd resigned himself to the

fact that the recordings weren't going to reveal anything significant. 'We're coming to the end of Chester's session anyw—'

'Wait!' Elliott shouted, sitting bolt upright. 'Rewind that!'

Will and Chester had climbed high enough up the hill that they could look across to the house, although it was far in the distance.

'Bart! Are you there, Bart?' Will called as Chester dawdled along behind him.

They heard a squeak and someone stepped from behind a large oak.

'Stephanie!' Chester burst out.

She had a mobile phone in her hand, and was wearing a dark blue mac with the collar turned up. She'd tied a ribbon around her lustrous red hair to keep the wind from blowing it about. Will noticed that she was wearing a pair of black high heels, which seemed more than a little incongruous given that they were in the middle of nowhere.

'Oh, hi,' she said begrudgingly, trying to conceal the phone behind her back. 'What are you doing up here?' She nodded. 'Wait – I know – you're searching for this dog-thing Parry's lost. Gramps has been looking for it too.'

'We are,' Will replied. 'The dog-thing's gone missing.'

'Well, I haven't seen it,' Stephanie said indifferently. She looked the boys over with a slight suggestion of a sneer, then whisked her head away from them as if they had no right to be there.

'And what are you doing here?' Chester said, in an effort to be friendly.

She didn't reply, glaring at him as if it was impertinent of him to ask.

'You were using your phone, weren't you?' Will said in an accusing tone.

Realising she'd been caught out, Stephanie's manner softened. 'I'm trying to get a signal on this stupid thing,' she confessed, producing her mobile from behind her back. 'Gramps is, like, totally unreasonable – he says Parry has these enemies, and that phones are totally forbidden on the estate.' She shrugged. 'And I'm, like, *who* do I know who'll even care?' She gave Will and Chester a coy look. 'You won't tell Gramps, will you? Or Parry?' she added, as if she'd already won them over and her secret was safe.

'Course not,' Chester agreed readily.

'So who were you calling?' Will said, his eyes narrowing with suspicion.

'I'm trying to pick up texts from my friends, but the signal's so weak. There's this, like, massive party in London tonight – they'll all be there, and I'm, like, stuck here in this . . .' She tailed off, as if it was unnecessary to say what she thought of the estate.

'A party?' Chester said.

'Yes. Some cool guys we know from Eton are coming. And also some from Harrow. Can't believe I'm totally not going.' The despair in her voice had pushed it up an octave. 'Where do you both go?' she asked quickly.

'School?' Chester said. He was starry-eyed as he spoke to her, finding it very difficult to string more than a few words together.

'Highfield,' Will told her.

She frowned, moving her hand as if describing an area on a

map. 'That's sort of north . . . north of London, isn't it?' She bit her lower lip as if she pitied the two boys.

'No, not there,' Will laughed. 'It's really pronounced High-*feld*. It's in Switzerland.'

She looked confused. 'In Switzerland? I haven't heard of—'

'No, you probably haven't,' Will interrupted, puffing his chest out. 'It's a bit, like, exclusive. And sort of, like, expensive. It's a totally cool place – we have skiing every morning before lessons.'

'Really? My parents have never taken me skiing,' she admitted with a glum expression. 'I really want to go.'

Unseen by Stephanie, Chester was frantically shaking his head and mouthing *No!* at Will. But Will wasn't to be stopped.

'And my friend here is, like, a megastar on the slopes. Our ski teacher thinks he's so awesome at the downhill slalom jumps it's a dead cert he'll be on the next Olympic team.' Will made a swooshing sound and moved his arms in the way he'd seen skiers do on television.

'Really?' she squeaked, spinning round to Chester so quickly she almost caught him gesticulating at Will. 'Downhill slalom jumps! That's, like, awesome!' She fluttered her eyelashes at the bemused boy. 'Now I can say I've met an Olympic skier.'

'Um, I'm not really that good,' Chester mumbled. 'And we've really got to go now.' He grabbed hold of Will's arm and yanked his friend down the hill with him. 'What d'you say all that for?' Chester asked. 'Why did you lie to her?'

'She's so stuck up. Eton. Harrow. She thinks we're useless just because we don't go to those places. Actually, the truth is we don't go to school *at all*, because an army of homicidal crazies that, like, live in the ground want to tear our heads off. Would you rather I'd told her that?' Will argued. 'Do you think that would, like, be better?'

'Stop saying "like" all the time, will you?' Chester said in a long-suffering voice. 'I think she's nice.'

Will looked over his shoulder to find that Stephanie was still watching them. He waved, and she waved back enthusiastically. Will bent his knees and swayed from side to side as if he was on skis, making more swooshing sounds. Stephanie laughed shrilly, but not unpleasantly.

'And bloody stop that too!' Chester huffed, stomping off down the hill.

Once Elliott had reviewed the last of the films for Drake, she'd made her way back to her room. As she sat at the glass-topped dressing table, she ran her eyes over the items Mrs Burrows had badgered Parry into buying for her. There was something so gratifying about the little bottles of nail varnish, which she now began to arrange beside her eyeliner, foundation and lipsticks. And there was the bottle of Mrs Burrows' own perfume that she'd given to Elliott.

Elliott held the moulded glass bottle so it caught the light, then sniffed at it. Of all the items on the dressing table, the perfume meant the most to her. It evoked memories of her mother, who always made such an effort with the rather unsophisticated scents sold at the perfumier's shop in the South Cavern. Elliott smiled, remembering how she'd had mixed feelings about the Colony perfumes after being told by the perfumier's son, a boy her age, that they were prepared by blending fermented fungal juice with Hunters' urine. To this day she didn't know if he'd been telling the truth.

Putting the perfume bottle down, she yawned and stretched. Her time in the Deeps seemed like an age ago and, after this recent sojourn at Parry's house, she felt like a completely different person. She'd had a respite from the life-or-death struggle that had been her existence for so long, of not knowing what lay around the corner, be it a hostile renegade, a Styx, or some predator on the prowl for its next meal. Topsoilers took so much for granted, living their lives in such a benign environment with all the food they could eat.

But, above all else, the months at Parry's house had allowed Elliott the opportunity to be clean. After all the years of grime and filthy clothes she might have overdone it with her long baths, which she sometimes took two or three times a day, but it was a luxury she'd never experienced before.

And she'd always known, deep down, that this couldn't last.

That eventually something would come along to disrupt it. And that *something* was trundling inexorably towards her, Will, Chester and every one of them right now, and she had no choice but to switch back to her old self. For her own sake, and for the sakes of those she loved.

With a sigh, her gaze drifted to the long rifle propped beside the dressing table. She reached over to retrieve it, working the bolt to make sure the chamber was empty. Through her bedroom window she had a view of one of Parry's statues on the lawn at the back of the house, a reproduction of Saint George in his mortal struggle with the dragon. She put her eye to the scope, adjusting it to compensate for the range, then settled the crosshairs on the dragon's head. There was a click as she dry-fired the rifle.

'This is all I know,' she said, as she lowered the weapon to her lap. She ran a finger over the dented barrel and the numerous nicks in the wooden stock. Many of these marked moments of peril, challenges over which she'd managed to prevail.

So far.

She twisted around on her seat to take in the Elliott in the dressing-table mirror, the one with tidy hair and spotless skin, dressed in a red Angora sweater and a knee-length skirt. As she continued to stare at her reflection, it did seem as though there was another person there. Someone who wasn't her.

The sensation was so powerful that when Elliott shook her head, she almost expected her reflection to remain still, and possibly even to begin talking to her.

'And I don't know you.' As if uneasy under the stranger's gaze, Elliott looked quickly away from the mirror. Rising from her seat, she slid the rifle onto the dressing table. As the bottles and items of make-up were pushed aside, some falling to the floor, she went to fetch her old clothes.

The moment Will and Chester entered the house and saw Elliott at the foot of the stairs, they knew something was wrong. Not only did she have her rifle with her, but the feminine clothes were gone, and she'd cropped her hair short again. The Elliott they'd relied upon for so many months while they were underground had been restored to them.

'Uh-oh,' Will exhaled. 'Looks like trouble.'

Chester was about to ask her what was going on when Elliott ordered, 'In there,' and pointed at the drawing room.

The boys found that everyone else was already assembled in the chairs around the fireplace, with the exception of Parry.

Will gave Drake a questioning look.

'Waiting for my father,' he said.

Then Parry stormed in and, without a moment's delay, began to speak. 'Every call made from the phone in the study is logged.' He brandished several pages in his fist. 'As you might guess, the line isn't there for anything remotely sensitive. It's for routine, day-to-day stuff – ordering up oil for the central heating and suchlike.'

He put on his reading glasses to examine the top sheet. 'A number cropped up on the log not long after you all arrived. I didn't think much of it at the time, but I had another careful run through and found two further calls to the same number. The duration of each of them was around a minute. And they were nothing to do with me.'

'But none of us were allowed in the study until very recently,' Mrs Burrows said, turning to Drake. 'Are you sure it wasn't you?'

'I wasn't even here when the second and third calls were made,' he replied. 'The only explanation is that someone's been sneaking in and making these calls in secret.'

Everyone looked at each other.

'But why would any of us do that? And who were the calls to?' Mrs Burrows asked.

'London. And the number's unobtainable now,' Parry said.

Drake stood up. 'I'm afraid I do know who it was, but I don't want you to blame him. It wasn't something he was doing consciously.'

'You said "he"?' Will burst out.

Drake nodded. 'And the calls stopped after he was purged by Danforth.'

As he wondered if it was him, Will shifted uneasily on his feet. 'So the Styx programmed me – or someone – to make—'

Drake waved him into silence. 'Elliott and I watched all the films from the purging sessions. I regret to say,' he wheeled around to face Chester, 'the upshot of it is that you mentioned a couple of the digits from the phone number, along with some Styx words that Elliott was able to translate.'

'What . . . no!' Chester cried, blanching. 'Me?'

'Yes, you. Most likely the Styx conditioned you to call in and report our location. You may have even made some calls to them without knowing it long before we arrived here,' Drake said, without reprimand. 'So the odds are they probably have a good idea of where we are right now.'

'But . . . I wouldn't do that!' Chester tottered back a step.

Elliott went over to him, taking his hand. 'You mustn't blame yourself. You couldn't help it.'

'No, it wasn't me,' Chester said, his voice uneven. 'I'd remember something.'

'No, you wouldn't,' Drake said gently.

Chester just looked at him, his eyes swimming with tears as he tried to speak, to say something to defend himself. 'Oh, God, I'm so sorry,' he blurted and ran from the room. Mr Rawls followed after him.

'That went well,' Parry said without any suggestion of humour, then addressed everyone. 'So now we're on a condition of high alert, and we can't stay here much longer. Our location is blown.'

'But if it's the Styx, why haven't they attacked already?' Will asked.

'I don't know. Perhaps we're on their "To Do" list and they'll get round to it when they have a spare moment,' Parry replied a little sarcastically. It was evident that he wasn't taking this latest development well. 'I've already warned Wilkie and the others, and Danforth is running a full systems check on the CCTV and thermal sensors around the estate to make sure they're fully operational.'

Drake took over. 'What's for sure is that we must be a prioritised target for the Styx. They won't want us popping up at an inopportune moment and gatecrashing their party. When – and it's not *if* – they show up here, we'll have to leave in a hurry. So everyone should pack. And you should all check out a weapon from the armoury in the basement.'

Parry grimaced. 'A damned nuisance.' He began to mutter to himself. 'There's too many of us. We'll need more water and food to keep us ticking over in the alternative location, and I can't do that with a wave of a magic wand.' Thwacking his walking stick hard on the floor, he hurried from the room, still complaining to himself.

Chapter Six

Will cradled his Sten in his lap. 'I feel better now I've got my old friend back.' He glanced up at Chester. 'But are you okay about that Darklighting stuff?'

Chester gave a small shrug. 'What freaks me out is that I can't remember a bloody thing about making any calls. Nothing at all.' He frowned. 'Even that time in the cottage in Norfolk with nut-job Martha . . . there was a phone there . . . maybe I rang the Styx from it. I couldn't have told them much because I had no idea where I was. When she bashed me over the head, I thought I was trying to call my parents. But maybe I wasn't, and maybe she was right t—'

'Don't,' Will said. 'You'll end up going crazy yourself if you don't just forget it. It doesn't matter now. It's done. And remember what they stuck in my head. That was worse.'

'You're right,' Chester agreed. 'C'mon, it's your move.' They were in the drawing room and on their second game of chess as a log crackled comfortingly in the fireplace. Drake had asked them to stay up until the early hours, in case unwelcome visitors decided to call at the estate.

Will's hand had wandered to his queen, but he withdrew it

as his concentration shifted to the dancing flames. 'Talking about Martha, remember all those times we played chess in her shack?' he said.

Chester nodded.

Will's gaze was still lost in the fire. 'We really thought Elliott was going to die,' he said.

'You like her a lot, don't you?' Chester asked casually, assessing his position on the board.

Will didn't answer straight away. 'Yes, I suppose I do. But you do too, don't you?'

'Mmmmm . . . I don't think she's as keen on me as she is on you,' Chester said, still surveying his pieces.

'I'm not sure about that,' Will mumbled, then focused on the game again with a grunt – it hadn't been going his way.

'You should say something to her,' Chester suggested.

Will finally moved his queen, then spoke with candour because he felt that he could trust his friend. 'No, not with everything else going on. It would make things too . . . too complicated.' Will glanced at Chester as it occurred to him that he could have broached the subject because he himself had strong feelings for Elliott, and his friend wanted his blessing. But when Chester remained silent, Will assumed this wasn't his motivation. 'I have to tell you, I'm not sure I'm cut out for all this relationship stuff,' Will confessed. 'Not after what went on with my parents.'

Will had been thinking about Dr and Mrs Burrows. Stuck in their lethargic and loveless marriage, they'd led separate lives for years. He couldn't forget the acrimony between them when he and Dr Burrows had returned to Highfield. Mrs Burrows had made it quite plain that she wasn't prepared to take her husband back.

'Which ones?' Chester asked.

'Huh?' Will replied.

'Which parents? You mean your real ones?' Chester said.

This prompted Will to think about his biological parents and what Cal had told him; how Mr Jerome's allegiance had been not to his wife when their infant son was losing his life to chronic fever, but to the laws of the Colony. Driven mad with grief, Sarah Jerome had deserted her husband when she'd done the unthinkable and escaped Topsoil.

Although it seemed irreverent to do so, Will laughed out loud.

Chester looked up with surprise.

'Take your pick,' Will said. 'They were all as bad as each other.'

They heard hurried footsteps in the hallway and Parry appeared at the door. 'Multiple signals!' he bellowed at the boys, his paging device bleeping so rapidly it almost became a solid tone. He went to the gong on the hall table and began to beat it, the urgent rhythm filling the house. Then he tore into his study with the boys following behind. Mr Rawls, still manning the telex, was already on his feet. Parry went straight to the monitor on his desk. He jabbed at the keyboard, flicking through different camera views. 'There! Got one on infra-red!' Parry shouted. 'They're inside the wall.'

Will could clearly see a dark form flitting under a tree. He drew in a sharp breath as, caught on another camera, a man stood in full view with the main gates of the estate behind him. 'Look at the weapon,' Will said, instantly recognising the long barrelled rifle with its bulbous night scope that the Limiters used. 'It's them!'

'Oh, God,' Chester gasped. 'It is!'

'Well, it's certainly not the vicar doing his rounds. And there's another team,' Parry pointed out as a camera showed at least four men as they crept in the lee of a wall. 'We've got several breaches of the perimeter – all to the south.' Parry looked up as Drake entered with Colonel Bismarck. 'Did you catch that?' he asked his son. 'They're here.'

Drake nodded once. 'Time to bug out.'

Stepping from behind his desk, Parry consulted his watch. 'The Styx are on foot, so it'll take them eight – maybe nine – minutes to get here. Stick to the evac procedure we discussed,' he said to Drake. 'Draw them east, while we take the storm drain to the Bedford. And if Sparks isn't waiting for you, just go without him. He can look after himself.'

'Jiggs and Danf—?' Drake began.

'Jiggs likes to do his own thing, and Danforth's already left,' Parry interrupted, holding up his pager. Then he swept his arms at everyone in the study. 'Now, out – out – GET OUT!' he ordered. He went down on one knee beside his desk and flipped open a panel set into the floor. Inside a small recess was a key in a slot, which he turned. 'I've primed the charges. They'll not get a thing from this room.'

Drake, Will, Chester and Mr Rawls met Elliott and Mrs Burrows at the bottom of the staircase.

'I sensed something was heading our way even before I heard the gong. I told Elliott to get dressed,' Mrs Burrows said. 'I take it we're leaving.'

'Yes,' Drake confirmed. 'All of you grab your kit.' He surveyed the Bergens and weapons lined up at the back of the hallway. 'My father will take you to the Bedford.' He threw a look at Colonel Bismarck, about to say something, but then seemed to check himself and addressed Will instead. 'Got your lens handy?' he asked the boy.

Will pointed at the top of his Bergen.

'Good,' Drake said. 'We won't be using lights for most of the way, and I could do with a co-driver. You up for that?'

'Sure . . . yes,' Will answered, flattered that he'd been picked instead of the Colonel.

Having collected his Bergen and a couple of bags of equipment for Drake, Will didn't have time to say goodbye properly. Giving his mother a quick hug, he turned to Elliott, but she was too busy getting herself ready to notice him. Then he and Drake rushed from the hallway and down the corridor to the kitchen. To Will's surprise, Drake left the lights on in the room as he crossed to the back door, and even switched on the exterior light outside.

'You're going to wave this about once we're mobile,' Drake said, handing him a powerful searchlight. 'We want them to see us.'

'We do?' Will asked.

'Didn't I tell you we're the hare?' Drake said with a chuckle. 'We're going to draw the Styx after us, and give Parry a chance to slip quietly away in the Bedford.'

They went towards the rear of the house where there was a shed that Will had never bothered to investigate. As Drake swung the doors open, Will smelt petrol, and in the small amount of moonlight he could make out an angular vehicle. It had a windscreen but no roof.

'My old jeep,' Drake said, throwing his equipment into the back. 'Had it since I was a boy.'

'Whoa!' Will recoiled as a bizarre face loomed at him from out of the darkness.

'Keep your pants on, laddie,' Sweeney growled. He turned

100

to Drake, who was already behind the steering wheel. 'Heard our guests coming up the drive. Caught snatches of something I didn't recognise – might be words, but it sounded bloody ugly.'

'They'll be speaking Styx,' Will said. 'That's what their language sounds like.'

'Ah,' Sweeney said with a rumbling laugh. 'The Stickies talk funny then.'

'Both of you get a move on. Jump in!' Drake ordered. He was about to start the ignition when he hesitated.

'Go ahead,' Sweeney sighed, pulling his hat down over his ears. 'Vehicle electricals aren't too painful for me, although the current in the alternator puts my teeth on edge something rotten.'

'No, I wasn't thinking about that,' Drake said. 'Why would Limiters speak during an operation? They're too damned good for that.' He shrugged, then started up the jeep, turning the headlamps on full beam. 'Time to shine that searchlight around,' he told Will.

Revving the engine to make as much noise as possible, Drake reversed the jeep out of the shed, then raced around to the front of the house and onto the drive. The wheels were churning up the gravel as Will pointed the strong beam down the hill where the Styx would be advancing.

'That should do it, Will. No way they'll have missed that!' Drake shouted above the roaring engine. He threw the jeep down the other side of the house, flooring the throttle to ensure it cleared a drainage ditch. Landing with a crash on the other side, they cut across several fields until Will saw a fence up ahead. But Drake didn't stop, slamming straight through it and down an incline. 'That's the new north gate,' he laughed. 'Torch off now, Will. Time to go dark.' He flipped his lens down at the same time as he extinguished the jeep's headlamps. 'Silent running from here on in, chaps,' he said.

Everyone filed after Parry as he swept down the flight of stairs to the basement. He hurried through the dimly lit and dusty corridor, taking them past the gym, the wine vaults and finally the armoury. As he came to a door of reinforced metal-plate at the end of the corridor, he stopped to check everyone had kept up.

'Why doesn't that surprise me?' he asked, as Colly poked her head out from behind Mrs Burrows.

Not waiting for an answer, he turned back to the door and, from across it, lifted out an iron locking bar laced with cobwebs. 'I might need some help with this,' he said to Chester, indicating the grips on the side of the door. As they both heaved, it wouldn't budge. Then, on the second attempt, the door burst open with a scatter of rust and dirt. Chester was greeted by a blast of damp air and, as Parry's torch beam cut into the darkness beyond, he could make out some kind of brick duct.

'This chute leads down to the main drain. But mind yourself – it's a mite slippery at the best of times,' Parry advised Chester, then gave him a hand through the opening. 'Just slide yourself down it, nice and steady,' Parry added to the boy.

Chester found himself on a slimy incline of around forty-five degrees. With his bulky Bergen on his back and his Sten hooked over his shoulder, he shone his torch into the pitch black below as he edged down on his bottom. He hadn't gone very far when the slope became so wet and slippery he couldn't control his descent. He tried to lean back and dig his heels in to slow himself, but it was no use. He skidded down the slope, building up speed until, with a large splash, his feet hit several feet of water.

'Oh, just brilliant,' Chester grumbled, wiping the foul-smelling water from his face. As he straightened his Bergen on his back, his torch beam fell on a huge brown rat. At Chester's cry of alarm, the rat took fright and scampered off. Parry had heard the cry and was calling to Chester.

'Are you all right?' he shouted down the chute.

'Why do I always *always* end up back in places like this?' Chester asked himself with a shiver. He shone his torch up at Parry, shouting, 'Yes, I'm fine!'

Then, as the others slid down the chute, he helped them, making sure they didn't injure themselves as they landed. It didn't seem to present any problem to Mrs Burrows, who was using her new supersense. Parry came last, speaking to them as soon as he touched down. 'This is the main storm drain connecting the lake to the river – nice example of Edwardian hydro-engineering. But now we need to get our skates on.' He immediately began to jog through the muddy water.

They all followed him, their lights ricocheting off the sides of the old tunnel built of ancient brick. As he ran with a limp, it was clear that Parry found it taxing to move at speed. But Mr Rawls was just as slow, losing his footing several times and falling into the water. Chester was there to help him up each time.

In less than ten minutes, they'd reached the end. The wind chilled them in their sodden clothing as they emerged into a culvert, its almost vertical sides overgrown with ferns and other vegetation. Some twenty feet away, as the culvert widened out, Chester spotted the dark outline of a lorry. With his shotgun in his hands, Old Wilkie appeared from around the side of the vehicle, and he and Parry immediately began to talk to each other in hushed tones.

As the others approached the canvas awning over the back of the Bedford, Stephanie suddenly poked her head from under it. They were all soaking wet and splattered with mud and, for a moment, she regarded them with a look of consternation. Then she saw Chester. 'Hi, it's you! Gramps didn't tell me you were coming too.'

'Er . . . yeah,' Chester replied.

'Isn't this sooo exciting! Nothing cool ever happens in this dump, and I, like, so adore this spy stuff. Guns and top-secret journeys in the night. It's like being in a movie!'

'Aren't you going to introduce me to your friend?' Elliott enquired.

Chester was halfway through some mumbled introductions when Stephanie noticed Colly and gave a small whoop. 'You found your dog-thing!'

'Keep it down back there,' Parry growled.

'Ooooh, sorry,' Stephanie replied, just as piercingly, clapping her hand over her mouth as she pulled a silly face. 'I'm always getting myself into trouble with my loud voice.'

'It's not *the* dog-thing,' Chester told her. 'It's the . . . er . . . the other dog-thing. There are two of them.'

Stephanie nodded, aware that Elliott was staring up at her.

'Anyway, I want you to come and sit next to me. I want my skier next to me,' Stephanie said. 'Whoosh, whoosh!' she added, moving her hips and laughing brightly.

'Whoosh?' Elliott repeated, frowning.

'Skier?' Mr Rawls asked.

Chester gave them a helpless look, then swung his Bergen into the Bedford, and clambered up after it.

'And I'm not, like, sitting anywhere near those dead pigs and cows,' Stephanie said adamantly. Now he was under the awning, Chester saw that against the rear of the lorry cab a dozen or so crates and blue plastic drums had been stacked. And above them, animal carcasses wound in some kind of cloth had been suspended. 'Ewwww! See what I mean,' Stephanie burst out as she pointed at the gently swaying carcasses. 'They might drip something totally yucky on my coat.'

'No . . . yes, they might,' Chester agreed, wondering exactly how much she'd been told about their current situation.

'Are we leaving now?' Colonel Bismarck asked Parry as he came over.

'Yes, everyone needs to get in the Bedford. After a couple of hundred yards, the culvert drains into the river, which is running high for this time of year. So we're all going to get wet,' Parry told them. He addressed the Colonel. 'And I'd like you to ride shotgun.'

'*Ja*. Of course,' the Colonel replied, patting his assault rifle.

Once they'd all loaded their kit on the lorry and the tailgate had been secured, they arranged themselves along the benches on either side. Joining Old Wilkie in the cab, Parry fired up the engine, and they rolled down the slope until they'd fully emerged from the culvert. Then Parry dropped a gear and everyone was thrown around as the lorry climbed over a gravel bank and into the river. Although it was difficult to see anything much in the darkness under the canvas awning, they could hear the water washing over the bed of the lorry and slopping around their feet.

'Ohhh!' Stephanie gasped dramatically, lifting her boots up as she gripped Chester's arm.

Drake drove the jeep off the track and a short distance into the trees. Then he used a machete to lop off some branches, which Will helped him to lay over the vehicle to conceal it.

They both returned to the track where Sweeney had been waiting. The earflaps of his army hat were tied up, and his head was angled to one side as he faced the direction they'd just come from. 'Nothing yet,' he told Drake, opening his shoulder bag. 'Brought some welcoming gifts for your Stickies.' He took out a massive foot-long combat knife, gripping it between his teeth like a pirate as he continued to rummage in the bottom of the bag.

'You don't carry a gun,' Will observed.

'Never been big on them,' Sweeney said, a grin just visible behind the knife in his mouth. He held out one of his huge hands and closed it as if gripping a throat, his knuckles popping like champagne corks. 'Prefer to work with these. I can be more creative with them.' Then he found what he'd been looking for in his bag. 'Ah, here we are.' He held up a pair of grenades. 'Fresh pineapples.'

'Thanks,' Drake said, taking one as casually as if he was accepting a bar of chocolate. Then he and Will positioned themselves on one side of the track, Sweeney the other, and they lay in wait. Drake had told Will that he should concentrate on the area beside the track because any Limiter worth his salt would never approach straight down it. So, with his

Sten gripped in his hands, Will kept careful watch. The tree trunks and shrubs were orange-hued through the lens over his right eye, which allowed him to see the surroundings as clearly as if they were in daylight. He wondered how it looked to Sweeney with his enhanced vision.

After an hour of listening to the patter of rain, Will's excitement had dulled. At the beginning, his heart had been thumping with anticipation at the prospect of catching the Limiters on the hop, but the damp was penetrating his clothes and making him very uncomfortable. Will suffered another two hours of this misery until Drake finally led him back to the path.

'Still nothing?' Drake asked as Sweeney appeared.

The huge man shook his head. 'Not a flippin' sausage.' He gave Will a passing glance. 'Except for young laddie here yawning and shifting about on his rump like he'd sat on an anthill.'

'Sorry,' Will mumbled.

'They've had plenty of time to catch up,' Drake thought aloud, looking down the track. 'There's no way they could have missed us as we left, so they certainly knew which direction we'd taken.'

'Perhaps they've dug in around the house, hoping we'd be stupid enough to go back,' Sweeney suggested.

Drake examined the grenade Sweeney had given him. 'Maybe,' he said.

After he'd reversed the jeep out, Drake waited while Will and Sweeney climbed into it, then they sped off again, still heading away from Parry's estate.

'Trees . . .' Will mumbled to himself as mile after mile of the forest sped by. There wasn't much to look at and, all the time, Sweeney was in the back, with his strange circled eyes tightly shut and his shoulder bag on his knees.

Will suddenly realised how cold he was, and wound his scarf up around his face, but it didn't do much to help. Telling himself he should relax because the Limiters couldn't possibly know the lie of the land as well as Drake, Will gave into his fatigue and fell asleep.

As Drake took the jeep around a bend so fast that it tipped on two wheels, Will woke with a start, hanging on for dear life. The first signs of dawn were approaching, a cobalt blue seeping into the sky. They careered around another bend and hurtled down an incline. At the bottom of the slope Will spotted a ford running across the track, but he was distracted by a shout from Sweeney. He turned, but the man and his shoulder bag were nowhere to be seen.

The vehicle slewed to a halt as Drake slammed on the brakes.

'Who *is* that?' Will whispered.

Some thirty feet in front of them a woman was standing in the middle of the ford. She was signalling with a torch.

Will heard Drake say 'Mrs Rawls' as he crunched the gears into reverse and gunned the engine.

Will couldn't work out why Drake wasn't backing the jeep up the track as fast as it would go. 'What are you waiting for?' he asked urgently. 'This has to be a trap.'

'Too late. We're already in it,' Drake replied in a low voice. He left the engine running, but slid from his seat, keeping low. Will did the same, his Sten at the ready.

Mrs Rawls called out to Drake several times but he didn't acknowledge her, panning around the trees with his Beretta as he edged cautiously towards the ford.

'What now?' Will asked.

'We improvise,' Drake whispered. Using his teeth, he pulled the pin from the grenade to arm it. But he kept the grenade firmly in his hand as he spat the pin out, then met eyes with Will. 'Just watch my back,' he said.

Will hadn't needed to be told as he pointed his weapon at the track behind them.

'Drake, it's okay!' Mrs Rawls shouted, still waving the torch.

Other than Chester's mother, there was no sign of life anywhere. And there was no sign of Sweeney either, but then Will hadn't expected there to be. The old soldier was doing what he'd been trained to do.

'It's all right!' Mrs Rawls shouted as she lowered the torch. 'Really, Drake – it's all right!'

'Emily,' Drake replied, still scouring the trees, 'who's with you?'

'Hello, Drake,' Eddie said as he stepped from behind a tree on the other side of the ford. He began towards Mrs Rawls.

'Stop right there!' Drake ordered, aiming his handgun at the Styx's head. 'I thought it had to be you.'

Eddie slowly raised both hands, opening them to show they were empty. 'I'm unarmed. I just want to speak to you.'

Although he was meant to be watching the rear, Will had never seen the former Limiter before and couldn't resist a peek at him. The man was rake thin like all Styx. He was wearing a dark brown three-quarter-length coat and Wellington boots, and on his head was a flat cap. If it hadn't been for his sunken cheeks and jet-black eyes, he might have passed as a country squire out for a walk.

'This isn't an ambush – if it was, I wouldn't be standing

here talking to you right now,' Eddie said, dropping his arms. 'It's crucial I speak to you. It's more important than any grudges you and I might still bear each other.'

Drake stood poised on one side of the ford with Eddie on the other, Mrs Rawls halfway between them, the water rushing around her ankles.

'How did you know I'd be coming this way?' Drake demanded.

'A tactical guess,' Eddie answered. 'I've had the house under observation, and naturally I recce'd the outlying areas.'

'Naturally,' Drake put in sarcastically.

'This wasn't an obvious escape route, so I calculated it would be the one you'd take.' Eddie glanced at Mrs Rawls. 'You know, they tried to activate Emily for the City offensive, but I intervened. She's been well looked after.'

'Is that true?' Drake asked. 'He saved your life?'

'Yes,' Mrs Rawls confirmed, with a smile and a nod. She certainly didn't look the worse for wear or under any form of duress.

'And I've brought her back for you,' Eddie said. 'A peace offering.'

Mrs Rawls began to step towards Drake. 'Sorry, Emily, that's quite close enough. You may have been Darklit,' he said. 'Will, keep your weapon on her.'

'Hello, Mrs Rawls,' Will mumbled awkwardly as he swiv-elled his Sten towards her. 'How are you?'

'Very well, thank you, Will,' she replied.

'She hasn't been Darklit. At least not by me,' Eddie spoke up.

They stood there, the only sounds the gurgle of the stream and the odd bird call in the distance.

'Okay, where are the others?' Drake asked. 'You didn't run the surveillance on the house or a full recon on the surrounding area without more manpower.'

'Absolutely correct,' Eddie answered, beginning to raise his hand. 'If you'd permit me?'

'Be my guest,' Drake said.

Eddie clicked his fingers.

There was a rumble as engines roared into life from both up ahead and from behind on the track.

With the cracking of crushed undergrowth, two large American military vehicles trundled into view.

'Humvees?' Drake said, looking alarmed.

They ground to a halt, blocking both ends of the track. They were painted a matt green and the windows were tinted.

As their engines fell silent, their doors swung open.

Styx dismounted from the vehicles. Others emerged from between the trees. Will could count eight in total.

'Limiters?' Drake asked, even more alarmed.

'They are,' Eddie replied.

None of the Styx soldiers were in their dun-coloured combat uniforms, but instead wore an assortment of Topsoiler clothes: Barbour jackets, parkas and walking boots. One was even in jeans. But with their craggy faces and hollow eyes, the soldier elite were unmistakable as they came nearer. None of them were carrying weapons, but that didn't make them any less threatening to Will. His stomach churned with fear. The last time he'd encountered them in such numbers his father had been brutally gunned down by one of the Rebecca twins.

'Where do you want us?' Eddie asked.

Drake inclined his head in Eddie's direction. 'By you, where I can keep an eye on everybody.'

The Limiters dutifully marched to the bank and formed up in a line behind Eddie. Will noticed that one of the Limiters had bandages across much of his face, and his left eye seemed to be stitched shut. It made him look all the more gruesome.

'Is that the lot?' Drake said, his handgun pointed at the group.

Eddie seemed hesitant as he inspected his men behind him. He was about to speak when Drake interrupted him.

'Sparks – you can come out now,' he said, barely raising his voice.

'Aw, and I was just getting into my stride,' came the response, and a low chuckle echoed around the trees. Sweeney swaggered onto the track. He had two Limiters with him, one on each shoulder. 'Bagged myself a pair of Stickies. Bit slow off the mark, aren't they?' He was carrying them as if they weighed nothing.

Eddie jerked his head in the stocky man's direction.

'You didn't hurt them?' Drake asked.

Sweeney grinned. 'Nah, they weren't armed, so I didn't think I ought to. They're sleeping the sleep of the fairies.' He considered each of the insensible Limiters on his shoulders in turn. 'Pig-ugly fairies.' Then he looked across at Drake. 'So where should I put them? Next to Big Chief Sticky?'

'No, just drop them there,' Drake said, smiling at Eddie, who was peering at Sweeney with interest. 'Say hello to Sparks, an old friend of mine. I've got more friends like him.'

Eddie raised his eyebrows, clearly astonished that the Styx soldiers had been taken unawares.

'One is still unaccounted for,' he said.

'Jiggs,' Sweeney put in.

'Jiggs is here?' Drake asked, amazed.

'Sure. He knocked another of these bozos out for the count.'

'Good man,' Drake said. He gave a dry laugh as he surveyed all the Limiters standing patiently in line. 'What's with the big turnout, Eddie? Nature ramble?' he asked coldly. 'I can only assume all these Limiters have come over to you now? But how do you know you can trust them?'

'They are loyal to me,' Eddie confirmed, no trace of doubt in his voice. 'Remember I told you that there were others who feel the same way I do. These men have all defected to me because of their convictions. They believe that the current escalation isn't right, and must be stopped.'

As Drake's gaze passed over Will, he noticed that the boy's face was strained. 'Are you okay, Will?' he asked.

Will wasn't. He was wondering if any of these Limiters had been on top of the pyramid, watching as Dr Burrows was murdered. He'd been highly critical to Chester about Drake's short alliance with Eddie when they'd mounted an operation together in the Eternal City, although he hadn't said anything directly to Drake about it. He found it impossible to believe that there was such a thing as a good Styx.

'Will?' Drake repeated.

'Yes . . . fine,' Will lied through his clenched teeth.

'So you're Will Burrows,' Eddie said gently. 'I've heard much about you.'

'Really,' Will grunted, unnerved by the attention from the Styx.

'And about your family: Tam, your mother Sarah . . . and Cal, your brother. And it is in relation to him that we have an apology to make to you.'

'Cal?' was all that Will could say.

'Yes, about his Hunter. I believe the animal's name was Bartleby.'

'*Was?*' Drake burst out, but Eddie continued.

'There was a serious and inexcusable lapse in protocol at one of the observation posts that I established on the hills surrounding the estate, and your Hunter got the better of the team manning it,' Eddie said. 'The Limiter on duty watch allowed the animal to steal up on him, and attack.'

'What are you talking about?' Will demanded.

'Unfortunately, Bartleby was killed.' Eddie pointed his claw-like finger at the Humvee parked further down the track behind Will. Will turned and began to walk mechanically towards the vehicle. He didn't want to see what was waiting for him, but felt compelled to look.

There was a shape on the flat bonnet. Will hinged up the lens from over his eye – with the advent of dawn it was becoming unnecessary.

As he came to the vehicle, he saw the shape was Bartleby. His fore- and hindlegs were bound with rope, his carcase stretched across the front of the vehicle as if the big cat was a trophy kill from a hunting trip.

Similar to the colour pervading the dawn sky, Will could clearly see the network of cobalt veins under Bartleby's slate-grey skin, which seemed to have lightened in death. And Bartleby's amber eyes had also lost all their intensity and were now pale as sour milk, their lenses opalescent as they stared into space.

But above all else, Will found it impossible to accept that the cat was motionless. He'd always been so full of life, always prancing everywhere in his permanent quest for something to eat, always up to no good like some mischievous child.

'Bart,' Will whispered. Part of him almost expected the cat to wake up, just as he had so many times before when Will had disturbed him during one of his naps. But he knew that wasn't going to happen. Extending his hand, he rubbed one of the Hunter's chunky paws. 'Poor old Bartleby,' he said, his throat tight with emotion. 'Poor old chap.'

He was muttering these same words and shaking his head as he made his way back to the ford. He dragged his feet, his body limp with grief and frustration.

Everyone was watching him, but no one spoke until Eddie broke the silence.

'I am truly sorry for this accident.'

'You're sorry, are you?' Will growled.

He could hear his dead brother's voice shouting in his ears,

Cal's voice, hungry for revenge, saying, 'Kill the White Neck bastards! Go on, Will, let them bloody have it!'

Will realised there was nothing to stop him. He could gun down Eddie and these soldiers, and there'd be no comeback. He wasn't breaking the law. Drake and Sweeney could bury the corpses in the forest, just like Bartleby's would probably be buried too.

'You're sorry?' Will said again, daring the man to respond. '*How* flipping sorry is that?' He thrust his Sten threateningly at Eddie.

He itched to pull the trigger.

He had tears in his eyes now.

'You people take everything away from me. Again and again. All you do is kill. I . . .'

He tensed his finger.

'Will!' Drake burst out.

'Easy . . . don't do anything you might regret, laddie,' Sweeney said as he swept in and seized the barrel of Will's Sten, deflecting it towards the ground. Will didn't resist as Sweeney gently pulled the weapon from his hands. 'Never act out of anger.'

'I want to make amends,' Eddie continued.

Drake was nonplussed. 'What?'

Eddie waded through the ford towards him. 'Let me dispose of that for you,' he offered, indicating the grenade still in his hand. 'You have no need of it now.'

Drake looked at Eddie blankly.

'I'm hardly going to use it on us,' Eddie assured him. 'I'm not suicidal.'

Drake frowned, but then to Will's complete amazement he allowed the Styx to take the grenade from him. The oddest thing was that Will could detect not animosity between Drake and Eddie, but something entirely different. Camaraderie. Friendship, even. It rankled with him.

Eddie returned to the line of Limiters and presented the grenade to the Styx with the bandaged face. He accepted it mutely.

'This soldier wants to express his regret,' Eddie announced, then the Limiter began to march a little way up the track and into the forest.

'No!' Drake shouted as he realised what was about to happen. He swung round to Sweeney. 'Sparks! Your ears!' he yelled.

Just as the last word left his mouth, the Limiter pitched forward onto the grenade. There was a muffled explosion. Will saw the flash as the Limiter's body was lifted from the ground. Everyone was showered with earth and wood splinters. As a tree groaned and keeled over, Mrs Rawls screamed.

'Ouch!' Sweeney complained, his hands still cupped over his ears. 'That was loud.'

'That was unnecessary,' Drake said grimly to Eddie.

Eddie's face, and those of the other Limiters, wore their normal, inscrutable expressions. 'No, that was the price for dereliction of duty,' Eddie explained. 'And I've also just answered your question, Drake. Every one of these men will show me unquestioning and absolute obedience. They are completely loyal to me. That's why they're here. They'll do anything I ask of them.'

Eddie then addressed a wide-eyed Will, who was still half crouched from the explosion. 'As I said, we are extremely sorry for the Hunter's death. Now the responsible party has been punished, I hope it has gone some way towards making amends.' Eddie swung round to face Drake. 'And now can we talk, please?'

'As long as you don't pull any more stunts like that,' Drake said.

The Sten looked like a toy in Sweeney's huge hands as Will and Drake left him to keep watch over Mrs Rawls and the Limiters. Eddie had made the tactful suggestion that they talk in the Humvee on the far side of the ford, which spared Will from seeing Bartleby's body for a second time.

Will climbed into the front passenger seat. He'd never been in a Humvee before, and was peering around at the spacious interior.

'Are you all right?' Drake said to Will, as he settled into one of the back seats.

Will turned and nodded, but Drake was already examining the weapons rack mounted behind him in the rear of the vehicle. It housed almost a dozen Styx rifles and state-of-the-art Topsoil weapons. And beside it was some expensive-looking communications equipment.

'Bet you had to flog a few diamonds to pay for this lot,' Drake said as Eddie climbed into the seat beside him.

'I've a couple more of these vehicles in London,' Eddie replied. 'And some armoured pers—'

It took Will completely by surprise when Drake lashed out, punching the Styx full in the face.

'That was for Darklighting me,' Drake said, rubbing his knuckles.

Eddie's eyes were watering as he fumbled for something in his hip pocket. He produced a handkerchief, using it to dab his nose. Will could see a smear of blood on his top lip.

'I suppose that I deserv—' Eddie started to say.

Drake lashed out at him again, if anything hitting him with even greater force this time. His handkerchief went flying, and blood was now flowing freely from his nose.

'And that?' Eddie asked, sounding even more nasal than ever.

'That was for Chester,' Drake growled. 'It was a low-down dirty trick to Darklight him too.'

'What?' Will exclaimed. 'Then it wasn't the real Styx?'

'No, it wasn't, was it, Eddie?' Drake accused the man.

The Styx nodded. 'I suppose I deserved that too,' he said. He didn't exhibit any resentment at the way Drake had just treated him, his voice impassive. 'It was underhand of me, but I needed a means to keep track of you. So when you left Chester alone in my flat, I applied a little light conditioning. It was nothing drastic.'

'You make it sound as though you gave him some sort of hair care product,' Drake commented drily, then shook his head. 'So we bugged out of my father's house for no good reason. Why in God's name didn't you just knock at the gate?'

Eddie sniffed in an attempt to clear the blood from his nostrils. 'I needed to get your full and undivided attention. If I'd simply shown up, you wouldn't have taken me seriously. And you seem to be overlooking the good turn I've done you. After you tossed Emily Rawls back into the pond, I stepped in to save her, and now I've delivered her safely back to you.'

'Back into the pond? What does he mean?' Will asked Drake.

'It was her choice,' Drake defended himself, but Will could see that Eddie had him on the back foot. 'Emily was dead set on helping, and I needed a way to keep tabs on what the Styx were planning next.'

'So you're saying that what I did to Chester was worse than leaving his mother to the wolves,' Eddie levelled at Drake, then took a breath. 'But, look, this isn't getting us anywhere, and I have to brief you on a matter wh—'

Drake was clearly angered by Eddie's accusation, and now cut him off belligerently. 'What's so damned important you've gone to all this trouble to speak to me? If it's about your daughter, you're wasting your time. She doesn't want to know.'

'Yes . . . and no,' the Styx answered in a measured way. 'No, I didn't come for Elliott, but have you observed anything different about her? Any changes?'

Drake frowned, not understanding why Eddie had asked the question. 'Well, she's growing up fast,' he replied. 'Same as any normal girl in her teens.'

'Normal girl,' Eddie repeated in barely a whisper, opening and closing his hand stiffly. It was a small but uncharacteristic sign of anxiety, and one that Will and Drake immediately picked up on. The Styx then locked eyes with Drake. 'I'm going to tell you something that no human has ever heard before. It will explain why my people have ramped up their operations here on the surface.'

'Go on,' Drake urged, crossing his arms as he leant back. 'I'm all ears.'

'I need to tell you about . . .' Eddie said, faltering for a moment as though his lips were refusing to obey him, '. . . about *the Phase*.'

Manned by two New Germanians, the factory gates swung open and Captain Franz steered the Mercedes to an area of tarmac designated *Visitors' Parking*, where he pulled up. In a flash he'd left his seat and was at the rear of the car to let the Rebecca twins out. He then hurried ahead to do the same again, opening the door into the office building. But, for a moment, the Rebeccas hung back in the parking area as they admired the ranks of expensive cars.

'Makes you proud,' Rebecca One said as she spotted a Bugatti Veyron next to a Ferrari Enzo.

Her sister hummed in agreement, then they continued to the office building where Captain Franz was still propping the door open.

'Very kind. Thank you,' Rebecca Two said as she slipped by him.

'Very kind. Thank you,' Rebecca One repeated in a gushing Marilyn Monroe voice as she passed the captain, topping off the impersonation with a small curtsey.

Rebecca Two ignored her sister's taunt as a Limiter in full combats strode forward to meet them. 'I see from the cars they're all here,' she said to him. 'Show them into the board-room.'

Moving quickly on from the reception area, the twins passed along a corridor and through an open doorway. It was a sizeable room, dominated by a table some twenty feet in length with chairs arranged around it. The Rebecca twins made their way directly to the head of the table and sat down. Captain Franz positioned himself behind them as if he was standing to attention, his hands behind his back.

In less than a minute, a procession of fully grown Styx women began to enter the boardroom. They came from all walks of Topsoil life and their appearances differed accordingly. Some had kept their raven-black hair, but others had bleached or dyed it, and their clothes were just as varied. Far from hiding away in the shadows like their male counterparts, many of these women had insinuated themselves into prime areas of Topsoil commerce and the upper echelons of government, and were regularly in the limelight. They were important and valued members of English society, many of them key decision makers in their chosen fields.

There were forty women in total. And although their appearances were diverse, the one thing that they all had in common was their exceptional beauty. With their high cheekbones and piercing eyes, they were all incredibly tall and slender. In Topsoil terms, each and every one of them was stunning.

A woman with short cropped black hair sashayed to the chair at the opposite end of the table from the twins and settled into it, crossing her legs elegantly.

'Hermione,' Rebecca One greeted her.

Hermione smiled.

'I caught the spread they did on you in *Hello!*' Rebecca One continued. 'You looked simply fantastic in the photos.'

'Yes, I was pleased with how that shoot turned out,' Hermione replied. With homes in London, Paris and New York, she was the guiding light at one of the world's leading PR companies.

Another woman, with shoulder-length blonde hair and dressed in a black Vivienne Westwood suit, took the place beside Hermione. Moving with the grace of a cat, she slid down in the chair, propping one of her Jimmy-Choo-shod feet on the edge of the table.

'And hi, Vane,' Rebecca Two said to her. 'It's been a long time.'

'It has,' she replied.

Although it was difficult to tell at first glance, Hermione and Vane were twins just like the Rebeccas, and had always been role models for the young girls.

'We saw you've been busy with your latest show,' Rebecca Two said to Vane.

The woman gave a small smile. She was the main presenter on a reality television series which was topping the ratings. 'It doesn't take much to amuse the average Topsoiler,' she said, her voice dripping with scorn.

Hermione rubbed a shoulder under her jacket, casting an eye around the boardroom. 'What a dive this place is. Wholly unremarkable.'

Rebecca Two nodded in agreement. 'Yes, it's perfect, isn't it? And out back,' she said, inclining her head to her right, 'there's nearly an acre of controlled environment.'

Rebecca One took over, addressing all the women. 'And in that acre we've already prepared three hundred subjects for you.'

All the woman reacted immediately, purring with approval. And all of them, without exception, had begun to breathe more heavily as their faces became flushed. Several were kneading their shoulders.

But a woman standing in the midst of the group behind Vane and Hermione seemed less than impressed. 'Is that all?' she said curtly. Her appearance was dowdy in comparison to the other women; she wore no make-up, and as she took off her officer's cap, her hair was a mousey brown. Dressed in her khaki uniform, she was one of the highest-ranking women in the British Army. 'Because I know where we can obtain many more candidates than that,' she said, referring to the soldiers under her command. 'And they're all in tiptop physical condition.'

Rebecca One answered quickly. 'There's no need for them. The same number again is going through processing and will be ready for you soon. That should be adequate even for your voracious appetite, Major.'

A woman in a dark blue suit took a step forward from the group. She had come direct from the Harley Street optometrist's clinic where she administered regular Dark Light sessions to many leading politicians and businessmen. 'Can I make a start on him?' she asked, widening her dark eyes as she ogled Captain Franz. 'He's a sweet morsel.'

'I saw him first,' Hermione laughed, uncrossing her legs as she ran her tongue over her perfect teeth.

'You're both mistaken. I think you'll find that he's mine,' Vane said.

'No,' Rebecca Two answered a little too sharply. 'He's useful to us.'

'Really?' Hermione said, her eyes flashing as she noticed how defensive the Rebecca twin had become. 'And in what way could this Topsoiler ever be deemed "useful"?'

To defuse the situation, Rebecca One clapped her hands together and rose to her feet. 'If everyone is ready,' she announced, 'then please follow us.'

The girls led the way, the Styx women behind them. Their heels clicked on the lino as they left the carpeted area and trooped down the corridor leading to the first of the warehouses. A pair of Limiters, the fearless soldiers of the elite Styx regiment, was stationed at the entrance of the former factory. But they didn't seem to be so fearless now, cowering and pulling back as far as they could from the horde of women. As she passed, Hermione leant towards one and growled at him. The Limiter nearly jumped out of his skin. 'Men are such wimps,' she chuckled throatily.

But the rest of the women didn't utter a word as they stepped onto the factory floor. The industrial humidifying units were rattling away to themselves, and the air was thick and warm. Much of the interior, lit only by the occasional tripod-mounted luminescent orb, was in gloom.

And across the factory floor were three hundred hospital beds arranged in a grid, each bed with a person stretched out on it in a state of unconsciousness. The scene resembled some mass dormitory of slumbering humans, consisting of Topsoilers and Colonists, and even a handful of New Germanians who had been brought in to make up the numbers.

Rebecca One stood before the group of women. 'This is . . .' she began to say, but then noticed most of the Styx women weren't paying any attention whatsoever to her. Drawn by the irresistible, primal drive present in each of them, many were already edging towards the beds. Rebecca One held her hands high in the air and addressed the women at the top of her voice. 'This is one of the greatest moments in our long history, and we're proud to have been able to . . .' She trailed off as she realised it was useless; the assembled group of women were barely listening as their eyes darted over the beds.

'Once you're done in here, you can move on to the other two warehouses, where the rest of the candidates will be waiting for you,' Rebecca Two added. 'Don't worry if you can't manage them all, as more of our sisters will be joining us later.'

'We'll try to leave them a few scraps,' Hermione said. A ripple of muted laughter ran through the group, but most of them were too full of anticipation to join in.

'So let the Phase begin!' Rebecca One proclaimed in a shout.

The women fanned out across the factory floor, some running in order to claim the humans in the outlying corners for themselves.

'We've come a long way since Romania,' Rebecca One said. 'It's so much easier now we have the technology to scrub their minds,' she said, referring to the intensive Dark Light treatments the people on the beds had been subjected to.

'Yes, it's far less messy than hobbling them. Even with their ankles shattered, they might still try to resist,' Rebecca Two said breathlessly, as she watched Hermione approach one of the nearest beds.

As the Styx woman sidled up to the senseless human, she shed her jacket, then her blouse. Straddling the body, Hermione arched her upper body and threw her head in the air, unleashing a primordial and piercing shriek which rose to the corrugated roof and seemed to fall back down to the factory floor again.

There was already blood on her back. But as she'd begun to shriek, two slits opened up across the upper edges of both her shoulder blades, the flesh tearing apart.

From these slits, jointed insect legs pushed out. They twitched as if they'd just been born and were taking their first breath, then they snapped open to their full length.

A pair of insectoid limbs, black and shiny and glistening with blood and plasma, and covered with small bristles.

Hermione was still shrieking, but the sound was swelled by the other women as, astride their victims, they began to shriek too. They shrieked until the combined volume was unbearable in the confines of the factory, the sound resonating through the very fabric of its walls.

Then, as Hermione threw her arms forward at the

insensible human, the insect limbs also whipped over each of her shoulders. With their pincers they gripped the man's temples on either side, holding him steady for what was about to come.

Hermione was breathing in staccato bursts as she lowered her head closer to the man's and stuck her thumbs into his mouth, stretching it wide open. A tube suddenly burst from her mouth. More than a foot and a half in length, it immediately found the man's gaping mouth.

'It's a wonderful thing to behold,' Rebecca One slurred, intoxicated by the spectacle before her. 'We're so lucky to see this.'

The fleshy tube was similar to the ovipositor found at the tip of the abdomen of many insects for egg laying, but far larger. And Hermione's pulsated as something was squeezed down it by the peristaltic movement of the muscles.

It was a pod the size of a box of matches. An egg case.

As the tube pushed further into the man's mouth and forced its way down his throat, a reflex action made him cough and he tried to move his head. But, with a final slurping sound, the egg case was deposited deep inside him, and he became still again.

Hermione's insect limbs unhooked themselves from the man's temples. She raised her arms and stretched them elegantly, then slid from the man. She immediately moved to the next bed, where a woman lay.

'One down, five hundred and ninety-nine to go,' Rebecca Two said.

Chapter Seven

'And from each of these egg sacs or pods,' Eddie continued, 'more than thirty Styx are spawned. They go through a larval stage, consuming the living flesh of the human host. And when they've depleted the host's ravaged carcase, they burst out, and—'

'Burst out?' Will asked, looking more than a little queasy.

'Yes, they rupture it and crawl out in search of more food. In the following days, they need an ample supply of fresh meat in order to fully develop. Once they've absorbed sufficient protein, they form cocoons, for the pupation stage. And within a week or two, they hatch out, and a brand new army is ready to swarm.'

Drake was frowning. 'You say "Styx" are produced. What do you mean, exactly?' he asked.

'Like me, like Limiters,' Eddie answered.

Drake's frown deepened. 'After only two weeks? How can a fully formed adult be produced in only a matter of weeks? How can that be?'

'They possess the intelligence of a fully developed Styx male, but they have no emotional faculties. They have no need of them. They've been brought into this world with a single purpose – to kill. And they're incredibly good at it, because they have no qualms about dying. We call them the Warrior Class. They'll work their way through the Topsoil population, using whatever weapons are available and slaughtering as they go, until they're ordered to stop. Or until there's no one left to kill.'

There was a shocked silence in the Humvee until Will spoke. 'It's like the ichneumon wasp,' he whispered in horror. If it was possible with his unpigmented skin, his face seemed to have turned even whiter than usual. 'I saw this TV programme about them once. They lay eggs in a living animal, which hatch out and b—'

'It's more than that,' Drake interrupted, turning to Will. 'You remember that last time we were in Highfield with your father? When he wanted to catch a glimpse of Celia from the rooftop?'

'Sure, I remember,' Will said. 'In Martineau Square.'

'Well, I rather glibly made a comparison between the Styx and viruses then. I had absolutely no idea how close I was.' Drake turned to Eddie. 'At a guess, when the spawn grows in the host, it assimilates not just its proteins, but also some of the host DNA into its genome, doesn't it? And isn't that the reason why current Styx physiology mirrors our own?'

Eddie nodded. 'Our scholars believe that there was a Phase in prehistoric times, which brought about the extinction of the dinosaurs. And we most certainly weren't humanoid in those days. The scholars tell us that the human resemblance came later, after a second Phase during Neanderthal times.'

Will uttered a barely audible, 'Wow.'

'Wait . . . this is all getting a little too fantastic,' Drake said, holding up his hands. 'Where's the proof for all this, Eddie? How do I know what you've just told us is true?' he challenged, although not aggressively, as he tried to deal with what he'd just heard. 'We've only got your word f—'

Eddie made a move to reach inside his jacket. In a heart-beat, Drake had drawn his gun and was aiming it straight at the Styx.

'You know I'm not armed,' Eddie said, holding completely still. 'I want to show you something.'

'Go on,' Drake said, his gun still on the Styx.

From an inside pocket Eddie slowly eased out a book, its cover creased and worn.

'*The Book of Catastrophes*?' Will asked, as he regarded the battered volume in Eddie's hands, which was bound in some type of ivory-coloured parchment.

'No, this is from long before that,' Eddie replied. 'Only a handful of copies of this book survived from the fifteenth century. No Colonist has ever laid eyes on it, and it's unlikely there'll be another above grass. I had this particular copy smuggled out of the Citadel for me.'

Putting his handgun away, Drake shrugged. 'So what is it?'

'Well . . .' Eddie thought for a second. 'The Styx title for it means "from one comes many". There isn't an exact match in the English language, but I suppose the best word for it would be "Propagation", or better, perhaps, "Proliferation".' With a finger, he traced the three sides of the inverted triangle tooled into its front cover. 'Yes, the *Book of Proliferation*,' he decided, then held it up to Will and Drake. 'And this isn't leather. It's bound in skin. Human skin.'

'O-k-a-y,' Drake exhaled. 'I suppose that about sets the tone.'

Eddie opened the book and was carefully turning the pages, which rustled like old leaves. 'Ah, here it is,' he said, rotating the book so Will and Drake could see the illustration, a crude woodblock print.

It depicted a man lying on the ground, his body bloated and misshapen, as a woman's thin face hung over him. The rest of her body was partially concealed by the shadows, and difficult to make out.

Will was squinting at the picture. 'It sort of looks like she's got wings on her back . . . but those must be the insect limbs you talked about,' he said.

'Correct.' Eddie swivelled the book around again and glanced at the page of meticulously written text. 'This is a record of our last Phase. It documents what took place in the mid-fifteenth century in Romania,' he told Will and Drake. 'It was during the reign of the Prince of Wallachia, who achieved notoriety for his wholesale slaughter of p—'

Will couldn't stop himself from jumping in. 'Vlad . . . Dad told me about him. You're talking about *Vlad the Impaler*, aren't you?'

'I am,' Eddic confirmed. 'And the folklore surrounding him has given rise to the improbable vampire stories and films that seem to be so in vogue at the moment. But the reality is somewhat different . . . the reality is that our Phase started the myth. You see, the prince offered us protection on the under-standing that in return we'd wipe out the boyars, his arch enemies, for him. His part of the bargain was to provide somewhere secure for the Phase to take place . . . and an ample supply of human bodies.'

'I bet he gave you that, all right. My dad said he killed thousands, after roasting and skinning them and hacking off their arms and legs,' Will remembered. 'And he liked to stick their heads on stakes.'

'That was just window dressing to divert attention from what we were up to,' Eddie said. 'The prince was actually a very cultured and gentle man.'

Drake was frowning. 'Let me get this straight. If there was a Phase back in the fifteenth century . . . then . . . what happened? We're not all dead or in servitude, so what went wrong?'

'The prince reneged on us,' Eddie said. 'He was persuaded by his bishops that we were ungodly, and that we had to be stopped. So he ordered his knights to storm the catacombs in the palace where the Phase was under way. Our newly spawned Warrior Class were still either in the larval or pupation stage, so the knights met no opposition, cutting them to shreds and burning their remains. In fact the only resistance was from our womenfolk, but the knights eventually corralled them down one end of the catacombs, where they put them to death.' Eddie almost smiled as he added, 'So rather than portraying him as a cruel despot, history should instead recognise Vlad – the so-called Impaler – as one of its greatest saviours. The irony is that he *saved* all humanity.'

Drake steepled his fingers as he absorbed this. 'So what you're saying is that conventional forces – armed only with rudimentary weapons – stopped the Phase? So with modern equipment, it shouldn't be a problem.'

'If – and only if – you can find where the new Phase is taking place, and destroy the Warrior Class before they spread,' Eddie answered. 'Before or during pupation.'

'Why?' Drake cut in.

'Because the Warrior Class can reproduce too. When they

get out, their numbers become—'

'Exponential,' Drake interjected. 'So they're male and yet they can reproduce.' He was suddenly struck by a question. 'But why is this new Phase taking place right now?'

'As I told you, a number of factors have to be present before a Phase is triggered, and even our scholars don't know exactly what they are. Perhaps one of the factors is simply our biological clock. The time was—' Eddie stopped, correcting himself, '– *is* right. And I know it is because I can feel it, and so can all those Limiters who've come over to me.'

Chapter Eight

With Captain Franz standing like a shop dummy behind them, the Rebecca twins had been watching on a security monitor as Hermione and the other Styx women worked their way through the humans, impregnating them with egg sacs.

Rebecca Two spotted activity at the factory gates on another monitor. 'The food drop's arrived,' she observed.

'It's about time. I bet the sisters are famished. Let's see if I can override this thing,' Rebecca One said, pressing the function keys on the keyboard until she found the view she was looking for. 'Here we are.' The articulated lorry was backing up in the loading bay. As soon as it stopped, the trailer was opened and a squad of New Germanians began to hurriedly empty its contents onto a series of barrows. 'Meals on wheels,' the twin joked. 'You are my sunshine,' she began to sing quietly to herself as she switched back to the camera inside the steamy factory space. Using the swivel stick on the desktop controls, she zoomed in on the connecting doors from the loading area. In less than a minute, the doors swung open and in came two New Germanians with a laden barrow. Behind them, a Limiter stood guard in the entrance.

Smelling the food, a horde of Styx women had been lurking just inside the doors.

Rebecca One laughed maliciously. 'This should be good.'

Vane rushed one of the New Germanians, clawing him to the ground with amazing speed. The rest of the women immediately swarmed on both him and the other soldier, tearing at their bodies. They were so Darklit, the two soldiers did nothing to fight back.

'I suppose we promised our sisters fresh meat,' Rebecca Two reflected as she watched the carnage. 'You can't get fresher than that.'

Even the Limiter didn't escape the women's attention.

'Wild!' Rebecca Two exhaled.

Like an attacking spider, Vane had moved with such phenomenal speed that the trace she'd left on the security monitor wasn't much more than a blur.

In a single leap, she'd reached the Limiter and, before he knew what was happening, her insectoid legs lashed his eyes. Staggering blindly, he tried to use his rifle to fend her off, but Hermione was already on his back, her teeth in his neck.

'The female of the species is always the deadliest,' Rebecca One said under her breath.

'Ha! Those two!' Rebecca Two chortled as she watched. Vane and Hermione were ripping the Styx soldier apart, limb from limb, while another panicked Limiter quickly sealed the doors to the factory floor behind them. 'They're so picky about what they eat.'

As the Bedford trundled along the path of the river, the water level receded so at least their feet weren't being swamped. Then the lorry tyres spun as they climbed the bank and were back on some sort of track.

After a while Chester felt a pressure on his upper arm. Stephanie had drifted off, her head against him. Careful not to disturb her, he took out his torch, shielding it as he tried to make out the time on his watch. Before he turned the torch off, its stray beam flicked over Elliott who was sitting directly opposite him. She was wide awake, and staring at him and Stephanie. It might have been down to the angle of the torch beam, but her expression was grim and unamused.

Despite the fact that he was protected by the darkness, Chester felt himself colour up, as if he'd been caught doing something he shouldn't.

It was true that he wasn't sure how to respond to Stephanie's interest in him, particularly as he assumed that it was mainly due to the false picture Will had painted of his prowess as a skiing champion.

And Chester felt awkward about the pace at which everything was moving, as if he was being swept along by an actual river. What it came down to was that he didn't know how Elliott really felt about him, or how he really felt about her. There had been times when they seemed to be close, but more recently, during their stay at Parry's house, she'd distanced herself from him, and everybody else.

Chester was just confused.

And he was very relieved when the Bedford eventually came to a grinding halt, which roused Stephanie.

'Where are we?' she yawned, sitting up.

'Don't know,' Chester grunted, aware that he was probably still under scrutiny from Elliott.

With a crash Parry opened the tailgate. 'Everyone out,' he said.

Following behind Colonel Bismarck, Chester jumped from the lorry, and found that they were under a shelter made of rusty corrugated sheets. He wandered a few paces into the open, squinting at the sky, where the dawn light was beginning to streak its way between the clouds. 'What a surprise – it's raining,' he complained, blinking as the drizzle fell in his eyes.

'That's a Morris Minor!' Mr Rawls announced, and Chester turned to look at the old car hidden behind the lorry. It resembled an overripe and very large grape, not just because of its globular shape, but because of the dull patina on its paintwork.

'It's Danforth's,' Parry informed them. 'At least he arrived without mishap.'

Once everyone had gathered up their equipment, they followed Parry along a path surrounded on both sides by thick undergrowth. Chester noticed that Elliott had come to a stop, and that she was grimacing and rubbing her shoulder under the strap of the Bergen. Concerned for her, he retraced his steps back to where she was. 'Are you all right?' he asked, and placed a hand on her arm.

She jumped, drawing away from him, then met his eyes. 'Stephanie's very pretty. You never mentioned that you'd met someone on the estate,' she said.

'I . . . er . . . I didn't think it mattered,' Chester gabbled. 'And I really don't know her at all.'

'I do,' Elliott replied. 'She's everything I wanted to be. And everything I hate about myself.'

Chester had no idea how to respond to this, but Parry had spotted they weren't keeping up. 'Hurry it along, you two,' he called, then continued to strike out along the path. Within a few minutes Chester caught sight of some open land before them.

'Move quickly along here,' Parry urged.

They'd emerged in a gulley at the foot of a mountain, much of which was covered with grass and sheep-cropped vegetation. However, towards its upper reaches, the soil had been scoured away by the elements, and large slabs of striated rock stood proud like the remains of ancient fortifications. Chester saw that the gulley was taking them towards a line of electricity pylons.

Parry called everyone around him on the side of the gulley. 'Once we're over the top, we'll be in an exposed position. It's very unlikely there'll be anyone in the valley below, but just in case Wilkie's going to send you across one at a time. Understood?'

Everyone nodded, then Parry climbed out of sight. When it was Chester's turn, Wilkie gave him a pat on the back and the boy clambered up the side. With the wind and rain in his face, he began to jog the forty feet across to where Parry was crouched down beside one of a pair of structures at the base of the nearest pylon. As Chester came nearer he could see that these were two squat, grey-painted transformers approximately twenty feet square and covered in cooling fins. On top of them were what appeared to be elongated goal posts, from which cables extended to the pylon above.

The transformers were both encircled by a chain-link fence with razor wire strung along the top. Parry ushered Chester through a gate in the fence so that he could join his father and a very fed-up Stephanie.

'This is so not cool any more,' she said, as water dripped from the end of her nose.

Finally, as Old Wilkie joined them inside the fence, Parry moved towards the nearest of the transformers, from which a steady hum was emanating. On the transformer a sign warned *DANGER OF DEATH. KEEP AWAY. HIGH VOLTAGE WILL KILL*, with lightning strikes either side of a red skull and crossbones.

'Danger indeed,' Parry said, placing a hand on the structure. There was a whiplash crack as electricity discharged. Despite the fact that Parry's hair was damp, it stood on end. His appearance would have been rather comical if everyone hadn't thought he was being electrocuted.

But he was completely unharmed. 'Nothing to be worried about,' he laughed. 'An electrostatic charge to see off the overcurious.' He selected one of the fins on the side of the transformer and pressed a catch on it, then slid open a small hatch.

They all ducked in though the hatch, entering a claustrophobic chamber on the other side. Parry used his torch to see as he pressed a series of digits into a small keypanel. The moment he'd finished, a red light blinked on above a grille beside the keypanel. From it a man's voice issued the demand, 'The prime sequence.'

'You know precisely who I am. Do we really have to go through this charade every time?' Parry replied tetchily.

'Of course we do,' the grille snapped, adding 'sir,' as an afterthought.

Parry blew through his lips, then recited, 'The beast deep within the mountain slumbers until the kingdom calls, and then it shall arise to do the king's bidding.'

'Affirmed,' the panel said. 'Now sequence fourteen, if you please, sir.'

Parry thought for a moment. 'There is a pleasure in the pathless woods, there is a rapture on the lonely shore, there is society, where none intrudes—'

'And sequence eight, please,' the grille interrupted.

'We're all frozen to the marrow, bloody hungry and bloody knackered. If you don't open up, Finch, I'm going to blast my way into the Complex,' Parry threatened.

There was a pause, then something clicked to the side of the panel and a crack of light appeared.

'Finally!' Parry exclaimed, heaving the door open so they could make their way down a ramp with rusted iron handrails to either side. They descended into a low-ceilinged room.

'This is the only way in or out of the Complex,' Parry told them, tipping his head at the substantial-looking door that appeared through the dim torchlight. 'That's armour plate,' he said. 'It would take a ton of explosive to even make a dent in it.' Then he pointed at the gun-sized slits in panels of grey metal set into the concrete walls flanking the door. 'And behind those are the twin guard rooms where the sentries would be stationed,' he continued.

'What exactly is this place?' Mr Rawls ventured.

'The Complex was the base for Operation Guardian,' Parry answered. 'It's so hush-hush that *them upstairs* have probably forgotten that they're meant to have forgotten that it ever existed.'

'So it's like that fallout shelter Will found?' Chester asked.

'No, it's more than that,' Parry said. 'Back in the years before the Great War, the aristocrats running the country decided that they needed a safe haven. Somewhere to put their families and portable valuables in the event of invasion. So they built the Complex with their own money – I suppose you could regard it as an underground castle for the very rich. Later on, when things were getting sticky for us in the Second World War, the War Cabinet commandeered it, expanding its role to include a command centre for the Resistance.'

'Operation Guardian?' Mr Rawls guessed.

'Precisely. Every town in the south-east and every major region throughout the British Isles had its own pre-recruited Resistance team waiting in the wings. The historians will tell you that the moment the Germans crossed the Channel, each team was to open their sealed orders and follow them to the letter.'

Parry shot a glance at Colonel Bismarck, who merely nodded. 'But what the historians don't know is that these teams weren't entirely autonomous. Major initiatives were to be orchestrated from the tactical ops room right here in the Complex, known as the "Hub". It's still here, and we still call it that.'

'So what's the Complex used for now?' Mr Rawls asked.

'It's kept ticking over just in case it's needed at some time in the future,' Parry answered. 'And I reckon that time has come.'

He stopped speaking as they all heard a clanking sound. It seemed to be coming from behind the armour-plate door, although it was difficult to tell because it was so distant. The sound came again, only louder this time, then was repeated several more times.

Then the large door in front of them slowly ground open. Chester and Colonel Bismarck shone their torches into the square passageway, its walls painted cream white and its floor a waxy green. But their beams didn't penetrate very far down it, and beyond was an ominous and unbroken darkness.

Then lights came in the far distance.

'How long is it?' Chester asked, as he squinted at them.

Parry didn't reply as more banks of strip lights flickered on, coming closer each time.

They heard a whirring noise from somewhere in the unlit portion of the passageway.

'What's that?' Mr Rawls asked, stepping back with concern.

'The last remaining Knight Protector,' Parry chuckled.

The strip lights came on in the room where they were all standing.

In the same instant an elderly man on a mobility scooter shot into view before them, executing a sliding stop on the lino flooring with a squeal.

Stephanie giggled.

Behind him more than a dozen cats, all of different colours and ages, were scampering along the passage as they hurried to catch up with him.

'Sergeant Finch,' Parry said, going over to give the old man a hearty handshake. As if somehow he'd shrunk, Sergeant Finch's fawn beret seemed to be several sizes too big for him, flopping forward over his bushy white eyebrows. He was dressed in a khaki-coloured cardigan, and a pair of crutches was tucked into a sling at the back of his scooter.

'Commander, 'ow very good to see you again, sir,' Sergeant Finch grinned. 'Apologies for not getting up, but me legs aren't what they used to be.'

'You and me both,' Parry said, raising his walking stick.

Sergeant Finch glanced down at a cat that had made itself at home between his feet on the scooter. 'An' apologies for the formalities at the front entrance. You know I 'ave to follow protocol.'

'Of course you do,' Parry assured him.

Sergeant Finch was looking around at everyone. His gaze came to rest on Colly, who'd taken several tentative steps from behind Mrs Burrows to sniff at one of the more courageous cats. 'That's not a dog, is it, Commander? Can't 'ave no dog running loose down 'ere. Not with my c—'

'Don't worry – she's a cat too. Just rather a big one,' Mrs Burrows spoke up.

It was odd to watch Colly towering over the other cats who, smelling one of their own, were rapidly overcoming their fear. They began to throng around her, rubbing themselves against her and mewing.

'What will they think of next?' Sergeant Finch exclaimed. ''Ad no idea that cats like that were being bred back in the world!' Shaking his head, he leant forward in his seat to take some clipboards and a batch of cheap biros from the pannier attached to his handlebars. 'First things first. I need you each to sign this form in triplicate before I can allow you to go any further.'

Parry pulled a face. 'Oh yes, I forgot all about the paper-work.'

'So what is this?' Mr Rawls asked as he took a clipboard and scanned the form.

Sergeant Finch wagged a finger at him. 'No, no, sir – you can't read it. You're not permitted to read it. It's the SOSA – the Special Official Secrets Act,' he explained.

'What?' Mr Rawls burst out. 'If I can't read it, then how do I know what I'm agreeing to?'

'You don't,' Parry said, smiling. 'It's so top secret that you're only allowed to read it *after* you've signed it.'

'Barmy,' Mr Rawls muttered, dashing off his signature, then turning to the next copy on the clipboard.

After everyone had completed the requisite forms to Sergeant Finch's satisfaction – including Mrs Burrows, who had to be shown where to sign – they all followed him down the passage. It was several hundred feet in length, and along the sides were racks of battered metal helmets, gas masks, bicycles that looked as though they dated from the 1940s, and similarly old-fashioned radios in canvas haversacks.

As they went, Sergeant Finch used a control on the handle-bars of his scooter to activate the section doors in the passageway behind them. With a press on each numbered red button, another slab of heavy metal would grind across with the clanking noises they'd heard before, sealing the way out.

'So Danforth's here already?' Parry asked.

'Yes, the Professor's in the Hub, sir,' Sergeant Finch replied. 'He's been connecting up his new gizmos.'

Parry nodded. 'We'd better go and check on how he's doing.'

'Yes, sir,' Sergeant Finch acknowledged, the wheels on his scooter squeaking on the lino flooring as he picked up speed down the slight incline. Colly trotted along quickly in front of the human contingent, all the cats flocking after her in a herd. The Hunter seemed to be more animated than she had been in a long time, but that was probably because a playful kitten kept attempting to jump on her with its tiny claws extended.

Danforth barely glanced up as they entered the Hub, transfixed by the screen of his laptop. 'You need to see this,' he said. 'It's the main item on all the US channels.'

The Hub was a large circular space, and in the middle were five banks of long desks, on which were old telephones and oak boards dotted with clunky-looking dials. Down one whole side of the Hub were Perspex screens which extended the full height from floor to ceiling, and on which various maps of the British Isles had been painted in heavy black outlines. Chester hovered by one which showed the south of England and right across the Channel to the French coastline.

Danforth was at the very front of the room. From a panel in the wall next to him spilled a tangled spaghetti of cables, and these twitched as he fiddled with something behind his laptop. 'If I can just get this redundant piece of junk to work,' he muttered, waving a hand in the direction of a large screen on the wall above him, 'we'll all be able to watch in glorious Technicolor.'

The screen suddenly swam with rapidly moving jagged lines. 'Almost got it,' Danforth said as the image of a person loomed from the static, then was gone again. Changing a setting on his laptop, Danforth announced, 'And if we apply a little attenuation . . . hey presto!'

'CNN?' Parry asked as he frowned at the picture on the

screen – a presenter behind a desk – although as yet there was no sound. 'Is this what you wanted us to see?'

'Yes,' Danforth replied. 'The item's running on all the news channels over in the US. CNN, Fox, ABC – take your pick.'

Sergeant Finch was gawping open-mouthed at the picture. 'Is this the TV? I've never 'ad the TV down 'ere before.'

'The whole electricity pylon up top was designed to be a powerful radio antenna, but there are also a couple of satellite dishes concealed in it. I managed to tap into the feed from one of them,' Danforth said. 'And . . . with a bit of Heath Robinson ingenuity . . . finally . . . we should have sound.' There was an ear-splitting screech from the speakers around the walls as he tweaked another setting on his laptop.

Everyone had gathered before the large screen, except for Mrs Burrows who was kneeling beside Colly as she kept the over-zealous kitten away from her.

The presenter wore a grim expression. *'Only now are details being released by the Department of Homeland Security about the explosion which killed three members of the Senate and four other people outside a government building on Capitol Hill late yesterday. Erroneous reports had been circulating that a car bomb had been responsible for the explosion.'*

There were shots of American military personnel manning a barricade across a road. Then the camera zoomed past them for a close up of several burnt-out cars, around which people in white forensic suits were milling.

'But this is now known not to be the case. Security footage has revealed that the explosive device was carried by a middle-aged man, who appears to have been operating without accomplices.' The presenter came on screen again. *'A few hours ago at a media briefing, Homeland Security released this statement.'*

A woman was at a podium, a sea of reporters in the long room before her. *'The alleged bomber has been identified as an American citizen.'* A loud ripple of amazement went through the reporters as hands shot up. *'Please – I'll be taking questions in a moment,'* the spokesperson said, and waited for the reporters to quieten down again. *'Thank you,'* the woman continued, as the clamour subsided. *'Identified as an American citizen who has been resident in the United Kingdom for the last five years, where he was working on television documentaries.'*

Mrs Burrows was on her feet.

'A recent photograph of the alleged bomber has been circulated,' the spokesperson continued, as a picture flashed up on the screen.

'Can you see him? Will you describe him? Please!' Mrs Burrows demanded anxiously.

Everyone in the Hub was looking at her, except for Parry.

'Late thirties, hundred and sixty pounds, longish curly hair, beard . . .' Parry began.

'Ben,' Mrs Burrows gasped, realising it had to be the American television producer she'd befriended in Highfield.

Parry didn't need to complete the description as the spokesperson continued. *'According to the passenger logs at JFK, Benjamin Wilbrahams arrived on a flight from London in the early hours of yesterday morning, and then drove a hire car from the airport to Washington DC. Although all commercial flights to and from the United Kingdom have been suspended for the last fortnight, Wilbrahams was on one of the special US Air Force repatriation flights. He was subjected to a full security check before being allowed to board. Although a device was not detected in his luggage or about his person, it is believed that he might have had it concealed inside his body, similar to the Human*

Bombs, despatched from England to other European countries, which have been all too numerous in recent weeks.'

The reporters at the media briefing in the long room were now completely silent.

The studio presenter reappeared on the screen. *'Following the oil spill debacle on the East Coast, hostility towards Britain has never been higher than in the last year. And this incident, in which one of our own citizens has somehow been coerced into perpetrating a horrific act of terrorism on American soil, has taken anti-British sentiment to a new high. There have been demonstrations outside the British Embassy in New York and several British consulates across the country.'*

The picture switched to a heaving crowd bristling with placards.

'Our American sons gave their lives to help England conquer Germany in the last war. And this . . . this is how they repay us!' a man fumed as he brandished a fist at the camera.

'Just look at all the terrorist factions they've let into their country. This was going to happen – it was only a matter of time,' another man said.

Then a woman began to chant, *'Nuke the Brits! Nuke the Brits!'*

'Very clever. The Styx have made sure there'll be no help coming from our cousins across the Atlantic,' Danforth said.

'That's enough,' Parry decided. 'Turn it off.'

As the screen went dark, everyone turned to Mrs Burrows. 'They used Ben. He must have been Darklit to oblivion,' she said quietly, her head bowed. 'He didn't deserve to die like that.'

Parry cleared his throat uncomfortably. Exchanging a glance with Old Wilkie, he went over to Stephanie. 'I think the time has come for you and me to have a proper chat.'

Stephanie didn't respond with any of her usual shrill exuberance, but instead nodded meekly. Chester felt a surge of sympathy for the girl – it was obvious that she hadn't yet been told quite how serious the situation was.

'And the rest of you check in with Sergeant Finch as to your rooms,' Parry said. 'At least you'll be comfortable here – the sleeping quarters in the level below aren't far off a five-star hotel.'

Chapter Nine

Will had never seen Drake look so worried, as he drew his gaze up to Eddie's face and then spoke. 'Tell me something,' he said. 'How do you know for certain that this so-called Phase is really taking place? Have any of your men seen it with their own eyes? And where's it going on?' he asked in quick succession.

'Oh, it's going on all right, but we don't know where,' Eddie replied. 'If you're a Styx it's the most powerful force you ever encounter . . . you can sense it with every single cell in your body. All my men can. We've known it was on the way for a while. And the Styx women, wherever they are, will have felt it long before us. The urge is far more powerful in them. It's the irresistible and overwhelming summons to reproduce. It's . . .' Eddie paused as he chose the right way to express himself, 'it's as though a clarion call is transmitted through the air . . . a chemical trigger.'

'Pheromones,' Drake suggested, drawing in a breath.

Eddie appeared to be so deep in thought that he hadn't heard. 'The trigger instigates . . . coordinates . . . the Phase, whether anybody wants it or not. Our women transform into something different, something terrifying. And what they unleash – the Warrior Class – wipes the board clean of any species that aren't regarded as food stocks. *Out with the old.'*

'Us included?' Drake said.

'Yes, any lifeform that poses even the remotest threat to Styx dominance will be eradicated. That means open season on all humans.' Catching a movement outside the Humvee, Eddie noticed a red squirrel as it shimmied down a tree trunk. He pointed at it. 'In the same way that species was once the dominant one, before the grey variety pushed it out.'

'But this Warrior Class you're talking about – they're still only physical. Even if they're some kind of mega-Limiter, well-armed Topsoilers could stop them, couldn't they?' Drake asked. 'Particularly if we get ourselves organised.'

'That's a monumentally big *if.* They thrive on chaos. They *are* chaos,' Eddie said. 'And if you engage them, and somehow manage to gain the upper hand, there's the possibility of a second stage.'

'I don't think I want to hear this,' Drake groaned, as Eddie hunted for a page in the Book of Proliferation, then held it up.

'What the hell are those?' Will asked.

The woodcut illustration occupied a full page, but was divided into three boxes, which showed the sky, the land and, right at the bottom, an area of water covered in spume and waves, which was probably meant to suggest the sea. And in each of the boxes were inexplicable creatures. Other than the deadly teeth and claws, the only aspect the creatures had in common was that the artist had attempted to show they were transparent or semi-transparent. Apart from this, each creature seemed to be adapted for its environment; the uppermost one with two sets of bat-like wings, the middle one with three pairs of legs, and the aquatic one with fins.

'If all else fails, the success of the Phase is guaranteed by this,' Eddie said. 'This is the back stop . . . this is the *Armagi.*'

'The Armagi?' Drake repeated carefully.

'It's the basis for the word Armageddon, which has nothing to do with a place where some mythical final battle is going to take place, as many faiths would have you believe. But it is sort of the end . . . the end of the humans' time on Earth,' Eddie said.

'*Sort of?*' Will repeated, almost wanting to laugh because he couldn't cope with what he was hearing.

'According to our legends, the Armagi are continually adapting organisms, capable of regenerating an entirely new body from even a tiny piece of tissue. You take one apart, and you give rise to a legion. In scientific terms you could describe them as entire clusters of neoblasts, with the gift of being able to differentiate into whatever configuration of genocide machine is required at the particular time.' Eddie closed the book with some force. 'So even if you manage to get to the end of the first act – the Warrior Class – the second act will bring the house down. Without knowing it, Vlad the Impaler's knights forestalled the Armagi because they cremated every single living cell when they torched the catacombs.'

'So we catch the Warrior Class before they're able to disperse. And we use fire too,' Drake reasoned. 'We cremate everything – the Warriors and the Styx women.'

'I know you might not think it's as important as all this, but can I ask something?' Will spoke up.

Eddie gave him a nod.

'Is this why the Rebeccas have so much power over the Styx?' Will said.

'All our women possess an ascendancy over male Styx, but the Rebecca twins are from our ruling family.'

'Right . . . and . . . um . . .' Will began, but seemed uncomfortable with what he wanted to say next.

'Go on,' Drake encouraged him.

'Well . . . where does all this leave Elliott?' the boy asked.

Eddie looked blankly at him. 'Where does it leave her? I honestly don't know. Of course, she's what the Colonists uncharitably call a "Drain Baby" as she's a part-human, part-Styx hybrid. But which genotype is the dominant, I couldn't tell you. All I can tell you is that she must be kept in isolation if the Phase is affecting her in any way. She'll be a danger to anyone around her.'

Will swallowed nervously. 'Right,' he said, wishing he hadn't asked.

Sweeney was still guarding the Limiters when Will returned to the ford. The soldiers were all standing in precisely the same spot, and only Mrs Rawls had moved. She was sitting on the bank with her legs drawn up.

'So the pow-wow's over. What's the skinny?' Sweeney asked.

'You wouldn't believe it if I told you,' Will replied.

Sweeney touched the grid just in front of his ear. 'Actually I caught most of it. Crazy stuff.'

'You did?' Will said, glancing over his shoulder as he estimated how far away the Humvee was. 'But it must be . . . what . . . a hundred feet?'

'Piece of cake,' Sweeney grinned.

As Will turned back, he was suddenly aware that eight pairs of Limiter eyes were on him. Now he knew what they knew. He coughed uneasily. 'So you heard Drake wants to get going right away – and we're taking Eddie along with us in one of his Humvees,' he said to Sweeney.

Sweeney jutted his chin at the line of Limiters. 'Sure, but what do we do with this sorry bunch?'

'We let them go,' Will said.

'So they're our pals now?' the big man smiled.

'S'pose so,' Will replied, as he turned to address the Limiters. 'Eddie wants you to go to London and wait there for his orders. He said you should take the jeep and the other Humv . . .' As he peered down the track at the second vehicle, he could make out the Hunter's body on the bonnet. His mind suddenly went empty.

'You were saying,' Sweeney prompted gently.

'Bartleby,' was all the boy could manage as he gave Sweeney a helpless look.

Sweeney nodded, then addressed the Limiters, 'Listen up, all you Sticky Boys. You're going to do the decent thing and give the laddie's cat a burial. I want a proper hole dug – no skimping. You owe him that.' Sweeney caught Will's eye. 'Okay?'

Will nodded gratefully.

Sweeney stuck a thumb in Mrs Rawls' direction. 'And what about the filly?'

Mrs Rawls opened her mouth to object at being referred to in this way. She evidently thought better of it, and resorted to giving Sweeney a murderous look.

'Mrs Rawls is coming with us,' Will said, then went off to collect his Bergen from the jeep, as well as a couple of holdalls Drake had left behind.

Once he'd returned, Sweeney reached out an arm. 'Let me take the weight off,' he said, hooking the Bergen and holdalls with his fingers and hoisting them from Will as if they contained nothing more than feathers. 'And you can have your peashooter back,' he added, passing the weapon over. Although Sweeney didn't have a gun on Mrs Rawls any longer, Will noticed that he was careful to keep close to her as they walked.

'Will,' Mrs Rawls said, 'now all the macho posturing is over, I want to know about my family. No one's told me a thing about Jeff and Chester, but I'm assuming they're both somewhere safe? Is that right?'

'They certainly should be,' Will assured her. 'And we'll be joining them soon.'

'Thank you,' Mrs Rawls said, looking relieved.

But the moment they arrived at the Humvee, Drake took one of the holdalls from Sweeney and approached Mrs Rawls.

'Emily, I can either continue to treat you as a potential hostile and keep you under restraint. Or I can give you a clean bill of health by making sure you're not Darklit. It's your call.'

Mrs Rawls inclined her head towards Will and gave him a smile. 'I was wrong about the macho posturing. He's at it again.' Then she turned to Drake. 'I don't want to be in handcuffs when I see my family,' she said. 'Do what you have to.'

Drake delved into the holdall and extracted a small device. It appeared to be a pair of glasses connected by a cable to a small cylinder.

'Did Danforth make that?' Will asked.

'Yes, the new improved Pocket Purger,' Drake replied. 'I know I've said it a million times, but the man's a genius.'

155

'Certainly is,' Sweeney said. 'He offered to give my bonce an overhaul once, as if I was his blessed Moggy Minor.'

'Well, he certainly miniaturised the original purger,' Will observed.

Drake nodded. 'Will, I need you first.' He held the cylinder in front of the boy's face.

'Me? What for?' Will asked warily.

'Just keep your eyes open, and watch the birdie,' Drake replied. He depressed a button on the cylinder and an intense purple beam shone straight into Will's pupils.

He immediately recognised the colour; it was identical to that of a Dark Light, although this time it was having absolutely no effect on him. He screwed up his eyes, but only because of the brightness of the beam. 'What now?' he said.

'Anything?' Drake asked. 'No feelings of nausea or discomfort?'

'Nope,' Will replied.

'Good,' Drake said, as he released the button and the beam went out. 'You see, you're the control. I didn't expect any reaction, which proves you're squeaky clean. Now for you, Emily.' Drake held the cylinder directly in front of her and clicked the button again.

Letting out a sharp breath as if she'd been punched, her body went rigid as a plank. Sweeney used his lightning reactions to catch her before she fell.

Eddie was watching the proceedings intently. 'Fascinating technology. I assume you developed it on the back of your work on my Dark Light,' he said. 'But I promise you, Drake – I haven't given Emily any programming.'

'No, maybe not you,' Drake said. 'But there's something knocking around in her head. I don't know what it is, and I

156

can't take the risk. Put her on the back seat, Sparks,' he told Sweeney. 'Hold her tight – I don't want her thrashing about and hurting herself.'

Mrs Rawls was more than a little disoriented as Sweeney manhandled her into the Humvee. Sliding in beside her, he looped his gigantic arm around her shoulders. 'Locked and loaded,' he confirmed.

Drake leant in through the open door of the Humvee, the glasses attached to Danforth's device in his hand. 'This is the business end,' he said, as he made sure the glasses were securely over Mrs Rawls' eyes. 'I nearly forgot – don't want her biting her tongue. Anyone got a handkerchief?'

'Here,' Sweeney offered, producing a rather dirty rag from his combat jacket, which Drake folded over several times.

'Open wide,' he directed Mrs Rawls. Still groggy, she obediently did what she was told, allowing Drake to place it in her mouth. 'Now just try to relax. This shouldn't take long.' He flicked another switch on the cylinder, and purple light leaked from around the sides of the glasses.

Will winced as Mrs Rawls' guttural cry reverberated through the forest.

The Second Officer was buckling up his Sam Browne belt as he shuffled out into the corridor. Rather than go home he'd just spent his second night in one of the cells in the interrogation wing of the police station, sleeping on a pile of prison blankets heaped on the cold flagstones. He still hadn't forgiven his mother and sister. Not after they'd killed his little dog and served it up to him in a stew. As he came to the end of the whitewashed corridor and entered the reception area, he was swinging his arms in an attempt to de-kink his muscles.

'Hello,' he called out, as he arrived to find it deserted. 'Sir? Hello? Anyone?'

There was no response, so the Second Officer raised the flap in the counter and went to the doorway of the First Officer's room. 'Oh, you are here,' he said to his superior, who was bent over his desk, his head in his hands. 'Is it the gut rot, sir?' the Second Officer asked sympathetically.

'No,' the First Officer replied after a moment, then straightened up.

The Second Officer recoiled as he saw the man's battered face, his eye so swollen that it had almost closed up. 'What happened? Who did this to you? How many were there?'

'It was in the Hold,' the First Officer sighed. 'I was squaring the prisoners away for the night when that bloody Mulligan started on me.'

'Mulligan?' the Second Officer asked. 'Bill Mulligan – the cabinet maker?'

The First Officer glanced down sheepishly. 'No, his mother.'

'Not *Gappy* Mulligan,' the Second Officer burst out. 'But she's ninety if she's a day! How did she—?'

'I know,' the First Officer grunted, rolling his head as if he'd never live this one down. 'She was mouthing off about the Styx and – with no warning at all – she let fly at me. Got a vicious right hook, too.'

'Gappy Mulligan,' the Second Officer repeated. He was so flabbergasted that he flopped down in the chair in front of the First Officer's desk. He hadn't been invited to sit, and when he'd realised what he'd done, he found that his superior was squinting at him through his good eye. 'Oh, sorry, sir,

I didn't mean to—'

'You stay right there,' the First Officer said. 'You know, Patrick, I think we've reached the point that we can do away with the usual decorum.'

The Second Officer was astonished for a second time. His superior officer had never – *never* – before addressed him by his Christian name. Indeed, even the Second Officer's own family referred to him as 'the Second Officer', rather than by his real name, because the laws of the Colony demanded it.

'I . . . I . . .' the Second Officer stuttered.

'This is no time to be a stuffed shirt, Patrick,' the First Officer said, taking his pipe from a desk drawer and opening a tobacco pouch. It was also absolutely forbidden to smoke in the station. 'Face up to it. Half the Colony is slowly but surely starving to death in their homes, while the other half is missing God knows where,' the First Officer continued, as he filled the pipe bowl with tobacco. 'And the half that's starving to death will probably end up killing each other as they fight over whatever scraps they can plunder from the food stores, and . . .'

The First Officer used his flint lighter to ignite the tobacco before he went on '. . . and you and I, we'll be stuck bang smack in the middle of it all. Some toothless hag – just like Mulligan – is going to bludgeon us to death with her handbag, and all for a mouthful of salted toadstrip.' He took several large puffs. 'The joke is, Patrick, *we're* all that's left. A thin blue line holding back a tide of total and absolute anarchy. We're caught between the devil and a cold, dark sea.' He shook his head stoically. 'No, the outlook's not good for us, old friend. Not good at all.'

The Second Officer had been half listening as he racked his

brains to try to remember his superior's real name, but it wasn't coming to him. Then something the First Officer had said struck him. 'Sir, what was that about people missing? Has there been an incident?'

Like everyone else, the Second Officer had heard the rumours, but he was inclined to believe that it was pure hearsay and that the people were somewhere in the sprawling shanty town in the North Cavern.

The First Officer blinked as smoke wandered into his good eye, then he located a message scroll by his elbow and pushed it across the desk. 'The Fifth Officer submitted a report while you were resting. You and I have both fielded a couple of unsubstantiated claims about missing citizens, but this is different. One of our own is unaccounted for. No one's seen hide nor hair of the Third Officer for twenty-four hours.'

'But he's been doing the beat in the North,' the Second Officer said, referring to the rural cavern. 'I saw him not long ago. Isn't he over there right n—?'

'He didn't report for duty this morning,' the First Officer interrupted. 'And he hasn't been home. Word is something went on in the North overnight and, whatever it was, my guess is he got caught up in it. Look at this edict from the Styx,' he said, jabbing his pipe stem in the direction of the scroll. 'We're being refused access.'

'The North? Off limits to us?' the Second Officer said. 'Why? We're police officers.'

The First Officer nodded. 'Highly irregular, isn't it?'

The Second Officer read the message. 'Why in Earth would the Styx impose a full restriction order?' He got to his feet with a sudden snort of indignation. 'I'm going down there to take a look for myself,' he resolved on the spur of the moment.

'Really?' the First Officer said, his eyebrows arching with a detached amusement as the strong tobacco began to work on his strained nerves. 'Then you're a braver man than I am, Patrick.'

No one came out to check the Second Officer's credentials as he approached the Skull Gate, but that didn't necessarily mean he hadn't been observed by a Styx. He passed through it and, twenty minutes later, he reached the final incline down to the South Cavern where he could look out over the streets and houses. As the thrumming from the Fan Stations resonated in his ears, it seemed to be louder than usual, as if it was the only sound in the whole of the city.

Even when he entered the built-up area, he had the sense that he was the last person left in the Colony. There would normally be somebody out at that time in the morning, as they went to their place of work or opened up their shops ready for the day, but now the streets were completely empty.

Despite the fact that he wasn't on speaking terms with his mother and sister, the Second Officer was so concerned that he stopped off there first. Finding that the front door was locked, he managed to drop his key with a clatter on the top step as he tried to open it. As he bent to retrieve his key and then stood up, he again became aware of the eerie calm all around him.

With their curtains drawn, the windows in the terrace opposite were dark and unfriendly, like many black eyes glaring at him. For a while the street had been crammed to capacity with New Germanians, but the Styx had since taken them Topsoil. Over the weeks, he'd heard the New Germanian troops being mobilised at all sorts of odd hours during the night, their feet beating a tattoo on the pavement in perfect unison. But even though they'd now gone, very few Colonist families had been allowed to move back into their homes. He was beginning to wonder if they'd ever return, and if his street would ever be the same again. Particularly if something untoward had gone on in the North Cavern.

He finally let himself in and went inside. His first port of call was the kitchen, and, not finding his mother or sister there, he tried the sitting room, then the bedrooms upstairs. The beds were unmade, the covers pulled back.

Of course, Eliza might have taken their mother out somewhere, but the Second Officer couldn't imagine quite where at that early hour. He was trying to stop himself from thinking the worst – that the Styx had paid a visit – as he descended the stairs. Pausing in the hallway, he heard a sound which seemed to come from the empty kitchen, and immediately ducked into the sitting room to fetch Will's spade from the sideboard. If there were thieves in the house, he was going to give them a damned good hiding.

The Second Officer crept into the kitchen and listened. There was another sound. He went to the far end of the kitchen and slowly opened the door into the small vestibule. He tiptoed across it to a second door, which led to the coal store. As he pressed his ear to the door, he was sure he heard a scrabbling noise. *Maybe a rat*, he thought to himself.

But then he was certain he could hear whispering.

Two-legged rats, he told himself.

Counting silently to three, he flung the door open and tore in with a roar.

Someone moved in the shadows. He saw the whites of their eyes.

He raised his spade, ready to strike.

'OOOH MY GAWD!' his mother wailed, her hands up to protect her face.

Eliza screamed.

'What . . . ?' the Second Officer cried, not believing his eyes.

In their nighties, both his mother and sister were black with coal dust as they cowered in the far corner.

'What in God's name are you doing in here?' the Second Officer demanded, adrenaline still pumping through his body.

His mother began to cry.

'We thought it was the Styx at the door . . . coming for us,' Eliza managed to say.

Both she and the old lady were still shaking as the Second Officer led them back into the kitchen and sat them down. He looked at them, so terrified, their faces and clothes thick with dust, then looked at the kitchen floor and the trail their bare feet had left on the tiles. The tiles that the old lady laboured day in, day out to keep so spotlessly clean that one could eat off them.

And he couldn't be angry with them about the little dog any longer. But he *was* angry; he wanted someone to pay for what was going on in the Colony. Everything was falling apart. And this previously loyal Colonist, this upholder of order, knew precisely who was responsible.

'This has to stop,' he whispered under his breath. 'The Styx have to be stopped.'

He made sure his mother and sister were safely tucked up in bed, then set off for the North Cavern. He went through still more deserted streets, not seeing a soul. Not even any Darklit

New Germanians. Some streets he went down stank power-fully of raw sewage. Now the regular work details had been suspended, nobody was going below the city to make sure the sluices were flowing freely. There must have been blockages in the main drains, and as a result the whole system was backing up.

'What have we come to?' the Second Officer mumbled to himself, as he suddenly stopped. Sure enough, at the mouth of the passageway into the North Cavern, there was a single piece of thick rope strung across the entrance, an official notice forbidding entry suspended from it. As the breeze rocked it gently, he considered the black-edged warning sign, then stepped over the rope and went in.

And, as he emerged into the cavern, there were no longer any luminescent orbs on stands – they'd all been taken away, so he used his police lantern to light the way. Either side of the main track, there were only empty fields. No shanty town, no evidence that anyone had ever been there.

The Second Officer thought that he saw something. A movement. He tensed, fearing the worst, that he'd bumped straight into a Limiter. But after a few moments, when no one appeared, he carried on.

A little further down the track, he stopped again and shone his lantern before him.

'Oh, G—!' he gasped.

A shape, black and amorphous, rose from the ground. The Second Officer was absolutely convinced his luck had run out, and that this time it could be nothing else but a Limiter.

The flapping wings immediately told him he was wrong. He'd disturbed a small flock of Miner Birds, which had been picking over the ground. They were unsightly-looking scavengers, with raggedy black feathers and spindly bodies, rather like etiolated sparrows. With no sound but the beat of their wings, they took flight, returning to their nests high in the canopy.

Holding his chest and breathing heavily, the Second Officer took a moment to recover his composure, then began a thorough investigation of the area where the town had stood. It was strange to think that the last time he'd been here, he'd been examining the three bodies while the Third Officer himself had watched on. But it was a different story now; he couldn't find a single clue to help him.

'Hopeless,' he complained, kicking at the sodden soil in sheer frustration. Then he froze. As though the ground had been raked over, just under the surface there were unusual deposits. A darker, almost black material seemed be mixed in with the soil. And it was nothing to do with the Miner Birds or the cultivation of pennybun crops. He knelt down to take a pinch of the material between his fingers, then held it to his nose.

'Ash,' he said, sniffing. 'Burnt timber.'

Whoever had cleared the area, they'd razed the town to the ground. They'd done a thorough job. As only the Styx could.

He stood up, directing his lantern around him.

'But what happened to the people?'

He was still half expecting to hear the crack of a rifle and feel the sharp pain in his neck as a Limiter executed him for contravening the Styx edict. But there didn't seem to be any of the ghoulish soldiers in the cavern either.

He continued to comb the area, going over the ground inch by inch. He was coming across pieces of broken crockery and glass, then he found a spent rifle cartridge. It smelt of cordite. It had been fired recently. But the people in the shanty town couldn't have been burnt along with their huts. He couldn't believe that. And if they'd been taken away by the Styx, then where had they gone?

He saw something glint as his lantern beam flicked over it. He almost knew what the object was before he stooped to retrieve it. It was a brass button, with the motif of the crossed spade and pickaxe cast into it. The three-hundred-year-old crest of the Founding Fathers of the Colony. And this button could have come from only one place.

From a policeman's tunic.

From the Third Officer's tunic, to be precise.

With the button gripped tightly in his hand, he returned to the main track. He walked faster and faster as it became clear to him what he had to do. He crossed the South Cavern, returning to the incline that he'd only descended a couple of hours previously. He continued up past the Fan Stations, then came to an abrupt stop.

Making sure he hadn't been followed and that there was no one in the tunnel up ahead, he ducked into the dark side passage. After thirty feet the passage opened out into a small chamber. In its centre was a penned enclosure, with straw scattered across the floor of bare rock. Although the Second Officer could still detect the smell of pigs, it had long ago been emptied of its occupants, slaughtered to feed the army of New Germanians.

But the Second Officer hadn't gone there for the pigs.

At the far side of the chamber, he found where the door blown open by Drake and Chester had once been. It had since been shored up with huge chunks of rock, and most likely the Labyrynth tunnel on the other side had also been collapsed in, so that no one could ever again use it to enter into the Colony.

The Second Officer counted his paces as he followed the chamber wall along to his left, then stopped to examine the ground with his lantern. He found the depression, filled with pieces of rock, and began to excavate it, trying to make as little noise as he could.

Then he saw what he'd come for. It was a black box, the size of a pack of cards, with a wire aerial trailing from it.

'Look on it as a last measure,' Drake had told him. 'If you ever need help, for any reason, I'll do my best to come.'

At the time the Second Officer hadn't given much thought to it. After half of the Laboratories had been demolished by their explosion, it had been vital that Drake and Chester escaped from the Colony with Mrs Burrows as quickly as they could. And the Second Officer himself had also been more than a little preoccupied about quite how he was going to convince the Styx of his innocence.

He knew that he should have reported the device and had it removed, but his knowledge of it wasn't going to be easy to explain away. So, in the end, he chose to simply forget about its existence.

Until now.

He inspected the device's shiny black casing. Its appearance was similar to the beacons that Drake had provided to Will to mark his way down to the inner world, but this one was different. It also emitted a radio signal that was detectable through the crust, but on a completely different wavelength.

With his clumsy fingers, the Second Officer located the microswitch on the side of the casing and slid it into the *On* position. Then he placed the beacon carefully back into the depression, and made sure it was well buried again.

He didn't know quite when – or even if – Drake would pick up the signal, but he also didn't know where else to go for help. He regarded the beacon as a message in a bottle, which he'd just cast into the ocean in the hope that it would be found, and that he'd be rescued.

That the entire Colony would be rescued.

Chapter Ten

As Mrs Burrows entered her quarters, the intercom beside the door was buzzing. She snatched the handset from the cradle.

'Yes, it's done,' she said. 'It wasn't easy – I reduced my breathing almost to nothing and moved slower than a snail so she wouldn't hear me. She didn't, and it's a damned good thing because I would've been hard pressed to explain what I was doing in there.'

She listened to the caller for several seconds.

'I will,' she confirmed, moving towards the cradle as if she thought the conversation had come to an end.

'Bartleby?' she gasped, turning in the direction of the oak desk in the small study at the end of the room. Between the two pedestals of drawers that formed its base, Colly was sitting like a Sphinx, her large amber eyes fixed on Mrs Burrows. 'Yes, it's a terrible shame, but I suppose he was only doing what any wild animal does – he was following his instincts.'

Mrs Burrows twirled her finger around the flex of the handset as she listened to the caller. 'Don't worry, we'll be there when you arrive,' she said, then hung up.

With a very human sigh, the Hunter lowered her muzzle onto her forepaws.

'I know,' Mrs Burrows said. 'But you've got so much to look forward to.'

'Elliott,' Mrs Burrows said, speaking softly in the darkness.

The girl was instantly awake, rolling from her bed with her long rifle in her hands.

'What is it?' she asked urgently. 'What's wrong?'

'No, it's nothing to be concerned about,' Mrs Burrows assured her. 'Only Will and Drake have arrived, and I thought you'd want to see them. They're up in the Hub.' Mrs Burrows didn't give Elliott the opportunity to decide whether or not she wanted to come as she switched on the lights to the room.

Parry hadn't been misleading them when he'd said that the accommodation was comfortable. Elliott's and Mrs Burrows' rooms were next to each other, the doors labelled *Gov 1* and *Gov 2*. The quarters had evidently been intended for cabinet ministers, the interiors resembling something you might find in a luxurious ocean liner, with mahogany furniture and brass fittings, but minus the portholes.

The main room in each quarters was some thirty feet square, with its own en-suite bathroom and a small adjoining study just large enough for a writing desk and a couple of chairs. Everything in them – the cupboards, carpets, linen – was the very best that early twentieth-century Britain had had to offer. The only modern addition to the rooms was the ugly plastic trunking that had been run along the top of the skirting and by the sides of the doors, where intercoms with incongruous aluminium faceplates had been installed, so that each room had a communication link with the Hub.

'Do I need to get dressed?' Elliott asked. She was wearing a baggy white T-shirt that she'd found in the wardrobe, along with a pair of blue shorts far too large for her.

'Maybe a dressing gown,' Mrs Burrows suggested, hugging herself inside hers, which was cut from a thick blanket-like material. Far from being airless, if anything the quarters were rather chilly as fresh air pumped in through vents in the ceiling.

When Elliott was ready, Mrs Burrows said, 'All set?' and they left the room together.

'Chester!' Elliott exclaimed, surprised to see him slumped against the wall in the corridor. Elliott's voice roused the boy and, with much grunting, he hauled himself to his feet. He yawned so cavernously it looked as though he might dislocate his jaw.

'Oh, hi . . . sorry . . . I was in such a deep sleep when Mrs Burrows came to get me,' he said, rubbing his eyes. 'Only had a couple of hours.'

They went down the corridor, then turned into a lobby where the lifts were located.

'Level 2,' Chester read through another yawn. He was squinting through one eye at the floor plan on the wall. As Sergeant Finch, with his bevy of cats in tow, had taken them down in the lift to show them to their quarters, he'd told them that the Complex had six levels in total. He had also told them that all the power for it came from the nearby electricity lines outside, the clever thing being that because it was taken straight from the grid, no one could tell that current was being siphoned off for the secret establishment.

'Which lift did he tell us to avoid?' Mrs Burrows asked, as

she stood in the middle of the lobby. Sergeant Finch had warned that one of the lifts was liable to break down, but she hadn't been able to see which of them he'd been referring to.

'Here,' Elliott answered, leading Mrs Burrows by the hand to the closed doors. 'Just remember not to take the first on this side.'

'Thank you,' Mrs Burrows said.

Chester summoned a lift and one arrived almost immediately. 'Going up,' he mumbled, and stepped to the side to allow Elliott and Mrs Burrows to enter, then reluctantly followed them in.

The lift picked up speed as it ascended, then abruptly shuddered to a halt. The main light above them went out and another blinked on, bathing them in a dim yellow glow. A pre-recorded man's voice calmly announced, 'Emergency Lighting'.

'Oh, bloody brilliant,' Chester complained as he repeatedly pressed the button with H on it to try to get them moving again. 'Rather have taken the stairs . . . haven't trusted lifts ever since that wonky contraption under Will's house.'

But the moment he'd finished speaking, the lift sprang back into life and continued on its way up.

'So Drake and Will . . . are they all okay? Nothing happened on the way here?' Elliott asked Mrs Burrows. The girl was rubbing her shoulder as if it was painful.

There was no time for an answer as a bell tinged and the doors slid open. The three of them exited, passing down several passageways to reach the Hub. The illumination on the way was similar to the emergency lighting in the lift.

'I wonder why it's so dark?' Chester asked as they stepped into the Hub.

The first person they saw was Danforth, lit by the glow of not just his original laptop, but another five of them arranged on trestle tables around him. He'd obviously continued to work on whatever he was doing as many more wall panels had been opened, and a bewildering number of cables spilled from them and around the legs of the tables. Noticing that Chester, Elliott and Mrs Burrows had entered the Hub, he peered up briefly. 'Main power's going to be off for a while,' he said, without any further explanation.

'Will! Drake!' Elliott shouted, as she spotted them on the other side of the Hub, and hurried over.

'I don't believe it!' Chester cried as he saw who was in his father's arms. Mr and Mrs Rawls were standing at the mouth of the entrance tunnel.

'Chester!' Mrs Rawls shouted, widening her embrace to include him as he dashed over to her. Chester clung to her, feeling her face was wet with tears of happiness and relief.

'You found her! Thank you!' Chester said to Drake. 'Thank you so much!'

Drake nodded, then turned to Elliott. 'We need to talk,' he began, his voice serious.

Elliott noticed Will had stepped a little closer to her, and also the way in which he was peering nervously at her back – at the long rifle slung over her shoulder, she assumed.

'What is it?' she asked, immediately aware that something was amiss. She took a couple of paces away from Will and Drake. 'Why won't you tell me?'

Then she happened to glance down the long entrance tunnel. Two figures were making their way towards the Hub along it. The larger of them – the hulking form – was unmistakable even at the distance. 'Sweeney,' Elliott said, but she didn't recognise the second, smaller figure. 'Who's that with him?'

'Elliott . . .' Will said, edging closer to her. 'We've got—'

'Jiggs . . . is that Jiggs?' Elliott demanded, squinting down the tunnel. Although there had been the odd mention of him, nobody had actually laid eyes on him yet, although they assumed they would before long.

Elliott shook her head slowly.

'No,' she said.

She shot a glance at Drake.

'No! Not him!'

Will saw the way she'd set her jaw, and the look of deadly intent in her eyes.

'Elliott, give me the rifle,' Drake asked, trying to seize hold of her, but she was too fast.

She ran towards the figure.

Towards her father.

Part Two

Maelstrom

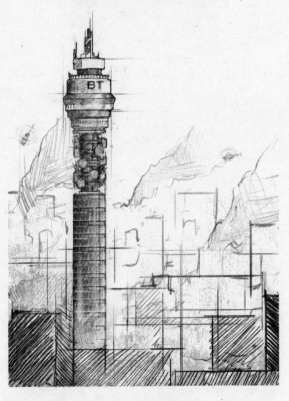

Chapter Eleven

Vane pushed herself off the Colonist she'd just impregnated. With slow, reptilian precision, she extended her leg to the floor beside the bed where she planted a foot. The tube-like ovipositor was retracting into her mouth as she slid her other leg across the limp body, then stood up.

The Colonist on the bed was a middle-aged woman, who had only recently been brought up from the subterranean city. She'd been one of the unlucky inhabitants of the shanty town in the North Cavern, taken from there at gunpoint by the Limiters, and Darklit until nothing remained of the conscious centres of her mind.

And although effectively brain dead, the Colonist's chest now began to heave and she coughed soundlessly as the egg sac induced involuntary spasms in her air tract. In a few cases, the troublesome human hosts would actually bring up the egg sac, and that meant starting the process all over again. Vane watched the woman until she was satisfied that the implantation had been successful, then looked from one end of the warehouse to the other. The Styx women had been systematically working their way through the humans, and maybe as many as a hundred had already been impregnated.

Vane's insect limbs twitched, then came together above her head. They oscillated against each other, faster and faster, until they were producing an unbroken sound similar to that of a cricket. Vane silenced the limbs, angling her head as she listened out. Barely a second later, a hollow rattle drifted back from somewhere else on the floor as Hermione replied in kind.

Vane and Hermione continued to communicate, homing in on each other as they headed towards the beds at the entrance to the warehouse.

Through the steam and subdued lighting, they spotted each other. They met around the bed of a young man, the very first human to be impregnated.

Although both Vane and Hermione had been feeding on the raw meat and drinking regularly from the vats of viscid sugar solution provided for them at various points across the warehouse floor, the Phase had drastically changed their appearance. The relentless production of egg sacs had sent their metabolic rates soaring through the roof, so much so that nearly every ounce of their body fat had been burnt off.

They barely resembled the strikingly beautiful women they'd been before the Phase had begun. Under their torn and bloodstained clothes, their physiques had been pared down to not much more than muscle and bone. Their faces were unnaturally angular, as if an artist had attempted to recreate them by using an assortment of hard planes.

'Time to check on our young,' Hermione announced in the rasping Styx language. If Will and Chester had been there to see her appearance as she spoke, it would have explained why the Styx's tongue had always sounded so inhuman to them. It was inhuman, and they were inhuman.

'Yes, it will be time,' Vane replied, eagerly rubbing her bony hands together. As she did so, the musculature and ligaments in her arms slid against each other under her taut skin like a mechanical model.

Hermione moved closer to the young man and leant over him. She paused to wipe her chin. The glands in her throat hadn't yet stopped producing the lubricative fluids required for the multiple impregnations, and these were now overflowing from her mouth and dangling from her cracked lips in sticky necklaces.

Undoing the top button of the man's shirt, she slid her hand inside it.

'Yes,' she sighed.

She very gently took out a pulsing, ivory-coloured larva, some five inches in length. It was similar in appearance to a giant maggot, although far stubbier. Holding the Styx Warrior larva in both hands, she lifted it up to her face to examine one end. 'Who's such a pretty little thing? Who's just perfect?' she cooed.

The eyes hadn't yet developed, but a small mouth opened and closed. As it did so, something caught in the illumination from one of the nearby overhead lights. The Warrior larva's fangs shone with a pearly whiteness, like a baby's milk teeth. They were snapping together as she held the grub against her chest, looking down at it lovingly.

Vane had also reached under the man's shirt and into his pleural cavity, which had been exposed as the grubs burst from his body. She took out not one, but two larvae, cradling them in her arms as they wriggled against her, like lively puppies.

'Yes, they are perfect,' Vane said, her eyes flooding with tears of happiness and fulfilment. One of her larvae began to make a high keening sound. Almost immediately the other larva in her arms and Hermione's also joined in.

The man's body on the bed started to move as though he'd miraculously been brought back to life. But he was well and truly dead. The movement was the other larvae as they tried to gnaw their way through his jeans and worm out from his shirt sleeves.

'The little ones are ravenous,' Hermione said. 'They're our first born. They're special. I think we should spoil them.'

Vane nodded in agreement. 'They deserve a special treat.' She placed her larvae back on the bed and strode across to the very corner of the warehouse. There she peered into the shadows, at the group of Colonists and New Germanians. Most of them were simply stretched out on the floor, but a few were sitting up. And although they'd had their minds wiped by Dark Lights, the Limiters had taken the precaution of erecting a pen around them in case any of them still had the ability to wander off, like bewildered cattle.

Vane opened the gate to the pen and heaved a thickset man to his feet. 'Let's be having you,' she said.

It was the Third Officer, still in his police uniform. 'Good. Nice bit of flesh on you,' Vane said, yanking him towards her. He could barely walk, his feet landing on their sides or clumsily knocking against each other. But Vane half-dragged, half-carried him until she was back at the bed. Hermione had ripped open the clothes on the corpse so that the other larvae – as many as thirty of them – no longer had to fight their way out.

Vane pushed the Third Officer down onto the mattress.

The larvae's teeth clicked like many pairs of castanets as they wriggled towards his living tissues. The two *Styx* women watched on, their hearts bursting with pride as their babies began to gorge themselves.

Eddie and Sweeney had both come to a standstill in the long entrance passageway, but Elliott was very much on the move. She was striding towards her father, and closing in fast.

Everyone in the dimly lit Hub had their eyes on her – Parry, Danforth and, even though they'd just had their emotional reunion, Chester and his parents.

Will couldn't see Elliott's expression, but from the way she'd talked about Eddie in the past, he thought the odds were stacked against this being a happy reconciliation between father and daughter. Quite the opposite, in fact – Elliott had taken the side of her Colonist mother and had even killed Limiters down in the Deeps. Will really didn't want to think about how she was going to react now she was finally coming face to face with her father again.

'She's armed,' Will pointed out to Drake with some urgency.

Chester had quickly made his way over and Will gave him a glance to see if he was similarly troubled. 'You know, she might use that rifle on him,' Will said to him. But his friend didn't answer – he seemed to be completely preoccupied with Elliott's progress along the passageway.

'Well, isn't *anyone* going to do *anything*?' Will demanded frantically, directing the question at Drake. 'Just in case?'

'Stand down,' Drake whispered. 'Let her keep the rifle.'

As Will saw the big man next to Eddie turn slightly, he

realised Drake was speaking to him. Although Sweeney was some forty feet away, he had heard the directive with his incredibly acute hearing. Will watched as Sweeney gave the tiniest shrug.

'I say again – *stand down*,' Drake whispered. 'But step in if you see a blade.'

Will thought Sweeney gave a wink in response, but he couldn't be sure. In any case, he was too intent on Elliott – if there was going to be an incident, it was going to be now.

Some ten feet away from her father, Elliott shouldered her rifle, aiming it squarely at him.

Eddie stood his ground, not shifting an inch.

'Drake . . .' Will said, panic creeping into his voice.

Maybe Elliott was expecting Sweeney to intervene with his lightning-fast reactions, because she seemed to falter slightly in her step as she stole a quick glance at him. However, Sweeney showed no signs of doing anything.

As she came closer still to Eddie, she lowered the rifle from her shoulder, but made as if she was going to lash out at him with the stock.

In the event she didn't, lobbing the weapon at Sweeney who caught it with ease in his enormous hands.

Instead she stopped before Eddie. She shook her head, then slapped him across the cheek with such force that the sound carried all the way back to the Hub.

'Ooh, bet that stung!' Chester said, cringing slightly.

Elliott struck her father again, slapping his other cheek with equal vehemence.

'Eddie's been getting a lot of that lately,' Will said. This elicited a sidelong glance from Drake, before he whispered another directive to Sweeney.

'I think we're out of the woods,' he said. 'You can give them some space now.'

Sweeney started down the passageway towards the Hub. Much to Will's amazement, Elliott and her father had begun to talk, albeit Elliott was shouting.

As Will considered what had just taken place, he was puzzled. 'How could you be sure she wasn't going to shoot him?' he asked Drake.

Mrs Burrows opened her hand, revealing the contents to her son. 'That would be difficult . . . without these.'

'Bullets?' Will said, then realised why his mother had them. He glanced at the long-barrelled weapon Sweeney was holding as he ambled into the Hub. 'So Elliott's rifle wasn't even loaded?'

Drake nodded. 'Eddie's vital to us right now – I couldn't afford to let anything happen to him. So I rang ahead and asked your mum to make safe the rifle. She's just about the only person I know with the ability to sneak in and do it without waking Elliott up.' Drake looked directly at Will. 'You don't think I'd leave something like that to chance, do you?'

'Thanks for telling me,' Will grumbled, annoyed that he'd been left in the dark. 'And you'd better make sure they're back in her rifle before she finds out. Otherwise she'll never trust you again.'

Parry had come over. 'So we're allowing the enemy onto the base now,' he said disapprovingly to his son. 'Are you handing out tickets? It's getting like bloody Piccadilly Circus down here.'

'Eddie's not our enemy, and what Will and I learnt from him this morning explains exactly what the Styx are up to,'

Drake said firmly. 'And it's worse than any of us could ever have imagined.' He produced the Book of Proliferation from an inner pocket and passed it to Will. 'I want you to gather everyone together in one of the briefing rooms and bring them up to speed. And that includes Old Wilkie and his granddaughter, the Colonel and Sergeant Finch – they all need to hear too.'

'Me? You want *me* to do it?' Will said, aghast. He wasn't sure yet if he himself was wholly convinced by what Eddie had told them, and he also felt that he lacked Drake's authority to deliver such an Earth-shattering revelation.

Drake nodded.

'So I tell them everything?' Will asked.

'Everything,' Drake confirmed.

Will couldn't have felt more uncomfortable with Drake's answer, because in telling everyone about the Phase he'd also implicate Elliott. The fact that the Phase could change her into something alien and hostile hadn't been out of his thoughts since Eddie had revealed it in the Humvee that morning. She was Will's friend, and he'd been doing his best not to view her any differently. And if Will was the one who broke the news about Elliott to everyone, it would make him feel very disloyal towards her.

'You really mean *everything*?' Will asked again.

'Yes, chapter and verse,' Drake answered a little tetchily.

'Why are you lumping this on the lad? What's so important that you and this Eddie fellow can't give us the sitrep yourselves?' Parry demanded of his son.

'Because I have something I need to see to right now,' Drake said, as he inclined his head towards the entrance tunnel where Elliott and Eddie were deep in conversation.

Elliott's voice was no longer raised, and from the way it was going between her and her father it certainly appeared as though there wouldn't be any trouble between them. Nevertheless, Drake was far from relaxed. This was made even more evident when he drew his Beretta from its holster, and made sure it was loaded before replacing it.

Parry seemed to realise that his son had other priorities and didn't push the point. Drake took a step towards the entrance tunnel, but then stopped and swung around to his father. 'Tell me – does the medical bay in this place have an X-ray machine?' he asked.

'Check with Finch, but I'm pretty sure it does. The bay was fully re-equipped in the seventies,' Parry replied. 'Even if the machine needs some coaxing to get it working, Danforth's your man. He'll be able to do it.'

Parry stayed behind to summon Stephanie and the others from their rooms using the intercom, while Will and Chester began to walk towards one of the briefing rooms just off the Hub. Will was carrying the Book of Proliferation rather gingerly in his hand – he didn't much relish the thought of touching the human skin on the cover.

'So what's this about, Will?' Chester asked, leaning his head conspiratorially towards his friend. 'And what's with Drake and the pistol? Doesn't he trust Eddie?'

'The gun isn't for Eddie. It's for Elliott,' Will replied.

Chester stopped dead in his tracks as Will continued towards the briefing room.

The dim half-light of the room seemed highly appropriate as Will recounted what Eddie had told him and Drake. When he'd finished, Will glanced at the sombre faces around the table. Nobody spoke – there was only the sound of the steady rush of air coming in through the vents.

Parry was the only one not looking at him. With a small torch, he was examining the Book of Proliferation, squinting at the pages through his reading glasses. Then he raised his head to Will. 'I don't know this Eddie chap from Adam, but if this is just some tall tale, it's a mighty elaborate one. And it does explain why the Styx have become so active; they didn't have any choice in the matter.'

One of Sergeant Finch's many cats leapt up onto the table. Its tail switched from side to side as it strolled regally towards the old man in his mobility scooter. The sight of the animal reminded Will that he had something else to add. 'I don't know how I forgot,' he said sadly, 'but there's one more thing I need to tell you. Bartleby's dead.'

Coming on top of the revelations about the Phase, there was no immediate reaction from anyone in the room, until Mrs Burrows spoke. 'Bartleby would never have deserted Colly, not voluntarily,' she said.

'Eddie told us it was all an accident,' Will said. 'Bart surprised one of his Limiters, who reacted on instinct. The man's been punished.'

Hunching forward, Chester thumped his elbows on the table. 'I hope he bloody well has,' he said angrily.

Will nodded. 'Actually, the Limiter killed himself. Right in front of us, he blew himself apart with one of Sweeney's grenades.'

'It was just awful,' Mrs Rawls whispered.

Stephanie made an 'Erm' noise, and raised her hand as if she was in a classroom. Old Wilkie was about to tell her to be quiet when Parry intervened. 'Let the girl talk if she wants,' he said. 'We're all in this together.'

Stephanie took a breath. 'Will, what you've told us sounds sort of like something from a horror movie. I totally accept the Styx are real enough and everything, specially as you brought one home with you. But this stuff about eggs and reproduction and these monsters wiping out human beings . . . how do you know it's true? It seems so – like– *out there*,' she said, raising her hands and wiggling her fingers in mock terror. 'Other than what Eddie Styx has told you, and this Monster Booky-wook of Monsters he's got,' she gestured in Parry's direction, 'you don't know for certain it's true. You don't have any other proof, do you?'

Will was about to say something, then closed his mouth.

'So?' Stephanie pushed him.

Will knew then that he couldn't avoid opening up about Elliott. While he'd been briefing them all, he'd tried to make as little eye contact with Chester as he could, hoping that his friend wouldn't work out the implications for her until Will had spoken to him in private.

Will swallowed. 'Elliott,' he said quietly. 'Elliott could be the proof.'

Chester murmured something, but Stephanie was quick to follow up. 'Why Elliott?' she demanded.

'She's half Styx, isn't she? And she might be old enough for the Phase to alter her.' Will made himself look at Chester. His friend's face fell as he realised the significance that Elliott's mixed parentage could have for her.

Stephanie had put her hand up again. 'But she's looks normal – she can have babies like . . . like normal people, can't she?'

'Yes,' Will replied.

Stephanie was shaking her head. 'So you're saying Elliott could still change . . . but wouldn't she know this might happen? I mean she *must* have known about all this Phase stuff?'

'Elliott wasn't brought up by the Styx, so – no – she didn't know. It's a secret they've kept completely to themselves. And the Colonists don't know anything about it,' he replied. 'Eddie did tell us that Styx women can give birth like normal people, but the Phase is something else altogether. It's a really powerful force . . . instinct . . . that affects the Styx race. And the Phase only shows itself when it takes control of their wom—'

'So does that make her dangerous to be around?' Stephanie interrupted.

'I . . . we don't know yet,' Will replied. 'But I suppose that's what Drake's trying to find out right now by X-raying her.'

'You mean he's finding out whether Elliott's turning beetle on us or not?' Stephanie asked, with a genuine shiver.

Will nodded. He couldn't really be angry with Stephanie for being so outspoken. It was only what everyone else in the room was thinking, even if they weren't saying it.

'Poor sweetie,' Stephanie said sympathetically. 'I do hope she doesn't.'

Referring to the floor plan on the wall in the Level 4 lobby, Will and Chester found their way to the medical bay. Neither of them would have dreamed of entering while Elliott's examination was still in progress, so instead they installed themselves on a bench in the corridor outside.

Danforth eventually emerged, but there wasn't an opportunity to ask him anything as he tore off in the direction of the lifts. Before long he was back with a large briefcase that Will recognised – it was full of tools and electronics testing equipment. And as Danforth swept back into the medical bay, through the open door Will caught a glimpse of Elliott being led by her father. Although everywhere else in the Complex was still on emergency lighting, the medical bay didn't seem to be affected at all, the interior bright and well illuminated. So before the door slammed shut, Will had been able to see that Elliott was walking barefoot on the lino, and dressed in some sort of loose-fitting hospital garment, which made her look very small and vulnerable. And she'd also appeared to be incredibly agitated. Will didn't know if Chester had seen her too, but made no remark to him.

As Elliott's examination went on, the boys listened to the low drone of voices, not being able to make out distinct words, but imagining the worst.

The drone of male voices continued, but then there was a scream. It was Elliott. The scream wasn't particularly loud but Will and Chester both jumped.

'Bartleby,' Chester abruptly blurted out, pretending to scratch a callous on his palm. 'It's strange now he's gone for good, isn't it? I miss not having him around.'

The Hunter's unfortunate demise certainly wasn't what was preoccupying either Chester or Will at that moment, but it was less painful to talk about than Elliott's situation.

'Bartleby. Yes,' Will answered, not really knowing what he was saying. 'I miss him, too. I suppose he was sort of part of the team.'

There was another, quieter cry.

Will didn't want to imagine what they were doing to her. His feelings swung from anger that she should have to endure

191

this, to helplessness that he couldn't do anything to stop it.

'Colly's been very quiet lately,' Chester said, giving the door to the medical bay a sidelong glance.

'She dotes on Mum,' Will said, straightening up on the bench. 'You know, she's been complaining about her back a lot lately.'

'Huh?' Chester asked, turning to his friend.

'Elliott has,' Will said, his eyes glued to a faded poster on a notice board by the entrance of the medical bay. It had a pretty, smiling nurse pictured on it, and a man in a bowler hat, also smiling, as it proclaimed GIVE BLOOD. SAVE LIVES. in bold red letters. 'I just hope that her back trouble isn't due to the Phase.' Will couldn't get the image from the Book of Proliferation out of his head, of the woman with the pair of insect limbs.

'Me too,' Chester replied glumly.

Sweeney thumped open the door of the medical bay, and came out. Still holding Elliott's rifle, he sat between the boys on the bench, which creaked under his weight. Both Will and Chester were looking at him, eager for any news.

'Your girly's passed the first part of her physical,' Sweeney said, a grin crinkling his singular face. 'Passed it with flying colours. Nothing much out of place there.'

'Thank God,' Chester exhaled.

'So what's next – the X-rays?' Will enquired.

Sweeney nodded. 'I had to get out – they play havoc with the circuits in my bonce.'

The three of them listened to the high whirr as the machine was activated, followed by a muted thump as the radiograph was taken. This happened once more, then Danforth bustled out of the medical bay. 'I'm going to develop these. You need to go back in now,' he told Sweeney.

'Yes sir, of course, sir,' Sweeney mumbled sarcastically, as he watched the Professor sail down the corridor to another office. It was almost impossible to read Sweeney's expression, but there seemed to be no love lost between him and Danforth.

'I'll leave this with you,' he said, handing the rifle to Will and then trundling into the bay.

It seemed ages before Danforth reappeared, wafting two X-ray plates in the air before him to dry them. He completely ignored the boys as he went back into the bay.

'I can't stand this,' Chester said. Getting to his feet, he began to walk up and down. 'It even smells like a hospital down here.'

Will remembered how Chester's younger sister had died in hospital after a road accident, and how much he loathed them as a result.

'If you don't want to hang around here, I'll come and get you when she's finished,' Will offered.

'Yes, think I might nip upstairs for some water,' Chester said, leaning against the wall. 'I'm incredibly thirsty.'

Will noticed that his friend was sweating heavily and looking distinctly peaky.

'Actually, Will, I think I'm going to be sick.' With that Chester broke into a run towards the lobby, leaving Will watching the empty corridor where he'd been.

Ten minutes later the door to the medical bay opened, and there was Elliott, with Drake beside her. She was still in the hospital gown, her clothes in a bundle under her arm.

'Oh, Will,' she said, dropping her clothes as she rushed over to him and hugged him tight.

'I think we're in the clear,' Drake said.

As Elliott continued to cling to Will, hiding her face in his chest, he felt something across her shoulders. It was a large piece of gauze, taped into place, and there was blood soaked into it. Will stared at Drake in shock.

'Yes, we attempted a limited surgical exploration,' Danforth said, the X-ray plates rolled in his hand like a baton, as he stepped into the corridor with Eddie. Danforth's tone was so dispassionate he could have been discussing one of his gadgets. 'We found evidence of features that are clearly related to the Phase, but they're only vestigial. Given that she's a human/Styx cross, it may be that she's carrying the recessive Phase gene or genes, but the traits will never reveal themselves in anything more than a partial manifestation.'

Danforth held up the rolled X-ray plates. 'However, bearing in mind her age and the fact that she's still in the throes of adolescence, it's something we'll need to keep a close eye on for the future.'

'But she's okay? Really okay?' Will asked Drake, ignoring Danforth.

'Yes, she is,' Drake exhaled.

Maybe it was due to the intense stress he'd been under, but Will began to chuckle. 'So my best friend isn't a bug after all?'

As this set Drake off, Elliott raised her head to peer up at Will through her tear-filled eyes.

'You bastard,' she laughed, then kissed him on the cheek.

'YOU BASTARD!' The grating cry reverberated around the quiet of the police station.

'Gappy Mulligan?' the Second Officer asked.

'Gappy Mulligan,' the First Officer confirmed. 'It'll be

aimed at me. She was telling me how I should free her . . . and the rest of the prisoners while I'm about it.' Scratching his chest vigorously through his shirt, unbuttoned at the neck, he glanced in the direction of the Hold. 'I must've left the aisle door open. I should go and close it.'

'Don't bother. It'll give them a bit of air in there,' the Second Officer said. He was studying his hand as the two men played poker on a desk in the main office.

The First Officer had finished scratching his chest, but was examining something intently between his thumb and forefinger. Lice were a permanent problem down in the Colony. Grimacing, because he wasn't sure if he'd caught one or not, he pressed his fingers together and then wiped them on his leg. 'You know, we haven't got much food left in the store, and I don't know about you, but I'm a bit tired of playing skivvy to the prisoners now everyone's refusing to work here.'

The Second Officer had been concentrating on his cards, but now looked up sharply. 'Smoke! I smell smoke!' he shouted.

They both leapt to their feet and began sniffing. Of all the things a Colonist feared most, a fire was top of the list. Throughout the three-hundred-year history of the underground society, there had been several outbreaks that had got a grip, and the deaths that ensued were not from the fire itself, but smoke inhalation in the enclosed caverns and tunnels.

'You're right!' the First Officer yelled.

They both dashed through the opening in the counter.

At the entrance to the station – the only way in or out – huge flames were licking up over the swing doors.

'MY GOD!' the First Officer cried, rushing to the cabinet where red-painted buckets of water were kept for this very eventuality. 'Patrick – free the prisoners! We're going to need help to put this out!'

Dense smoke was already wafting into the Hold as the Second Officer quickly went along the row of cells and unlocked them. The occupants – Gappy Mulligan included – didn't need to be told what to do. They formed themselves into a chain stretching between the entrance and the small room in the station with a fresh water faucet. Then they passed the filled buckets to the First Officer, who was throwing them at the blaze. He'd shed his tunic and wound some material over his nose and mouth as he continued to do battle with the flames. All the prisoners were coughing and their eyes watering as they worked tirelessly, passing the water-filled buckets forward.

After several minutes, they'd managed to douse the swing doors sufficiently to open them, but still they didn't stop. The water was making a sizzling noise as it fell on the large pile of timber outside at the top of the steps.

Finally the fire was out. The First Officer, his shirt and uniform trousers soaked, was supporting himself against the counter as he broke into a racking cough. The prisoners were all coughing and trying to catch their breath too, as the Second Officer began to inspect the damage. Grateful for the cool breeze outside the station, he examined the charred pile of timber. From the smell there was little doubt in his mind that an accelerant had been used to start the blaze. Then the Second Officer spotted an old can that had been discarded by the side of the steps, and carried it back into the station with him.

'Petrol,' he announced, placing the can on the counter by his senior officer. 'They were serious about burning us down, but there's nothing on this to show who it was.'

'You don't say,' the First Officer replied, laughing and coughing. 'I would have expected them to paint their name on it, as a bare minimum,' he went on, sarcastically, then turned to the rabble of prisoners. 'Listen, you lot, you can all go,' he declared. 'You're free.'

The Second Officer leant towards him. 'Sir, don't you think that's a bit hasty? I mean—'

'Give it a rest, Patrick. Are you worried the Styx will come down on us for releasing a motley bunch of losers, whose crimes don't amount to much more than rustling the odd chicken to feed their families?' the First Officer asked, then turned to all the prisoners. 'No offence meant,' he added quickly. 'I'm very grateful you all mucked in to help with the fire.'

Gappy Mulligan was grinning, but a muscular-looking man with mad, staring eyes didn't look so happy. He was known simply as 'Cleaver', named after the digging implement used everywhere in the Colony. 'Losers?' he said indignantly. 'I'll 'ave you know I didn't steal no bloody chicken. I'm up for disord'ly conducks, and a' unpr'voked attack with a' axe.'

The First Officer guffawed loudly. 'Is that an admission of guilt, Cleaver?'

Cleaver was confused by this at first, but quickly caught on. 'No, sir, no way I dun what they said I dun. No, sir. I'm inn'cent a' a newborn sluice fish.'

A petty thief with rat-like features, who was sitting on an upturned bucket at the end of the reception area, found this funny. He tittered loudly until Cleaver glowered at him.

The Second Officer still wasn't comfortable with his senior

officer's pronouncement. 'Are you seriously going to free them?' he asked in a low voice so the prisoners wouldn't overhear him. 'They've all got charges to answer to.'

The First Officer had no qualms about letting the prisoners know what he was thinking. 'Patrick, we haven't heard a squeak from the Styx in nearly three days now,' he said loudly, sweeping a grimy hand at the brass message tubes across the room. 'And nobody's seen one in the streets in as many days. For all we know, they've gone . . . they've scuttled the Colony.'

The prisoners gasped.

'And you seem to be forgetting the fire . . . an attempt was just made on our lives – by some of our own people. That's how far things have gone.' For a moment he stared thoughtfully into the Second Officer's eyes. 'Where's your warrant card, Patrick?' he asked. 'Fetch it for me.'

The Second Officer did as he was bidden, going to his tunic where he'd left it on the back of a chair and retrieving the warrant card from it. As he handed it to the First Officer, the man plucked the quill pen from the pot on the counter. The Second Officer and the prisoners listened to the scratching of the pen, then the First Officer handed it back. 'Congratulations,' he said.

The Second Officer read what he'd written on the warrant card. 'No!' he exclaimed.

'Yes, I'm handing my chips in. I've had all I can take. I'm resigning and going home to take care of my family,' the First Officer said. 'So now you're in charge.'

The Second Officer reeled.

'Take these, Squeaky,' the First Officer said, detaching a large bunch of keys from his belt and lobbing them to the man with the rat face. 'In the evidence room, on the bottom shelf, you'll find a case of Somers Town malt. Bring it back here, will you? We're going to toast the new First Officer's promotion in style.'

Chapter Twelve

Parry looked every bit the military leader as he strutted up and down in front of the map displayed on the big screen in the Hub.

He now turned to everybody. 'Right . . . the Phase is under way at this very moment so the clock is ticking fast. We need some positive action to find it and put a stop to it. We need to move quickly!'

'We do,' Drake agreed.

'So let's analyse what we know,' Parry said. 'The Phase will be taking place on the surface, because that's one of the pre-conditions. And it's somewhere . . .' He twisted to the map of the UK on the screen, '. . . somewhere here, and probably at a single location.'

'Yes, that's correct,' Eddie confirmed.

Parry tugged thoughtfully on his beard as he went closer to the screen and pointed with his walking stick. 'But can we reasonably assume it's in the London area? It might be in the Home Counties, or anywhere in the country for that matter? Would the Styx bother to venture further than a hundred miles from London?'

'London and its environs make sense,' Eddie said. 'Unless they chose somewhere remote because it would be more secure.'

'That doesn't help us at all. It's like searching for a poisonous needle in a haystack,' Parry grumbled to himself, tugging even more forcibly on his beard. 'But we do know that the Styx need an ample stock of human bodies for the breeding process. Unless they're abducting Topsoilers willy-nilly, that means Colonists and maybe New Germanians are being used as the living hosts. Which would suggest somewhere around London, because they wouldn't want their supply chain to be stretched too far.'

'Particularly not with the disruption to the transport network *they're* responsible for down in the south east,' Drake put in. 'Getting around isn't as easy as it used to be.'

Parry drew in a breath. 'Everyone put their thinking caps on. How, precisely, do we find the Phase site?' he asked, then spun to Eddie. 'Can't we snatch a Styx from the London streets and interrogate him?'

'Even if you could find one, you wouldn't get anything,' Eddie replied.

Parry wasn't to be deterred. 'Okay then – what if one of your men returned to the Colony? He could gather the intel we need down there.'

'No, I told you – my men have cut all ties with our people and covered their tracks,' Eddie said categorically. 'One couldn't just show his face as if nothing had happened. He'd be executed the instant they laid eyes on him. It would give us nothing, and simply put them on notice that there's a splinter group of disaffected Limiters.'

Parry went on tugging his beard until his fingers came

away with a tuft of hair. 'But what are the Styx doing at the Phase site that will put up a smoke trail we can spot?' He looked pointedly at his son, then at Danforth who was copying the Book of Proliferation page by page on a scanner so he'd be able to translate it with Eddie's help. 'Come on, you two – you're the tech specialists. Any bright ideas?'

Danforth glanced up from the scanner, but didn't reply, and Drake was slowly shaking his head.

'The Dark Lights,' Eddie suggested. 'Thanks to Drake we can locate them. And my people, wherever they are, are likely to be using them on an intensive basis.'

Drake was quick to answer. 'But we've already considered that. Yes, we can detect Dark Light activity by using mast arrays, but it only works over relatively small areas. In order to increase the search radius, I'd need microwave antennae mounted up somewhere high, so there'd be uninterrupted line-of-sight out across the country.'

'You mean a whole cluster of bloody powerful parabolic dishes, and directional to boot,' Danforth added in a patronising tone.

Drake gave him a weary nod; although the Professor was arguably one of the most brilliant minds on the planet, at times his sense of self-importance was difficult to stomach. 'Then, in theory at least, we could identify any major Dark Light hotspots two or three hundred miles or even further from the centre of London,' Drake said.

'Well, that's a start,' Parry said optimistically.

'We'd also need to dispatch roving teams with battery-powered mobile detectors to help us pinpoint the precise coordinates of any hotspots.' Drake paused as he pursed his lips in a moment of contemplation. 'Yes, we might strike gold, but it's a hell of a long shot.'

'Hell of a long shot,' Danforth echoed, as he turned to a new page in the Book of Proliferation and placed it face down on the scanner.

'High-powered parabolic dishes in clusters,' Parry summarised. 'Now we're getting somewhere. But where would we find that sort of set-up in a hurry? The City? Canary Wharf?'

Sergeant Finch mumbled something.

'What?' Parry boomed, wheeling towards him. 'What did you just say?'

Sergeant Finch was taken aback by Parry's reaction. 'It's just what you were saying . . . it made me think of the *Backbone Chain*,' he suggested sheepishly.

'What's the Backbone Chain?' Drake asked quickly.

'It was a network of purpose-built concrete towers erected across the country by NATO to preserve communications after a nuclear strike,' Parry said. 'The nearest tower to us here is at Kirk O'Shotts, and then there's one at Sutton Common, and another at . . .'

Parry and Sergeant Finch looked at each other, speaking at the same time. 'The Post Office Tower,' they choroused.

Parry strode over to Sergeant Finch and placed a hand on his shoulder. 'You bloody genius!'

'You're talking about the BT Tower in London?' Drake asked.

Parry waved his walking stick impatiently. 'Stuff and nonsense! They will keep changing the blessed names of everything! Yes – the BT Tower – and we can get into it using the old emergency protocols, can't we, Finch?'

Sergeant Finch was grinning. 'We certainly can, sir – and I've got a cousin who used to work there, back in the good old days wh—'

'Raise him right now on one of Danforth's satphones. Haul him out of bed, if necessary,' Parry ordered. 'And you two,' he said, setting his gaze on Drake, then Danforth, 'how many mobile detectors can you rustle up for me at short notice?'

Danforth groaned; he didn't seem to be particularly enamoured by the thought of doing any work. 'How many do you want?' he enquired begrudgingly.

'How many can you give me?' Parry said.

'But how can we mass-produce them here?' Drake put in.

'Simple as pie – if somebody gathers up all the Geiger counters in this place,' Danforth replied, 'I can adapt them with components from the stores on Level 4. It'll be bloody tedious to say the least, but you can help me, Drake.'

Drake raised his eyebrows. 'You can do it? With components here in the Complex?'

'In my sleep,' Danforth replied resignedly.

'And once the mobile detectors are ready, we'll ship them down south and send patrols out. Your men can lend a hand,' Parry said to Eddie, 'but there aren't enough of them. It looks as though I'm going to have to bring the Old Guard into play. We'll need quite a few bods to cover the country.'

'And we need to get ourselves down to London,' Drake said, 'to the BT Tower.'

There were shouts from outside the police station and someone mounted the steps, taking them three at a time. The man reached for the counter as soon as he came in, propping himself against it as he tried to catch his breath.

'You have to come – been an accident,' he wheezed. It was one of the Colonists from the Quarter, a shopkeeper called Maynard. He peered with disbelief at the scene that greeted him – the former First Officer, in his sweat-stained shirt and with his braces hanging from his waist, holding court with all the prisoners as they supped from their tankards of Somers Town whisky. Maynard met Cleaver's eyes, but when the grizzled visage smiled back at him, revealing his darkened stumps of teeth, he quickly looked away.

'Wass all the rumpus 'bout?' the former First Officer drawled, trying to pull himself up in his seat.

Maynard frowned. 'It's my son – the magic's got him. I need your help.'

'I don't work here any more,' the former First Officer said, thrusting his tankard in the new First Officer's direction and managing to slop drink over himself, which elicited giggles from Squeaky. 'Ask Patrick.'

'Patrick?' Maynard asked. 'Who the hell's Patrick? And what's going on here?'

'It's all right, Maynard,' the new First Officer said as he emerged from what was now his office. He tried again to recall the former First Officer's name, but it wasn't there, so he pointed instead. 'He's taking a break, so I'll be in charge for a while.'

'Mole flaps!' the former First Officer exclaimed, his expression pained. Cleaver and Squeaky dissolved into roars of laughter at hearing him use the swearword. Even Gappy

Mulligan, who everyone had assumed had passed out from the drink because she was lying under the table, began to cackle. 'Nope, I ain't never coming back,' the former First Officer insisted. 'Never, never, never.'

'Never,' Squeaky added in his nasal squeak, laughing.

'I heard you say "magic",' the new First Officer asked. 'What do you mean?'

'No such fing,' one of the other prisoners commented, and was shushed immediately by Cleaver. 'Listen t'the man,' he urged, in his rumbling baritone voice.

'My boy and me and some others were planning to go through a portal, and up Topsoil to collect a bit of food for everybody. We've got some Topsoil money left, and we figured we'd use it to buy a few basics: bread and milk and the like. There's almost nothing left in my pantry, you know,' he said.

The new First Officer nodded sympathetically. 'I know how it is. We have to do something, although we should get ourselves organised first. But what do you mean by "magic"? What happened?'

'I'm telling you – it's Styx magic,' Maynard insisted.

'You'd better show me,' the new First Officer said, taking his truncheon from the peg on the wall and then going through the open counter.

'I've got to see this magic for myshelf,' the former First Officer slurred. He had somehow managed to get to his feet, all the prisoners rising with him – even Gappy Mulligan, although she was swaying unpredictably from side to side and singing softly to herself.

Danforth had restored power to the main circuits so the

Complex was no longer lit by the emergency lighting. After her examination, Elliott had gone straight to her quarters and refused to come out, despite Will and Chester's best efforts. So instead they took it in turns to bring her food and drink.

On one occasion, when Will had turned up with a mug of tea, he found her before the full-length mirror in the wardrobe door, simply rocking up and down on her feet as she looked at herself.

'Are you okay?' he asked, as she continued to regard her reflection.

'I'm not sure I know who I am any more,' she said to him. 'I thought I knew, but I don't.'

Before Will had time to ask what she meant, she fixed him with her piercing dark eyes. 'Do you think differently about me now?' she said, stretching an arm above her head in a balletic movement. Then she let it flop at the elbow, so her fingertips touched the bandage across her back.

'Of course not,' he replied without hesitation.

'But Danforth found early signs of the Phase in me, and that makes me feel like a monster. It makes me something ugly.'

'That's just silly—' Will began.

'But you don't look at me in the same way now,' she interrupted. 'When you held me earlier on, I could sense it.'

'That's a load of rubbish,' he puffed indignantly. 'And you know it is. You're just a bit confused.' He remembered why he'd come to see her in the first place, offering her the mug. 'You should drink this. Drake told me to put some extra sugar in it – he said it'll help you get over the shock.' She took the mug, but as Will tried to touch her arm in a gesture of reassurance, she snatched it away, spilling her tea.

He looked down at the tea as it soaked into the carpet.

'You're my friend,' he said. 'That will never change. You're Elliott. And that's all that matters to me.' Not knowing what else to say, he left the room.

The strange party had followed Maynard up through the tunnel network until they came to the portal. As the new First Officer threaded between the crowd gathered there, he saw Maynard's son was on the ground, some ten feet from the riveted steel door of the airlock. It was rather unfortunate because the boy was very chubby, and he'd fallen face down on the ground with his well-padded bottom sticking in the air.

'No closer,' Maynard warned, catching the new First Officer's arm. 'It's bewitched.'

The new First Officer heeded the advice. 'So what happened? Tell me precisely,' he enquired, as he saw the pickaxe lying on the ground beside the plump boy.

'We thought the Styx might have welded the portal shut, so we were preparing to force our way through,' Maynard replied. 'My boy Gregory was the first to reach the door. He's been very hungry lately, and a bit difficult at home. Anyway, he was rushing towards the door and just fell over – like the magic had struck him down.'

'Styx magic. They placed a curse on the portal,' a man in the crowd piped up.

'We're all doomed,' a woman wailed, which sent a ripple of disquiet through everyone gathered there.

'Poppycock! The Styx don't have magic,' the former First Officer drawled. 'Fat boy passed out from his hunger.' As he wheeled unevenly around, his eyes fell on the prisoner nearest to him. 'Cleaver, show them,' he said.

'Cleaver, show them! Cleaver, show them!' Squeaky and the other prisoners began to chant.

Delighted to be the centre of attention, Cleaver strode towards the portal in lumbering, confident steps. As he glanced over his shoulder at the other prisoners, they all chanted even louder, cheering him on.

'Cleaver, show them!' the prisoners continued.

'Shaver, clove them!' Gappy Mulligan screeched.

Cleaver was clearly basking in the moment, a big grin pasted across his face. He built up speed, his thick legs pumping as he ran. But as he came to where the plump boy lay, he too crumpled to the ground, as if he'd been poleaxed.

As if he'd run straight into an invisible barrier.

All the prisoners *ahhhed* with disappointment, their chanting immediately dying out.

'It's magic, I'm telling you. I did try to warn you. The Styx don't want anyone to escape,' Maynard said. 'So what now? We have to get my boy back and see if he's all right.'

'From now on nobody goes near *any* of the portals,' the new First Officer ordered the assembled people. 'Is that understood?'

The crowd murmured their agreement.

Turning towards the portal again, the new First Officer took off his helmet and scratched his head for a moment as he thought. 'Right . . . I'll need a grappling hook so I can drag these two out. And someone else fetch a doctor, if there's still one left in the Colony.' He regarded Cleaver's huge body, which dwarfed even the vastly overweight boy slumped beside him. 'And you'd better make that a big grappling hook,' he added.

Elliott had stripped her rifle down to give it a thorough clean. She was in the process of putting it back together again when Stephanie pranced past the open door of her quarters.

'Oh, hi there,' the girl said. 'I didn't know you had this room.' She was wearing a white T-shirt identical to the one Elliott had on, but Stephanie had tied the bottom in a knot so it looked rather more stylish on her.

'I'm so glad you're all right,' Stephanie said vaguely, eyeing the thick gauze on Elliott's back, which was difficult to miss. She had begun to follow up with, 'And not a . . .' but decided better of it and closed her mouth. For once.

Elliott made no effort to reply as she slotted the bolt back into the rifle's receiver, then worked it several times.

Uncomfortable with the silence between them, Stephanie announced, 'I shoot too.'

'Do you?' Elliott replied quietly. 'Not with anything like this.'

'Oooo, can I see?' Stephanie asked eagerly, entering the room in little steps, her hands outstretched.

Elliott sighed. 'I suppose so. Just be careful with it – it's heavy.'

Stephanie took the weapon and, without any hesitation, put it to her shoulder. 'It *is* heavy,' she agreed. 'At school I mainly use a .22 for target practice. What calibre is this?' she asked, sliding back the bolt. Elliott had risen to her feet to stop her, but it was unnecessary – Stephanie appeared to know what she was doing. 'I guess it's like a .303 or something,' the girl continued, peering inside the chamber.

Elliott nodded. 'You're close. It's a .35, and uses a special cartridge with a long casing, so it can take an extra load.'

'Right,' Stephanie said, turning her attention to the bulbous scope mounted on top of the weapon.

'That's a light-gathering sight; the only place you'll find anything quite like it is down in the Colony, where they're hand-built for the Styx. This is a Limiter rifle, and I've shot and killed at least ten of them with it. Maybe more, but I wasn't close enough to know if I'd hit the mark,' Elliott said. When Stephanie didn't react to this, Elliott frowned. 'I'm curious . . . do you mind if I ask you something . . . ?' she began.

'Totally,' Stephanie answered brightly, lowering the weapon to her hip and twisting from one side to the other as if she was spraying an invisible foe with a submachine gun. To make matters worse, she blew through her lips in an imitation of rapid gunfire.

'Ha,' Elliott swallowed, trying to resist the temptation to cuff the girl.

'What did you want to ask me?' Stephanie said, unaware of Elliott's scornful expression.

'Will briefed you on the situation, so you know about the Phase and how serious things are. And because you're with us, you're marked by the Styx. There's absolutely no way you can go home now,' Elliott said with over-brutal directness.

Stephanie looked enquiringly at her.

Elliott continued, 'You're okay with all that? Being holed up in this place until it's all over. Or if we *don't* deal with the Phase and beat the Styx, spending the rest of your life – however short it might be – constantly living in fear. Constantly on the run.'

Stephanie took a breath and passed the rifle back to Elliott. 'You couldn't make it more obvious you don't like me,' she said, flicking her beautifully groomed hair from her face. 'But I'm, like, not some little sissy who screams or faints at the first sign of trouble. I'm tough, you know.'

Elliott laughed harshly. 'You are, are you? You don't look it to me.'

Stephanie held the other girl's stony glare. 'Come on then. If you think I'm such a waste of space, why don't you have a pop at me?' Taking several steps back to give herself room, she kicked her shoes off. 'Try me.'

Elliott laughed again, then stopped herself. 'You're serious?'

'Totally, like, serious,' Stephanie replied.

Elliott put her rifle down. 'Well, if you insist, but Drake won't be pleased if I hurt you or anything.'

'I don't want to hurt you either,' Stephanie countered. 'Is your back better? I don't want to damage it.'

'Don't you worry about me. I've got Styx blood. I heal fast,' Elliott said. She squared up to Stephanie, who seemed completely relaxed. Then Elliott launched herself, grabbing the girl's neck with both hands.

Stephanie reacted with complete precision, swinging her arms up to break Elliott's hold, then hooking her leg. Elliott was spun around like a top, and dropped face down on the carpet.

Stephanie backed away, allowing the other girl to pick herself up.

'Where did you learn to do that?' Elliott asked, narrowing her eyes.

'Well, Parry was, like, this huge influence on my dad when he was growing up on the estate, and he got him into military intelligence,' Stephanie explained.

'Not another spook?' Elliott said.

'Something like that. Dad's been stationed in loads of trouble spots across the world, and my mum and brothers and me have followed him to most of them. I haven't exactly led a sheltered life.' She gave Elliott a small smile. 'Try me again, but really give it all you've got this time. Chester's not the only Olympic champion round here.'

'He's not?' Elliott replied, her confusion obvious.

'No, and if they had judo or aikido on *Britain's Got Talent*, I'd win hands down. Come on, grumpy – try and hit me,' Stephanie urged. She waggled her fingers, beckoning Elliott towards her. 'And do your worst this time.'

Elliott attacked in earnest. Her full-bodied punch was aimed directly at Stephanie's chin. But Stephanie deflected the blow, caught Elliott's wrist, and threw her onto her back in a single, fluid movement. It didn't end there – as Stephanie dropped to the floor beside Elliott, she had one of her arms in a lock. Elliott was pinned to the ground and completely in the other girl's power. 'Got you!' Stephanie said.

'NO!' Chester cried from the doorway.

The boy's sudden appearance distracted Stephanie sufficiently that Elliott managed to twist free. She swung her legs up and caught Stephanie around the neck in a scissor grip. Then Elliott heaved her to the floor, where the other girl was trying all she could to break free. But now Elliott had her in an iron grip.

Chester was reaching in to separate them. 'Stop it! Stop it at once!'

Elliott relaxed her grip, and they both sat up.

'Nice move – wasn't expecting that,' Stephanie complimented Elliott.

'What do you think you're both doing?' Chester demanded,

huffing with concern as the girls stared up at him.

'You sound like my dad,' Stephanie giggled.

'It wasn't for real,' Elliott said.

'It looked real enough to me,' Chester came back. 'Besides, you should watch out for your back,' he said to Elliott.

'My back's completely . . .' she replied, but stopped as Stephanie failed to stifle another giggle.

'What's so funny?' Chester demanded, becoming quite irate now.

'You didn't think we were fighting over *you*, did you?' Stephanie said.

Blushing, Chester made an about turn and fled from the room. Muttering to himself, he hunched his shoulders and stomped down the corridor.

As he was approaching the lift area, Will rounded the corner, a piece of paper in his hands. 'I was just on my way to find you,' Will said. 'I went up to the Hub and they're all busy with whatever they're doing, but I did speak to Sergeant Finch and . . .' Clearly excited about whatever was on the piece of paper, Will was about to show it to his friend when he sensed that all wasn't well with him. 'You don't look very happy. Are you all right?' Will enquired.

'Peachy . . . just peachy,' Chester spat, his face stiff with anger.

Will caught Elliott's and Stephanie's animated voices, then Stephanie's shrill laughter. 'Wow! Am I really hearing that?' he said. 'I never thought those two would ever hit it off. What are they laughing about?'

Chester pulled a face. 'I haven't the faintest idea – they're girls, aren't they? What did you want me for, anyway?' he asked curtly.

'This,' Will said, flashing the sheet of paper in front of his friend. 'Sergeant Finch told me there are some interesting rooms on Level 3. We should go and have a look.'

At Chester's insistence, they took the stairs rather than the lift. As they entered the new level, they immediately spotted a difference. There might still have been lino on the floor, but it was a rich blue in colour, and the walls of the corridor were covered with a fine gold-and-green patterned wallpaper.

'What's this all about?' Chester asked, looking around. 'I thought we'd been given the luxury floor?'

'You just wait,' Will replied, consulting his piece of paper as he walked ahead of Chester, checking what was on the doors. 'Ah, here we are,' he announced, pushing one of them open and turning on the lights.

Inside there was a suite of four interconnecting rooms, two with four-poster beds, their canopies swathed with red velvet, and on the walls tapestries depicting hunting scenes. The antique furniture was incredibly ornate and looked expensive – it was in a different league from anything in their own quarters.

'Was this for someone important?' Chester asked, running his eyes over the gilded chairs and a large divan.

'You're getting warm. It was for someone *really* important. Go on – have a guess,' Will challenged his friend, as they passed into a small side room, which was very basic and utilitarian compared to the bedrooms. With a butler's sink in the corner, it had several small pens along the longest wall.

'Any ideas?' Will asked.

'Nope,' Chester said, his patience growing thin. 'Come on, Will, stop messing around. Who were these rooms for? And why are we stopping in the kitchen?'

'It's not a kitchen. If I told you these pens were specially built for corgis, would that help?' Will said, stepping into one of them.

'Corgis?' Chester repeated, then the penny dropped. 'You're joking! This was for the Queen!'

'You got it! And that's not all!' Will exclaimed, leading him back through the rooms and out into the corridor again. He groped in his pocket for a key, which he slotted into the solid-looking door of the next room along. As it ground open on its chunky hinges, the boys stepped inside. Will turned on the lights, and he and Chester were met by the sight of a whole room of glass display cases on pedestals. The cases were empty but, from the satin-covered stands in the bottom of each of them, it was clear that they'd been constructed to house something specific.

'This is where the Crown Jewels would have been brought if we'd been invaded,' Will informed his friend.

Chester was smiling and shaking his head. 'That's wild. So what else is on this level?'

'Sergeant Finch said that all these rooms were for the VIPs,' Will said. 'And you've got to see this next one.'

Further down the corridor there was a door with PM painted on it. Chester was unimpressed because the room itself was rather cramped and completely unremarkable as he walked around it. On the desk there was a blotter where someone had begun to draw a wall, brick by brick, underneath which the sentence *Where are you, Mrs Everest, when I need you the most?* had been written. When he gave the desk drawers a quick check, Chester found nothing, so he took another look around the room, even going as far as investigating the lavatory. He came out brandishing a newspaper – an ancient, yellowed copy of *The Times*.

'This is old – 15th August 1952,' he said, then lobbed it onto the bed where Will was sitting. 'I give up – whose room was this?' he asked.

The plastic dust sheet covering the bed crackled as Will leant over and opened the bedside stand. He took out a bottle with a label that said *Hine*, and a box with *Aroma de Cuba* emblazoned on it. 'Brandy and cigars,' he said, holding both items up.

Chester could see that the bottle wasn't full, and the seal on the cigar box had been broken. 'That doesn't help – you'll have to tell me.'

'Winston Churchill was the last person to sleep in this bed,' Will announced.

Chester laughed. 'Well, I hope they changed the sheets!'

Will was looking at the cigar box and the brandy with interest. 'Sergeant Finch told me that these have been here since he was Prime Minister. He wanted to spend a night in the Complex to find out for himself what it was like. And he always had a gulp of brandy first thing in the morning to go with his first smoke,' Will said, as he bounced up and down on the mattress several times. Then he held the brandy bottle up to study the label. 'Why don't we drink this?'

'Why?' Chester asked, nonplussed.

'Because I've never been *really* drunk. I suppose I had that beer Tam gave me in the Colony, but it tasted foul.' Will was now staring at the thick brown liquid in the bottle as he swilled it around. 'Maybe it's something we should do. Just in case . . .'

'In case what?' Chester said, flopping down on the bed beside his friend. 'In case we don't make it through all this?'

Will nodded sombrely.

'That's a happy thought,' Chester whispered. He took the cigar box from Will and hinged the lid open, sniffing inside. 'These things must have been here for years. Don't they go off?' he asked, as he picked out one of the stubby cigars and rolled it between his fingers.

Will shrugged. 'Who cares – they're still cigars, and I've never smoked one. I've never smoked *anything* yet.' He rooted around in the bedside cabinet until he found a box of matches. 'Whitehall,' he said, reading what was printed on them. 'That follows.'

'I had a couple of lager shandies once on holiday with Mum and Dad, but that's it,' Chester admitted. 'And I've never smoked either.'

'Remember the Greys?' Will said, staring into the middle distance as he thought about the gang who had terrorised the smaller children at Highfield High School. 'Speed and Bloggsy necked cider and smoked cigarettes all the time. They'd done the whole lot, hadn't they, and that was more than a year ago!'

'They had girlfriends, too,' Chester said wistfully.

Will still had a faraway look in his eyes. 'If you think about it, Churchill led the country through the Second World War, and right now you and I are stuck in the middle of this war with the Styx. We're pretty important too. Who knows – without us, the country might not have a chance of winning? So don't you think we have a right to do we what want? Don't we owe it to ourselves to polish off what's left of his brandy?'

But Chester dropped the cigar back into the box and closed the lid. 'Tell you what, Will, when we do win, let's come straight back here and smoke our heads off and get really bladdered!' He stuck his hand out. 'Deal?'

'Deal,' Will agreed, shaking his friend's hand, then putting the brandy and cigars away again.

They were interrupted as the intercom system emitted a clear tone both in the room and outside the corridor. 'Everybody is to report to the Hub immediately. I say again – everybody is to report to the Hub immediately,' it ordered.

'That's Danforth, isn't it?' Chester said as he angled his head to listen to the voice.

Will nodded. 'If she shows up, I hope Elliott's forgiven him. She's in a funny mood, and he got a little carried away with the scalpel when he was investigating her.' As they walked back towards the stairs, Will added, 'In fact, I don't like to think what would have happened if nobody else had been there to stop him.'

'Yes,' Chester agreed. 'It's odd really, because although he doesn't look like much, when you get to know him better he's actually a really scary little man.'

Drake was laying out a variety of items on the desks as everyone converged on the Hub.

Will and Chester arrived first and were watching as Mrs Burrows, Mr and Mrs Rawls, Colonel Bismarck, then Elliott and Stephanie turned up. The two girls were chatting enthusiastically to each other as though they were long-lost friends.

'Here they are,' Chester muttered to Will as he twisted away from Elliott and Stephanie. 'Looks like they're getting really matey.'

'And Danforth's keeping well out of the way,' Will observed, watching the Professor, who had his eyes glued on the screen of one of his laptops. 'I'm telling you, I really wouldn't be surprised if Elliott has a pop at him when she gets the chance.' Will switched his attention to Parry and Sergeant Finch who were both busy talking on satphones.

'Form a line, please,' Drake said. 'The quicker we're done here, the quicker we can move out.'

'Where are we going?' Chester asked, as he and Will found themselves at the front of the queue.

'London,' Drake answered, preoccupied as he inserted a small glass cylinder into a stainless steel device, then rolled up his sleeve. 'Just in case anyone has misgivings about the shot I'm giving all of you, I'll go first.' Cocking the mechanism, he placed it against his upper arm and, when he pulled the trigger, it made a small click. 'Didn't feel a thing,' he smiled.

'But we've all had the vaccine for Dominion,' Chester pointed out. 'So what's this for?'

Drake cleaned the end of the device with an alcohol wipe, then cocked it again. 'We haven't seen any deployment of the Dominion virus yet, but the Styx have some other nasties they might unleash on the population,' he replied.

'How do you know?' Will said.

'Because I snitched a load of specimens before Chester and I totalled the Laboratories in the Colony. Some were locked away in a special vault, so naturally I had to have them. And I asked a contact to analyse the different pathogens I came back with. On the back of his findings he manufactured a vaccine cocktail against all of them.'

Will unbuttoned his cuff and pulled up his sleeve. 'Come on then. Better safe than sorry,' he said.

Drake hadn't been lying – the shot wasn't painful and after he'd administered it, he led Will to the next desk. 'Special Forces radio with a throat mike,' he told the boy, as he handed him one of the units. 'Chester's used a similar model before, so he can show you how it works.' Drake then dipped his hand into a plastic container and fished out what appeared to be a pair of small ear plugs, which he passed to Will.

Will examined them, then looked at Drake questioningly.

'Belt and braces,' Drake said. 'Celia and I were KO'd by a Styx subaural bomb on Highfield Common. I lost Leather-man and too many men that day. I'm not going to let it happen again.' Drake looked down for a moment. 'There've been a couple of reports that the Styx are using similar devices in London.'

He took a second pair of plugs from the container and inserted them into his ears. 'So these are a little something I knocked up while I was at Eddie's flat. They won't interfere with normal frequencies, but the moment they detect a sub-aural bomb, they kick in. They replicate its wavelength, but out of phase. So they'll counteract any audiosonics being used on you.'

'They'll protect us?' Will asked.

'Well, you'll still know you've been zapped – maybe you'll feel some dizziness and your vision might go a little funny – but at least you won't black out. These plugs will protect you long enough either to skedaddle, or to neutralise the source . . . the bomb itself.'

'Cool,' Will said, as he went to slip them into his pocket.

'No, you should get into the habit of wearing them. Put them in,' Drake said quickly. 'And I've finished with you now, so you can lend Danforth a hand to crate up the mobile detectors over there. We need them outside, ready for pickup by our transport.'

Will was about to ask what the transport was when Drake

221

turned and went back to the waiting queue. With a shrug, Will made his way over to Danforth. He slowed as he passed Parry, who was on a satphone. He seemed to be employing a similar passcode sequence to the one Sergeant Finch had used when they'd first arrived at the main entrance of the Complex – Parry was quoting lines of what sounded like poetry about waking slumbering dragons, then waiting for responses from whoever he was speaking to.

'Drake said I should help you,' Will began, announcing himself to Danforth. The Professor was so intent on the symbols scrolling down the screen, he took a few moments to look up.

'That's a classified government programme I've got translating the Book of Proliferation. And from what I've read so far, it's quite an eye-opener,' he said, tipping his head towards the screen. 'The document gives an insight into one of the oldest, most resilient and, arguably, most highly evolved species the world has ever known.'

'Really,' Will said indifferently. He wanted to spend as little time in Danforth's company as he possibly could. Chester was right – there was something incredibly unnerving about the man.

And Will was surprised when Danforth stepped from behind the table and nearer to him, albeit making sure he wasn't too close because of his phobia about human contact. 'So you're off to London on a wild frolic to hunt for Dark Light activity,' Danforth said, keeping his voice low. 'How do you feel about that?'

'I don't know anything about it yet – Drake hasn't briefed me,' Will admitted.

'Ours is not to question why, ours is but to do or die,' Danforth said, misquoting the poem by Tennyson. 'How very admirable you're willing to throw your life away for the cause.'

'Well . . . no . . . we've got to do everything we can to stop the Phase, haven't we?' Will met the Professor's intense pupils through his glasses, but the man didn't answer.

For a moment the Professor and the boy held one another's gaze, as if trying to delve deeper, to understand each other. In Danforth Will again sensed something akin to Dr Burrows' obsessive dedication to the pursuit of new knowledge. A cold shiver passed down the length of his spine; he could almost imagine he was back with his dead father. But there was a stark difference. The Professor's eyes were completely devoid of any warmth or compassion – no one mattered to him. No one at all. And that frightened Will.

Danforth began to smile, but it wasn't a pleasant smile.

'Why – what's wrong with the plan?' Will asked, hoping to find out more about it.

'Well, it promises to be interesting,' Danforth said, his smile transforming into a sneer. 'Look at what we've got here.' He indicated everyone in the Hub with a sweep of his hand. 'A leftover from the Third Reich, a Styx turncoat, a man with a microwave oven in his head, and a bunch of trigger-happy teenagers like you. And to top it all off, there's a commando old enough to claim his bus pass calling the shots. How can we *possibly* go wrong?'

All of a sudden, Mrs Rawls' anxious voice made everyone look. Drake had finished with Chester, and was about to give his parents their shots.

'No! I won't let my husband and son have any part in this!' she exploded. Chester and Mr Rawls were standing either side of her as she remonstrated with Drake. 'Hasn't my family done enough for you already?'

'Dissent in the ranks,' Danforth commented. 'Doesn't bode well either.'

As directed by Danforth, Will began to cut a roll of khaki material into strips, which he wrapped around each of the Geiger counters before stacking them in a crate. The Geiger counters appeared to be the same as the ones Will had seen left at various points around the Complex – rather battered, with chipped grey enamel casings. The only difference he could spot in the ones he was packing up was that some type of stubby antenna had been added to them, and the analogue dials had been replaced with modern LED displays. But Will really didn't feel like speaking to the Professor to find out what they were going to be used for.

The heated discussion with Drake came to an end, with Mr Rawls and his wife leaving the Hub. Will saw Chester heading over to him.

'That was embarrassing,' his friend said.

'What's the matter?' Will asked.

'Mum doesn't want Dad or me to be put in danger again. She's a bit strung out by everything at the moment,' Chester replied. 'So Dad and I are still coming, but Drake's promised we'll only be there in a support role. No front line stuff. And Mum's stopping here with . . .' He didn't go as far as to mention Danforth's name, but the Professor was too engrossed in his laptop anyway to hear.

'Oh,' Will said. He'd been counting on his friend being with him when they faced whatever they were going to face in London.

Chester leant towards Will and whispered into his ear. 'Don't worry though, Will. I'm not about to wimp out after all we've been through together.'

Chapter Thirteen

Everyone had been ordered to report with their weapons and equipment to the area by the twin guardrooms at the far end of the entrance tunnel.

This was it. The moment they were all leaving.

Drake had given everybody white parkas with fur-lined hoods, and thick trousers of the same colour. Although the clothes were a little bulky to move around in, he said they'd be grateful for the insulation they provided when they went outside.

As Will looked at everyone in these white combats, he saw their vacant expressions, and how fidgety they were. He knew precisely what they were feeling. They were trying to hide their fear.

In the relative safety of the underground Complex, the threat posed by the Styx Phase felt so far away. Like some nightmare that might fade from memory if one stopped dwelling on it.

Why us? Why can't someone else deal with it? Will asked himself. There must be somebody else out there who knew what was going on, somebody better placed to fight it.

Given the choice, Will knew that he would simply turn around and just march back down the long tunnel again. The Complex might be very far from the real world, but it had been the closest thing to home that he'd known in a long time.

But then he looked again and noticed what lay behind Drake's and Eddie's expressions. Their eyes spoke of duty and quiet determination and doing what had to be done. Will told himself that he should try to emulate these men, and draw strength from them. He'd been so immersed in his thoughts that he hadn't heard Drake speaking to him.

'Have you got your earplugs?' Drake asked for the second time.

Will nodded.

From his mobility scooter Sergeant Finch was helping Drake to give each of them a detailed equipment check before they were allowed to pass up the slope and into the darkness of the entrance chamber. Will had emptied his Bergen and arranged the contents neatly on the floor next to his belt kit and Sten submachine gun. Drake now praised him.

'Perfect turnout,' he said. 'We'll make a soldier of you yet.'

'One last thing – comms check,' Sergeant Finch reminded Drake, as he squinted at the list on his beloved clipboard while a cat slept on his lap.

Drake put his hand to his headset. 'Testing – one – two – three,' he whispered.

'Got you loud and clear,' Will confirmed.

'Good kid, but now turn it off to conserve the juice. And that's you done.' Drake turned to Chester and began the process with him. Will repacked his Bergen, but held back for his friend, who clearly embarrassed as his mother seemed

226

reluctant to let go of him.

Will's heart went out to her as she clung to her son, speaking softly to him. Against all odds the Rawls family had been reunited, and it felt wrong that Chester and his father were about to be separated from Mrs Rawls again.

Will threw a glance at his own mother as she stood not looking at anyone, in some sort of ethereal detachment. Will and Mrs Burrows hardly constituted a family any longer. They were more like fellow combatants.

Then Chester was coming towards him. 'Poor old Mum. She really doesn't want us to go,' his friend confided in a low voice. The boys entered the chamber together, finding that Parry was already in position beside the sliding exit panel.

'Sweeney's coming with us, isn't he?' Will said to Parry, realising that he hadn't spotted him by the guardrooms.

'He's watching the crates outside,' Parry replied. 'And before you ask, Wilkie's not part of the detail either. He's . . .' Parry simply trailed off as he looked at the dial of his luminous watch.

Before long, everyone was packed in the chamber. Shoulder to shoulder in the enclosed space and laden down with their weapons and heavy Bergens, they were getting hotter and hotter in their Arctic Issue uniforms.

Parry's radio suddenly crackled into life. 'Five clicks on a north by northwest flight line,' it announced. 'Acknowledge. Over.'

Flight line, Will thought, wishing he could catch Chester's eye, but it was impossible in the darkness. Nobody had been told how they'd be making the journey to London. Drake had said it was on a need-to-know basis.

'Acknowledged,' Parry replied into the radio. 'The LZ will

be painted. Over and out.' As he hooked his radio back on his webbing belt, he must have sensed that both boys were bursting to know what his exchange had been about. 'These days we don't use visible light to mark landing zones, but infra-red beacons,' he explained. 'The pilot can see it a mile off through his dropdown.'

'Right,' Will replied, as if he understood exactly what Parry had said, which he didn't. But at least he now knew they'd be flying down south.

'It's time,' Parry said to everyone. 'I know you're all weighed down with kit, but you must keep up with the Colonel as he leads the way to the LZ. Our window is very tight, and we can't afford to be late.'

Parry slid the hatch open and the boys shuffled aside to allow the Colonel to slip past and outside. Then they all followed into the whirling flurries of snow.

'Jeez, it's freezing!' Chester exclaimed as the cold air filled his lungs.

They moved quickly, one following the other, through the gate in the chain-link fence and then downhill, their boots thudding on the frosted ground as they jogged along.

Ahead of Will were Chester and the Colonel. Directly behind him came Parry, then he could make out the vague forms of the rest of the party: Mr Rawls, Eddie and Elliott, Stephanie, Mrs Burrows and, last of all, Drake.

A gale was sweeping up the mountainside and whistling through the overhead electrical lines as they passed beneath them. There was barely any moonlight due to the thick cloud cover, so Will found it impossible to make out anything much ahead. He could see Mr Rawls was struggling to keep up, and began to wonder how far they still had to go. Were they heading towards the valley floor itself? But some twenty minutes later the ground levelled out, and the Colonel began to slow. Will saw that Sweeney was crouched beside a number of crates that contained the mobile detectors he'd helped to pack.

'Stay put,' Parry ordered. Then he and Drake moved off. Standing some forty feet apart, they held up devices that resembled torches, although they gave off no discernible light.

Everyone was looking up when there was a sound as if the sky had fallen in. It was so tumultuous and unexpected, it was impossible not to duck.

The helicopter had been flying so low that there'd been no warning whatsoever as it appeared directly over them. As the immense downthrust from its powerful rotors whisked the snow blizzard aside like confetti, the massive piece of war machinery hovering no more than forty feet above their heads was quite terrifying.

As it taxied into position between Parry and Drake and

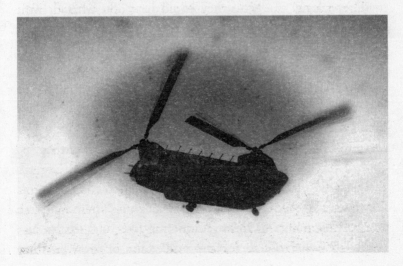

began to descend, it tipped back. It maintained an angle of forty-five degrees and the moment the wheels at the rear of the fuselage touched down, a ramp swung open between them. Over the sound of the helicopter's engine, Parry and Drake were yelling at everyone to get on board. There were subdued red lights marking the edges of the ramp to guide them, and as Will climbed it he glimpsed army insignia on the fuselage. Drake, Sweeney and the Colonel hauled the crates up the ramp and then it thudded shut, and they were airborne.

Will took the place beside Chester and strapped himself in. With seats down both sides, the interior was easily twice the size of a train carriage, but there was no sign of the crew. Will and Chester watched as Parry moved to the front of the helicopter. The boys caught a momentary glimpse of the two pilots bathed in the green glow of their instrumentation before the door to the cockpit closed again.

Seeing their interest, Drake came over and leant between them, speaking loudly so they could hear. 'So what do you think of our ride?'

'Wild!' Chester replied.

'What type is it?' Will shouted.

'It's a Chinook from No. 27 Squadron on its way back to Hampshire. Dad called in a few favours and managed to hitch us a lift. Of course, our presence is completely unofficial, and there'll be no record of us being picked up on the flight log.'

Will and Chester nodded.

Drake gestured towards the window behind the boys, and they both swivelled around to look through it. There were one or two tiny points of light glimmering like stars in the distance, but otherwise there were just eddies of snow twisting into the darkness. 'Keep buckled up as it's going to be a bumpy flight. We're tree-hugging all the way to avoid radar as much as we can,' he told them.

'Yeah, we're really shifting it,' Will said excitedly, as they zipped over an illuminated stretch of road.

But as Drake went back to his seat, Will's initial enthusiasm quickly evaporated. The beat of the engines and sudden changes in altitude brought back memories of the last helicopter flight he'd been on.

Although it was difficult to tell in the dim light, Will was certain that he caught both Elliott and Colonel Bismarck looking at him. He wondered if they were also thinking about the journey they'd taken together in the inner world. It was shortly after Dr Burrows had been gunned down by one of the Rebeccas, and Will had been so beside himself with rage and grief, he'd had to be strong-armed onto the aircraft by two New Germanian soldiers.

And then, to make matters worse, Will had proceeded to blame Elliott for his father's death. He could see the glint of her eyes as she sat opposite him in the helicopter, and felt so ashamed of his behaviour. But more than this, he couldn't stop thinking about his father's violent end on the sun-soaked pyramid.

He was still lost in these thoughts when Chester poked him in the ribs, a big grin on his face as he gave the thumbs up. Will could only manage a weak smile in response. But at least someone was enjoying the flight.

Will wasn't sure if he'd nodded off, but it seemed no time at all before the engines changed in pitch. Then he glimpsed many more lights through the windows as they reduced altitude. Before he knew it, there was a jarring bump and the helicopter had touched down.

Parry and Drake were there, shouting at everyone to disembark over the sound of the rotors, which were still turning. The crates were quickly offloaded and, in less than a minute, the helicopter lifted off again.

Will's ears rang in the silence. They'd been dropped in a field where the snow was coming down even heavier than ever, and there was nothing visible around them.

Then, from a far corner, a single pair of headlights flicked on for an instant. Parry signalled back with his torch, and suddenly multiple lights raked across the field.

The vehicles began to approach, one at a time. The first was a camper van, followed by a Land Rover, then a Volvo estate and a whole succession of rather nondescript cars. Parry spoke to each driver as Drake and Sweeney loaded a crate into the back. Then the vehicles continued on, their wheels churning the snow as they went.

As the last of them disappeared into the night, Parry spoke to Eddie, who was waiting beside a single remaining crate of detectors. 'This is where we part company. Good hunting.'

Eddie gave him a nod in response, then looked at Elliott. 'Do you want to come with me?'

Elliott paused, throwing a half glance at Will through the steady fall of snowflakes. 'Okay,' she replied casually.

Will's jaw dropped; he hadn't expected for one second that she'd accept the invitation. He felt betrayed and abandoned by Elliott, and although he would never have admitted it to himself, a little jealous of her newly established relationship with her father. And he realised how much he relied on her being at his side, just as he did with Chester.

Parry struck out for the edge of the field, but Will didn't

move. Drake nudged him in a friendly way with his arm. 'It's all right, old mate, before you know it she'll be back with us again,' he assured him.

'Um, right . . . yes,' Will mumbled, realising how obvious his feelings must have been. He hunched forward, pretending to cough so he had an excuse not to speak to Drake as he began to walk beside him.

Battling the blizzard as they went, everyone followed Parry through several fields until they came to a fenced-off area. Here he opened a gate. On the other side was a raised, snow-covered mound the size of several tennis courts. Will tried to make out where they were, but there wasn't time as Parry led them briskly around the edge of the mound, then down some ice-crusted steps and through a door.

They were grateful to be out of the freezing wind and snow as they filed after Parry, descending several more flights of basic concrete steps. Then they came to a battered metal door with a sign that proclaimed *Pump Room*.

Chester went through before Will. 'Look at this!' he whispered to his friend.

They were on a platform, complete with a Tube train waiting in the tunnel. The platform wasn't that different from the old-fashioned ones still in use on the London Underground; the walls were tiled, although it was impossible to see what colour they were due to the thick crust of dirt and efflorescence on them. And the platform was littered with massive drums of armour cable and rotting wooden boxes filled with engineering components that were more rust than metal.

Will spotted a board with *Alert Status* just visible at the top, beneath which were a pair of hooks, although there was nothing suspended on them. And as he scanned further along the platform, he couldn't see anything to indicate the name of the station.

'We must be near London?' he asked Parry.

'No, that's a good thirty miles away. We're in Essex.' Parry waved a hand at the roof. 'We're directly under Kelvedon Reservoir, and you won't find anything about this place in any of the history books,' he said. 'This was known as the "First Circle" of the defence infrastructure, so the government could decamp from the capital if things got sticky. When it was built, this train link originally ran all the way to Westminster.'

'So that's where we're going?' Will said.

Parry shook his head. 'The last mile's been out of commission for years – due to flooding.'

Will had turned his attention to the train. There was illumination coming from inside the two carriages directly in front of them, although their windows were almost opaque with dirt.

'It's been maintained by a few of the Old Guard, more as a hobby than anything else,' Parry said, then swung around as a whistle rang out from the far end of the platform and the train doors creaked open. 'And there's one of them now.' The man was too far away for Will to see him clearly as Parry waved to him and shouted, 'Everyone in!'

The interior of the carriage consisted of a wooden slatted floor, on which there were a few heaps of tattered tarpaulins.

'We have to keep the speed down because of the state of the track, so the journey takes about an hour. You should try to get some sleep,' Parry advised, as everybody took their Bergens off and chose somewhere to put themselves.

Drake took over. 'The golden rule is to catch some shut-eye

whenever there's an opportunity. You never know when you'll get the chance again.'

'So we've had a helicopter, and now a train,' Chester said to Will. 'What next?'

'Maybe a boat,' Will suggested, lying down with his head against his Bergen and trying to make himself comfortable. As the doors ground shut, he gave a large yawn. 'Yes, a boat. We haven't been in one of those since the Deeps.'

'No way. I hate boats,' Chester said in a disgruntled voice. 'Boats and lifts and going underground.' He wiped the moisture from his face, then stifled a sneeze. 'And being cold and wet. I hate that too.'

'What about insects,' Will added. 'Don't forget insects.'

'The station's coming up,' Drake shouted.

Will's eyes flicked open, but it took him a moment to work out where he was as he saw Chester's slack face not two feet away from him.

'Oi, ugly! Wake up!' Will said, prodding his friend. 'We're here!'

Chester looked dazedly around at the grimy floor. 'Damn it. I was dreaming that I was on holiday,' he complained. 'In Center Parcs again, with Mum and Dad.'

'Sorry to disappoint you,' Will said.

They disembarked from the train to find themselves on a platform similar to the one they'd left from. As they trooped down it, there was a figure waiting for them by the exit. Although his face was obscured by a ski mask and he had a sidearm on his belt, he didn't look the slightest bit intimidating. As he puffed away on his pipe, he gave the impression that he was even older than Parry.

'Thank you, Albert,' Parry said, giving the man a pat on the shoulder as they went through what Will knew must be a blast door from its thickness, then up a flight of circular stairs. The stairs went on forever, spiralling around and around, until they came to a door at the top, which led into a dark corridor. There were brown carpet tiles on the floor, many of which were loose, and office furniture was stacked down one side of it. At the end of the corridor was a small service lift, which Parry summoned. It wasn't big enough to accommodate them all, so Parry took Will, the Colonel and Stephanie with him.

'Where exactly are we now?' Will asked as they ascended.

'You'll see,' Parry replied. The doors rattled open, and Will squinted because of the light as they followed Parry from the lift. 'It's criminal this place isn't used for anything much these days,' Parry said. 'There was once a restaurant a couple of levels below where we are now, with a rotating floor.'

'We're in the BT Tower,' Will gasped.

'We're in London!' Stephanie squealed with glee.

Daylight poured in through the windows running around the outside of the floor which, except for the central area housing the lifts, was completely empty.

And through these windows was a breathtaking vista – the London cityscape. Will went over and peered down, seeing rooftops covered in snow and people in the streets. As he walked slowly around the windows, he spotted a group of army lorries down in Charlotte Street, but otherwise nothing looked out of the ordinary. Until he reached where Parry had come to a stop.

'My God. Who'd've thought we'd ever witness that,' the old

man exhaled, transfixed by the view through the window.

Three or so miles away, in a stretch from Westminster to the City, several thick columns of black smoke rose into the sky. Will spotted the legions of helicopters hovering over the stricken areas, and became aware of the constant howl of sirens in the background.

'It's anarchy out there,' Parry said. 'The Styx have achieved what I never thought possible. We're at war with ourselves.'

Drake and the rest of the party had come up in the lift. As they joined the old man at his vantage point, they too stared through the windows. There was a moment of shocked silence.

'Are you all right, Mum?' Will asked, as he saw his mother reel back.

Her fists were clenched, and she'd turned quite pale. 'Too many people,' she whispered. 'I can feel their hate and their fear. It's worse than the last time we were here.' She was backing towards the centre of the floor. 'It's too much to take . . . and a man has just come up in the lift.'

Somebody cleared their throat, and they all turned to find an elderly man with a handlebar moustache, dressed in blue overalls, standing there. He began to read from a card. 'The dragon sleeps . . .'

'Oh, don't bother with that claptrap,' Parry said, striding forward and grasping the man's hand firmly. 'Sergeant Finch's cousin, I presume.'

The old man nodded, then there was a small high-pitched noise. He patted his ear and it stopped. 'Hearing aid's acting up,' he explained. 'I'm Terrence. . . Terry Finch.'

'Look this way for a moment, please,' Drake said, holding Danforth's Purger in the old man's face. The blast of purple light reflected in his rheumy eyes, but there was no reaction from him.

'Did you take my picture?' Terry asked.

'He's clear,' Drake said, putting the Purger away. 'No Dark-lighting.'

'We're just making sure you're one of us,' Parry said.

Terry clearly hadn't heard Parry as he cupped a hand to his ear. 'One's enough?' he enquired.

Parry spoke even more loudly than usual. 'Has the requisition order been served on the security staff downstairs? We don't want to be disturbed up here.'

'Come again?' Terry said.

With a sigh, Drake leant towards the old man. 'Terry, take me to the Transmission Room,' he shouted. 'I need to set up.'

In another part of London, Harry trundled downstairs, his head raked awkwardly forward on his shoulders as he negotiated the steps. But that day his posture was nothing unusual. He'd been that way for some twenty years, after a High-Altitude, Low-Opening or HALO parachute drop had gone badly wrong, leaving him with mostly titanium for an upper spine. 'Janey, I'm going out. And I'm taking the car,' he called. 'Okay?'

'Sure, Dad,' his daughter replied, tearing her eyes from the book she was reading to catch a glimpse of her sixty-five-year-old father as he rotated his whole body to locate the keys – he had no option with the limited articulation in his neck.

He appeared at the sitting-room door. 'You don't remember where I put those spare Hi-Power mags, do you?'

'Yes, on the mantelpiece,' she replied. 'In Mr Clowny.'

'Thanks,' her father said, and she watched as he went over to the garishly coloured ceramic clown and lifted up its bowler-hatted head. Dipping his hand in, he took out two magazines for his handgun. He paused before replacing the lid, then also retrieved the long dagger he'd hidden in the clown.

'The Sykes-Fairbairn too? You will take care out there, won't you, Dad?' Janey said, concern on her face.

'I'm not about to let a few idiots kicking in shop windows spoil my day,' Harry replied defiantly.

'What's going on is a bit more serious than that,' she replied. 'Anyway, I wasn't talking about the riots – I meant the weather. It must be several degrees below zero out there.'

In a woolly hat and scarf and a thick green jacket, he was dressed in what he usually wore when he went fishing. But he didn't appear to have his fishing rod or tackle with him. In any case, it certainly wasn't the time of year for fishing, so she assumed it must be the other activity with which he occupied his days. 'You off to the allotment?' she asked as an after-thought, as he left the room. The only response was the front door as it slammed shut.

Putting the book down, Janey rose from her chair and went to the window where she lifted the net curtain aside. There had been a couple of showers of new snow at first light, and everything outside was white and crisp with the cold. 'He can't be working on the allotment? Not in this?' she wondered out loud.

As she continued to watch, Former Lieutenant Harry 'Hoss' Handscombe energetically cleared the snow and ice from the car windscreen with a scraper. 'So where's the silly old stick off to?' Janey asked herself affectionately. She shrugged, then went over to the television to try a few channels. They were all still off-air, so she settled back in her chair, immersing herself in her book again.

Harry drove for ten minutes, then turned into a supermarket car park and drove around it, shifting his whole body from the waist up as he peered through the windscreen. Like most shops in London, the recent panics had caused such a run on food that it had very little actually left to buy. Consequentially, the car park wasn't full, and it didn't take him long to find what he was looking for.

He parked his car, but not too close to the battered Land Rover in the corner. Harry was looking at the picture of a green dragon taped to the top of the windscreen as he walked to the vehicle with his peculiar stiff-backed gait. The driver's door opened the moment he arrived, and a woman of around the same age as him stuck her head out.

'Good to see you again, Hoss,' she said. She didn't smile, but her strong grey eyes were friendly.

'You too, Anne,' he replied as they shook hands. 'You know, I often think of Ian. I miss him.'

She nodded. 'He was very fond of you too. After you had your accident, he used to joke that you'd been trying your best to save your family the expense of a funeral, by hitting the ground so hard you buried yourself.'

'One thing I don't miss about the old sod is his sense of humour,' Harry laughed, then turned serious. 'How was he at the end?'

'He came to terms with the illness. He told me he'd reconciled himself to it because he'd got what he wanted – to die at home, rather than in some godforsaken jungle, like so many of you three decades ago. But enough of this maudlin nonsense . . . how's the arthritis?' she asked, changing the subject.

'Not bad, considering. Takes me longer and longer to get going in the morn—'

He fell silent as two police cars raced into the car park. Harry slipped his hand in his jacket pocket, closing it around his Browning Hi-Power. But as he and Anne watched, the cars drew up beside the supermarket. Police officers jumped out and then hurried inside the building.

'Probably just more fisticuffs at the counters,' Anne muttered. She was staring at the police cars. 'But you don't know who you can trust these days, do you? Except us OAPs, because everybody's written us off already. We're invisible.' She chuckled as she laid her sawn-off shotgun by her feet again.

'We live in uncertain times,' Harry agreed. 'I still find it preposterous that they've called on the army to patrol the streets.' While he'd been talking, Anne had retrieved an object wrapped in khaki cloth from behind her seat. 'That's for me, I presume?'

'Yes, with love and kisses from the Commander,' she replied. 'Parry told you the drill?'

'Yes, he briefed me,' Harry confirmed.

She handed him the converted Geiger counter. 'Happy hunting, Hoss,' she bade him. Before she closed the door, he glimpsed numerous other khaki bundles stacked in the rear of the Land Rover.

Back in his car, Harry placed the mobile detector carefully on the passenger seat beside his GPS unit and Browning Hi-Power, then covered them with a newspaper.

'It's going to be a long day,' he said to himself. He checked the fuel gauge as he drove off. He'd need to find a petrol station that actually had stocks so he could fill up his car. He had some way to go yet before he hit the motorway that would take him out of London and to the quadrant he'd been assigned by Parry.

'A long day for the Old Guard,' Harry said.

Back in the Hub, Danforth was coordinating operations as Drake controlled the parabolic dishes on the BT Tower using his laptop. Drake had a map up on his screen, and each time a report of Dark Light activity came in from any of the Old Guard or Eddie's men with their mobile detectors, it was relayed through to him from Danforth. Then Drake would concentrate on the area using the dishes mounted on the tower, and the exact location could be triangulated.

The operation wasn't helped because there were several power outages which shut down Drake's dishes. And each time, he had to wait for the electricity supply to be restored, and also allow the system to reboot before he could start over again.

It was several hours before he called out to Parry. 'I think we might have something here,' he said, inclining his head towards the map on the screen. 'We're finding signals all over, but there's a location in the west where the level is spiking off the scale. We've got ourselves a major Dark Light hotspot there.'

'Near Slough,' Parry noted, as he peered at the cluster of red dots pulsing on the map. 'Should we mobilise and get over there?'

Drake shook his head. 'Not yet. We don't want to waste

our time if it's nothing to do with the Phase. Danforth's sent some teams in for a recce.'

After he'd exited from the motorway, Harry passed through two roundabouts and was on his way to the industrial estate when he spotted the Army road block up ahead. He quickly scanned around; there were grass verges either side of him and not a building in sight. It was too late to consider turning back, so he made sure the mobile detector was turned off and out of view as he approached the barrier.

An armoured vehicle was parked at the side of the road, which he recognised as a Viking, and in it a soldier was manning a .50 cal machine gun. It was aimed directly at Harry, who immediately knew that something wasn't right. Even with the current levels of civil unrest and heightened security, this was rather excessive for an elderly man out for a drive.

The soldier at the barrier waved him down and came over. 'Can I ask what your business is, sir?' he demanded brusquely.

'I'm on my way to fetch my granddaughter from a party,' Harry lied.

'Your granddaughter. Really. Would you mind stepping from your vehicle, sir, and keep your hands where I can see them,' the soldier ordered.

'Is there a problem up ahead?' Harry asked, trying to see the road past the barrier.

The soldier's voice grated with impatience. 'Get out of your car.' He brought his assault rifle to bear on Harry. 'Now!'

Harry climbed out, holding his hands in front of him.

'Up against the vehicle,' the soldier said, twirling a finger to indicate that Harry should face the other way. 'And spread your legs.'

Harry complied as another soldier joined the first and began to give him a thorough pat down.

'I see you're Parachute Regiment,' Harry said. 'You're a long way from RHQ?'

The soldier searching him had finished checking his legs all the way down to his boots, and now quickly straightened up. He grabbed Harry roughly by the shoulder and spun him around. 'And what would you know about that, Gramps?'

Harry was unruffled. 'Because I was in the Paras too. I served from 1951 t—'

'Show me some identification,' the soldier snapped.

Harry slowly took out his wallet and handed it over. The soldier found his driver's licence and examined it. 'Harold James Handscombe,' he read. He oozed disdain, and had a way of looking away immediately he'd spoken to show how little Harry meant to him.

But then the words came that Harry was dreading.

'Stay there,' the soldier with the assault rifle said. 'We're going to give your vehicle the once-over.'

Alarm bells were ringing like crazy in Harry's head, and his nerve endings tingled as if raw electricity was passing through his body.

'Of course,' he said, as he glanced at the driver's seat, calculating how long it would take him to reach the Browning Hi-Power hidden under it. The timing would be tight, and even if he did manage to retrieve his weapon, the odds weren't stacked in his favour; he'd have to disable the nearest soldier first, then deal with the other two.

It was a long time since he'd shot anyone, but the old

instincts were never far away. One thing he knew for certain – the situation was going to turn nasty. For Harry, this was more than just a hunch – he was acting on all his years of being in tight corners.

The soldiers' eyes were slightly glazed; if Parry hadn't briefed him about the Styx and their mind control techniques, Harry would have guessed the men were on drugs. And the way the soldiers were conducting themselves was completely beyond the pale.

The soldier was moving around the front of the car. 'The boot's open?' he asked.

'It is,' Harry said. But before the soldier even reached the boot, Harry knew there was no way that he wouldn't discover the mobile detector, the GPS, and eventually the handgun under the driver's seat.

The soldier had reached the passenger door and was opening it.

He bent to look under the newspaper in the foot well.

As he registered the modified Geiger counter, he opened his mouth to shout a warning to the other soldier.

Harry knew the game was up.

He moved as fast as his less-than-agile body would allow him.

As he pivoted around on the ball of his foot and reached towards the driver's seat, in the corner of his eye he saw something curious.

The soldier with the assault rifle simply folded to the ground. And as Harry stooped to peer at the other man through the car, he saw he was sprawled on the road.

Harry stood up. Even the soldier in the Viking was slumped over the heavy machine gun.

Eddie, and three of his men with tranquiliser rifles, stepped down the snow-covered verge, towards the incredibly confused Harry.

'Professor Danforth thought you might need some help,' Eddie said.

Half an hour later the call came in. It was Eddie. Parry stood beside Drake as he spoke on the satphone. When the call was over, Drake briefed his father.

'We're on to something. Eddie found Limiters and teams of compromised soldiers manning checkpoints on the roads into the industrial estate. The area was completely tied up, but he and his men have cleared a way in.'

'Sounds promising,' Parry said.

'It gets better. Eddie's on the estate with some of the Old Guard. They've been surveilling a sizeable factory where the Limiters are thick on the ground, and there's also a high degree of vehicle activity. They've seen at least two refrigerated trucks make deliveries of what could have been meat – the last one's just gone in. So it could be food for the Warrior grubs. I reckon we might have struck the mother lode.'

'What's Danforth's take on it?' Parry asked.

'He agrees that the Dark Light usage is exceptionally concentrated at that location. He thinks it's a go. He's sending Eddie the schematics for the factory right now.'

Parry took a second to make up his mind. 'Everyone!' he yelled across the floor. 'We're in business.'

PART THREE

Assault

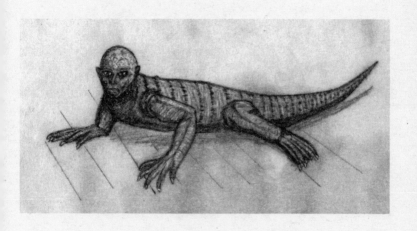

Chapter Fourteen

'This is cushy. I could get used to the corporate life,' Rebecca One joked, as she sipped her Diet Coke through a straw.

'Sure could,' Rebecca Two agreed.

The Styx twins were in the boardroom, lolling around in the upholstered chairs with their feet on the table.

Rebecca One ran her eye over the plates of sandwiches that she and her sister had barely touched. 'I've had all I want of these.'

'Me too. Would you please clear the table and bring us a couple of ice creams, Johan?' Rebecca Two asked. She watched Captain Franz as he collected the plates, then headed for the kitchen.

Rebecca One slammed her Coke can down on the table. 'Will you stop treating him with kid gloves? You don't *ask* him to do things for you – you *tell* him. And he's a Topsoiler – don't use his first name,' she said. 'I worry about you, you know. You've got to sort your act out.'

Slurping her drink, Rebecca Two made no response.

With a back swipe, Rebecca One sent her Coke can

hurtling across the room. 'Doesn't matter anyway. We'll probably have to dispense with him sooner rather than later.'

Rebecca Two avoided her sister's gaze.

Captain Franz returned with two tubs of ice cream. Rebecca One took hers, but then threw it straight back in his face. He barely blinked as it struck him. 'This is vanilla. I wanted chocolate. Get me a chocolate one right now!'

'You didn't say what you wanted,' Rebecca Two pointed out, as Captain Franz shuffled away.

'What *are* you like?' Rebecca One said. 'It's up to us to show the Heathen who's boss.' She was shaking her head in exasperation when her mobile phone suddenly rang. Taking her feet from the table, she went to her coat to retrieve it.

'I don't know this number,' she said, as she examined the display. 'And who would be calling me right now, anyway?' After a moment's deliberation, she answered the phone. 'How did you get m—?' she snapped, then fell silent.

'So who is it?' Rebecca Two tried to ask, as her sister continued to listen to the caller without saying a word.

Captain Franz had returned with the tub of chocolate ice cream, but Rebecca One waved him away. She was frowning. 'How do I know you're on the level?' she asked. A few moments later, she seemed satisfied with the answer. Still listening to the caller, she cupped a hand over the phone's microphone. 'Get your coat,' she whispered to her sister.

'What for?' Rebecca Two demanded, but her sister ignored her, already heading for the door.

Out in the corridor, Rebecca One again cupped her hand over the mouthpiece and spoke rapidly to her sister. 'Get Franz to bring the Mercedes round to the back. Tell him to keep the engine running.'

Rebecca Two almost exploded, she was so curious. 'Why? What's going on?' she hissed.

But her sister was moving down the corridor at speed as she wrestled her coat on. 'Tell me what you want out of this,' she said into the phone, as they turned a corner. They came face to face with the Limiter guarding the doors to the warehouse.

Rebecca One beckoned at him with her free hand. 'Your pistol – quick,' she ordered him, with that hushed urgency people use when they're in mid-phone conversation.

The Limiter obediently unbuttoned the flap on his holster and passed it over.

'Silenced. That's good,' she said, with a glance at the suppressor on the barrel. 'No, sorry . . . nothing,' she replied quickly to the caller on the phone. 'Just dealing with something here.' Her voice became hard with authority. 'All right, I'm convinced, and you've got yourself a deal. You have my word on it – scout's honour 'n' all that. We'll see you soon.'

She ended the call. Without missing a beat, she raised the handgun to the Limiter's chest and discharged it at point-blank range.

'What the . . . ?' Rebecca Two leapt back as, right in front of her, the Limiter sank to the floor. 'What did you do that for?'

Rebecca One barely drew breath to reply. 'Executive decision . . . no time to explain now,' she said.

Stepping over the Limiter's body, she threw open the doors. As the humidity and the stench of raw meat from the warehouse enveloped them, Rebecca One was already racing inside. 'Find Hermione and Vane,' she shouted to her sister. 'And fast!'

Parry took the first party down in the lift. He'd told everyone to change from their Arctic Issue parkas and into a variety of other less conspicuous clothes that had been provided to them back in the Complex. But as they entered the BT Tower reception area in their Sherpa jackets and thick corduroy trousers, they resembled a Victorian climbing party about to set out on an expedition.

Terry Finch was beside the rotating door as he kept a careful eye on Mortimer Street outside.

'You dealt with the staff then?' Parry asked, speaking loudly to the old man as he ran his eyes over the rather drab area and the unmanned reception desk. 'The Emergency Order obviously did the trick.'

'Well . . . they've gone to a caff around the corner until I give them the say-so to return,' Terry answered.

Parry frowned. 'You don't sound too sure – was there a problem?' he pressed the old man impatiently.

'One of the security gentlemen wanted to check with head office, so I stuck the official document in front of him.'

'And that worked?' Parry asked.

'No, he wasn't buying it, so I drew my Webley on him,' Terry said, with a mischievous grin, as he took a revolver from the holster in the small of his back. 'That worked like magic.'

'R-i-g-h-t,' Parry exhaled, his frown growing even more pronounced. He looked from Will to Drake. 'Make sure you've got your tranquiliser pistols handy,' he said, before he addressed Mrs Burrows. 'And Celia, can you keep a *nose* out for any trouble heading our way? I need to know what's waiting for us around the corner,' he told her.

'A very nice Italian restaurant about three hundred yards up on the left. The calzone's making me feel quite ravenous,' she said, smiling.

'Why doesn't anyone *ever* give me a straight answer?' Parry grumbled, as two old minibuses pulled up on the yellow line outside. The rest of the party had descended in the lift and, one at a time, they exited onto the street and loaded their gear into the backs of the vehicles.

The drivers of each minibus didn't speak as they threaded their way through London. Will saw for the first time just how far things had gone in the capital. Other than the groups of soldiers and policemen stationed around the place, Euston Road itself appeared to be quite normal and the traffic relatively heavy. But as he glanced down side roads, it was a different story. He spotted the odd burnt-out car, and huge piles of domestic rubbish that hadn't been collected in weeks. And as they passed the entrance to Regent's Park, the gates were blocked by fire engines as a whole row of the large white buildings blazed away.

They took a right off Marylebone Road and raced through several back roads because the driver of the first minibus had spotted trouble up ahead. Then they emerged at the start of the Marylebone Flyover, and sped up the incline.

They had all turned their radios on, so they could hear Parry's directions as he spoke into his throat mike from the first minibus, which was also carrying Stephanie, Sweeney and the Colonel. 'I've received a report that there's a disturbance in Shepherd's Bush, and the army are out in force there. So we're going to leave London on the M3, then cut across country to the M4. We'll maintain radio silence from now on, unless there's a hiccup.'

'Hiccup?' Mrs Burrows asked as there was a click and their earpieces went ominously quiet.

Drake swivelled around in his seat beside the driver to answer her, glancing at Will, then Chester and Mr Rawls as he did so. 'My old man means if they hit a problem, they'll open up with their weapons and take the heat so we can bug out. One of the vehicles *has* to make it through.'

'Gosh! I'm so glad I came with you,' Chester piped up.

One of the first to be born, the Styx Warrior larva was barely recognisable as the stumpy little maggot Vane had cradled in her arms only days earlier.

Having sprouted two pairs of legs and a muscular tail, its appearance bore more than a passing resemblance to a tadpole as it makes the transition into a frog. Only no lily pad could have supported this brute's weight; measuring more than three feet from tip to tail, it was more on a par with an overgrown Gila monster.

And as the Warrior larva had grown, building up reserves of protein for its impending pupation, food was all it thought about. It slept only sporadically, nearly every minute of its day spent trying to satisfy its insatiable hunger.

So when the Warrior larva chanced upon a pool of warm blood that had seeped under the doors to the warehouse, it began to lap at it energetically with its grey, darting tongue. The regular meat deliveries were all well and good, but not a touch on living or freshly killed quarry. Having licked the concrete floor clean, it began to investigate the source of the blood.

Like a dog outside a pantry, it scampered up and down as

it probed the gap under the doors with its tongue. As the larva's olfactory receptors picked up traces of the body on the other side, blood-flecked drool leaked from its maw. It snorted in frustration. It didn't know how to get at the juicy meal, and had begun to scuttle up and down again when it bumped into one of the doors. It observed how the unlocked door hinged open a fraction.

The Warrior larva paused for a moment, its slitted black pupils considering the barrier in its way. Then it began to ram its head against the door. The larva battered it harder and harder, until there was finally enough room for it to squeeze through. And it couldn't believe its luck as it surveyed the dead Limiter stretched out on the floor. The door had swung shut again behind it, but the Warrior larva didn't care – it had no intention of communicating its find to its sibling brothers. Keeping the whole body to itself was far too tempting.

It began to gorge itself on the delicious corpse. It was oblivious to its surroundings as it nipped off strips of flesh from the Limiter's face with its needle-like teeth, and gulped them down.

The minibuses parked at the rear of the two-storey building, and everyone clambered out and followed Parry inside. Eddie and one of his men were waiting for them in a room filled with cardboard boxes. Will looked for Elliott, but there was no sign of her.

'Your Old Guard have the factory surrounded. We haven't seen anything to suggest that anyone inside is aware of our presence yet,' Eddie reported to Parry. 'And we're ready to lock down the whole estate.'

'Perfect,' Parry said. 'Go ahead and seal the place. From

now on, nothing goes in or out.'

Eddie spoke to his man in Styx. After he'd hurried off, Eddie addressed Drake and the rest of the party. 'The floor below is a half basement used for storage. I've established it as one of four Objective Rally Points for the Old Guard. You can see the target location from there, but don't venture too close to the windows.' He turned back to Parry. 'And my surveillance team is waiting for you on the roof, Commander.'

'Excellent – I'll come and take a dekko. But first I want to hear from Celia,' Parry said, swivelling to Mrs Burrows. 'That thing you do – can you do it from here? Because I need you to tell me what's over the road. '

Mrs Burrows nodded, then tipped her head back. Will heard Stephanie's sharp intake of breath as his mother's eyeballs rotated upwards, so that only the whites were showing.

'People . . . humans . . . maybe five hundred and fifty . . . no, more, I think. Maybe six hundred – I can't tell precisely,' Mrs Burrows said.

'And Styx?' Parry asked.

'Yes . . . but not many. I don't know . . . three dozen or more?'

'It would be helpful to know the exact number,' Parry pressed her.

A bead of sweat broke from Mrs Burrows' hairline and trickled down the centre of her forehead. 'It's no good – I'm getting jumbled signals,' she whispered. Then a shudder ran through her as her eyes suddenly righted themselves. For a moment she seemed to be in a daze, then she turned to Parry. 'This is strange – it's as though I can't tune in.'

Parry stroked his beard thoughtfully. 'Don't worry – you've given me enough of a confirmation. All those people must have been bussed in for the breeding programme. What else

258

would they be doing there?' He began towards Eddie. 'Even if there's a full regiment of Limiters inside, we've got to get the job done.'

'No, wait!' Mrs Burrows said sharply. 'You don't under-stand – there's something in there that doesn't *want* me to find it. Something more than Styx. Something dark.'

Parry merely nodded.

'Okay, everybody downstairs with me,' Drake said to Will and the others.

Eddie held up a hand. 'Before you go . . . Elliott's in the roof-top Observation Post and, if it's all right with you, she's made a request.'

'What's that?' Drake said, as Will and Chester exchanged glances. They both began to move towards Eddie, believing that Elliott would want them with her.

'She's asked that Stephanie join her up there,' Eddie said.

Will froze as he heard Chester whisper, 'Wha—?'

Once up on the flat roof, Stephanie and Parry kept low as they approached the parapet with Eddie. The former Limiters were there in force, and had strung a light-blue camo net a few feet above the parapet so that their silhouettes wouldn't be outlined against the sky.

'Commander,' Harry Handscombe said, as Parry ducked under the camo net and they shook hands vigorously. 'Piece of luck, wasn't it – me locating the target so early in the running?'

'Certainly was,' Parry said, smiling at his old friend. 'But not so lucky that you almost got yourself slotted by those Darklit troops. I never asked you to stick your neck that far out, you know.'

Harry would have shaken his head if he'd been able, but instead gave Parry a wry grin. 'Enough of the neck jokes, you old reprobate!'

Parry moved to the edge of the roof, his binoculars in hand. He checked the position of the pale sun to make sure there'd be no telltale reflection from his lenses before he began to scrutinise the factory opposite. 'Ah, yes, there they are,' he said under his breath, as he located the Limiters and New Germanian guards patrolling the parking area.

Stephanie had been standing back from the parapet, not sure what she was meant to be doing, when Elliott beckoned her over. As she crept to Elliott's side, Stephanie eyed all the former Limiters with some trepidation.

'Don't mind them. They may look pretty spooky, but they're on our side,' Elliott confided in her.

'Cool,' Stephanie swallowed, then frowned at Elliott. 'But why do you want me here? Your two boyfriends are, like, gagging to be with you.'

'Back in the Complex you told me that you could deal with anything. So here's your chance to prove it.' Elliott wasn't being confrontational, and Stephanie recognised this as the girl continued to speak. 'In a moment, we're going to neutralise every single living thing outside that building opposite.'

'Neutralise?' Stephanie said.

Elliott inclined her head. 'We're going to snipe all those men as quickly and as cleanly as we can. Will you help me?'

'Is this some sort of sisters' thing?'

'If you want to call it that,' Elliott shrugged. 'I never had a sister.'

'You want me to shoot people too?' Stephanie asked, glancing at Elliott's long rifle, which she'd camouflaged with white tape, and now had a chunky silencer affixed to the end of the barrel.

'No, I want you to spot for me,' Elliott said, indicating the scope beside her. 'I'm relying on you to get a fix on the guards' positions, because when we open fire from up here, we can't afford any slip-ups. If one of them raises the alarm, we lose the element of surprise.'

'Okay, I suppose I could do that,' Stephanie said, going over to the scope.

Will was surprised by the sheer number of Old Guard present in the dimly lit basement. Although their faces were obscured by ski masks, he sensed the nervous expectation that hung over them as they chatted quietly amongst themselves.

'Shotguns?' he asked, as he noticed what some of them were carrying.

'We don't know what's waiting for us across the road,' Drake explained. 'For close quarter combat, a semi-auto twelve bore is right on the money.'

'And what are those tanks they've got?' Chester asked, as he saw a number of men had twin cylinders on their backs.

'Flame-throwers, for the final stage of the offensive,' Drake replied. 'You see, simply levelling the target building doesn't cut the mustard. Things have a way of surviving in air pockets under the rubble. We really don't want any of the Warrior grubs – if they're actually in there – to crawl out after we've left the scene. If a single one were to get loose, it could find more humans and make whoopee, and we'd be back where we started.'

'I see,' Chester said, as Will and the others listened.

'There's no alternative but to get inside and do the job up

close and personal. We have to make sure nothing is left alive,' Drake continued.

'You mean kill *everyone*?' Mrs Burrows interjected. 'What about the humans I sensed in there – they could be Colonists or innocent Topsoilers who through no fault of their own have got caught up in this. Can't we decondition them with Danforth's Purger, then take th—?'

'Not going to happen,' Drake cut her short, his face grim. 'We don't have that luxury. This operation is all or nothing – we have to stop the Phase in its tracks, whatever it takes.'

Mrs Burrows started to object, but Drake had moved away to speak to Parry over a private frequency on his radio headset. Once the conversation had finished, Drake returned. 'Everybody's in position around the target building, and we're on the final countdown.' He swung his Bergen from his back. 'I want you all to strip down to tactical kit – weapons and ammo only. Stow everything else here. Then you can watch the first stage from the windows.'

Armed with their Stens, Will and Chester went to the front of the basement and stood on tiptoe to peer through the dusty windows.

'Bloody Limiters,' Will growled as he saw a pair of them at the gates. 'They look like they own the place.'

'Those other men – do you reckon they're New Germanians?' Chester said.

Will gave Colonel Bismarck a glance as the man watched from another window. Some of the soldiers over the road were his troops from the inner world, and Will wondered what the Colonel thought about Drake's no-prisoner policy. And Will also knew that if the Colonel hadn't been shocked from his

Dark Light programming by the explosion in the City, right now he could be one of those brainwashed soldiers patrolling around the factory.

His thoughts were interrupted as Parry's voice came over the headsets. 'Alpha, I say, Alpha,' he enunciated clearly, initiating the first stage of the operation. 'Remove the designated targets on my mark.' He paused for a beat, then began to count down. 'Five – four – three – two – one – FIRE!'

There wasn't a sound, but the men that Will could see in the car park simply dropped from sight.

Up on the roof Stephanie swivelled the spotting scope round. 'Next target's on the move – he's turning – he's going towards the entrance,' she said, her voice becoming shrill with the urgency.

'I see him,' Elliott replied calmly, then pulled the trigger. Her silenced rifle bucked in her hands, but the only sound was a small rush of air. As the round found its mark, the Limiter pitched forward, his head exploding scarlet over the white snow.

'Ohhh,' Stephanie said, putting her hand to her mouth. 'That was totally a bull's eye.'

'Bravo,' Parry's voice announced. 'I repeat – Bravo. We've cleared the sentries.'

'Right, all of you outside,' Drake ordered.

Having taken off the top of the Limiter's cranium as if his head was a hardboiled egg, the Warrior larva was scooping out the last of the man's brain with its prehensile tongue. Its eyes flickered in ecstasy at the delicious grey matter, as the larva's hyper-efficient digestive system absorbed the proteins just as quickly as it could gulp them down.

Will and Chester began across the road with Drake and Sweeney flanking them, and Colonel Bismarck, Mr Rawls and Mrs Burrows following behind.

'Look at that.' Will was referring to what must have been a hundred men from Parry's Old Guard as they advanced in a line. And those were only the ones he could see; he knew there must be at least the same number again around the other sides of the factory. 'I didn't realise there were so many of them.'

Drake had overheard Will. 'Yes, the perimeter's in. My old man's running the show by the textbook,' he said, his eyes full of admiration as he watched his father join the line of Old Guard further along the road. 'He's even sent a couple of units into the sewers, in case anything tries to use the drains to make a break for it.'

The snow on the tarmac helped to deaden any sound the Old Guard made as they closed in. And as they reached the boundary fencing around the site, all that could be heard was the occasional bluster of the wind.

But then there was activity as the main doors to the office building swung open. A Limiter emerged, clearly in a hurry. Something had rattled him. But he'd only taken a couple of paces before a crossbow bolt struck him in the neck. As he dropped to the ground, all the Old Guard seemed to be holding their breath, but no one else followed him through the doors.

'Charlie,' Parry's voice crackled over the radio. 'I say again, Charlie. Before we lose the advantage of surprise.'

Drake signalled to Will and the others to come with him

through the gates and into the car park. The Old Guard were all around them, running to the various entry points of the factory that Parry had assigned them.

'Stay well back,' Drake ordered, as he and Sweeney moved into the main entrance of the office building, covering one another. There was no one in the reception area, so Drake immediately advanced along the corridor leading from it, Sweeney checking the rooms on either side as they went.

'The boardroom,' Drake whispered into the throat mike as Sweeney slipped through the last of the doors. 'I saw it on the ground plan.'

With their Stens at the ready, the boys kept their distance as Drake had told them, with Mrs Burrows, the Colonel and Mr Rawls bringing up the rear. A couple of the Old Guard had also entered the reception area, but they remained by the doors.

As Sweeney emerged from the boardroom, he and Drake inched further down the corridor. They stopped as a small explosion shook the whole factory, followed by the rattle of automatic weapons.

'Delta, Delta, Delta!' Parry's urgent voice came over the radio. 'The gloves are off!'

Unscrewing the silencer from his Beretta, Drake turned to address everybody. 'The Styx know we're here now, but we're still going to take it nice and easy,' he said.

He and Sweeney continued down the corridor until they came to a corner. Sweeney moved ahead, his back to the wall, as Drake slid along the opposite side.

Sweeney suddenly raised a fist, and Drake froze. The big man pointed to his ear, then up ahead. He'd heard something.

*

The Warrior larva could have pulverised what was left of the Limiter's skull with its powerful molars, but other softer and juicier parts of the corpse were too inviting. It was moving towards the Limiter's legs when it heard the explosion and the ensuing gunfire.

It paused momentarily, but then the smell of the blood from the two bullet holes Rebecca One had left in the man's chest became too much for it to resist. The larva crept back up the Limiter's body and began to lick at these, then nibbled the meat on the man's ribs.

'What's that?' Sweeney whispered to Drake.

Dappled with blood, the ivory-coloured tail had been sweeping from side to side, and visible to both of them. Then, as the creature clawed its way up the Limiter's corpse, the tail disappeared from view.

And whether the larva had heard or smelt the two humans approaching along the corridor, it now reluctantly stopped feeding and lowered its body in readiness.

Sweeney was straining to hear what was there. But it was impossible with all the noise coming from the other parts of the building.

'Careful,' Drake whispered, taking tiny steps forward.

There was no fear in the larva's mind – it wasn't capable of that. All it felt was the excitement that more food, with beating hearts, was coming its way. It suddenly broke from cover and hurtled into the corridor.

'Jesus! Contact!' Drake cried, as the Warrior larva scuttled straight past him like a lizard, opposing legs clawing the carpet.

The speed at which the creature was moving was phenomenal, but so was Sweeney's reaction time. He managed to get a shot off, clipping its tail. And although Sweeney was back at the corner of the corridor in the blink of an eye, with the retreating hindquarters of the larva squarely in his sights, he was unable to take a second shot. Will was right in the line of fire if the bullet happened to go wide.

The single shot might have slowed it a little, but the Warrior larva was still haring straight down the middle of the corridor.

'Stop it!' Drake yelled.

Later, he asked himself if the reason he hadn't opened fire on it was not because of how quick the creature was, but because of what he'd seen. It was true that the Warrior larva had been moving at a blistering speed, but its appearance might have also been a factor.

The sight of its head was enough to make his heart miss several beats.

Will's and Chester's jaws dropped as they reacted in the same way.

Although its torso was amphibian in appearance, its head was something else entirely.

Something shocking.

The larva's head was that of a human child – with distinct human features. Covered in off-white scales, the eyes, nose and ears were perfectly formed, albeit the mouth was filled with shiny white spikes for teeth, and its tongue was at least a foot in length as it flicked out.

And worse still, as Sweeney had winged it, the wail it emitted could have been that of a human infant.

As the Warrior larva bolted towards the main doors, one of the Old Guard had heard Drake's warning and was moving rapidly to intercept it. He brought his shotgun up, but the larva simply sprang clean over his head.

'Crikey!' he shouted. But the old soldier still had his instincts, and tried to take the shot as he tipped backwards. He missed the creature completely, the light on the corridor ceiling exploding into a million pieces, showering him and the boys.

'Stop it!' Drake yelled again.

Then Mr Rawls was the only obstacle in its path to freedom through the main doors.

Again the Warrior larva sprang.

The second member of the Old Guard tried to shoot it in mid-air, but he missed, the round shattering a vase on the reception desk.

Mr Rawls had stepped back. The Warrior larva tried to alter its trajectory by rotating its tail, but it wasn't enough. It slammed into Mr Rawls, gripping his chest with its claws.

'Colonel! Shoot it!' Drake shouted, realising that the larva was dangerously close to escaping.

But the New Germanian couldn't open fire for fear of hurting Chester's father.

Despite the weight of the Warrior larva on him, Mr Rawls had managed to remain on his feet. He was staggering backwards as if he was doing some form of bizarre limbo dance.

'Help! Help! Help!' he was jabbering as the larva bit down on his shoulder. Mr Rawls screamed in shock and pain.

'Get it off him!' Chester cried, aiming his Sten, but knowing there was no way he could use it.

Something flashed through the air.

The Warrior larva slid from Mr Rawls, a knife embedded up to the hilt in its neck. As the creature flopped to the floor, its limbs were still moving, but only in a weak reflex action.

'Evil-looking thing,' one of the Old Guard muttered.

'Nice kill, Colonel,' Sweeney said. 'I thought the Sticky bug was outahere.'

Colonel Bismarck went over to the Warrior larva. Placing a foot on the creature's back, he yanked his knife out. *'Ich war es nicht,'* he said. He put the knife back into the scabbard on his belt, then glanced over at Mrs Burrows. 'It was Celia. She helped herself to my knife.'

'Mum!' Will exclaimed. 'How did you do that? You can't even see!'

Mrs Burrows shrugged as Drake examined the creature, which was still twitching. 'Better make sure it's dead. Who knows what these things are capable of?' he said.

Much to everyone's astonishment, the Colonel simply raised his boot and brought it down on the larva. There was the most ghastly crack of bone as its childlike head split open.

Will and Chester looked away.

Drake opened a channel to Parry on the radio. 'Tell everyone that the mature Warrior bugs are fast and highly mobile. They can clear some height too.'

Parry was shouting as he replied. 'We already know that,' he said. There were yells and the sound of shotguns blasting in the background before Drake ended the connection.

Then Drake turned to Mrs Burrows. 'Can you get Jeff across the road and have that bite looked at?' he asked her. As she took him away, Will and Chester followed Drake and Sweeney to the end of the corridor, where they tried not to look at the dead Limiter on the floor, less one brain. The boys could hear the Old Guard on the other side of the doors as they began to work their way through the warehouse. They were killing anything that moved, the terrible screams coming thick and fast.

'Stay here and make sure nothing else gets out,' Drake ordered the boys, as he and Sweeney prepared to enter.

'Don't you want us to help?' Chester offered.

'No, the clean-up inside won't be a pretty sight. I wouldn't wish it on . . .' Drake trailed off as his radio bleeped. 'Parry again,' he murmured, opening up the private frequency.

'When Jiggs was with you he noticed something,' Parry shouted.

'Jiggs – with us?' Drake replied, frowning at Sweeney, who shook his head. 'None of us saw him.'

'Well, he spotted a CCTV camera in the corridor where you are,' Parry continued. 'He says there's a security room up on the second. Check it out, will you?'

As the exchange came to an end, Drake addressed Sweeney. 'Hold the position here, Sparks. I need to investigate this.'

Drake tore back down the corridor, the boys following so they could see what he was up to. Drake came to a stop outside the boardroom, where he peered up at a camera mounted just below the ceiling.

'Yes, there it is.' He turned to the reception area and addressed Colonel Bismarck. 'Jiggs has located the security room a floor up,' he said. 'If the system in this place has been left running, the footage could be very useful to us.'

Drake immediately went upstairs with the Colonel to investigate, leaving Will and Chester to relieve Sweeney by the warehouse doors.

'I may be coming back this way. Don't blow my head off,' Sweeney said with a grin, then ducked inside the warehouse.

Now alone, the boys stood guard with their Stens, listening to a soundtrack from the darkest of nightmares. They heard piercing screams. It was incessant. As though babies and young children were being slaughtered in their thousands.

'I know they're not human . . . but I'm so glad we're not in there,' Chester whispered.

Will just nodded.

The air was thick with steam, and the only relief to the murky darkness was the occasional muzzle flash as weapons discharged.

The squad was working its way in from the corner, the men with infra-red goggles checking under the beds on which a few desiccated human remains lay on blood-caked mattresses. The heat-detecting equipment the men were using was essential. The younger larvae were easy to miss as they slithered under animal carcasses or took refuge in any nook or cranny they could find.

But the mature larvae were the real problem.

'Heads!' one of the squad shouted, as he caught heat traces on the metal cross-beams running just under the roof.

As lights raked where they were hiding, several Warrior larvae scattered. They used their newly developed limbs to full effect, darting along the beams as automatic fire peppered the roof space.

One of the larvae was hit, falling to the ground where it writhed and screamed at ear-piercing volume until it was put out of its misery.

That was when the squad encountered their first Styx woman.

'Getting strong readings here,' one of the men warned, as he approached a pile of beds heaped in a mound so high that it was almost touching the roof. 'Could be a nest.'

As the squad advanced, a young Warrior larva nosed out from the bottom of the pile. It was dispatched with a single shot from a handgun, bursting open with a splatter of lacteous fluid.

A second larva was spotted not far from the first.

A member of the Old Guard lined up his weapon on it.

He didn't take the shot as someone yelled, 'Christ – watch it!'

She was poised at the very top of the mound of beds, her insect limbs vibrating together in a low hum. The Styx woman had crept out, much as a spider emerges when prey lands on its web. Her bloated midriff and her sinew-thin arms and legs only added to this image.

'Back off from my children!' the Styx woman ordered, leering at the squad as fluid dribbled from her mouth.

With her arched, angry eyebrows and her black, swollen lips, her exaggerated feminine features were like some burlesque mask.

'Blimey, I swear that's my ex-wife!' one of the Old Guard quipped, but nobody felt like laughing.

'Lower your weapons, men. I say again – lower your weapons,' the Styx female commanded the squad of Old Guard. There was such authority in her voice that before they knew it a number of the veteran soldiers had actually begun to comply, responding to the training entrenched in them during their lengthy military careers.

'No! Hold to!' someone shouted and, for several beats, neither side made a move.

The Styx woman and the squad of Old Guard frozen in the moment.

Then, as the young Warrior larva began to slither back into

its hiding place, the member of the Old Guard adjusted his aim on it.

With a banshee howl, the Styx woman flew at him. In less than the blink of an eye, she'd landed in front of him. Using both her arms and insect limbs, she wrenched the assault rifle from his grip.

She knew her weapons. In a blur, she'd flipped the H&K MP53 around and was pointing it straight at his chest.

She began to pull the trigger.

But another man had acted with equal speed to her.

Sweeney kicked the assault rifle, deflecting the burst away from the man's chest. The rounds hit the floor, ripping holes in the concrete.

The Styx woman swore as she swiped at Sweeney's face with her insect limbs, but he ducked low, avoiding them. And, as he came up again, he had the MP53 in his hands.

The Styx woman hadn't expected that.

Now disarmed, she did the only thing she could. She seized hold of the man who'd been about to kill the Warrior larva, wrapping her arms and insect limbs around his body. She squeezed him hard, several of his ribs cracking at some volume. His feet were lifted from the ground as she swung him in front of her, shielding herself from the rest of the squad as they came to the rescue.

There were just too many for her.

In all the darkness and confusion, shooting her wasn't an option – they might hit the man in her grip. With Sweeney shouting directions, it took ten members of the squad to prise her loose.

As she strained and shrieked and hissed at them, they held her.

'Three . . . two . . . one!' Sweeney counted down, and they slung her back against the mound of beds. Then the whole squad opened up on her, the rapid rates of fire shredding her body.

As she died, the former major from the British Army screamed one last time.

When the sound of gunfire had finally petered out, Parry proclaimed 'Echo' over the radio. Everyone withdrew from the factory grounds and formed a cordon in the road again.

There was a low rumble, as if something massive was being dragged along the ground. Fire began to lick the insides of the windows, and burst from the vents in the roofs like red spears.

'Incendiaries,' Drake said, as he carefully wrapped a jumper around a computer hard drive that he and the Colonel had retrieved from the security room. 'Nothing will survive those temperatures. Which is the general idea.'

Whistles blew. 'To the rallying point,' men shouted, and everyone moved en masse to the far end of the car park on the other side of the road.

They gathered around Parry, who was standing on a weapons crate with some sort of device in his hand. In addition to Eddie's men, who kept themselves to themselves in a small group, there must have been at least three hundred of the Old Guard there. Still wearing their masks, they stood in silence.

'I know this has probably been one of the oddest missions I've asked you on . . . and probably one of the most harrowing,' Parry said, throwing a glance over the road. 'But I want to thank all of you for your professionalism. It's been an impeccably executed op—'

Someone yelled, 'Blowing your own trumpet again,

Commander?' There were hoots of laughter and the whole mood of the gathering was at once transformed. Some of the men were lighting cigars, while others took out hip flasks and began to hand them around.

Parry tried to get some order back into the proceedings, although he was smiling. 'An impeccably executed operation, like the ones we used to mount back in the day. Some of you have taken your fair share of knocks, but I'm pleased to report that there hasn't been a single fatality on our side.'

Everyone looked over to a Land Rover with its rear doors open. Although there were two men on stretchers inside it, there were another ten or so outside in the process of being treated, most having dressings applied to what were only minor injuries.

'There's Dad. I'd better see how he is,' Chester said, spotting his father in the group behind the Land Rover. He rushed off, leaving Will by himself.

Parry continued, 'And I call that a resounding success!'

The crowd echoed their agreement.

'Although the job is far from done and we've still got to root out the Styx here on the surface, today . . .' he said, taking a breath, 'today we've diverted a catastrophe of global proportions.'

'It's over. We really stopped the Phase,' Will whispered to himself. With everything that had happened in the last hour, he'd rather lost sight of what they'd just accomplished. 'We've bloody done it.'

Parry was still talking. '. . . and I don't think I'm the man to do this,' he said, holding up the device in his hand.

There were shouts of 'Go on, Commander!' but he shook his head.

'No, I'd like my very old friend, who put his neck on the block for us today . . .'

There was a groan from the crowd.

'. . . to do the honours,' Parry went on. 'Show yourself, Hoss!'

A tall man pretended to hide himself in the crowd.

'Come on – it's not like you to be shy,' Parry teased.

Will watched as the man lumbered from the ranks, noticing how he had to swing himself around to look at his comrades on the way over to Parry.

The man took the device from Parry, and held it high. 'This is for all of us. And after dealing with those creepy crawlies in there, I'll never complain about the pests on my allotment again!'

There was a roar from the crowd.

'Just a word of warning,' Parry said, managing to make himself heard as he scanned the crowd and found Will. 'For those of you who haven't seen much action, never look up when you're this close to a major detonation. Now, go ahead, Hoss.'

Harry hit the button and there was an almighty explosion. Part of the roof of the main warehouse blew heavenwards, fire belching from the opening. Engulfed by flames, the rest of the roof collapsed in on itself, followed by the walls, until very little of the structure was still standing.

Will found out why Parry had seen the need to warn him. After a few seconds, pieces of flaming debris began to drop not far from the car park, landing on the snow-covered ground and hissing away. But the Old Guard didn't mind, cheering loudly and jumping aside to avoid them.

As someone nudged his back, Will spun round to find Elliott behind him.

'Hi there,' he said, happy to see her.

'Hi,' she said, but she seemed preoccupied and didn't return his smile. For a moment her gaze crept to the far horizon, in the opposite direction to the burning ruins of the factory.

'Why did you want Stephanie with you?' Will asked, trying not to show that he minded.

'Because she's one of us now. Someone's got to show her the ropes,' Elliott replied distantly. 'And because I have this feeling . . .' She was rubbing the nape of her neck.

Before Will had the opportunity to ask what she meant, she announced, 'Ah, here they come.'

Eddie and Stephanie were strolling over, and part of Will was sad. It was different now that all these other people were involved. It wasn't just him, Elliott and Chester up against the Styx with Drake to lead them.

Some of the Old Guard, fuelled by whatever was in their flasks, were talking and joking boisterously among themselves. Others, their arms on each other's shoulders, were singing what sounded like a victory hymn.

They met the tyrant's brandished steel,
the lion's gory mane;

Something dawned on Will. As tough as the last year had been for him, he realised that without the Rebecca twins and the Styx and the constant danger, he would never have the friends he had – the very best friends – friends he could count on however dire the situation.

And if the Styx were beaten and the threat removed, everything would change.

... they bowed their heads the death to feel;
who follows in their train?

Perhaps they'd all go their separate ways, living lives completely apart from one another. Elliott had her father back now, and Chester his parents. As for Drake, he'd probably go off and find himself another cause to champion.

And what sort of life would Will lead once all this was over? Where exactly would *he* end up? Back in Highfield with his mother and her turbocharged nose? He couldn't see how that would work out. Worse still, he'd have to start school again.

The prospect of returning to a normal life filled him with the darkest dread.

'My father's going to give us a lift part of the way in the Humvees,' Elliott said, yawning. 'I just want to get home to the Complex again.'

'Yes, home again,' Will said.

Chapter Fifteen

The Bugatti Veyron shot across the grass fields of Windsor Park, narrowly missing a clump of trees.

'You're going too fast,' Rebecca One said, as the car launched from the top of an incline, then slammed back onto the ground again, jarring her and Vane.

'Slow down. I think we're he—'

With a snarl, Vane yanked the steering wheel round as she stood on the brakes. The car went into a 360-degree spin, its tyres spewing out snow.

As the engine stalled, Vane burst from the car, her insect limbs slashing the air.

Rebecca also stepped from the car, and Vane immediately rounded on her. 'What have you done?' the Styx woman screeched.

Vane began to cough, then doubled over. With a gush of yellow fluid she vomited something from her mouth.

It was an egg pod.

She dropped to her knees, taking the pod between her hands and holding it before her as if she was praying.

'What a terrible, *terrible* waste,' she said huskily. 'My

babies need a host. They're going to die.'

Driven by Captain Franz, the Mercedes sped across the grass and pulled up beside the Veyron. Hermione was also in bad shape, stumbling from the vehicle as Rebecca Two opened the door for her. And the Styx woman had to be helped the short distance over to her sister.

As they saw each other, Hermione and Vane didn't speak, but their insect limbs clicked together in communication. Still on her knees, Vane held up the egg pod to her sister. Hermione shook her head, her expression one of deepest despair.

Vane rose unsteadily to her feet, then the pair of adult twins swung on the younger ones.

'Why did you do this? You've ruined it for all of us,' Hermione accused Rebecca Two.

'I didn't sanction anything. I don't know why we're here,' the girl replied, turning to her sister.

Vane began to stride towards Rebecca One as if she meant to do her harm. 'Why did you make us leave our babies, and all those hot bodies?'

Rebecca One was unfazed. 'That's why,' she said, spinning around on her heels.

In the distance smoke drifted up into the sky.

Vane and Hermione tried to absorb what they were seeing. Still in the thrall of the Phase, their faces were gaunt, their almost translucent skin stretched tight over their skulls, and their eyes purple-rimmed.

'I tried to tell you in the car, but you weren't listening,' Rebecca One said softly.

There was a distant flash, then the sound of an explosion rolled towards them.

'That was our factory?' Vane asked.

Rebecca One let out a shuddering sigh. 'Yes, it's all gone. All our warehouses will have been taken out, and everyone along with them.'

'NO! NO! *NO!*' Hermione screamed at the top of her lungs.

'But how did you know this would happen? Was that the call on your mobile?' Rebecca Two asked.

Her sister nodded. 'Yes. It was a warning,' she said, her voice cracking. 'That little creep, Will Burrows, along with Drake and that half-breed Elliott, and all the others we should have buried months back – they're behind this. They're to blame.' She was fighting back the tears, and took a moment before she went on. 'I knew the force of numbers against us were too great. In the time we couldn't have done anything.'

'If we can be got at like this, we're not safe anywhere,' Hermione said.

'It's Romania all over again,' Vane added, her voice hollow. 'Now there aren't enough of us to see the Phase through. It's over.' She opened her hand and let the egg pod fall to the snow.

'No, it's not over,' Rebecca One said resolutely. 'I wish I could have saved more of the sisters, but at least I got both of you out.' She went to Vane and Hermione, and laid her hands on their arms. 'And we're going to split you up to help improve our chances.'

'Why? To do what?' Rebecca Two asked.

Rebecca One didn't look at her sister, switching her gaze between Vane and Hermione. 'There might still be time to do something Topsoil. I don't know if it'll work, but we can attempt to induce some of the younger sisters. Then we might have enough of you to get the Phase under way again.

'But the main thing . . .' she said, letting go of Hermione but still leaving her hand on Vane, '. . . is that you and I are going somewhere where these vile Topsoilers can't touch us. Somewhere where we'll have all the time in the world. Somewhere where the conditions for the Phase should be perfect . . . just *perfect*.'

Chapter Sixteen

Drake had connected the hard drive from the factory security system up to a laptop. He then typed wildly on this for several minutes before sitting back and stretching his arms. 'I could do with some extra pairs of eyes over here,' he said.

Will, Elliott, Parry and Sweeney gathered around him. 'I've broken the decryption – it was nothing special. This drive contains the last twelve or so hours of footage from the onsite CCTV.' He leant forward and typed in several more commands. 'And I'm now going to run the output in a mosaic on the main display, so each of you pick yourselves a couple of cameras to watch. It'll be playing back far faster than normal viewing rate, so the moment any of you spot anything interesting, just holler.'

Will and the others lined up in front of the screen, and waited with bated breath. 'Lights! Action!' Drake said, pressing a key. A grid of ten different monochrome images came on screen and began to play jerkily.

Will was scrutinising his two scenes, both of which he thought he recognised. The uppermost seemed to be of the factory reception area, and the second showed a stretch of the corridor leading from it. The reception camera was angled so that he had a view through the glass doors of the entrance, where it was evidently still night time.

The others had divided the rest of the scenes between them, but Parry didn't seem at all happy with his choice. As he watched what the two cameras inside the main warehouse had captured, he edged a little closer to the screen to scrutinise one of the bodies in the beds, which seemed to be stirring. Sergeant Finch had wheeled himself beside Parry and was also watching intently with him, a cat purring on his lap as he stroked it absentmindedly.

But as both Parry and Sergeant Finch continued to peer at the body, it began to writhe violently. From the neck to the groin, it burst open, and Styx Warrior larvae wriggled out. If it could have been made any worse than it was, the fact that it was being shown at an accelerated speed didn't help.

Parry recoiled as Sergeant Finch shouted, 'God's holy trousers!' so loudly that the cat on his lap took fright and bolted. 'It's like a flippin' sausage splittin' down the middle when you overcook it,' he added.

'It's an abomination,' Parry croaked. 'What I saw in the factory was bad enough, but *that* defies description.'

'Focus, Dad, focus,' Drake urged him. 'We need confirmation that we finished the job.'

This sent Parry into a mumbled tirade, of which the others could only catch, 'Teaching your grandmother to suck eggs, are you?', before he straightened his shoulders and began to concentrate properly again. In the semi-darkness, flickering images of the Styx women would suddenly come into view, scuttling around like insects as they either went about impregnating more humans, or fed on fresh meat.

'Got a Limiter in mine, but he's not in uniform,' Elliott announced, as her camera revealed one of the Styx soldiers guarding the main gate. 'Two Limiters,' she corrected herself, when a second soldier came into view. As she saw increasing numbers of them, Eddie came over to watch with her, but made no comment.

Chester was in the small canteen just off the Hub where he was making tea for everyone, while his mother prepared some sandwiches.

'Gone very quiet out there,' he observed, half glancing through the open door. Then he went back to topping up the last of the mugs with water from the kettle.

'I'm just so glad you made it back safely,' Mrs Rawls replied.

'I've got a car entering by the front. Time is 9.15,' Elliott reported as an expensive-looking vehicle appeared at the main gates, and was allowed through.

Drake nodded. 'The registration number might be useful, but I won't stop the playb—'

'More cars,' Elliott interrupted him.

Chester scooped out the tea bags from each of the mugs with a spoon, then added the milk.

'I'll take these through and hand them out. How are you getting on over there?'

Mrs Rawls didn't answer, her back to Chester as she continued to make the sandwiches.

Chester stepped nearer to her. 'Are you still only on the butter?' he asked with surprise. He couldn't understand why it was taking her so long.

'I'm just so glad you made it back safely,' she said again.

Chester shook his head. 'Mum, are you okay?'

She didn't answer, meticulously spreading butter on a piece of bread, which was already thickly buttered.

'I've got both Rebeccas in the corridor,' Will announced with a shudder. 'I think one's talking on a mobile phone.' Then the Rebecca twins disappeared from the scene.

'I'll slow the playback a bit,' Drake said, typing on the laptop.

'Too late, they've already gone out of view – but I'm pretty certain that one was speaking on her mobile,' Will said.

'I've picked them up in the main warehouse. Keep the playback at that speed,' Parry said. 'This is interesting. They're moving rapidly . . . but what are they up to? See that – they're hauling a couple of the Styx women out with them!' He struck the floor with his walking stick. 'They've taken them out of the warehouse!'

'Now I've got a Rebecca with a Styx woman heading towards the front entrance,' Will said.

Elliott took over. 'And I've got one of the Rebeccas around the back. She's got a Styx woman with her too.'

Drake squinted up at the big screen. 'Styx women? You're sure about this?'

Elliott's voice was uncharacteristically flat as she replied, 'Yes. I had a clear view of her insect limbs.'

Will spotted more activity in one of his scenes. 'Me too.'

Drake shook his head. 'This isn't good. Keep your eyes peeled – we need to know what else went on before we pitched up.'

*

'Mum? Tell me what's the matter? Are you upset because Dad was injured?'

Chester laid a hand on his mother's shoulder, but she shuffled sideways along the work surface, to the next piece of buttered bread. She began to spread even more butter on it. 'Isn't that overdoing it a bit?' Chester said gently.

She remained silent.

'Because if you're cross he got hurt, it wasn't Drake's fault – he did his best to keep us out of any danger.'

Chester craned his neck, trying to see her face. She certainly didn't appear to be anxious.

'Why don't you go and join Dad? Mrs Burrows is putting a new bandage on him, and I'm sure he'd really like it if you were there,' he said softly to her.

'. . . made it back . . . made it back . . . made it back,' Mrs Rawls mumbled, like a stuck record.

'What?' Chester couldn't understand it.

He thought for a second. 'They've forecast showers of chocolate frogs for tomorrow,' he declared confidently. 'We should catch ourselves a few, and eat them. What do you think of that? Chocolate frogs?'

Mrs Rawls sounded normal enough as she replied – only Chester had heard the same phrase too many times before. 'I'm just so glad you made it back safely,' she said.

Several of the monochrome views faded to black, as others were filled with a seascape of wavy interference. 'That's where we came in,' Drake said. 'The camera sensors are maxing out with the light from the explosions.'

Parry turned to him. 'So we're pretty sure the twins bugged

out.' He shook his head as if appalled with himself. 'No pun intended. And they extracted two of the Styx women.' He looked at Drake. 'Their timing was very convenient. Are you thinking what I'm thinking?'

Drake raised his eyebrows.

Parry went on, 'The call on the mobile could have been to warn them that we were about to enter stage left.'

'So there's a mole in the Old Guard?' Will thought aloud. 'Or one of Eddie's Limiters is a traitor?'

'That's not possible,' Eddie said.

As everyone had been talking, Chester had emerged from the kitchen and was standing beside Drake. 'I need to speak to you,' he said, with a concerned expression.

'Hold on a minute, Chester,' Drake replied, rewinding to the moment when Will had seen the Rebecca twin enter the corridor, then freezing it. 'You're right – she's definitely on a call. If the system clock on the CCTV has been set at the right time, we'll be able to tell roughly when the call took place. Danforth can try to trace the incoming number through the nearest transmitter.'

'Drake,' Chester said, his voice shaky with desperation.

'Where is the Prof, anyway?' Drake asked, as he resumed his typing on the computer.

Chester slapped the screen of the laptop shut, almost catching Drake's fingers. 'Why won't you listen? Something's not right with my mum.'

'What do you mean?' Drake said, only now realising how upset the boy was.

'She's acting weird and just saying the same thing over and over again when I speak to . . .' Chester was gabbling, then trailed as off as Drake and Elliott exchanged urgent glances.

They both seized their weapons, and began to move rapidly.

In an effort to catch a glimpse of Mrs Rawls in the canteen, Will had edged towards the centre of the Hub. But instead, he'd spotted something else rather incongruous.

'There's Danforth,' he said, pointing into the entrance tunnel. All the section doors were open, and the small man was standing a distance down it.

At that moment, the Hub completely powered down, and they were all plunged into total darkness.

'Is it the Styx?' Mrs Burrows said, sensing something was wrong. Will hadn't seen her enter the Hub, and of course the darkness made no difference to her.

'No, we don't know that. All of you stay where you are,' Parry ordered, trying to keep everyone calm.

'Where's Emily off to?' Mrs Burrows asked.

The emergency lighting blinked on. And, sure enough, in the pale yellow glow suffusing the passageway, Mrs Rawls was striding purposefully towards the Professor.

'Mum!' Chester shouted after her.

She hadn't reached Danforth when she came to an abrupt halt and wheeled around.

'What's she wearing?' Chester asked in a choked voice as he saw his mother was dressed in some sort of bulky vest.

Elliott had her rifle trained down the passageway. 'I might be able to wing him,' she whispered loudly enough for Drake to hear.

Drake gave the slightest shake of his head, then called out to Danforth. 'What *is* this? What's going on?' he asked.

'Plan B,' the Professor laughed. 'I didn't think you'd be on my tail so soon.' He was holding something in his hand. It wasn't a weapon.

'What do you mean, *your tail?*' Drake demanded as he began towards him.

'Might I suggest that you keep well back?' the Professor threatened, brandishing the control in his hand. 'I Darklit Mrs Rawls when Sergeant Finch was having his nap. It may have been a little rushed and not as polished as I'd have ideally liked, but the task I've programmed into her is simple enough. She's sporting enough explosive in her vest to bring the roof down if I tell her to detonate. And if anyone fires a shot at me, or even comes too close, she also knows what to do. It's *boom* time.'

'DANFORTH!' Parry bellowed. 'What the *hell* do think you're playing at?'

'Don't raise your voice at me, Commander, old chap. I've overridden all the systems in the Complex, so please be civil to me. There isn't anything you can do.' Danforth touched the control in his hand, and the section door between him and Mrs Rawls began to close across the passageway. Mrs Rawls didn't move, standing as still as a statue. Danforth touched the device again, and the door immediately reversed direction, rolling back into the wall. Sergeant Finch was trying the buttons on the handlebars of his mobility scooter, but they no longer had any effect.

'Explain yourself, Danforth!' Parry yelled, his voice like thunder.

'You can't win,' the Professor proclaimed. 'The Styx are ushering in a new dawn. You know I finished translating the Book of Proliferation while you were down in London. It's a blueprint for what comes next . . . after the human race. And what I found when I investigated Elliott – well – it opened my eyes. So it's nothing personal, Parry . . . it's evolution, and

I want to be on the winning team.'

'So you're jumping ship and joining the other side? Is that it?' Parry shouted. 'Sounds pretty personal to me, you damn fool!'

'Why shouldn't I?' Danforth replied. 'I've had it with my own kind – they had the benefit of my life's work, and all the thanks I got was an enforced retirement and house arrest in some Scottish backwater. It wasn't right, but I don't expect you to understand, Parry.'

'No, I bloody don't,' the old man roared. 'We all did what our country asked of us, and none of us expected medals in return.'

For the first time, Danforth lost his cool repose, his voice going up an octave as he rocked from foot to foot. 'I didn't expect flaming medals. I expected *gratitude*.' He took a breath, calming himself. 'All I wanted was someone to say "Good work, Professor Danforth – you made the world a better place with your ingenuity." But instead I received a gagging order in a buff envelope, and a one-way ride in a police car to your mouldy old estate, Parry.'

'So, like some whining brat, you've decided to betray us,' Parry said.

'It was a simple matter to trace the Rebeccas' mobile phone number. It was too late to salvage their operation in the factory, but I made them an offer they couldn't refuse. They didn't. Once the new order is established, they want me to take over the development of their technology. It's a job made in heaven!'

'You're deluding yourself,' Eddie said. 'They don't need you.'

Danforth's confidence wasn't shaken by this. 'Far from it,

I've been guaranteed a place with the new kings of the castle.'

Eddie's voice was its normal monotone, but Will could have sworn a vindictive note crept into it as he responded. 'When you show up, they'll simply execute you. You're a Topsoiler.'

Danforth laughed drily. 'On the contrary, I'm on the protected list, while the rest of you – including any turncoats like you, Eddie, old fellow – are most definitely the endangered species, along with the poor old pandas.'

'So you've told the Styx where to find us? Are they on the way here?' Drake demanded.

Danforth shook his head. 'No. Call me sentimental, but I didn't want your blood on my hands. They didn't ask where you were – probably because the game's moved on, and all of you will be dead within a matter of months anyway.' He smiled to himself. 'Don't think that your antics at the factory have made one iota of difference. You can't stop the inevitable, and the Phase is meant to be. It's progress.'

He drew himself up to his full height, a conceited smile playing on his lips. 'The Styx need me. My detailed examination of the Book of Proliferation showed them how they could have done things differently . . . done things better.'

'What are you talking about?' Drake said.

'Well, where else has conditions identical to the surface, with a supply of fresh human hosts, and where there won't be any interference from Neanderthal Topsoilers like you lot?'

There was a moment of silence, then the Professor rapped his forehead with his index finger. 'You never think anything through, do you? On my advice, the Rebeccas are relocating the Phase to where it should have been staged in the first place

– down in Colonel Bismarck's inner world. Did not one of you dimwits anticipate that? The conditions down there couldn't be more ideal.'

Danforth consulted his watch. 'Anyway, it's high time I went to meet my new chums.' Taking a step back, he waved the control in the air. 'None of you are going to follow me because I'm going to lock this place down long enough to get clear. And my able assistant here, the delectable Emily Rawls, is my insurance that you don't try to force your way out.'

In the darkness at the very edge of the Hub, Will became aware of a dim, slowly moving presence. He was about to alert Drake when Mr Rawls broke from the shadows, stepping into the soft yellow light of the passageway. He'd clearly come straight from having his dressing seen to, as his shirt was still unbuttoned.

'Emily! It's me, my love. It's Jeff.' Increasing his pace, Mr Rawls extended his arms towards his wife.

'No, Dad!' Chester shouted.

'I'm warning you! Call that moron off!' Danforth said, retreating further down the passageway.

But Mr Rawls didn't stop. 'Emily – it's me . . . Jeff. Don't listen to that man,' he pleaded with his wife.

'Jeff, get back! That's an order!' Drake shouted.

'This isn't good,' Parry whispered.

Will saw Danforth operate his control. He was shaking his head as the section door slid across the passageway in front of him.

Mr Rawls was still striding towards his wife, but he'd slowed to a crawl as he talked gently to her, his voice calm, soothing.

As he reached her, Mrs Rawls swung to him.

Her expression was vacant.

'Mum! Dad!' Chester cried in desperation, and began to sprint towards them.

'Take cover!' Parry yelled. He seized the handles of Sergeant Finch's mobility scooter and rammed it towards the lift area.

There was a searing flash of light, and the bone-shaking roar of an explosion.

Will was thrown into the air, slamming against one of the desks and losing consciousness.

Then there was just darkness and dust in the Hub.

And the rumble of tons of earth and rock on the move, as the mountain reclaimed the entrance tunnel as its own.

The only way in or out of the Complex was sealed.

Chapter Seventeen

Will came to on the floor. He was laid out on several blankets, and covered in a fine dust. He was forced to wipe this from his eyes before he could open them properly, but this didn't do much to help because there was scant light in the room. On a nearby table someone had connected a bulb in a portable holder to what looked like a car battery, and it was flickering only very dimly.

As Will sat up, his head throbbing viciously, he was seized by a coughing fit. Once it had passed, he became aware of low, sombre voices. One of them was Elliott's.

'You should lie down for a while,' Colonel Bismarck advised, as he came into Will's field of vision. The New Germanian had a bag slung over his shoulder with a large red cross on it.

'How did I get here?' Will asked, still in a state of confusion.

'You're in one the briefing rooms. You had a bad knock,' the Colonel said, indicating Will's forehead. 'I stopped the bleeding and bound it, but you need to rest.'

Will felt the bandage as he tried to remember what had

happened. 'The explosion,' he mumbled, as it began to come back to him.

Despite Colonel Bismarck's protestations, Will had made his mind up that he was going to get to his feet. In the penumbra cast by the feeble light of the bulb, he saw Chester and Elliott sitting in chairs at the other end of the room.

'Hey!' Will exclaimed, overjoyed that his friends were safe.

Then a memory – the split second before the explosion – dropped into place like the last piece of a jigsaw puzzle. He remembered Chester's parents in the entrance tunnel. They were together. Mr Rawls was holding his wife, but the memory didn't lead anywhere, dissolving into a spiral of fire and darkness and nothing.

As if a powerful gust of wind had propelled him forward, Will sought the edge of the table for support. 'Hey,' he repeated, only this time it was more like a gasp.

'Hello, Will,' Chester replied, his voice expressionless. 'How are you feeling?'

'Head hurts . . . bit dizzy. And my ears are ringing,' Will answered.

'Mine too,' Chester said. 'I've got a burn on my arm, but it's not too bad. I was lucky.'

Will moved down the side of the table, meeting Elliott's eyes as she looked up. He could see that she'd been crying, her tears leaving tracks in the grime on her face.

Chester was sitting ramrod straight and gripping the arms of the chair as if he was on a rollercoaster ride.

Will cleared his throat. 'Chester . . . I . . . I don't know what to say. I'm . . . so . . .' He took another step, extending his hand towards his friend's on the chair, although he didn't touch him.

Chester had been staring straight ahead at the flickering bulb, but now he focused on Will's hand. His jaw began to quiver as if he was about to give in to his grief. But then he pulled his head up, his face blank as he stared at the light again.

Will remained before him, his hand still outstretched, fingers slightly splayed. He knew only too well how he'd felt when his father had been gunned down in cold blood by the Rebecca twin, but in that split second the explosion in the entrance tunnel had claimed both Chester's parents.

Will wanted to say something to fill the silence. 'Is everyone else okay?' he asked, regretting his choice of words immediately he'd uttered them. *Is everyone else okay? Why the hell am I bothering my friend with this right now?*

'Yes, I think so,' Chester confirmed. He glanced fleetingly at Elliott who nodded in confirmation, then moved his gaze back to the light. 'Sergeant Finch lost some of his puss cats, though. That was sad.'

If Will could have felt any worse, this response did it. His friend was expressing sympathy for the cats when he'd suffered the worst loss imaginable. Chester had always been close to his parents, particularly after the untimely death of his sister. And Mr and Mrs Rawls had doted on their sole surviving child, only to have him snatched away from them when Will had taken him down to the Colony.

And through no fault of Chester's, his parents had been sucked into the whole nightmare with the Styx, and now they'd paid the ultimate price for their unwitting involvement. Will felt such a crushing weight of responsibility that he wanted to throw himself at Chester's feet. He wanted to beg his friend for forgiveness.

But he didn't.

Instead, he reached again for Chester's hand, this time actually making contact. Chester didn't move as Will's fingers brushed his tightly clenched fist on the arm of the chair.

It was an awkward act, and Will didn't know where to go from there. He wasn't Elliott – he couldn't hug his friend. Mumbling, 'I'm so sorry,' he took his hand away and stumbled from the room. He had to get out, he had to escape.

In the pitch black of the passage, he came to a stop. 'Oh God . . . why did this have to happen?' he croaked, his throat constricting with regret and self-reproach. 'Why did they have to die? Why them, and not *me*?'

He edged backwards until he found the wall – the wall beyond which his poor friend was trying to deal with his loss.

What twisted Will into knots was that however much he wished for it, he couldn't make things right again for Chester. He couldn't bring his friend's parents back. It felt precisely to Will as if he was in the throes of one of the fevered nightmares he'd suffered in early childhood, when he'd wake up with the unshakeable feeling that he'd done something monumentally wrong. Although he'd never known what his crimes had been, the guilt was as powerful as any knife twisting in his guts.

Will's forehead still hurt badly, but he swivelled around and pressed it hard against the wall. Then he began to slam it repeatedly on the unyielding surface, grateful for the stinging relief of the pain.

'No, no, no, no.'

Will stopped as blood ran into his eyes, making him blink. As he did so, he caught shouting from the Hub, then a crash. Drake was yelling something. The thought that someone might need help made Will pull himself together, and he began to feel his way along the passage and then into the Hub.

Although a few clouds of smoke still hung in the air, emergency lights had been positioned around the area so Will could immediately see the extent of the damage. A film of fine grey silt coated everything in sight, and many of the desks had been blasted over – those closest to the mouth of the entrance tunnel blackened by flames.

Stepping over the debris strewn across the floor, Will made his way towards the tunnel. Some twenty feet along, it was completely cut off by massive slabs of rock that had fallen through the reinforced concrete roof. The jagged ends of air conditioning ducts and wiring conduits hung loosely from the ceiling and walls like slashed arteries. And much of the surviving length of tunnel was mottled with carbon patches where fires had evidently been put out.

'We're lucky to have survived,' Parry said, as he appeared beside Will and surveyed the damage with him.

'Chester's parents . . . is there any way they could have escaped?' Will asked, staring at the rocks.

Parry shook his head. 'Danforth probably made it out because he was on the right side of the blast door, but not them, I'm afraid.'

Will was silent for a moment. 'Can we dig our way through this?' he said eventually.

'I reckon it would take a team with specialist excavating equipment two or three weeks to clear it.' Barely pausing for breath, Parry asked, 'What sort of shape is Chester in?'

'I honestly don't know,' Will replied, turning to Parry. 'I think he's still in shock.'

Parry scrutinised Will's face. 'You're covered in blood. The

Colonel told me he'd cleaned you up,' he said with surprise.

'It's nothing,' Will mumbled. He was hardly going to admit that he'd made the injury worse by slamming it against the passage wall. He turned to peer at Drake on the other side of the Hub, ankle-deep in electrical cables where Danforth had been working before. As Drake shouted something across to Sweeney at another panel, he sounded panicked. 'We're in trouble, aren't we?' Will said to Parry.

'Other than the fact we should be out hunting those Styx twins and their women, yes, we're in serious trouble down here,' he replied. 'Danforth has done a hatchet job on all the Hub systems. Everything's shut down.' Parry's voice was so low and grim, Will had a job to hear him as he spoke.

'Everything?' Will asked.

Parry sighed. 'All we've got are a couple of satphones with no means of getting a signal, some industrial batteries, and a single laptop that's still functioning.' Parry took in a breath, then released it slowly. 'Maybe I'm giving Danforth too much credit – and when I see him again, rest assured that I'm going to throttle the little bastard – but I don't believe he wanted us dead. I don't believe he ever imagined that it would come to Mrs Rawls detonating the explosive vest.'

'You don't?' Will asked.

'No, he only wanted to contain us long enough so he could get clear. But Danforth's nothing if not thorough; he set charges to knock out every last one of the backup generators. They're all down.'

'So there's no power at all?' Will said. 'Why did he do that?'

'In case we tried to reroute the supply to the blast doors down there, I suppose,' Parry said with a wave of his walking stick at what remained of the entrance tunnel. 'We've checked and double-checked – all the generators are crippled and completely beyond repair. Which has the secondary effect that there's no power for the air recirculation system. And, in any case, the fire ate up quite a chunk of the available oxygen. On a rough calculation of what's left, I'd say we've got a fortnight at the outside. Maybe less, because there are so many of us.'

'We're going to run out of air,' Will whispered, trying to deal with this piece of news.

As Parry began to walk slowly towards Drake, Will went with him. 'What about the vents where the air comes in? Can't we open them up manually?' Will suggested, adding a further thought as it occurred to him: 'And couldn't we climb out through them?'

'That would be a great idea . . .' Parry began, poking at something on the floor with his walking stick, then stooping to pick it up. It was a mug, and as Parry swilled it around, Will could see that it still had some tea in the bottom. '. . . only there aren't any. The Complex was built on the principle that it can be completely closed off from the outside environment. It's hermetically sealed . . . not a molecule gets in or out.'

'So where does the air come from then?' Will asked.

'When the Defcon is raised, the entrance tunnel is locked down, and air is provided from the reservoirs – the pressurised tanks on each level.'

Will looked hopeful. 'Then we're okay because—'

'The tanks are empty,' Parry cut across him.

'This doesn't get any better, does it?' Will murmured, as they came to Sergeant Finch on his mobility scooter. His head was bowed as he stroked a tiny cloth bundle in his lap. It was one of his dead cats, and a kitten from the looks of it.

Stephanie was kneeling beside Sergeant Finch. She looked very un-Stephanie-like, her hair all over the place and her face smeared with dirt. She briefly met Will's eyes, then went back to what she'd been doing. He watched as she covered up the corpse of another cat. There were at least six of the small furry bodies, each with tea towels laid over them. These pitiful little corpses were evocative of television news footage Will had seen following dreadful accidents or terrorist attacks. In spite of the fact that these were cats and not people, the sight was still sickening because blood had soaked into the white cotton of the tea towels.

Will kept his voice low as he and Parry continued towards Drake. 'Does anyone come to check on Sergeant Finch? I remember you saying something about food re-supplies?' he asked.

Parry shook his head. 'Yes, there's a two-monthly rota when a member of the Old Guard makes a drop off at a bothy just round the mountain from here.'

Will frowned at the unfamiliar word. 'Bothy?'

Parry gave a small shrug. 'It's a disused stone hut. The Old Guard have no idea who the supplies are for, due to the security restrictions, so the food will just sit there until it rots. And because of budget cuts, the obscure engineering department within MI5 that services this Complex only despatches a team here once a year. As the next visit isn't scheduled for seven months, I'm sorry to say, Will, we're on our own.'

Will had another idea as he heard a cat howling and glanced over his shoulder at Stephanie. 'What about Old Wilkie? Won't he be beginning to wonder what's happened to us?'

ASSAULT

'Maybe, but he doesn't know our location. Again, due to the security restrictions, I blindfolded him when I dropped him some sixty miles away from here. And I also ordered him to maintain radio silence.'

This led Will to another thought. 'Jiggs! What about J—'

'He's in here with us,' Parry replied, moving away. Will was left squinting at the shadows in the Hub, asking himself where the elusive man was right now.

As the days passed, Chester seemed to spend every waking hour simply staring vacantly into space. And on the rare occasions he did fall asleep, he'd wake up screaming for his mother and father. Although Mrs Burrows sometimes sat with him, Elliott had taken it upon herself to make sure he was never left by himself. To begin with, she'd tried to take Chester's mind off his grief by talking to him, but after he continued to show no interest whatsoever, she just sat silently beside him.

So Will found himself on his own. He floated around in the darkness of the Complex, feeling like a fifth wheel because there wasn't anything in particular he could do to help anyone.

And Chester wasn't alone in staying awake; Drake and Parry hardly slept a wink as they struggled to come up with a way out of the Complex, or a means to summon assistance. Mrs Burrows put out canned food in the kitchen for everyone to help themselves, and when Will ventured in there he would often stop to listen to Drake and Parry's lengthy discussions. They sometimes had Colonel Bismarck, Eddie or Sergeant Finch in attendance, but father and son would be doing most of the talking.

The first initiative Will overheard was Parry's proposal to

blow open the doors to one or more of the other levels, so additional air would be released. When he'd tried to explore them, Will found out for himself that the third, fourth and fifth levels had each been sealed off by their own autolocking blast doors after the explosion in the Hub. When Will had asked Parry why this was, he'd said it was a measure to protect anyone in them if the integrity of the Complex was compromised.

Drake had immediately come out against Parry's idea, arguing that it wouldn't provide them with an appreciable amount of extra air. And, after many calculations, it was decided that using explosives in the belly of the Complex would be too risky, and probably consume much of the extra air anyway as they went off.

After more fruitless discussions, Drake and Eddie began to pursue a second initiative. With Sergeant Finch's help, they had located the microfiche plans of the Complex. Will didn't know what a microfiche was, so watched with interest as Drake managed to get Danforth's document scanner running on a string of industrial batteries. Once Drake had scanned the microfiches – as Will found out, these were postcard-sized transparencies with miniature photographs of various documents – he was able to increase the magnification sufficiently that they could be read on the laptop screen.

Drake and Eddie took turns to scour this documentation – mostly architects' drawings of the Complex's structure, and wiring schematics down to the very last detail. Neither of them had said what they were looking for, but they still spent hours poring over them.

Another initiative had been to use the radio antennae concealed in the electricity pylon on the mountain outside to send out a Mayday distress signal. However, after firing up one of the Hub radio transmitters, it became clear that Danforth had anticipated this. Despite trying everything he could think of, Drake didn't get anywhere. Danforth had either used circuit breakers or planted more explosives to put the antennae out of action.

It all looked pretty bleak, and the discussions between Drake and Parry became increasingly lacklustre as the ideas ran out.

But after hearing Parry refer to an arsenal on Level 6 – the lowest floor of the Complex – Will made up his mind to go down there and have a proper scout round. Besides, he was certain it was already becoming harder to breathe up in the Hub. This may have all been in his mind, but it was beginning to make him feel a little claustrophobic.

He'd gone via his quarters to collect his luminescent orb and was en route for the stairs when he bumped into Stephanie. She was back to her old self; she'd washed her hair and smelt fresh. Will noticed that she was even wearing make-up. In all the grime and gloom of the Complex, she shone with a radiance that made Will's heart skip a beat.

'You look fantastic,' he found himself saying.

'Thank you, Will,' she said, with a small smile. 'I think I've really done my bit for Sergeant Finch.' Will knew that she'd spent days keeping the old man company because he'd been so distraught following the death of his cats. 'He's a sweetie, but . . .' leaning conspiratorially towards Will, she continued, '. . . he's a bit smelly. So I thought I totally deserved some time out. Some quality *me* time.'

She asked Will where he was off to and insisted that she go too. Will realised how grateful he was for the companionship.

'It's really spooky, isn't it?' Stephanie said with a mock shivering sound as they reached the very bottom of the stairwell and could descend no further.

The start of Level 6 was in stark contrast to the layout of all the other floors because there was no main corridor – just an open space in which the floor, walls and regularly spaced columns were all of bare concrete, stained in places by streaks of rust water. Will's luminescent orb created shifting shadows as they passed between the columns.

'It's like a goth's bedroom or something,' Stephanie giggled as she caught sight of a large grinning skull on a cobwebbed warning sign.

'Yeah,' Will said indecisively, wondering why Stephanie felt compelled to fill any silences between them. 'But do you think it's easier to breathe down here?' he asked, as he came to a stop.

She noisily sucked in a mouthful of air. 'Think it might be,' she replied.

'Drake said carbon dioxide is lighter than oxygen. So maybe there *is* more oxygen down on this level?' Will thought aloud, trying to remember the outcome of the debate between Drake and Parry.

Stephanie made a contemplative 'Mmmm' noise as they came to some shadowy structures that reached almost to the ceiling.

'These are the water tanks,' Will said, playing his luminescent orb on the storage vats on either side of the floor. 'Pretty massive, aren't they?' he said, going over to the nearest one and thumping its side with his open hand. It reverberated like a sepulchral bell. 'Sounds full.'

'So at least we won't, like, die of thirst,' Stephanie said.

As Will investigated the areas between the vats with his light, she was uncharacteristically silent for the moment.

Then, as they moved deeper into the level, passing between the backup generators Danforth had put out of action, she slipped her hand into Will's. He must have started slightly because she gave a small laugh.

'Um,' he said awkwardly, careful not to direct the orb in her direction because he didn't want her to see how uneasy he was.

'I really like you, Will,' she said softly. 'You know that, don't you?'

Will was advancing down the walkway, but not at any great speed because Stephanie was still hanging on to him. He didn't answer immediately, then replied, 'I . . . I like you too.'

'You're just like saying that to be nice to me. But that's okay.' She began to take little trotting steps beside him, her high-heeled leather boots ratattating on the concrete, as if she was about to speed up and wheel in front of him. Sensing this, Will also sped up slightly.

'I'd really like to spend more time with you, Will,' Stephanie whispered. 'It's not as if Elliott's around much, is she? She doesn't have to know anything.'

When Will didn't respond, Stephanie lowered her voice even further, almost sounding a little tearful. 'And if it all goes badly wrong for us and we never escape from this place, does anything really matter any more? Except for the time we have left?'

They came to a series of closed doors and Stephanie squeezed Will's hand several times, clearly with no intention of letting go. Although he was pretending to be wrapped up in his exploration of the level, Will's mind was racing. He couldn't help but remember how pretty Stephanie had looked back in the stairwell.

He cleared his throat. 'This is the arsenal. It was locked last time I was here,' he said, as light from his orb fell on an open doorway. 'Let's take a look inside.'

'Sure, let's,' she said, brightening up. Her other hand was now on his forearm.

Will was picturing her clear blue eyes and the way her mouth crinkled at the edges when she smiled. His pulse quickened. Maybe she was right – it didn't matter now. Will knew how much Chester liked her, but his friend was hardly in any frame of mind to bother about that now, and probably wouldn't be for a long time. And Elliott was clearly more interested in looking after Chester than being with him. If they were all going to run out of air in a week or so, then everything was different, and Stephanie was right. Nothing at all mattered any more.

Except for whatever time they had left . . .

Before Will knew what he was doing, he'd increased his grip on Stephanie's hand and was pulling her into the room with him.

Once inside, they stopped. Will had dropped the lumines-cent orb to his side, and Stephanie was in front of him, not much more than a grey shadow. She slid her hand up his arm.

'You know, you're very special,' she said.

'Don't wha-ever y'do light a mash in here,' a low, slurred voice advised. 'Bad bad mishtake.'

Stephanie squealed.

Will spun in the direction of the voice, whipping up the orb to see who was there. The room was large, with row upon row of racking shelves, which housed all the weapons and explosives in the Complex.

'Who's that?' Will demanded, trying to sound as confident as he could. 'Who is it?'

'Jusht little ol' me,' the voice rumbled, still slurring. 'If you light a mash, we'll all be blowed up. Cos of the munishuns.'

Will stepped towards the source of the voice, Stephanie now clinging onto him because she was terrified.

The light from the orb fell upon a man slumped lopsidedly on some sacks.

'Sparks!' Will exclaimed. 'What the hell are you doing here?'

'Shame thing you four are,' he drawled. 'I jush wanted to be on my loneshome-oneshome.'

Will and Stephanie were looking down at him in astonishment. Sweeney's shirt was unbuttoned to his stomach. What appeared to be two small metal terminals sprouting from his sternum were connected by wires to an industrial battery at his side, which he was hugging. Sweeney followed their gaze to it.

'Yesh . . . don't really have to charge myshelf up like thish,' he said, his eyes slow-blinking as he spoke. 'Butsh I thought I could do with a top up of the old resherve cells. Jush in cayshe.'

'Sparks, you sound really weird,' Will ventured. 'You haven't been drinking, have you?'

'No, shir! Never touch the schtuff! It'sh the extra juice – hash thish effect, shomtimes. Makesh me a touch woozy,' Sweeney replied. He attempted to sit up, but didn't get very far. 'Y'know . . . I earwigged everyshing you were shaying.'

'Everything?' Will said, throwing a quick glance at Stephanie.

With his free hand Sweeney tried to point at them, his arm swinging wildly. 'Yesh . . . and lishen . . . if the worsht comes to the worsht . . . and we cash in our schips . . .' Grimacing, he shook his head with comic gravity. '. . . then we *should* all throw ourshelves in those water tanksh. Nearly drowned onsh in a shubermarine. Not shush a bad way to go. Better than shuffocation.'

'But, Sparks, we're going to get out of this place. It's not over yet!' Will said, shocked to hear the old soldier talking that way. 'Are you sure you're okay?'

'Shure I'm shure. Now take the weight off, shonny. Schtay with me a while. Tell all your friends to join ush, too.'

'But there are only two of—' Stephanie began, falling silent as Will caught her eye.

'Of course we'll stay with you,' Will said. He pulled some of the empty sacks over so that he and Stephanie could sit on them. Although there was plenty of room on the sacks for the two of them, as she adjusted her position Stephanie's leg touched Will's. And she left it there, while Will tried his best to have an exchange with Sweeney, who was making very little sense.

'Can I ask what name your booking's under?' the spritely receptionist in a pink tracksuit enquired.

She pulled a pencil from her tightly curled hair, allowing herself a curious glance at the confident young girl standing before the desk, a handsome if dopey-looking chauffeur at her side.

Then, twirling the pencil between her thumb and fore-finger as if it was a small baton, the woman used the mouse to scroll through a page on her computer screen. 'I assume it's for a relative? Your mother or father perhaps?' The receptionist had seen the top-of-the-range Mercedes draw up outside, followed by a coach, so it was clearly someone important. And as they didn't take children, the reservation couldn't be for the slip of a girl in front of her. 'If you can ask them to come in, we'll make sure their room's ready.'

'That's neat,' Rebecca Two said, watching the trick with the pencil as it helicoptered round and round in the receptionist's hand.

'Oh, thank you. It's something I picked up from an old boyfriend,' the receptionist said distantly. She was intrigued to find out who was about to grace their exorbitantly expensive establishment but, as she reached the end of the booking schedule on her computer and saw that there were only a few regulars yet to check in, she frowned. 'We are terribly full at the moment. What was the name of the booking?'

'Booking?' Rebecca Two repeated, as the Old Styx strolled into the reception, and then peered around at the photographs of various activities offered at the exclusive health farm in the depths of the Kentish countryside. The photographs were of people swimming in the Olympic-length pool, having massages and facials, and jogging in a group in the extensive grounds surrounding the converted stately home.

'Yes, the booking. I assume it'll be for you, sir?' the receptionist asked, directing the question at the Old Styx. He'd wandered to the large windows at the rear of the reception area that looked out onto the swimming pool, and was watching the morning aqua-aerobics class which was in full swing.

'Sir? Hello?' the receptionist said, as the grizzled looking man didn't bother to reply. She bit her tongue. However exasperated she was becoming with the two odd-looking people, she had to be careful because the chances were that the man was an important new client.

She studied his profile as he turned to a notice board where all the day's activities had been posted. With his hair raked back, the elderly man was dressed in a black ankle-length leather coat. That made the receptionist think he might be some famous film director – or, as she scrutinised him further, maybe a musician. She tried to recall the names of the members of the Rolling Stones – they all looked as thin and drawn as he did. Yes, maybe this man *was* one of them. But not the singer with the luscious mouth and the hips – she'd have known if it was him.

The coach outside could be their tour bus, and maybe his reservation had been made under a pseudonym. That wasn't uncommon as celebrities came to the health farm to escape the limelight and get themselves performance-fit again.

So the receptionist waited patiently, spinning her pencil and quietly humming *T-i-m-e is on my side* to herself. The last thing she wanted to do was offend whatsisname if she could possibly help it.

A gaggle of woman chatting breathlessly to each other chose that moment to pass through reception on their way to a Pilates session.

'How many people do you have staying here?' the Old Styx demanded when they'd gone.

The receptionist was quite unprepared for the severity of his cold, dead eyes on her. Little black holes that made her want to look away. Made her want to run away. 'One hundred and twenty guests at full capacity, but we also have a substantial number of people with day-passes coming in for classes and the gym.'

The Old Styx nodded. 'And are all your guests chronically obese like those women we just saw?'

Not unsurprisingly, the receptionist was rather taken aback by this question. 'I don't think that's—'

'There's ample human flesh for our purposes,' the Old Styx interrupted her as he spoke to Rebecca Two.

'What?' the receptionist exclaimed, now looking at him with incomprehension.

The Old Styx had plucked a walkie-talkie from his coat and was speaking on it in the strangest language the receptionist had ever heard.

'Sorry. It's just not your day,' Rebecca Two said, without emotion.

There was a crash as the main doors burst open.

The receptionist's pencil went spinning across the room as something slavering appeared behind Rebecca Two and Captain Franz.

With a rasping roar Hermione cannoned into the desk, bowling it over. The receptionist was thrown onto her back. As she lay stunned on the floor, Hermione leapt on top of her.

Giving a wail of relief as she gripped the sides of the young woman's face, Hermione's ovipositor sunk inside her, deep into her trachea where the egg pod squeezed out.

Hermione's head was up in a second, gluey saliva spilling from around the ovipositor. 'Need another . . . quick,' she rasped. 'So many babies in me.'

Glancing fearfully at Hermione, the Old Styx had retreated well out of the way. He was at the main doors, where a squad of Limiters had turned up to collect their orders.

'I reckon we should try through here first,' Rebecca Two said to Hermione, making for the door the Pilates women had taken.

'We might be on to something,' Drake declared, as they all gathered around the laptop. With the exception of Chester who couldn't be persuaded to leave the briefing room, and Elliott who didn't think he should be left alone, everyone was present.

It had been nearly a fortnight, and there was no doubt about it any longer – the air was more rarefied and it was becoming harder to breathe.

Will peered around at everybody. As their eyes reflected the glow of the computer screen, the sense of anticipation radiating from them was tangible. At least here was some hope. Not one of the other ideas had come to anything, and Will had begun to think only a miracle could save them now.

'Eddie and I have been going over the original construction plans for the Complex with a fine-toothed comb,' Drake said. He scrolled through a succession of pages on the screen. 'Here are some cross-section schematics of the mountain to show how this installation sits inside it.' He settled on an illustration and tapped the screen with his finger. 'You can see there's a substantial margin of rock around the Complex, to protect it.'

'That was the basic idea,' Parry mumbled.

Eddie took over from Drake. 'Nothing jumped out at us at first, but then we cross-referenced these construction plans with a geological survey undertaken in the fifties.'

Drake opened another window on the screen, which

showed more cross-sections of the mountain, but without any sign of the Complex. 'This report referred to several areas towards the mid-contours of the mountain where the erosion was particularly marked.' Drake indicated one of drawings. 'And we noticed that on the northern face of the mountain – just above the small ledge you can see there – the erosion was quite considerable. Add another sixty-odd years of water action and frost damage, and even more of the rock will have been worn away.'

'The freeze-thaw cycle,' Will chimed in, then wished he hadn't as Parry gave him a sharp look.

'So how does all this help us, exactly?' the old man asked.

'Time and water erosion wait for no man,' Drake smiled as he went back to the first window and dragged an image from it. 'It helps us because if you overlay the geological report with the construction plans, the area of accelerated erosion is . . .' He pointed at the plan, '. . . right next to the external wall at the end of Level 2.'

'So it's the most vulnerable point in the Complex,' Eddie said. 'And if we were to plant every last piece of explosive against that wall, there's a slim chance we could blow a way out for ourselves.'

Parry whistled. 'High-stakes stuff,' he said. As he leant on a neighbouring desk and began to tug his beard in thought, Will noticed that everyone's eyes were on him. Stephanie even had her mouth open and was shaping words as if she was willing him to decide that the scheme was feasible.

Parry was shaking his head when he eventually spoke again. 'I see what you're saying, but the volume of explosive material in the arsenal will be a limiting factor. And even if we ploughed ahead with every last stick, if the plan fails all the remaining oxygen in the Complex will have been used up. We'd have brought forward the last curtain call.' With a sniff, he crossed his arms. 'Besides that, what's left of the Complex might just come crashing down on our heads.'

'Er . . . Commander,' Sergeant Finch began. 'Aren't you forgetting someth—'

'No, Finch, I'm not!' Parry snapped savagely at him.

Drake was looking from his father to Sergeant Finch and then back again as he tried to work out what their exchange had been all about. 'If there's something you two aren't telling us, I think we have a right to know.'

Parry was on his feet in an instant. 'No,' he barked. 'There are some things that *nobody* has a right to know. And Finch here has spoken out of turn, when he doesn't know the whole story.'

Mrs Burrows' voice was quiet and controlled as she joined the conversation. 'Parry, we're the only people in the world who are aware that the Phase might still be under way. And we're the only ones who can do anything to stop it. So what can be so important that you're prepared to let us all die in this place?'

Parry was looking at the ground and tensing a leg as if he was racked with indecision. He suddenly raised his head to his son. 'Are you certain that we've got a chance with this cocka-mamie idea of yours? Are you absolutely certain?'

'Within the tolerances of the drawings we've seen, and on the assumption that more erosion has taken place . . . yes,' Drake replied 'The only real negative is that we could do with two or three times the amount of explosive to punch through the reinforced Complex wall *and* the mountainside.'

'You boys do like to use brute force, don't you?' Parry said, then thought for a moment. 'Okay, you'd all better follow me,' he decided, giving Sergeant Finch a nod.

As Parry directed, they collected sledgehammers, coal chisels and mallets on the way. The lifts were out of action so the Colonel carried Sergeant Finch on his back, while Drake and Sweeney hauled his mobility scooter down the stairs.

Once they were all on Level 6, Parry led them past the water tanks and to the arsenal at the very end of the floor. He strode through one of the aisles between the racking shelves until he reached a large metal cabinet against the wall.

'Several of you get to work and move any explosives and incendiaries within a twenty foot radius of here. Last thing we want is to ignite anything with a stray spark,' Parry said, with a wave of his hand at the shelves. Then he supervised his son and Sweeney as they slid the metal cabinet out of the way. The wall behind appeared to be no different from anywhere else, but Parry took up a coal chisel and mallet, and began to tap away at it.

It quickly became apparent that it wasn't just a solid slab of reinforced concrete. He'd located an area at the bottom of the wall that gave off a different sound as he chipped away at it. And he was working his way vertically up the wall when he stopped to address Will. 'You're good at this sort of stuff, laddie. Help yourself to some tools and find the other side of the doorway,' he said, pointing four feet or so along the base of the wall.

Will found that there was a wooden batten buried just below the surface of the concrete, and it didn't take much effort to uncover it. As the two of them continued to work, a rectangle the size of a pair of double doors was revealing itself. Once they were finished, they both stood back.

'Open Sesame,' Parry said. 'That's our way in.'

Having checked that the surrounding shelves were clear, Parry turned to everyone. 'Now we break down the concrete in the doorway.'

'What's in there?' Drake said. 'An explosives cache?'

Ignoring the question, Parry swung a sledgehammer at a bottom corner of the rectangle.

Sergeant Finch wasn't so reticent. 'Yes, the secondary store is 'idden there,' he said. 'A top secret store.'

'And the rest,' Parry muttered under his breath as he kept swinging. Both Sweeney and the Colonel joined in. The concrete was gradually yielding, but not as quickly as Will had thought it would.

'Can I have a go?' someone asked as they strode into the arsenal.

'Chester!' Will burst out, a big smile on his face. Elliott was following several paces behind, her expression one of concern.

'About time I did something,' Chester said as the Colonel passed his sledgehammer over and the boy set to work.

Sweeney was the first to break through, and stopped to take a look.

'No, carry on,' Parry said. 'Better that we clear it completely.'

Some twenty minutes later the Colonel was attacking the last piece of concrete at the top of the opening. As he swiped at it and it crashed to the floor, Parry used his torch to light the way as they all filed in behind him.

'There's more than enough here for what we need,' Drake said, taking in the sheer number of wooden crates as Parry flicked his torch beam over them. 'But this is nothing fancy – just your plain vanilla post-war explosive stock. So what was with all that melodrama earlier?'

'The best way to hide something is to hide it in something already hidden,' Parry announced as he spun around to face everybody. 'You cannot under any circumstances breathe a word of what you are about to learn – not to anybody.' He drew himself up to his full height. 'I am now going to ask you each to give your consent that, under the Defence of the Realm Act 1973, as revised 1975 and 1976, that you irrevocably and unreservedly yield to the powers contained within the act.' Parry then spoke their names in turn.

'Drake?'

'Whatever all that means, yes,' Drake said.

'Finch?'

'Yes, Commander.'

Colonel Bismarck – you are hereby granted full British nationality. I need your answer.'

'Can Parry do that?' Will whispered to Chester as the Colonel indicated that he agreed.

'And, likewise, Eddie the Styx, you are hereby granted full citizenship of this country. Do you agree?'

'Yes, sir,' Eddie replied.

'Mrs Burrows?'

'Yes, Parry,' she said gently. 'Why ever not?'

'Elliott – sorry, I forgot that you also need to be granted British nationality. Answer me, please.'

'Yes,' she said.

'Sweeney?'

'Yes, boss.'

Parry then addressed Will and Chester, who confirmed their agreement.

'Stephanie?' Parry said.

'Like, yes,' she replied.

'Right,' Parry said. 'You should be aware that if any one of you leaks information regarding this matter, under the Defence of the Realm Act, you will be liable to summary automatic execution without trial or any form of legal recourse whatsoever.'

'Execution?' Mrs Burrows said.

'I'd have full authorisation to kill you,' Parry answered matter-of-factly. And from the tone of his voice, everyone knew he meant it. 'After the nuclear disarmament treaty of 1972, it was resolved by a secret subcommittee within the Ministry of Defence that we were leaving ourselves at a howling disadvantage. So . . .'

Parry directed his torch beam into the corner of the room.

There were ten metal containers there, shining dully.

'Huh?' Stephanie said, wholly unimpressed after all the build-up.

'We stuck a few TNDs away in here,' Parry said, 'for a rainy day.'

'TNDs?' Will asked.

'Thermonuclear Devices,' Parry explained.

'Nukes . . . he's talking about nukes!' Drake said, staring at the containers. 'And he's got to be bloody joking!'

Parry and Sergeant Finch, armed with his ever-present clipboard, went around both the arsenal and the secondary cache, marking chalk crosses on the crates that contained the most potent explosives. Bit by bit, these were then loaded onto a trolley, which was pushed to the stairwell. Will and Chester took over from there, finding they had the unenviable task of lugging each crate up the eight flights of stairs to Level 2 where another trolley was waiting for them.

It was hard work as the wooden crates were heavy, and the boys were suffering from the lack of air. As they laboured up the stairs with the umpteenth crate between them, Chester seemed to be oblivious to the rope handles cutting into his hands. They finally cleared the stairs with their crate and placed it carefully on the trolley with all the others.

Leaning against the wall and breathing heavily, Will caught his friend's eye. Chester gave him a broad grin as if he hadn't a care in the world.

'You okay?' Will asked him.

'Just pleased to be doing something,' Chester replied. Regardless of the way he seemed to be coping, Will was concerned about him, but there wasn't much he could do right now.

Chester mopped his brow. 'Where's Drake got to? I say we take this load to him ourselves.'

'Sure,' Will agreed.

With Will pulling and Chester pushing, they wheeled the heavily laden trolley down the corridor. One of the wheels had begun to squeal plaintively. 'Reminds me of when we were emptying the wheelbarrow on Highfield Common,' Chester remarked.

As they came to the end of the corridor, they steered the trolley through a doorway and into the utility room Drake had identified. He'd said it was their best bet to punch a way through the mountainside.

The room was already piled high with crates, and Drake was in the process of embedding pencil-sized detonators into each one, which were connected by a skein of cables.

'Cool,' Drake said, glancing at the trolley. 'I'll unload it myself if you want to get on.'

'How many more do you need?' Chester asked, looking at the stacks of crates beside Drake.

'Enough to fill this room, then the one next to it,' Drake answered. 'I reckon that's another twenty or so trips with the trolley.'

'Twenty!' Chester exclaimed, laughing in an exaggerated way. 'Cool – we'll keep 'em coming,' he added as he left the room. They could still hear his laughter as he passed down the corridor, slapping the wall and saying 'More, more, more!'

'He's not himself,' Drake pronounced in a low voice, frowning.

'Are any of us?' Will shot back.

'Well, keep a close eye on him, won't you, Will?' Drake said.

It took the best part of a day to prepare the two rooms. Finally Drake walked the distance up the stairs and into the Hub, a drum rotating in his hands as he played out a cable behind him.

Parry had been concerned that even if the explosion blew a way through, it might also bring down the ceiling of Level 2 in the process, sealing their way out and negating the whole exercise. There was no way of closing the blast doors to the level, but at Parry's direction everyone piled sandbags around the two rooms in a bid to contain some of the inward force of the blast. Parry still wasn't satisfied that they were doing all they could on this front, so he oversaw the construction of another sandbag barrier halfway down the corridor.

The time had come. Everyone was waiting outside the small canteen off the Hub where Chester had first noticed his mother was behaving strangely. Drake and Eddie had picked it because they believed it would be a good place for them all to shelter from the blast.

'All systems go,' Parry said, and everyone trooped into the canteen, and the door was shut behind them. They watched as Drake untwisted the two glinting copper wires at the end of the cable, then connected them to the terminals on a detonator.

No one spoke. As Mrs Burrows stroked Colly, there was a chorus of anxious meows from the row of wicker baskets along the top of the work surface. Stephanie and Elliott had had a devil of a job rounding up Sergeant Finch's cats from their various hiding places in the Complex, but it was the least they could do for the old man.

Drake had told everyone to stow their Bergens in one corner, so they had their kit close by them. And in addition to the many fire extinguishers they'd brought into the room, Parry had ensured that there was enough food and water to last them a few days.

Drake tugged the wires to make sure they were firmly attached to the terminals, then nodded to his father.

Parry took a breath, and his voice gentle for a change. 'I don't think there's much to say, except bloody good luck to every one of us. I sincerely hope God's smiling on us today.'

'Amen,' said Sweeney.

Parry tapped his walking stick twice on the ground. 'Now can we all assume safety positions, please?'

Sergeant Finch was helped out of his mobility scooter and then everyone did as they'd been told, finding a place on the floor. They bowed their heads, their hands clasped behind the napes of their necks.

Will was watching as Drake wound the handle on the detonator to build up an electrical charge. As it went faster and faster, the whirring of the dynamo filled the room.

'That'll be enough,' he decided, hinging back the safety guard around the push handle.

'Okay?' he asked.

'Okay,' Parry replied.

'See you on the other side,' Drake said.

He rammed the handle home.

Chapter Eighteen

The lift rose through the levels of the Chancellery, the huge government building at the very centre of New Germania. As it came to a stop, the doors slid open and a pair of Styx Limiters stepped from it. Their boots beat in perfect unison as they marched over the highly polished marble floors.

The Chancellor's assistant was at her station, a Baroque gilded table with a telephone and a vase of wilted flowers on it. She was brushing her hair as she observed the two soldiers approaching. There would have been a time when she'd have been paralysed with fear at the sight of these ghoulish men with their skeleton-thin faces and jet-black eyes. Men that reeked of death and destruction.

But now she regarded them with a sleepy detachment as they paused in front of her table.

'Is he in?' one of them demanded in a growl.

She nodded with that sheep-eyed look that spoke of intensive Darklighting – along with almost every other inhabitant of New Germania, she'd been subjected to excessive amounts of the treatment, and it had all but fried her brain.

And her appearance had changed considerably since the day, several months before, when Rebecca Two and the Limiter General had made their first visit to the Chancellery. She still wore her efficient blue suit, but the dark roots of her platinum hair were showing, and her make-up carelessly applied.

She watched as one of the Limiters kicked open the large wooden doors to the Chancellor's office and they both stormed in.

Still brushing her hair, she listened to the commotion inside the room. Then the Limiters emerged, dragging the corpulent Chancellor, Herr Friedrich, between them. They must have caught him during one of his typically lavish lunches, as he still had a napkin tucked into his shirt.

'I'm going out for a while, Frau Long,' he managed to say before he was carted off down the corridor.

With two outriders blazing the way, the official limousine roared down Berliner Strasse, one of the grandest and usually busiest roads in New Germania. But other than this single vehicle, with its old-fashioned swept-back airflow styling and gleaming silver paintwork, there was no traffic now.

As the vehicle drew to a halt near the waiting delegation, the door opened. Placing a dainty combat boot on the chalk coloured road, Rebecca One emerged unhurriedly from the vehicle. And, just as unhurriedly, she made her way towards the delegation, inclining her head to listen to the forlorn drone of sirens resounding across the city.

Then she turned to survey the opposite side of the broad avenue across the central reservation with its palm trees, where a multitude of people were standing in several queues. There were so many New Germanians there that the lines wound up and down the baking surface of the road. And not one of the people spoke or made a sound, simply shuffling forward as the queues moved at an interminably slow rate.

Rebecca One blew through her lips. 'Water . . . somebody bring me some water,' she said, flapping her long black coat open to circulate air to her body.

A Limiter soldier in the delegation immediately removed a canteen from his belt and passed it to her. She took several long gulps before handing it back. 'This climate – it's too much,' she said, squinting at the ever-burning sun directly overhead in the sky. She lowered her eyes to the Limiter General who was waiting for his orders. She frowned slightly as she studied the sand-coloured fatigues he and the other Limiters were wearing. 'I leave you in charge and this is what happens. I know the heat is the reason you've ditched your uniforms, but I'm not sure I approve of the replacement. It's not really us, is it? A little too *beach party* for my taste.'

There was no change in the Limiter General's deadpan expression, but he was clearly troubled by her criticism as he looked down at the loose-fitting combat jacket and trousers. 'They're New Germanian Special Forces issue,' he explained.

'Don't worry about it now,' she said. 'But if you're the Master Race, you've got to look the part. Isn't that right, Chancellor? Isn't that what your wonderful Third Reich believed w . . .' She fell silent as she sought out Herr Friedrich, who was standing in the midst of the delegation. He was miles away, his head craned back as he watched a lone pterodactyl riding a thermal high in the sky. 'Hey, porky boy – I'm talking to you!' she barked.

The Chancellor, the former supreme leader of the nation of

New Germania, hiccupped with surprise. He too had had his fair share of the Dark Light, with the expected ill effects.

'Hello?' he said, frowning at Rebecca One.

'Oh, forget it,' she snapped. She swung to the Limiter General. 'Give me an update. How's Vane getting on?'

The Limiter General shook his head. 'She's exceeding all expectations.' He pointed at one of the institutional buildings that lined the road, a substantial ten-storey edifice of light granite. 'As you know, we filled the Institute of Geology with human stock.' He panned his finger along the other, similarly imposing buildings in the row, coming closer to where he and Rebecca One were standing. 'Then we did the same with the medical facility, and the universities of antiquities and prehistory. She's worked her way through the human hosts in all of them. That's three hundred and fifty bodies for impregnation and nearly double that number for sustenance—'

'Wait!' Rebecca One broke in. 'You're telling me that she's impregnated that many already? She's just one woman. How can that be?'

'Might I suggest you come and see for yourself?' the Limiter General replied. He and the rest of the delegation fell in behind Rebecca One as she stepped over the central reservation and cut straight through the queues. The people dumbly moved out of her way. One of them, an elderly man, his face bright red from exposure to the unforgiving sun, abruptly collapsed. Rebecca One hardly bothered to look at him as he lay where he fell.

'Yes, through there,' the Limiter General said as she reached the nearest building.

It was a huge botanical glasshouse, its facade nearly a thousand feet in length. 'Kew Gardens,' Rebecca One said under her breath as she noted the similarity with the Royal Botanic Gardens she'd driven past with Vane no more than a fortnight before.

The Limiter General held the door of the glasshouse open for her, indicating the stairs just inside. She mounted the cast iron steps, then she passed through another door and out onto a walkway spanning the entire width of the building. From the abundance of different trees, shrubs and flowers that Rebecca One could see below, New Germanian botanists had obviously been collecting specimens from the jungle and propagating them here.

The Limiter General and the Styx soldiers, two of whom had the Chancellor hoisted between them, held back as she moved to the middle of the walkway. There she peered down one side and then the other. Through the foliage she could see the numerous human bodies lying in the soil, already monstrously bloated by the Warrior larvae growing inside them.

'Outstanding,' Rebecca One said. 'But how's she managing to impregnate so …' She trailed off as she noticed that one of the bodies had already ruptured and young larvae were crawling in the rich peat of a planting bed. 'I don't believe it! It took almost a week for them to hatch Topsoil. But this has taken . . . what?'

'Twenty-four hours,' the Limiter General answered.

Rebecca One was silent for a moment. 'But how can the life cycle have accelerated to that extent?'

'We can only think that Danforth's pronouncement about the conditions down here was right. Perhaps the environment – the proximity to the sun and the high UV levels – acts to stimulate the process,' the Limiter General said.

'Even so . . . how can one woman be physically able to do

this?' Rebecca One asked. 'It's off the scale.'

The Chancellor was also peering over the side of the walkway. Some part of his mind that had survived the Darklighting was registering the carnage below – that his people were dying in the most horrible way. He began to sob.

'Oh, do stop that!' Rebecca One reprimanded him. She returned her attention to the scene below. 'Where is she?' she asked herself. Then she shouted, 'Vane! Are you there?'

At this the Limiter General and his men drew back. The last thing they wanted was to attract the attention of the Styx woman. They'd already witnessed the unfortunate deaths of their comrades as she'd been conveyed from one building to another.

There was a rustling and a head popped up between two date palms. Vane's blonde hair was matted with gore, sweat and the fluid slopping from her mouth. No change there. But the aspect that made Rebecca One's eyes widen was that instead of the single ovipositor, Vane now had an additional two of them swinging from her mouth. And her abdomen was hugely extended as her reproductive system continued to operate in overdrive to churn out new egg pods.

Vane gave Rebecca One an enthusiastic thumbs up, then rubbed her belly proudly.

'Go for it, sister! You're breaking all the records!' Rebecca One congratulated her.

The Chancellor was still sobbing, even louder than ever.

'Oh, Christ, you big baby,' Rebecca One groaned. 'Just chuck him over, will you?' she ordered the Limiters. 'Juicy fat treat on the way!' she called down to Vane.

Vane again gave the thumbs up, then there was a thrashing of the undergrowth as she began to move at speed.

The Limiters hiked the man over the balustrade of the walkway, his arms and legs flailing for the short distance down. His fall was cushioned by the soil in the planting bed, so he wasn't badly injured as he hit the ground, but sitting up and looking around himself dazedly.

'Check him out!' Rebecca One shouted to Vane. 'Enjoy!'

The explosion was so loud that several of them cried out. And the tremor so powerful that their teeth rattled and their vision blurred.

Then the concussive wave swept into the Hub. Will's ears popped. There was a sudden crash as if something large had struck the door from outside.

Saucepans clattered down from the shelves above. As a crack opened up across the ceiling, sprinkling dust on their heads, the caterwauling from the wicker baskets reached fever pitch.

Stephanie began to cry softly to herself as Sergeant Finch recited the Lord's Prayer in broken sentences. Will couldn't help but notice that Chester, his head still down, was trembling violently – the explosion was obviously bringing back unwanted memories of his parents' death. Elliott had noticed too, and was holding Chester tight.

As the blast subsided, there was a low groaning sound.

'I hope that's not the roof of Level 2,' Parry whispered.

Then, except for the confused calls of Sergeant Finch's cats, all was quiet.

Drake stood up, brushing the dust from his head. 'Bring lights and fire extinguishers,' he said.

The Colonel picked up Sergeant Finch, and Drake pushed

the door open. The Hub didn't look any different, but as they went down the stairs and out into Level 2, there wasn't much left standing – nearly all the interior walls close to the stairs had been blown away.

Drake and Parry were checking the roof immediately above them as they advanced further into the level, but the dense dust and smoke prevented them from seeing very far ahead. They all covered their noses and mouths with scarves and pressed forward, negotiating the rubble strewn over the ground. Eddie and Sweeney were blasting away with the extinguishers at small fires in their path.

As they made their way around a bath thrown on its side, the smoke cleared a little and Will caught sight of a chair. It was still the right way up, but every part of it was ablaze.

Holding up his fist, Drake came to a stop. He unwound his scarf. 'Feel that?' he shouted.

And they all did.

The air on their sweat-drenched skin felt cold. A breeze was coming from somewhere.

Filled with hope, they ventured further into the floor, where the corridor had previously been. In one place their way was blocked by debris, but Drake and Sweeney heaved aside a partition wall, enabling them to proceed further.

The fires were more numerous as they came closer to the end of the floor. They were using the extinguishers and kicking pieces of burning timber out of the way, when Drake yelled a warning and they all hastily retreated.

There was a crash as a whole section of the ceiling not ten feet in front of them simply dropped to the floor.

They waited, but as the rest of the ceiling seemed to be holding in place, Drake waved them on again.

They came to where the rooms packed with explosive had been. As they stepped around a large hole in the concrete floor, through which the level below was visible, they were all far too preoccupied to notice what lay ahead.

But Drake had sped up. As he led the group, he'd been the first to spot the jagged breach in the Complex's outer wall.

Then they all saw it, and clambered through behind him.

There were shouts of joy as, within a short distance, their feet ground not on shattered concrete, but on the rocky ledge they'd seen in the cross-section plans on Drake's laptop. They were high up on the side of the mountain, experiencing something that they hadn't known for weeks.

There was a huge open space above them.

The night sky.

'Stars!' Will yelled. 'We bloody did it!'

The Colonel was jumping up and down with Sergeant Finch still on his back, and they were both cheering.

'Oh, yes! Fresh air!' Stephanie cried. 'And snow!' she added as she held out her hand to catch the flakes.

Everyone was hugging everyone else. Will grabbed his mother and squeezed her hard. It had been a long time since he'd done that and it felt a little strange. But he was quite unprepared for what happened next as Stephanie suddenly appeared before him and gave him a kiss on the lips.

'Oi!' Will laughed.

As Colly scampered madly around, Will saw that Drake and Parry were already at the end of the ledge, where they were pointing at the tiny points of light from a distant village.

Chester hadn't moved very far from the jagged opening in the mountain. He tried to say something to Will, but a sudden gust of wind snatched his breath away.

'What was that?' Will shouted, but Chester averted his face as a flurry of snow fell in his eyes. He began to shake uncontrollably, although it wasn't from the cold. Now they'd escaped from their airless tomb in the mountain and were out of immediate danger, the stark reality of his parents' death was finally coming home to him.

He was gibbering to himself as his legs buckled. Elliott had already begun to move towards him, and was able to catch him before he hit the ground. Mrs Burrows was also at the boy's side, helping to support him.

Parry had been watching Chester as he collapsed. 'That snake Danforth is going to pay very dearly for his actions,' he promised in a growl.

'First things first. We need some transport,' Drake said. 'If it's true that we haven't yet neutralised the Phase, we've lost valuable time. The key thing now is that we cover all the bases.'

Parry was looking at his son, waiting for him to continue.

'We'll split into two groups; one to conduct a search up here on the surface,' Drake suggested.

'I'll coordinate that,' Parry said. 'I'll call on the Old Guard again.'

'And I'll lead the second group to the inner world. We can't take the risk that Danforth was spinning us a line about the Phase resuming there.' Drake abruptly wheeled to his father as he thought of something. 'Those TNDs,' he said. 'How many did you say there were?'

'I didn't,' Parry replied. 'There are twenty in total, starting with a couple at one kiloton up to the largest, which used to be known in intelligence circles as the *Party Stopper* – a single fifty-megaton device.'

'That's way too much – a pair of the one kilotons will be sufficient for what I have in mind. But I need a fast way to get them down to the Colony. From there I can take them on to your world, Colonel.'

Colonel Bismarck had come over to listen, and his distress was evident as he nearly let Sergeant Finch slide from his back. 'You intend to destroy it?' he asked.

'Nothing that extreme,' Drake told him. 'I just want to seal the two ways in that we know about.'

'*Gott sei Dank!*' the Colonel exclaimed, looking at the ground.

'Unless I'm left with no alternative,' Drake said, which made the Colonel's head jerk up. 'But time's short and I need a really quick route down,' Drake continued, directing the request at Eddie.

The former Limiter shrugged. 'There are any number of ways down to the Colony. You can take your pick.'

'We've got all the muscle we need,' Drake said, glancing briefly at Sweeney before he addressed Eddie again. 'But I really don't fancy lugging a pair of even the mini nukes down your usual convoluted routes. And, of course, the Norfolk river-route is out of the question – there are just too many of us with too much equipment to risk shooting the rapids. No, something with a lift would be perfect,' he joked.

Will's ears perked up. 'I think I might be able to help there,' he said.

PART FOUR

Nuclear

Chapter Nineteen

'Hello,' the young woman said, as she answered the door. 'Mornin',' Drake replied. He took a laminated card from the chest pocket of his blue overalls and passed it to her. 'I'm afraid there's a major gas leak in your house. We're the instant response team sent to locate it.'

'A gas leak . . . I haven't reported one,' she said, shaking her head. She pushed the laminated card back at Drake. 'There's no leak here, I can assure you. I'm surprised you people are still working – everybody seems to be on strike these days.' Her brow suddenly creased with annoyance. 'Look, this isn't a convenient time for me right now – I have to leave shortly to collect my son from my mother's. Can't you come back anoth—'

'Madam, I don't want to appear impolite, but our grid sensors flagged up this problem overnight. And they're rarely wrong about these things.' Drake planted his tool box on the ground by his feet as if he hadn't the slightest intention of leaving. 'If you don't allow us in to make our report, then we'll have to close down the supply to this whole street and several others on the same grid. Then I'll be back in an hour with a court order forcing you to allow us access.' He hugged himself, shivering a little. 'You won't be popular with the neighbours if there's no gas for their central heating, particularly with this cold weather.'

The woman immediately took a step back as if she'd decided to let Drake in, then looked curiously at Mrs Burrows beside him, who was sniffing the air. 'Do you both need to come in? Only I'm not comfortable w—'

'We do, I'm afraid,' Drake replied. 'I have my electronic sniffer in here,' he said, nudging the toolbox, 'but there's nothing like the human touch. My assistant, Celia here, is what we in the gas trade call a "Nose". She's a trained detector.'

'Really?' The young woman inclined her head as if she was about to question this, then seemed to accept it as she pulled the door fully open.

'Okay, Celia, tell me what we're looking at here,' Drake said, as they entered the hallway.

Celia stuck her nose in the air. 'The kitchen's there,' she said, turning towards the closed door on her left. 'But it's clean.'

'Clean?' the young woman said, sounding slightly offended.

'What Celia means is that the boiler's functioning properly and the problem's not in there,' Drake explained.

'The sitting room is to the right,' Celia continued. 'There's a gas fire in the hearth, but it hasn't been used for at least a year. It's one of the older models with a ceramic grille, and faux wood panels at either end.'

'That's right!' the young woman burst out. 'My husband says it's too expensive to use it, and we've got to get a replacement. But how do you know what it looks like?'

'She's one of the best Noses in the country,' Drake said. 'You see – she's only just getting into her stride.'

Celia flicked her shifting eyes to the top of the staircase. 'Airing cupboard at the back of the landing, with a lagged cylinder,' she went on. 'Three bedrooms – the main with two radiators, and two smaller bedrooms each with a single radiator.'

'Right again,' the young woman gasped.

'And . . .' Celia began, then stopped. Drake moved aside as she went to a narrow set of drawers up against the wall, on top of which were several pairs of gloves and a child's hat. Celia got down on one knee and felt underneath. She pulled something out, barely glancing at it as she passed it to the young woman, who took it gingerly. '. . . the remains of a rusk,' Mrs Burrows finished. 'Nothing to worry about – it dried out a long time ago, when your son threw it there, but it smells of mouse. One came in from the garden and had a nibble, and you don't want to encourage that.'

'No, I don't,' the woman said emphatically, as she held the rock-hard piece of rusk between her thumb and forefinger to examine it. 'Yes, you're absolutely right. There are small nibbles here at the end.' She looked at Mrs Burrows with renewed fascination. 'You're like a circus act or something!' The young woman straightaway realised that this might have been rather insulting to Mrs Burrows, and began to apologise.

Drake held up his hand. 'Don't worry – we get it all the time. A lot of people react the same way you have,' he assured her.

Mrs Burrows' brows formed a deep V. 'The real problem is in the cellar,' she said, pointing at the door. 'And it's a Category One. It's critical.'

'What's a Category One?' the young lady asked.

'Not good news, I'm afraid,' Drake said. 'Major fracture of the supply line – probably due to ground freeze. It's likely to have been spewing gas down there for some time, and into . . .' Drake swallowed as if he could barely bring himself to utter the next words, 'into an *enclosed space*.'

'Yes, I'd say the fault's been active for thirty . . . no . . . thirty-five hours,' Mrs Burrows informed him, sniffing randomly.

Drake whistled. 'Blooming heck! That long?' He whirled round to the woman. 'Look, madam, you have to leave the property right now. Our insurance doesn't cover us for customer fatalities. Please just gather your coat and what you need, and get away from here – well away. And don't operate anything electrical – even a mobile phone could set off the gas down there and blow us all into the next century.' He looked at Mrs Burrows. 'We'll have to make the cellar a containment area and flush it out before we can even start to think about digging down to the fault.' Then he turned back to the young lady again. 'I need a set of house keys and a number where I can reach you. I'll let you know the moment it's safe to return.'

'Of course. Anything you say,' the woman replied. 'I'll be at my mother's. And thank you for coming so quickly.'

As Will and Elliott watched the proceedings through the back window of the van, the woman hurriedly left the house, pausing only to scribble down a telephone number for Drake. Then she tore down the street, throwing the odd glance over her shoulder as if it might be the last time she'd ever see the place.

As Will's breath left condensation on the glass, he wiped it away with his sleeve so he could see his old home clearly. 'Number sixteen Broadlands Avenue. I used to live there,' he said distantly, as if trying to convince himself. He pressed his finger against the window and pointed, directing Elliott's attention to the upper floor. 'So weird . . . that's the Rebeccas' bedroom. The vile little snakes slept there, under the same roof as me,' he said, then swivelled round and slumped down against the door. 'This place was all I knew for so long . . . and now I can hardly remember it.'

Elliott hummed, but didn't say anything.

'I'm not going to ask what you lot are up to,' the bald man behind the steering wheel suddenly spoke up. It was Drake's mechanic from the under-the-arches garage in West London, who been brought in to supply them with the mock British Gas van, the overalls Drake and Mrs Burrows were wearing and also their identity cards. It was apparently one of the many services his 'clientele' expected from him, in addition to unregistered vehicles.

The mechanic had met them in a motorway services car park, where Will, Elliott, Mrs Burrows and Drake had trans- ferred from the Bedford to the van for the final leg of the journey to Highfield. 'But whatever your caper is, it's not strictly legit, is it?' the bald mechanic now added.

'Do you really want to know?' Will challenged him.

The mechanic rubbed his chin but didn't reply.

'If I said that we're trying to save the human race, would you believe me? And if we don't succeed, every single person on the surface will die,' Will said, completely straight-faced.

Elliott drew in a breath in surprise.

The mechanic grinned, showing his golden tooth. 'You're right, mate, I shouldn't go sticking my nose in your beeswax.

The less I know the better.' He patted his breast pocket, then chuckled. 'Anyway, the sparklies your Mr Jones gave me are all the answer I need.'

'Mr Smith,' Will corrected him, grinning. 'Mr *Smith* gave you the diamonds.'

At that moment, Mr Smith, who was actually Drake, rapped on the back of the van and then opened the door a few inches. 'The owner's out of the way. I called Sparks and the others – they'll be along when we've prepped the place. But in the meantime, we should—' Noticing the mechanic was listening, he checked himself. '—get the Christmas decorations inside.'

The Christmas decorations were in fact enough explosive to blast through many yards of rock. As Will entered the house, carrying two heavy bags laden with them, he stopped dead. He looked at Mrs Burrows. 'It's all different, Mum,' he gasped. 'The wallpaper's new.' He scuffed his boot on the floor – it was no longer covered with the stained carpet he'd known all his life. 'And this too. They've completely redone the place.'

Drake came up behind him. 'We need the gear downstairs, Will. Okay?'

'Sure,' Will replied, ambling towards the cellar door. 'This is where my dad disappeared every night,' he told Elliott, who was following behind him with a kit bag full of tools. 'Until he disappeared altogether, down to the Colony.'

The cellar was also very different now – very tidy and organised – with peg boards on the walls of carefully arranged power tools. And a partially disassembled vintage Triumph motorbike sat on an oily sheet in the centre of the room.

'Sweet,' Drake said, running a finger over the gleaming

chrome of the handlebars. 'But we need to shift all this out of the way, so we can get at those.' He looked at the shelves, on which there were pots of paint and decorating equipment.

Will and Drake worked quickly, while Mrs Burrows and Elliott between them dragged a mattress down from one of upstairs bedrooms. This was secured against the back door of the cellar leading to the garden, to help deaden any noise they might make while working.

Taking a pickaxe from one of the bags, Drake used the tip to lever the shelves from the wall. As he heaved the unit aside, the others gathered around to see. Behind it there was what appeared to be a stretch of perfectly ordinary wall, painted white.

'Right here,' Will said, going over and tapping the spot where he remembered the tunnel mouth had been. 'It was right here.'

Drake nodded. 'We'll do it the hard way to begin with, using good old elbow grease to knock a hole through. It'll make less noise,' he said. 'Everyone back,' he warned, then swung the pickaxe. Within a matter of minutes, he'd loosened enough bricks that a chunk of the wall dropped onto the cellar floor. A raft of hardcore and gravel slid from the small opening.

'Very clever,' Drake said. 'Precisely what you might expect to find. He continued until he'd increased the size of the opening. 'That's enough. Over to you, Will.' Breathing heavily, Drake turned to the boy. 'We need the spoil cleared away so we can see what we're up against. And you used to enjoy a spot of digging, didn't you?'

Will smiled. 'Sure, but this is going to take ages, isn't it?' He was remembering how many days he and Chester had toiled to re-excavate the tunnel the first time round.

'Not if I can help it,' Drake said. 'Just do your stuff, Will.'

'Okay,' Will replied. He chose a spade from the bag and expertly tested its weight in his hands. Then he spat on his palms. 'Watch out! I'm back!' he announced, and began to dig.

He worked like a whirlwind, only stopping to lift aside the larger pieces of rubble that he encountered. Elliott, Drake and Mrs Burrows had formed a chain and were passing the filled buckets to the end of the cellar where they emptied them out.

With a jarring clang, Will swore and straightened up. 'Bad news – I've hit solid rock. It's a bloody monster of a piece.' He wiped the sweat from his forehead. 'There was nothing like this when I dug the tunnel out.'

Drake didn't seem to be at all disheartened by this news, but before he could respond to Will his walkie-talkie crackled into life. 'Your Christmas turkeys have flown in,' the mechanic's voice announced, using Drake's code. A few moments later, there were footsteps on the wooden stairs, and Eddie descended into the cellar.

'Where are Sweeney and the Colonel?' Mrs Burrows asked. 'And Colly?'

'They're staying with the lorry until we need them,' Eddie replied.

'Hope they're keeping their eyes peeled,' Drake said. 'With that payload, we can't afford to take risks – any number of terrorists or rogue states would give their eye teeth for fissionable material in full weapon configuration. Besides that, Parry would go postal on me if I lost them!' He grinned. 'And while I'm on the subject of explosives,' he went over to one of the large bags that Will had carried into the house and zipped it open, 'it's time to use the charges. We'll just keep blasting until we're through.'

'You've already hit the first barrier?' Eddie enquired.

'You mean this?' Will said, as he turned to slap the uneven wall of rock.

'Yes. It will be approximately five feet in width, followed by more loose material, and then the same thickness of rock again,' Eddie pronounced.

'You seem pretty sure about that,' Drake commented, as he took two pads of explosives from the bag.

Eddie nodded. 'It would be more normal for the tunnel to be collapsed in along its full length, so there'd be no opportunity for anyone to use it again. Particularly after you and Chester came down it,' he said, glancing at Will. 'But there was nothing *normal* about this tunnel. We envisaged that we might need to bring it back into service again.'

Although Will was still contemplating the slab of rock blocking the way, his curiosity was piqued. 'Why? What was so special about it?'

'It was referred to as the Jerome tunnel,' Eddie told him.

Will's head jerked towards the former Limiter. 'The what?' he asked.

'It was named after your blood mother – Sarah Jerome.'

Will frowned.

'Do you think it was simply down to chance that a tunnel led straight to your house?' Eddie put to him.

'I don't know . . . I haven't really thought about it,' Will admitted.

'It was excavated specifically for you, Will, or more specifically, so that there was a quick means to reach you if Sarah showed herself. The Styx Panoply had made her recapture a priority, due to her growing influence as an anti-hero for the more rebellious elements in our city.'

'You mean in the Rookeries,' Will interjected.

'No, not just there, but across the rest of the Colony too. We wanted to reel her in and make an example of her. Of course, when we did eventually apprehend Sarah, the Rebecca twins had other plans for her.'

'Yes, they tried to make her kill me,' Will said quietly, as Eddie peered into the shadows behind him.

'And this tunnel also enabled us to maintain contact with the Styx females you call the Rebecca twins,' Eddie said. 'Particularly when they were first embedded in your family as infants. It enabled us to swap them over as and when we wanted.'

'So you were sneaking into our home, and we didn't know a thing about it,' Will said, stepping closer to Mrs Burrows.

'Mostly at night, to check on you while you slept.' With his boot Eddie rolled over a piece of brick lying on the floor. 'Later on, when Dr Burrows began to drill holes in our hatch, we were forced to reinstate the cellar wall.'

'I was there then!' Will exclaimed, shaking his head. 'I helped him do the drilling, so he could put his shelves up!'

'During his Darklighting sessions, Dr Burrows was given instructions about the existence of the tunnel,' Eddie said. 'We intended that he should discover it, and then be drawn down to the Colony. We knew it was almost a certainty that you'd follow him there, Will.'

'You're saying Roger was *conditioned* to do that?' Mrs Burrows asked. 'It wasn't something he did off his own back?'

'Not at all. In addition to the existence and location of the tunnel, we instilled in him both wanderlust and an overpowering hankering for exploration. Over a period of several years, these were introduced in the form of compulsions deep in his preconscious, ready for us to activate when we decided it was time he should be on his way,' Eddie replied matter-of-factly. 'He was highly receptive to our conditioning. Although I wasn't around to see it, I assume these very same compulsions later drove him to leave the Colony, enter the Deeps, and keep going until he reached the inner world. These actions weren't taken of his own volition, and were not something a man in his right mind would ever contemplate.'

Will let out a sharp breath. 'So . . . so Dad wasn't really some great explorer . . . and all the stuff he was so mad keen to discover . . . to record in his journal . . . that was because of you.' The boy's eyes were wide with disbelief as he tried to articulate the myriad thoughts racing through his head. 'Then, what I thought Dad was . . . wasn't really *him*. You made him that way. The Styx made him something he wasn't?'

'Yes. Like most Topsoilers, Dr Burrows was decidedly unmotivated until we Darklit him,' Eddie said, as he stared at the sightless Mrs Burrows. 'And, of course, we did precisely the opposite to you, Celia. We instilled utter and absolute apathy in you, because there was no role for you to play. It suited us that you did nothing . . . but watch your television.'

For a moment no one in the cellar spoke.

'And I thought I was the one with the dynamite round here,' Drake murmured, putting the explosive pads back into the bag.

As if she was on the verge of fainting, Mrs Burrows was swaying where she stood. 'I knew it,' she croaked several times,

'Mum?' Will said, as he took her arm to steady her.

'All those years . . . I felt as though I was fighting something that wasn't me. I felt as though I was losing myself . . . that I wasn't in control of my life. And I wasn't, because you Styx were dictating who I was. It was all a fabrication . . . a construct! Those thoughts . . . my thoughts were never my own!'

Whether he'd intended it or not, Eddie's response was completely without remorse. 'Yes. I thought that you would have already worked that out for yourself. After all, you managed to overcome the programming when you w—'

'You hijacked our lives,' Mrs Burrows growled accusingly. 'You soured everything with your games, and *all* because you wanted Sarah Jerome.'

'Well, not quite,' Eddie said. 'It was also an opportunity for the Rebecca twins to gain their experience of life amongst the Heathen.'

Nobody had noticed that Mrs Burrows had laid a hand on Will's spade.

With a sudden step forward, she swung it at Eddie. It struck his head with such force he was thrown on top of his daughter.

'Hey! No!' Drake yelled, wresting the spade from Mrs Burrows' hands. But this did nothing to stop her. She was still trying to punch the Styx as Drake pushed her back.

'Keep her away!' Elliott cried, supporting her stunned father. 'She's gone crazy.'

'Mum's not bloody crazy!' Will yelled at Elliott. 'These bastards are. They screwed with our lives! They ruined everything!' He was so furious that he was spitting as he shouted.

The anger seemed to have gone out of Mrs Burrows, but

Drake was now forced to step in between Will and Elliott, his hands outstretched as he kept them apart. 'Everyone just chill. We don't have time for family feuds. Not now.' He half turned toward Mrs Burrows. 'Celia, I want you to take some deep breaths, then go upstairs with Elliott and make tea for everyone. And you two,' he said, looking in turn at Will and Eddie, who was bleeding profusely from the temple, 'we're going to patch up Eddie's noggin, then plant the charges. You can settle your differences later, but right now time is running out for all of us. So is everyone going to behave like adults?'

Elliott hesitated, about to say something.

'I thought I told you to take Celia upstairs,' Drake said firmly.

That was enough for Elliott – she nodded a yes. And Mrs Burrows appeared to have regained full control of herself as she shuffled past Eddie. 'I'm sorry,' she mumbled. 'It was the shock – I really wasn't aware of any of that. It was the shock . . .'

Eddie wiped the blood from his eyes. 'That's quite all right,' he replied, then promptly collapsed.

Eddie was carried up from the cellar and laid out on the sofa in the sitting room. While everyone was fussing over him, Will slipped from the room. He lingered at the foot of the stairs for a moment. The banister had been freshly painted and was so white and clean and perfect that he felt he had to touch it with his grime-encrusted fingers.

He began to climb to the first floor. He'd been up and down the same stairs so many times in his life that, with each step, different memories from his childhood filtered back to him. Saturday lunches, when whichever Rebecca twin was there would prepare a huge fry-up for the family – eggs, sausages, mushrooms, bacon and waffles – all dripping with unhealthy fat. Will smiled; it was strange that the Rebecca twin had never seemed to partake of the food herself. Maybe even then she had been trying to kill them all off?

And Will remembered his mother's lengthy phone conversations with Auntie Jean. He would sometimes sit on the bottom step of the stairs and listen as the two sisters rabbited on about the latest turn of events in some TV soap or other. But when Auntie Jean began to monopolise the conversation with her long lists of what she'd eaten that day and how her unpredictable digestive system was coping with it, or what her precious poodle, Sophie, had got up to, then all Will heard was his mother saying, 'I know . . . I know . . . I know,' in a bored voice. On a couple of occasions, Mrs Burrows had even nodded off while her sister was still talking.

But as he reached the landing, Will realised that what he'd accepted as normal family life was far from it, and what he was remembering might as well have been scenes from a play. If it wasn't enough that the part of his sister had been shared by two girls – if *girls* was the right word, because they weren't even human – the Styx had been directing and manipulating everything in the house with their Dark Light sessions for years.

'None of it was real,' Will whispered.

And even the stage on which this farce had been performed was no longer there. As he surveyed the landing before him, everything was different. The fitted shelving unit had gone, the paper ball lampshade replaced, and the brand-new carpet didn't have those patches in it where the weave was completely worn away.

With the sensation that he was dreaming, Will crossed to

the room at the front of the house. He'd always been strictly forbidden from entering because it had been 'Rebecca's' bedroom, but now it was being used as a study. Will cast his eye over the desk and the expensive computer, his gaze settling on the cork notice board on the wall behind. In the many photographs pinned to it he recognised the woman who now lived in the house. The pictures had been taken in a variety of different locations, and in most of them she was accompanied by a man who was probably her husband.

Will leant over and pulled one of them from the board, the drawing pin securing it flipping onto the desk. In the photograph the woman and her husband were toasting each other with half coconuts, which had little cocktail umbrellas and stripy straws in them, and a fire-lit beach was visible behind their relaxed, tanned faces.

Then there were all the baby photographs, so Will knew what he'd probably find when he went into his old bedroom. Sure enough, there was a cot, soft toys everywhere, and the walls were a washed-out azure with fluffy cloud stickers slapped all over them. Not the slightest trace remained of Will's tenure of the room. Not the shelves where he'd kept his collection of finds, nor the posters he'd taped to the ceiling, of the Roman centurion and the Fire of London. He went to the window, where a mobile of brightly coloured caterpillars and butterflies was gently swaying in an air current.

He poked a finger in the face of one of the smug-looking caterpillars. 'Don't bite me! Don't bite me!' he said in a whimsical voice.

'I'm a Styx Warrior larva, and I *am* going to bite you,' he replied to himself, assuming a monster's gruff voice.

'No! Ow! Ow! Ow!' Will said, chuckling to himself as he

jabbed at the caterpillar and it bounced around on its length of string. Then he became distracted by the sight of the garden below. The lawn was under snow, but he could tell it wasn't overgrown as it had been in his time. And there were some recent additions to the garden: a paved area, a circular flowerbed and, in front of the new fence at the far end, a child's swing and sandpit.

Shaking his head, Will let out a breath from the side of his mouth. It wasn't *his* garden any more. It looked like a thousand others.

Perhaps it was better that he simply tore up his past and moved on.

At least what he was living now was genuine and not some Styx construct.

He heard Drake calling for him.

'Eat that, ugly bug!' he said, punching the caterpillar so hard that the whole mobile was spinning wildly as he left the room.

There was a rumble as the first detonation shook the building and the street around it. Everyone except for Drake had decamped from the house, and Will and Sweeney were watching from the back of the mock gas van.

'That felt like an earthquake,' Will said, as the van rocked slightly on its suspension. The only other signs were some snow sliding from the roof and a couple of car alarms going off further down the street.

After a moment Drake opened the front door, shrouded by a cloud of dust. He waved at the van. 'We're on again,' Sweeney said to Will. 'No, wait up – we've got a neighbour sticking his oar in.'

A man was hanging around on the pavement and peering at the house. Drake went over to speak to him, showing him his fake credentials.

The mechanic in the front of the van had been leaning over to watch the proceedings in his wing mirror. 'If he turns into a problem, I'll deal with him,' he said, as the curious neighbour scurried off. 'Otherwise I'll just hang on here until you or Mr Smith need something. And if you make it through to Australia, let me know. I've never been there.'

Will and Sweeney jumped out, but Will made a quick detour to the rear of the Bedford, pulling himself up on the tailgate to peer through the canvas awning. Elliott was sitting with Eddie, who clearly hadn't recovered yet from being struck with the spade. He appeared to be asleep, his eyes closed.

'How's he doing?' Will asked.

'A little concussed, but he'll be okay,' Elliott replied. 'Styx are pretty thick-headed.'

'Um – yes – that's good,' Will said, unsure whether Elliott was being serious or not. He was still feeling profoundly ashamed of the way he'd flared up with her after his mother's outburst.

And Mrs Burrows also seemed to be regretting her actions, as she sat meekly in the corner with Colly. The Colonel had a pistol at the ready as he stood guard over the equipment, which was covered in a tarpaulin and secured with rope. Will glanced at the shapes under the tarpaulin, thinking how strange it was to be that close to atomic weapons.

As he entered the house, he found Sweeney waiting for him in the hallway. 'Ready for round two?' the man asked.

'Yep,' Will said, waving his hand through the dust-laden

air. He noticed a picture had fallen to the ground and that several rather severe cracks had opened up in the walls. 'We're going to trash this place. What a shame, after all the work they've put into it,' he added.

The dust was even thicker in the cellar, where Drake was already shovelling the debris from the tunnel. Will and Sweeney set to work right away, helping him to clear the spoil so they could inspect what progress they'd made.

'We've gained another four feet or so,' Drake said. 'A couple more goes with the charges should get us through.'

'If the roof holds up,' Will said, as he inspected it for any signs of weakness. 'Not too bad,' he decided, running his hand over a small fissure in the rock.

'Yes, I'm placing the charges so they direct all their force into the face itself. If Eddie's right and the Styx didn't knobble the roof, we're going to be just fine,' Drake said. 'It's not as if it matters if it gives way after we've gone through.'

'Poor house,' Will said.

As arranged, a handful of Eddie's former Limiters turned up to help with the work on the tunnel. It was odd watching them labouring in silence, but Will was grateful for the extra manpower.

It took three more rounds with the explosives to punch a way through the rock plug in the tunnel. And, at the end of the process, so much spoil had been generated that in places it reached up to the cellar roof. Even the motorbike Drake had so admired had been completely buried. The only relatively clear area was a corridor from the bottom of the stairs to the tunnel entrance.

'Let's have a look, shall we?' Drake said, pushing aside the debris so he and Will could move deeper into the tunnel, past where the blockage had been.

'This brings back a few memories,' Will murmured, as they followed the passage around a corner. And there it was – the crescent-shaped chamber with walls of milky rock, that Will had first discovered with Chester.

As Will and Drake peered around, the beams from their miner's lights seemed to penetrate the translucent rock itself and make it glow. Much of the grotto floor was submerged under rust-coloured water. Will was wading quickly through this in his haste to reach the door he knew lay at the far end of the grotto when he turned to Drake. 'You know, I thought this place was the best thing I'd ev—'

'STOP!' Drake yelled, his voice booming within the confines of the chamber.

Will almost lost his footing as he threw himself into reverse.

In the blink of an eye Drake was beside him. 'Keep – Very – Still,' he said in a deliberate way that told Will it was critical he did precisely as he'd been told. 'Not an inch backwards – or forwards,' Drake added. 'You're hooked up.'

'What do you mean?' Will asked. Keeping his head still, he swivelled his eyes as far as he could. Drake's outstretched hand was poised by a taut wire, which extended horizontally across the cavern, and directly in their path.

'Jesus. I'm touching it,' Will whispered as he realised that the wire was actually resting against his chest. It was so fine as to be almost invisible. All that gave it away was the glistening droplets of moisture along its length as Drake's miner's light played on them

'Very bloody sneaky weaky,' Drake said. He traced where

the wire ran to the middle of the grotto, culminating amongst the wreckage of a machine which lay in the deeper water. Whatever the machine had once been, it was now a mass of corroded iron cogs in a twisted frame.

'So the tripwire's secured there . . .' Drake whispered, then moved behind Will so he could trace the route of the wire in the opposite direction. 'Always be on the look-out for secondaries,' he said, as he took extra care about where he was treading in the shallow water. He reached the grotto wall and extracted several items from a pouch on his belt.

Will couldn't see what he was doing. 'What's there? Can I move now?' he asked, barely daring to breathe.

'Mot . . . am . . . mufscle,' Drake replied, a screwdriver gripped between his teeth. He swapped it for the penknife he'd been using, then another minute passed before he finally announced, 'Okay. Done.'

The tripwire suddenly zinged away towards the ruined machine, and Will finally let out his breath.

'Here!' Drake lobbed something at Will. With a cry of alarm, he caught it. Many dull marble-sized ball bearings spilled from a small canister, dropping all around Will's feet with little splashes. Drake had removed a panel in the canister and a few remaining bearings rattled around inside it, against a stick of what looked like Plasticine.

'Styx antipersonnel explosive device mark 3. Guaranteed to ruin your day, or your money back,' Drake said. 'In future, Sweeney or I will take point.'

'You got it,' Will agreed, tipping the last of the bearings from the canister.

Because there wasn't enough room in the cellar, all their

equipment was taken into the sitting room and laid out so Drake could give it a last check. Will and Elliott were watching as Sweeney and Colonel Bismarck lugged the second of the two nuclear weapons into the hallway. Mrs Burrows immediately shut the front door behind them.

'They look heavy,' Will remarked. The stainless-steel box was only around four by six feet in size, but the two men were grunting with the effort as they carried it using the handles at either end.

'Okay. Everyone on me,' Drake called from the sitting room.

'Where do you want the second TND, boss?' Sweeney asked, as he and the Colonel entered, sidestepping around a coffee table.

'Over there will do – by the first,' Drake answered.

Will was at the door, peering at the impressive amount of kit inside the room. 'If that woman could see what was going on in her home right now!' he said.

Sweeney grinned. 'Yes, reckon she might be a little brassed off that her view of the telly was blocked by a couple of atom bombs.'

'Particularly if *Countdown* was on,' Mrs Burrows added, as Sweeney and the Colonel lowered the device beside the second one, and then straightened up, rubbing their hands.

Drake had been squatting beside a curious-looking piece of equipment laid on the coffee table. 'Come in and shut the door, Will,' he said, as if even now he didn't completely trust Eddie's men, who were still in the house.

'Right, before we set off there are a few things I need to say.' He indicated the devices in front of the television. 'Moving the nukes is going to be a real back-breaker until we reach the lower grav environment towards the centre of the Earth. The bombs themselves aren't that heavy, but because of their antiquated design there's a hunk of lead in the casings around them.'

'Then can't we just lose the casings?' Elliott proposed.

'The fissile plutonium in the bombs throws off too much radiation – we'd be glowing like neon signs before we'd gone any distance. But it might come to that yet,' Drake said, his expression grim. 'This mission isn't going to be a walk in the park.' He ran his eyes over Mrs Burrows who had Colly beside her, the Colonel, then Will, Elliott and Sweeney. 'And Eddie's not going to be with us on this one.'

'Because of his head?' Will asked, not looking at Elliott.

Drake nodded. 'He needs time to recover, but it's not that. I don't know what the current situation is in the Colony, but if the Styx are still there in any number, it's better he keeps out of sight. Anyway, he's more use to us here on the surface, where he and his men can work with Parry and the Old Guard to find the Styx women.'

'Unless they've all gone underground,' Colonel Bismarck said.

'True,' Drake concurred. 'What Danforth told us about resuming the Phase in the inner world might have been nothing more than a ploy to throw us off the scent. However, we need to find that out for ourselves.' He took a breath. 'Right, unless anyone has any questions, let's saddle up,' he said.

'I have,' Will said. 'What's that? A weapon?' He was looking at the device on the coffee table. Three slim metal tanks, each a metre in length, were welded together, with a pistol grip halfway down, and some sort of funnel or nozzle mounted at one end.

'A little something my mechanic friend outside in the van knocked up for me,' Drake replied. 'In fact, he's made me several versions of it.'

Will edged closer to the table to inspect the device. By the base of the nozzle, tubes from the three tanks were intertwined in a Gordian knot, on which there were a number of knurled knobs.

Drake picked up the device and, taking hold of the grip, slid back a catch and clicked the trigger. A blinding blue flame roared from the nozzle.

Will leapt back in surprise, raising an arm to shield his face from the heat. 'It's a flamethrower!'

'No, this isn't a weapon. I won't bore you with the principles,' Drake said, the flame phutting out as he released the trigger, 'but two high-octane propellants mix with oxygen to create a powerful propulsion device . . . a booster. So we don't have to rely on a Sten to produce the thrust to get us across the zero-grav belt, like you and your father did.'

'That's so cool,' Will said. 'I can't believe you know how to do that. It looks really complicated.'

'Nah – it's hardly rocket science,' Drake said dismissively, then frowned. 'No, I suppose it really *is* rocket science,' he added, correcting himself.

Having gathered up their equipment, Will and Elliott went down to the cellar. Eddie's men were waiting there – Drake had said that they'd collapse the mouth of the tunnel so the Topsoil authorities wouldn't find it.

Elliott spoke to several of them in the Styx language, then she and Will entered the tunnel, quickly moving to the far end of the crescent-shaped grotto. Will showed her the iron door with the three handles down one side that he and Chester had first discovered together.

'This was where it all kicked off,' he told her, rapping its battered surface with his knuckles. It rang with a low, resounding tone, until he touched it again, tracing around an area of shiny black paint with a fingertip, and remembering. 'There was no turning back when I found this door – well, not for me, anyway. I don't think Chester was happy about it at the time, but he still came along.'

'Poor old Chester – he's like that. He's a loyal friend to you,' Elliott said.

And look where it got him, Will was thinking as Drake appeared. 'You can open up. I've checked for Styx anti-personnel mines,' Drake said.

Will immediately clunked up the three handles on the side of the door, then stepped back. 'Ladies first,' he said to Elliott.

She leant on the door and it groaned open on its hinges. Then she stepped over the metal lip at the base of the door frame and went into the cylindrical chamber. Once they'd gone the short distance to other side, Drake joined them and Will cranked the three handles on the second door, which was identical to the first.

Then, without even troubling to glance through the hazy porthole, he heaved it open. There was a sibilant hiss as the air equalised.

'At least that means the Fan Stations are still operating, doesn't it? So the Colony's getting air,' Will said to Drake.

'I hope so,' Drake replied noncommittally.

Will and Elliott moved through the antechamber, the beam from Will's miner's light lancing the moisture-laden air. The walls themselves were a patchwork quilt of rusted metal plates studded with rivets.

Will caught his breath as he made out the shaft up ahead. There, waiting for them, was the cage lift itself, ready to take them down.

Will went to open the trellis door to the lift, but glanced at Drake to see if he should proceed.

Drake nodded, his miner's light bouncing up, then Will slid the gate back and went in.

'Safe as houses,' he whispered to himself, but this time he didn't feel like jumping up and down.

The equipment and nuclear weapons were ferried down in several trips because Drake didn't want to overload the old lift. When it had all been moved and everyone was down too, Will began for the door to the second metal chamber.

'Hold up,' Drake said. 'I need to investigate that airlock first. I haven't risked opening it yet, in case it's alarmed.' He turned to everyone. 'Weapons at the ready. And you should also have your tranquiliser guns close to hand in case we bump into any Colonists.' He paused for a moment. 'There's something you should be aware of. When we were last in London, I picked up a distress signal from the Colony.'

'What do you mean?' Mrs Burrows asked.

'I left a radio beacon with your friend the Second Officer. It was tuned to a specific frequency, and I told him to use it if things got difficult in the Colony and he needed help. Well, he did.'

Mrs Burrows looked troubled. 'Why didn't you mention this before n—'

'Because we had bigger fish to fry at the time,' Drake interrupted. 'So I've really no idea quite what we're going to find when we go through that airlock.'

Mrs Burrows was shaking her head as she placed her hand protectively on the Hunter at her side, who immediately began to purr loudly. 'I brought Colly along because I wanted to take her home. If I'd known what you've just told me, I'd have made other plans – I'd have left her with Sergeant Finch.'

'She'll be fine. She can come with us on the journey – she looks healthy enough,' Drake argued.

'Yes, she's healthy enough,' Mrs Burrows said a little curtly. 'But do you really expect her to have her litter on the hoof?'

Everyone turned to look at the Hunter who, aware of the sudden interest in her, stopped purring.

'Litter?' Will said.

'Yes, Bartleby's offspring,' Mrs Burrows answered. 'Why do you think she's put on so much weight?'

Drake sighed. 'Look, let's see what the situation is in the Colony, then we'll work something out. Okay?'

'Okay, I suppose,' Mrs Burrows said.

They all held back as Sweeney and Drake checked the door into the airlock for booby traps, then opened it.

As if she couldn't wait to find out what state the Colony was in, Mrs Burrows was right behind the two men.

Sweeney was halfway across the corrugated flooring when he suddenly missed a step and staggered. He was groping for the side of the airlock as if his legs couldn't support him. Drake was immediately on the case, pulling the larger man back with him.

'No! Colly!' Mrs Burrows shouted. The Hunter had collapsed beside her. She was out cold.

'Get the cat out!' Drake yelled at the Colonel and Will.

Sweeney seemed to recover as soon as he was helped towards the lift. Colly however remained completely unconscious.

'What is it?' Mrs Burrows said. 'We can't have this – she's pregnant!'

Drake pointed to his ear. 'It's a subaural field. They've put one around the door to stop anyone using it. Sweeney was wearing his plugs, but he's hypersensitive to most frequencies. And, of course, Colly had no protection at all.'

'But she'll be all right?' Elliott asked, running a hand over the cat's plump stomach.

'She should be,' Drake replied. 'Now, you're all going to get as far back as you can, because – in time-honoured fashion – the Colonel and I are going to blow our way through.'

Chapter Twenty

In Market Square, a large paved area at the centre of the South Cavern, people were gathering to hear what the Board of Governors had to say. Word of the forthcoming meeting had gone around, and most, if not all, of the remaining occupants of the subterranean city were turning up.

The Governors hadn't been much in evidence lately. But since the Styx had abruptly vanished, they'd crept out from wherever they'd been hiding, clearly with the intention of reasserting their authority over the Colony.

Before the recent troubles, the square had thronged with people on market days as they purchased goods from the numerous rows of carts. But now these carts had been wheeled to the side to make room, although a few people were standing on them to get a better view of the Governors.

And almost the full complement of Governors was present on a hastily erected platform. There should have been twelve of them, but one of their number was unwell; Mr Cruickshank was suffering badly with gout and hadn't been able to leave his bed. The rest, all decked out in their tall stovepipe top hats, formal black coats and grey pinstripe trousers, were sitting stiffly behind a long table on the platform. When it was time for the meeting to start, the eleven men removed their top hats from their heads and placed them on the table before them. Then, Mr Pearson, the most senior Governor, rose to his feet.

With his lugubrious expression and the painfully slow way he spoke, he began to lecture the people about 'Keeping order', and how it was 'a Colonist's duty to his neighbour to obey the age-old laws'. Sir Gabriel Martineau's name kept cropping up as Mr Pearson wittered on; he obviously believed that frequent references to the Colony's founder would resonate with the audience, and make them more compliant.

But although the crowd was listening, they weren't pleased with what they were hearing. The Governors had been the puppets of the Styx, merely putting into effect whatever the real ruling class ordained. And with the Styx out of the picture, it was inevitable that there wouldn't be the same degree of respect for these officials.

'We have . . .' Mr Pearson proclaimed, one hand tucked into his waistcoat as he wagged a finger at the rock canopy far above, '. . . we have known hard times for these past months. We have all been parted from family and neighbours, although we don't yet know the reason for this. And we don't know where they have been taken, or when they will be returned to us again.'

'Never,' a woman in the crowd muttered.

'And when our lords themselves return, you can be assured that we, the Board, will ask them these very questions,' Mr Pearson said in answer to the woman.

With this reference to the Styx, a ripple of disapproval spread through the crowd.

'And until the *status quo* is restored, we will ensure that our daily routines are back to normal, and that we are not troubled by outbreaks of lawlessness from the small handful of malcontents in our society,' Mr Pearson said. 'For down here, we have only each other. We are one big society, and we look after our own.'

With great ceremony, he turned to the Governors on his left, and then those on his right. All ten officials were saying, 'Hear, hear,' with great emphasis, and nodding like a row of drunken monkeys to show their agreement.

Mr Pearson addressed the crowd again. 'We have all been in the same boat. In recent months, we have all known the turbulent waters . . . we've been hungry, confused and frightened by the inexplicable changes taking place in our lives. But never you fear, the Board is here to reinstate law and order.' He paused, as if expecting a cheer from the crowd, but the only reaction was stony silence.

He cleared his throat, then went on. 'Our first act will be to find an open portal, so deliveries of Topsoil food-supplements are resumed forthwith. But, just as importantly, the production of our staple foods – those foods on which we rely so heavily – will also be restored. Livestock breeding and rodent collection are a priority and, as I speak, the penny-bun fields in the North are being prepared for sporing, and—'

'Ain't seen you doing no diggin',' a Colonist said loudly.

'Yeah, roll yer sleeves up yerself, Pearson,' a second added.

Mr Pearson ran a finger inside his starched collar and ignored the hecklers as he tried to continue. But in the depths of the crowd, a Colonist coughed at some volume. Although it wasn't a real cough.

The man had ducked his head and shouted the word 'Gazunder'.

The crowd tittered.

All but a few citizens of the Colony had dispensed with the rather archaic practice of using a Gazunder, or chamber pot – the porcelain bowl kept under the bed into which they could relieve themselves during the night if the need took them. Instead they would make the effort to go downstairs to the water closet, usually to be found at the back of the house.

But not Mr Pearson.

And, being one of the privileged class, Mr Pearson was too high and mighty to swill out his own urine in the mornings. Because of his high standing, he'd always had a servant – normally a captured Topsoiler, or if one wasn't available, some low ranking Colonist who'd been pressed into service in his household – and it would be their unfortunate lot to see to the distasteful task. And on some days it had been known for the Gazunder to be emptied rather late in the day, so its odours would circulate downstairs and permeate the rest of his house. It wasn't pleasant.

Another joker in the crowd took his cue from the first. He pretended to sneeze loudly, although he actually shouted the word 'Potty' for all to hear.

The braver members of the crowd erupted with laughter.

Someone had dared to utter the most senior Governor's nickname – he was widely known as *Potty* Pearson in the Colony. Or – on occasions – something rather more impolite than that.

This was a brazen display of lack of respect.

Mr Pearson's face went deep puce, and he bunched his fists. As he resembled an over-stoked boiler, one could almost imagine that steam was going to blast from his ears.

'I will not tolerate this boorishness!' he bellowed. 'First Officer! Detain those people!' Mr Pearson went even redder. 'Where are you, First Officer? Report to me right now! I want those responsible locked up in the Hold!'

The new First Officer appeared at the side of the platform, then clambered up onto it. The planks of the makeshift dais creaked and shook under his bulk, and several of the Governors gripped the table as if they thought they might at any moment be plunged into the great unwashed before them.

By this time, Will, Drake and Mrs Burrows had reached Market Square and were moving slowly around the edge of the crowd. They were receiving some curious glances from the people on the carts, but on the whole these Colonists were far too engrossed by the public display of insolence unfolding before them to take much notice. In any case, with all the New Germanian troops billeted in the Colony over the past months, they had become far more used to seeing outsiders in their midst.

'Do your job! Arrest them!' Mr Pearson insisted, stamping his foot, which caused the platform to shake all over again.

The First Officer scanned the faces in the crowd, noticing Cleaver and Squeaky close to the front. He hadn't yet informed the Governors that his predecessor had released all the prisoners detained in the Hold. And he wasn't looking forward to telling them.

Cleaver grinned, showing his missing teeth, and Squeaky began to jump up and down.

Another of the Governors leapt to his feet. 'Do what you're told, man! Apprehend those dissenters!' he shouted.

'But . . . arrest *who* precisely?' the First Officer asked. 'Which ones?'

'I know that voice,' Drake said, as he helped Mrs Burrows onto an unoccupied cart, which was covered with a few desiccated cabbage leaves. Then he climbed up beside her. Will was already on the cart, watching the stage intently and shaking his head.

The ranting Governor had turned on the First Officer, who was looking nonplussed. 'Just follow your orders, you useless fool!' he snarled.

'That stupid, stupid old fart!' Will exclaimed loudly, making no effort to keep his voice low. The Colonists close to the cart twisted around to look at him.

'Keep it down, Will,' Drake warned, but he was intrigued by the boy's unexpected vehemence. 'Why did you say that, anyway?'

'Because that stupid spod is my father.'

'Your *what*?' Drake said.

'That's Mr Jerome,' Will muttered. 'My real father.'

Mr Jerome was strutting across the stage towards the First Officer. As he reached him, he began to jab a finger into the chest of the taller and far bigger man. 'If you don't do what you're ordered, we'll clap you in irons too,' he promised.

The First Officer wasn't intimidated, just perplexed. 'But if I don't know who called Mr Pissy a Potty, then how can I arrest anyone?' he asked innocently.

Rather than cheer at the First Officer's fabulously confused sentence, a deathly quiet fell on the place.

'You blithering idiot!' Mr Jerome snapped, drawing his hand back as if he was about to strike the policeman.

All of a sudden, there was a commotion at the front of the crowd. Cleaver was surging forward, pushing through to the platform.

His voice dripped with the violence of which he was capable. 'Don't you lay a finger on 'im! 'E's my friend!' Cleaver rumbled, then pounded the stage with one of his sledgehammer fists. 'Or I'll come up there meeself and sort both you and Mr Pissy out.'

'Mr Potty,' Squeaky corrected Cleaver, bobbing up and down as he tried to see over his shoulder.

Mr Jerome hadn't backed off from the First Officer, his hand still poised in the air.

'I'm warnin' you,' Cleaver said, spoiling for a fight.

An ear-piercing wolf whistle from beside Will and Drake made them both start.

As every single person in Market Square, Colonist and Governor alike, sought out who was responsible for this, Mrs Burrows took her fingers from her mouth.

Drake bowed his head. 'Jesus, and I said we should keep a low profile,' he muttered.

'Isn't it time for a new start?' Mrs Burrows proclaimed in a shout. 'The Styx have gone, and you don't have to take them back. For the first time in three hundred years, you have the chance to run your own lives.'

Everyone considered this, then there were mutters of 'Yes,' and 'She's right.'

'Celia,' the First Officer said, beaming at her over the heads of the crowd. He had to take a breath before he went on, because he still couldn't quite believe his eyes. 'Tell us what to do. Tell us how to go about it.'

Mrs Burrows thought for a moment. 'Well, for starters . . . you can send those Governors packing,' she said. 'They haven't got your best interests at heart.'

Mr Jerome was craning his neck and squinting at who was

on the cart. 'Why, look at what we've got here. A bunch of loathsome Topsoilers sticking their nose into our business,' he said.

'Oh, put a sock in it, you old bore!' Will blurted, not able to help himself.

There was a pause, then Mr Jerome frowned. 'Seth? My son, Seth?'

Will curled his lip curled insolently. 'I'm no son of yours.'

Clearly in some shock at seeing Will again, Mr Jerome took a moment to compose himself. 'So . . . so my runaway son has returned home, and his friends are telling us what to do.' He laughed drily, then turned to the First Officer. 'Well, you can arrest them too.'

The First Officer had had enough. 'No, I won't,' he said simply.

Mr Pearson re-entered the fray. Seizing his top hat from the table, he brandished it threateningly in the First Officer's face. 'See this? We are the only authority here! You damned well do what Mr Jerome has ordered.'

'I told yer to leave my friend alone,' Cleaver exploded. 'I've 'ad it with yer! Why don't yer shut yer flippin' cake 'oles and let 'im say 'is piece?' Cleaver roared, leaning forward over the platform and swiping at Mr Pearson and Mr Jerome's ankles like an angry bear.

As the two Governors hastily hopped out of Cleaver's reach, the First Officer turned to the crowd. 'If any of you think those people on the cart are *just* Topsoilers, think again. The woman who just spoke was talking sense,' he said, point-ing at Mrs Burrows, his eyes gleaming. 'She was subjected to the worst Dark Light interrogation I've ever seen in my whole time as a policeman, and she came back from it. She didn't crack . . . she didn't tell the Styx what they wanted to know.'

The crowd murmured.

'And that man there . . .' he indicated Drake, '. . . destroyed the Laboratories for us. He put a stop to all the Styx's horrific experiments. I know because I was there. I helped him.'

The murmur became even louder.

'And the lad with them,' the First Officer declared, as he pointed directly at Will, 'is Tam Macaulay's nephew, and . . .'

There was a collective gasp from the crowd – they knew what was coming next.

'. . . and Sarah Jerome's son.'

Now people were cheering.

'Sarah Jerome, a brave woman who stuck to her beliefs and resisted the Styx for so long . . . for so many years. We could do nothing to help her when she was brought back to the Colony, but we can honour her spirit now. We can do things her way, and never let the White Necks rule our lives again.'

The crowd went wild. Filled with pride, Will wasn't at all embarrassed by the attention he was getting.

The First Officer raised his arms and the crowd quietened. 'So, Mrs Burrows, what should we do now?' he posed.

'You could appoint a committee to oversee the Colony – a temporary committee,' Mrs Burrows advised. 'You can hold an election later, but right now you need people in place who'll get things done. Your own people – people you trust.'

'Codswallop! *They* wouldn't have the faintest idea how to run things!' Mr Pearson shouted. 'This is sheer lunacy! That woman's a Topsoiler. Don't listen to anything she says!'

'First Officer, we want *you* to lead us,' a man suddenly yelled out.

'Me?' the First Officer spluttered.

As the suggestion gathered support, the First Officer waved the crowd to order. 'But . . . it can't be me alone. That wouldn't be right.'

'Pick Cleaver too!' Gappy Mulligan screeched. Waving a bottle, she was perched on a water butt on the far side of the square, and only just managed to stop herself from falling off.

The crowd seemed to be completely behind this suggestion, and jostled Cleaver until he clambered up onto the platform.

That was when the whole structure tipped to one side, the table, chairs and Governors sliding off. As their feet found the ground, to a man the Governors fled.

The applause from the crowd rattled every window in the city. Cleaver and Squeaky took the opportunity to help themselves to a pair of the Governors' discarded top hats, and were sporting them proudly.

'I wish every coup went off this peacefully,' Drake whispered. And he – like everyone else in Market Square – was filled with optimism for the future of the Colony. With no Styx to terrorise the population and with the opportunity to govern themselves, it would be a very different place to live.

A mile away, on the outskirts of the city, Elliott heard the echoed shouts and cheers of the crowd, but didn't know the reason for them. After Sweeney and Colonel Bismarck had failed to persuade her from going off by herself, she'd sprinted all the way down to the South Cavern, not encountering a single Colonist or, for that matter, Styx, as she went.

And now, as she entered her old neighbourhood, she

slowed to take in the surroundings so familiar to her.

The Colony was similar to an ancient but highly reliable piece of machinery that functioned day-in, day-out, because its inhabitants kept it running smoothly. By and large, each Colonist knew his or her place in the hierarchy, and like cogs in the machine they all did what was expected of them.

But this machine had evidently broken down. What Elliott saw around her was unprecedented chaos: streets strewn with foul-smelling rubbish, piles of wrecked furniture heaped in front of houses, and even people's personal belongings scattered in the gutters. There were signs of neglect and turmoil everywhere she turned.

Finally Elliott came to the terraced house in which she'd grown up. This was the house she'd left early one morning when she'd run away to the Deeps, leaving behind all she knew.

As a child she'd learnt to live with the lie that her aunt was her mother, but the risk of being outed as a Drain Baby grew as she grew. And although choosing to go to the Deeps was tantamount to committing suicide, the alternative would have been worse. Not only would Elliott and her real mother have immediately been put to death by the Styx for the illicit liaison, the rest of the family would most likely have been lynched for their part in the cover up.

And whispers had already begun to circulate in the neighbourhood about Elliott's dark eyes and Styx-thin physique, with one man attempting to extort money from her aunt in return for his silence. Elliott decided that she had to disappear from the Colony, so removing any grounds for blackmail or discovery.

Walking slowly up the path, Elliott's gaze strayed over the

lawns of black lichen to either side where she'd played as a child. From the state they were in, it was evident that they hadn't been tended to for some time. But unlike many others in the street, the house itself looked lived in. Elliott was encouraged by that.

She reached out and pushed on the front door. It wasn't locked, and swung open a few inches.

'Hello,' she called.

For a moment she was distracted by a huge roar from the crowd elsewhere in the city.

'Hello,' Elliott repeated, although she sensed that the house was empty. She raised her foot to step over the threshold, but then stopped herself. Inside there would probably be signs to confirm her mother still lived there. But Elliott knew that her reappearance and the way she looked now would just reignite the old suspicions, and her mother's secret would become known. There was little doubt in Elliott's mind that the age-old prejudices about Styx-Colonist interrelationships would persist.

And part of her was also reluctant to find out about her mother. The mission to the centre of the Earth was fraught with danger, and Elliott was only too aware she might not return from it with her life. Perhaps it was better to embark on it with the belief that her mother was still alive and well.

'I'll come back another day,' Elliott said out loud, pulling the door shut. Tucking her hand inside her jacket, she took out the bottle of perfume Mrs Burrows had given her and placed it carefully on the doorstep. 'That's for you, Mother,' she whispered, then turned from the house.

Chapter Twenty-one

'This is what I wanted you to see,' the First Officer said to Drake, Will and Mrs Burrows. Drake was keen to leave the Colony and continue their journey, but he also knew it was important to help the First Officer in any way he could now the city had declared its independence.

And, as they turned the corner, there was the Styx Citadel.

With its stark facade of roughly hewn granite, it was built into the cavern wall itself, extending all the way up to the canopy high above, where it disappeared into the ever-present clouds that swirled and lapped there. And never had any Colonist been known to set foot inside the forbidding building.

'This is the closest I've been to it,' Will whispered, as the black crystal windows marking the upper levels of the Citadel stared down on him like pitiless Styx eyes.

The First Officer stopped at the open gate in the iron railings, and a large man holding a pickaxe handle came out to meet them from the watchman's cabin. 'This is Joseph,' the First Officer said. 'He and another citizen have been guarding the compound around the clock, in case the White Necks decide to come back.'

Drake nodded at Joseph, who was deep-chested and stocky, typical of the *pure stock*, as they were known – descendents of the original army of labourers who had helped Martineau to build the subterranean city some three hundred years ago, and then populate it. Joseph was staring fixedly at Will, which the boy began to find rather unsettling.

'Very wise,' Drake said. He indicated the man's pickaxe handle. 'But you're going to need more firepower than that.' For a moment he considered the Garrison, a squat, two-storey building beside the Citadel, letting his gaze linger on the entrance. But then he struck out for the Citadel itself. When he was some forty feet away from it, he bent to pick up a stone, which he slung at its doors. The stone struck them, clattering down the front steps. As nothing happened, Drake began to move closer to the building.

'Stop!' the First Officer shouted. 'It'll knock you down!'

It wasn't just the portals that the Styx had protected with their subaural fields. The First Officer had already been called out to rescue several unconscious Colonists who'd been incapacitated by the one around this building.

Drake paid him no notice, mounting the steps at the entrance.

'How can he do that?' the First Officer asked, as Drake appeared to be completely unaffected by the field. He was checking all around the entrance, pushing on the huge stone slab where the doorway had previously been. Then he walked backwards from the building, examining the windows which began on the upper floors.

As he rejoined everybody, Drake was yawning and working his jaw as if he had chronic earache. 'There's an immensely strong field around it,' he said to Will and Mrs Burrows.

Then he addressed the First Officer. 'The Styx have brought down protective barriers inside the building and completely sealed it, so I have no way of telling if there are any left inside.'

The First Officer looked extremely uncomfortable at this. 'You know that it's rumoured there are various Topsoil routes down into the building, so . . .' he turned to regard the Citadel, 'so this might be where they return to take control of us again.'

'They can try,' Drake said.

'But you'll be ready for them,' Mrs Burrows chipped in.

'Let's investigate the Garrison building,' Drake suggested to Will.

'Um,' Joseph began. He still couldn't seem to keep his eyes off Will.

'What is it?' the First Officer said.

'Can I accompany you?' Joseph asked Drake. 'You see, I used to work there.'

The First Officer was about to object to this request when Drake reached into a pouch on his belt and took out a spare pair of earplugs. 'Put these in,' he said to Joseph.

As Drake set off towards the Garrison, Will and Joseph were following a short distance behind him.

'Seth?' Joseph began nervously.

Will turned to him. 'It's really *Will*. I'm not called that any more.'

'Sorry,' the man whispered, running his hand over the stubbly white hair on his scalp. Then he spoke with more assurance. 'I knew Sarah, your mother.'

'You did?' Will asked.

'We were friends when we were young.' Joseph frowned,

and seemed to have difficulty in continuing. 'The last time she was here . . . when the White Necks trapped her and brought her back, we saw each other again. I looked after her for the weeks she stayed in the Garrison.'

Although Joseph had lowered his head, Will could see that his expression was incredibly sad. And when the man gave Will a fleeting look, his pale blue eyes – with identical colouration to Will's own eyes – seemed to reflect the light as if they were brimming with tears.

'I think she knew what was coming,' Joseph mumbled. 'She could tell it wasn't going to end well for her.'

Will suddenly felt such a strong kinship with this massive man that he briefly put his arm around him as they continued to walk. Like Joseph, Will too was overcome with sadness, but at that moment they reached the entrance. Will could feel the buzzing in his skull – there was a field around the steel doors, but, surprisingly, they were unlocked.

They entered the building, and Will walked the polished stone floor that his real mother had once trod, with her friend beside him.

'I don't think she ever really believed a single word of what the White Necks were trying to fill her head with about you,' Joseph said in a low voice. 'She went along with them because she wanted to find you.'

'Thank you for telling me that,' the boy said.

'Are you two okay?' Drake asked, eyeing them curiously as he noticed they both appeared rather overwrought.

'We're just fine,' Will replied.

'Good, then let's put a stop to the subaural field in this place. I know there's an armoury in here, so if you show us where it is, Joseph, let's break in and see what the Styx have left behind,' Drake said. 'You'll want something a little more businesslike than that pickaxe handle if they pop up here again.'

Will, Drake and Mrs Burrows were heading back to the Quarter when Elliott appeared from nowhere.

'I thought I told you to stay put,' Drake said, clearly annoyed.

Elliott didn't reply, and Will noticed that she was purposefully avoiding his gaze. Perhaps all wasn't well between the two of them after Mrs Burrows had attacked her father and the angry exchange that had ensued. And Elliott didn't speak to him for the time it took for them to rejoin Sweeney and Colonel Bismarck, who had been guarding the nuclear weapons and the rest of the equipment.

Although the First Officer had had other matters to attend to and wasn't yet with them, he'd suggested that they wait for him at his police station. So that was their next stop and, once they'd moved all the equipment over there, they sat around in the main office, eating their rations. The nuclear weapons were safely under lock and key in one of the cells in the Hold, somewhere that held only bad memories for Will. So bad that he'd found himself unable to go into the dank and dismal place again.

When the First Officer finally turned up, strolling breezily in through the swing doors, he'd only made it a few feet when there was the frantic noise of claws scrabbling on stone from beside Mrs Burrows. If Colly hadn't been carrying so much extra weight, she would have undoubtedly leapt over the top of the counter. Instead she cannoned straight through the opening in it.

'My girl!' the First Officer bellowed, as the Hunter reared up and put her paws on his shoulders to lick his face. 'I thought I'd lost you for good.' Purring at deafening volume, Colly rolled onto her back, inviting him to rub her stomach. 'Who's Daddy's girl then? Who's Daddy's girl then?' he cooed at the animal in baby talk.

He looked up as Mrs Burrows came over to the counter. 'My Hunter was with you all the time!' the First Officer said to her. 'Thank you! And she looks so fit and well – she's really filled out.'

'It's a bit more than that,' Mrs Burrows said.

'Kittens! No?' he asked, as he examined the cat.

'Yes,' said Mrs Burrows.

A big stupid grin creased the First Officer's face. Still grinning, he stood up. He stuck a finger in the air as something occurred to him. 'And I have a little surprise for your son.' He trundled through the counter and into his office. Reappearing with something hidden behind his back, he went over to Will.

'Here,' he said, revealing what it was.

'Awesome!' Will burst out. It was his trusty spade – his favourite possession from his time in Highfield. He reached for it.

'Not so fast,' the First Officer said, teasingly putting it out of the boy's reach. 'It's yours on one condition: I want you to promise never ever to clobber me with it again!'

'Done!' Will said, taking his spade and inspecting the brightly polished blade.

Colly wouldn't leave the First Officer's side, and was now rubbing herself affectionately against his legs. 'I missed her,' he mumbled.

'She'll be stopping here with you when we go,' Mrs Burrows said. 'It wouldn't be fair to take her along.'

'Of course,' the First Officer agreed readily, stroking the cat's broad head and making her purr at even greater volume.

'Um, I'd like to make a proposal, Celia,' Drake began, putting aside his sandwich and rising from his chair. 'I've talked this through with Will . . . and we think you should remain behind in the Colony, too.'

'O-k-a-y,' Mrs Burrows said slowly.

'I've got all the manpower I need for the mission,' Drake continued. 'And you've already given us a glimpse of how useful you can be to the Colonists now the Styx are out of the picture. Not least that, with your supersense, you'd be invaluable as an early warning system if the Styx try to pick up where they left off. You'll be able to smell them coming.'

Mrs Burrows considered this for a moment. 'I can see the logic in that,' she said. 'Yes, I'll stay then.'

Will was surprised she'd decided so quickly, but the First Officer was overjoyed. 'Excellent,' he kept repeating, as he clapped his meaty hands together.

As everyone thought about going back to their sandwiches, Drake remained on his feet. 'There's something I need to air with all of you. And this involves you too,' he said, turning to the First Officer.

Drake slid a small attaché case from his Bergen and took it over to the counter, where he laid it on the worn oak surface. 'As you know, our objective is to seal the inner world with the nuclear weapons. So that the Phase – if it's been resumed there – is fully contained.'

Drake undid the catches on the attaché case. Inside there was a metal canister nestling in a foam inset, which he took out.

'During the year I was held prisoner in the Laboratories, I overheard the Scientists discussing a virus,' Drake said, then smiled. 'Academics do like to boast to each other.'

'It wasn't Dominion?' Elliott asked.

'No, not Dominion.' Drake unscrewed the top of the canister, and ever so carefully eased a small test tube from it. 'The Scientists knew exactly what they'd unearthed in the Eternal City. They'd trialled this on a range of subjects, and they were in awe of what it did.' Drake held up the test tube. 'This little baby is far more powerful and more indiscriminate than Dominion. Not just humans, but the Styx and many of the more developed lifeforms are susceptible to it. It's deadly with a capital D.'

'So you got it from the Laboratories?' Will said.

'Yes. When Chester and I raided them and fortuitously rescued Celia at the same time, I had the opportunity to grab it from the secure vault in the secondary path lab. That was why I was late on the scene and Eddie got the better of me.' Drake thought of something. 'By the way, none of you need to worry – you were all immunised against it when I gave you that shot back in the Complex. And when I was in London, I had my friend Charlie weaponise it – so it's now not just transmitted by direct contact, but by droplet nuclei transmission.'

'That being . . . ?' Mrs Burrows interjected.

Drake's eyes were slightly unfocused as he stared at the clear fluid in the test tube. 'It can spread in air . . . on the wind. And I doubt there's anything quite as lethal or as toxic anywhere on this whole damned planet right now, inside or out.'

'But you made it worse when you *weaponised* it . . . was that wise?' Mrs Burrows asked.

'Maybe not, but when we're on the ground in the Colonel's world, if all else fails I might need a bargaining chip. The Styx know what this virus represents. They know it will bring about what the scientific community calls an *Extinction Event* . . . and that means an end to their race, too.'

He turned to the First Officer. 'The reason I'm bringing you in on this is that I have enough vaccine for all your people. There's a chance – a slim chance – that if it's released in the inner world, it might eventually work its way up to the surface. And you'd be bang smack in its path if it does.'

'What about Topsoilers?' the First Officer asked.

'Parry's got the vaccine, too,' Drake replied as he slotted the test tube back into the metal canister.

Mrs Burrows was frowning sceptically. 'Enough for everybody?'

Drake closed the clips on the case. 'No, and there wouldn't be time to vaccinate everybody anyway. I don't have the slightest intention of letting it loose, but ask yourselves this . . .' He took the case back to his Bergen, then turned to everyone, looking at them each in turn: at Sweeney, Colonel Bismarck, Elliott, Will, the First Officer, and finally Mrs Burrows. 'What's worse, this deadly pathogen, or the Phase? Because I don't think there's much in it.'

Chapter Twenty-two

The Miners' Train chugged out of the station in the Colony as they set off on the first leg of the journey that would take them deep into the bowels of the Earth. Unlike the last time, when Will had stowed away in one of the open trucks, he was now in the guard's carriage at the very end of the train. And although the warped timber planking that formed the sides and roof of the carriage had numerous gaps in it, at least it offered a degree of protection from the smoke and soot spewing from the locomotive up ahead as it began to build up a head of steam.

Over the roar of the engine, Will could hear the pair of pure white stallions as they whinnied in the next carriage along. The First Officer had requisitioned them from one of the Governor's residencies – the official had kept them hidden away in his personal stables during the troubles, knowing that the starving masses would have devoured them given half a chance. The Governor was beside himself with rage when Cleaver had turned up with an official letter from the newly formed Colonists' Committee, although he'd had no choice but to let them go. The horses would be a real boon in the

Deeps; Drake wanted to cover the distance across the Great Plain as quickly as possible, and the railwaymen assured him that there was bound to be a cart somewhere in the Miners' Station to hitch them to.

The guard's carriage was dimly lit by a single shaded luminescent orb suspended at its rear. For a while Will watched the odd fiery spark as it found its way into the carriage, then traced a short streak in the air until it burnt itself into invisibility. Watching the brief lives of these sparks, he found himself thinking about the parting from his mother. Will didn't know quite what had changed between them, but she hadn't given him the send-off he'd had on other occasions. Mrs Burrows was aware of the risks her son would be facing, yet she simply hugged him in a perfunctory way, and wished him good luck.

And Will had to admit that this time he himself had felt differently about leaving her.

Perhaps they had both changed because of all they'd been through. Or, he asked himself, was it because he was growing up and didn't need his mother in the same way that he'd used to? He was still mulling this over as the rocking motion of the train began to make his eyelids feel heavier and heavier, and he drifted into sleep.

And, as the temperature gradient gradually rose the deeper they penetrated into the Earth's crust, none of them did much more than sleep and eat for the next twenty-four hours. Their journey was broken several times for the horses to be fed and watered, and for the huge sets of storm gates across the track to be cranked open to allow the train through.

As they finally drew into the Miners' Station, it was much as Will remembered it – a ramshackle row of rather unimpressive huts. He jumped from the guard's carriage, his boots crunching in the layer of iron ore, coke and clinker covering the ground. Drawing in a long breath through his nose, the arid air evoked the time when he, Chester and Cal had stolen through this very cavern. And Bartleby. They'd all been killed or touched by death, and that's why not one of them was with him at that moment.

He was still mulling this over as he began to walk towards the station huts, but then came to an abrupt stop. The old Will would have taken the opportunity to explore the huts, but he found that he had no desire whatsoever to investigate them. It just didn't seem important to him any more. Instead he helped Sweeney and the Colonel unload the equipment as Drake went off with the Colonist engine driver and his assistant in search of a cart. They quickly located one, and once the stallions were harnessed and the equipment in place, Elliott and Drake led the way from the cavern on foot as the Colonel drove the cart.

Will had shown the Colonel how to wear one of Drake's headsets, adjusting the drop-down lens over his eye so he could see the way clearly without the need for any light. Then Will had found himself a place to sit at the very rear of the cart behind the equipment, and put on his own headset. Now back in the familiar world of shifting orange light, he was quite content to watch the sides of the tunnel slipping by as Sweeney jogged along behind the cart.

Drawing on his enhanced senses, Sweeney was scanning the tunnel behind and checking the side passages for any lurking Limiters when his gaze fell on Will.

'Hey, lazy boy,' the huge man ribbed him. 'Don't strain yourself too much.' Will was framing a suitably indignant response when Sweeney continued, 'You know, I just *love* this place.'

'What do you mean?' Will asked, shifting uncomfortably as sweat trickled down the small of his back. 'It's hot and dusty . . . and just foul.'

'Sure,' Sweeney answered. 'But for the first time in a long time, I'm not getting any radio interference.' He touched one of his temples. 'You have no idea what it's like to have some tosspot of a DJ burbling away in your head all day and all night. Some weeks it's not too bad, but then it suddenly kicks in big time, and I have to listen to bleedin' Chris Evans prattling on whether I want to or not.' He curled his lip in disgust. 'But in this place, there's not a whisper . . . there's nothing. Just glorious peace and quiet.'

Will nodded to show he understood.

'Yes, siree, I can really see myself settling down here one day,' Sweeney said.

They hadn't encountered a single living soul – human, Styx or Coprolite – as they emerged into a vast cavern where the ground was peppered with large, teardrop-shaped boulders.

Will had taken advantage of the incline to stretch his legs, and was jogging behind the cart alongside Sweeney.

'Oh, God!' the boy suddenly burst out.

'Whassamatter?' Sweeney asked, as he peered around them. 'Got something?'

'No, it's not that,' Will assured him. 'I know where we are . . . and I hoped I'd never see it again. My brother died not far from here. And my real mum too.'

Sweeney was silent for several of his lumbering strides. 'That's tough, Will. I'm sorry.'

They crossed a path of well-worn paving slabs, and an hour later the huge opening in the ground came into sight.

'There it is . . . the Pore,' Will told Sweeney gloomily.

Drake and Elliott had come to a stop and were waiting for everyone to catch up.

'We've spotted something new,' Drake informed them. 'There appear to be some huts by the side of the Pore.'

Elliott had her eye glued to her rifle night scope. 'Three . . . three huts,' she confirmed.

'We know this area well, and they weren't there before,' Drake said. He'd spent years in this land of eternal night, latterly with Elliott, and as Will watched them both now he realised they were back in their element. 'We're going in to investigate,' Drake said, then he and Elliott moved ahead again. Colonel Bismarck followed at a distance, keeping the stallions to a steady trot, as Will and Sweeney remained on the lookout for any Limiters.

When they finally reached the Pore, the continual deluge of water from above splattered their heads and shoulders, helping to cool them. The ground by the basic huts was strewn with deflated hot air balloons, and beside them a wooden platform extended almost forty feet over the huge void. Will, the Colonel and Sweeney stepped around the sagging forms of the balloons as they moved to the end of it.

Sweeney whistled as he tried to see across to the other side of the titanic void and, not finding it, peered down. 'That's one . . . big . . . mother. You threw yourself down it, didn't you, Will?' he asked.

'Didn't have much choice at the time,' Will mumbled. It dawned on him that they were here to do precisely the same again. Unless Drake had a better idea, such as using one of the balloons to carry them down to the fungal ledge far below.

As Will began to retrace his steps along the platform, he was repeating to himself, 'I *really* don't want to do this.' And he really didn't – the prospect of taking a step off the edge and pitching headlong into that black nothingness again filled him with unremitting dread. He sought out Drake where he and Elliott were deep in conversation. They fell silent as he arrived.

'What's the plan now?' Will demanded. 'Are we really going to jump down the Pore? And how the hell are we going to know when we're deep enough to find the passageway?' He was furious that the two of them seemed to be leaving him in the dark, just as it had been all that time ago when they'd first rescued him, Chester and Cal on the Great Plain. After all he'd gone through, hadn't he earned the right to know what they were intending to do?

Drake caught the edge in the boy's voice. 'For lack of any other alternative, that was my original idea,' he answered. 'I agree that our chances of hitting the right fungal ledge at exactly the right depth are slim at best. Particularly as there isn't a radio beacon to guide us.'

Drake slipped a tracker from a pouch on his belt. It resembled a strange looking handgun with a dial on top of it and a small dish where the muzzle should have been. The tracker was able to detect the VLF or Very Low Frequency signals that the radio beacons broadcast. Will had planted these beacons at various points along the route he'd taken with Dr Burrows and Elliott when they'd somehow found their way through to the inner world the first time.

'Haven't seen one of those in a while,' Will said, as Drake aimed it at the Pore and depressed the trigger. It emitted a single click, then remained silent. Will frowned. 'That's weird,' he said. 'Is it working properly?'

'It should be. Don't forget the beacon you left at the jump-off point on the second pore is quite some distance from us,' Drake reminded him.

'Yes, by Smoking Jean,' Will said, recalling his name for it.

Drake nodded. 'And I also agree with you that it's going to be a bit hit-and-miss if we do a swan dive with the nuclear weapons tied to our ankles.'

Will was frowning. 'You don't have a plan at all, do you?' he accused Drake. 'You're just making this up as you go along!'

'That's the way it works,' Drake replied.

Will was shaking his head angrily. 'Wow, that's just great. So you don't actually have a clue what we're going to do next.'

'Will,' Elliott intervened, reaching out as if to touch his shoulder but then lowering her hand to point at the ground. 'Look at the tracks you're on.' It was clear that something heavy had passed that way because the rocks had been pulverised. 'Lots of Coprolite machines went by here.' She raised her rifle to peer through the scope. 'And I can see one of them way over there . . . around the side of the Pore. Drake and I think we should recce it.'

Drake indicated the balloons by the huts. 'The Styx must have been using those to get up and down, but from the state of them they obviously switched to another method some time back. And I ask myself what could that be – did they find or even *make* themselves an alternative route? I think we owe it to ourselves to find out, don't you?' He punched Will gently on the arm. 'Happier now?' he asked, smiling at the boy.

'Much,' Will replied, smiling back.

*

With Will beside him in the cart, Colonel Bismarck drove the stallions along the tracks by the edge of the Pore. Will was soon able to make out the Coprolite digging machine. The cylindrical body of battered steel shone like quicksilver as he squinted through his lens.

As they came nearer and the Colonel slowed the horses, there was no sign of either Elliott or Drake by the machine.

'Where are they?' Will asked, as Sweeney caught up with the cart. 'And why aren't they keeping in touch over the radio?'

'Wait here,' Sweeney replied, as he went to find out.

As Will saw him reach the digger, he too disappeared from sight. It was a good twenty minutes before the horses began to stamp the ground and become agitated. Then Will heard what he thought was the distant rumbling of a vehicle. And it sounded heavy.

'What's that?' he asked, angling his head and looking around. 'And where's it coming from?'

'There!' said the Colonel, pointing.

Where Will had last seen Sweeney, a Coprolite digger rose into view. As it came at full pelt towards them, the Colonel struggled to control the horses. It stopped, spinning a hundred and eighty degrees on the spot, boulders popping beneath the massive rollers that bore it along.

The rear hatch swung open, and Elliott and Sweeney dismounted into the cloud of smoke issuing from the machine's exhausts. 'Got ourselves a ride!' Sweeney called over to Will.

It turned out that Drake had found the Coprolite digger fuelled up and ready for use. Will didn't question it – he was just relieved that there was an alternative to jumping down the

Pore.

Once all the equipment was on board and lashed down, the Colonel freed the stallions, watching them gallop off. 'I do hope they make it back to the station,' he said with some regret.

Then everyone boarded the digger. The interior of the vehicle was fabricated from beaten metal – most of it was grimy except for several areas which shone brightly from their regular use. Will took in the display at the navigator's station, and the red glow coming from an inspection port in the boiler.

Then Drake, sitting at the front of the vehicle, pushed in and twisted a rod to engage the engine, and depressed a pedal. The digger lurched forward, and he steered it around to face the opposite direction. Will joined Elliott and Sweeney to watch from the open hatch at the rear of the vehicle as the digger's nose dipped down an incline.

'Some tunnel!' Will shouted over the thunderous din of the vehicle.

It was approximately forty feet to the roof, and easily as wide.

'The Styx rounded up some Coprolites and forced them to bore this out with one their mega-machines,' Elliott shouted back. 'But get a load of what's coming up!'

As they roared past, there were scores of the diggers parked at the side of the massive tunnel. Then there were what had to be spoil-movers from the scoops mounted on their fronts, and the long trains of trailers behind them. Will had never seen this second type of vehicle before, but he remembered Drake had told him that as the race of master miners dug into the rock, they were careful to in-fill crevices and open faults with the spoil as they went. They regarded the earth as a living entity, treating it with respect and not wanting to cause it excessive damage with their excavations.

Sweeney pointed. 'There!' he said.

Coprolites – a group of around thirty of them – were milling around. Although their mushroom-coloured and bulbous suits were almost indistinguishable from the surrounding rock, light poured from the luminescent orbs mounted in the eye openings of their suits.

'And some ex-Stickies,' Sweeney added.

Will saw the bodies of Limiters sprawled on the ground, and looked at Elliott, who nodded. It was clear a four-man team had been supervising the Coprolites. Will was wondering if Drake or Elliott, or both of them, had despatched the Styx soldiers, when Drake yelled from the front.

'Okay! Batten down the hatch and buckle up!' Then when everyone was seated and strapped in, he floored the accelerator.

The digger was capable of impressive speed. Sweeney, Will and the Colonel kept the boiler well fed and well stoked as they went, always heading downwards in this new tunnel.

They passed what must have been a Limiter checkpoint along the way. They only knew this because they could hear the bullets striking the thick crystal windscreen as the Styx soldiers tried to stop the digger. But their efforts were completely ineffectual, and everyone in the vehicle laughed and gave each other the thumbs up.

Elliott was in the co-driver's seat beside Drake, continually checking the tracker. When Drake eased off the accelerator to allow Sweeney to tend to the boiler, Will took the opportunity to undo his seat harness and come forward.

'We're dead on the signal,' Elliott shouted, showing Will

the twitching needle on top of the detector.

Drake leant over from the driving seat. 'If this tunnel has been completed all the way down, we're going to reach Smoking Jean in record time!' he said. 'Maybe a few hours!'

Will frowned. 'But the journey from Martha's shack to the submarine in Smoking Jean took us a week!' he pointed out.

'You were following natural fault lines then, and wandering all over the shop. This is *as the mole burrows*,' Drake said. 'It's direct.'

Despite the fact he was being jostled around by the vehicle, Will dozed off in his seat. He had no idea how long it had been until he was rudely awoken by shouting. He at once realised that they were no longer travelling down an incline, but were on the flat. Then he caught sight of a well-lit area through the windscreen.

'Yee-ha!' Drake yelled as he drove right at several Limiters in front of some sort of shack. They leapt from the path of the vehicle as the digger exploded through the structure.

'Straight ahead!' Elliott yelled, checking the tracker.

Multiple shots struck the digger all over its hull, then an explosion lifted it clean into the air.

As it landed, Drake was shouting and laughing as he kept his foot pressed firmly to the floor. There were rock outcrops in the way, but he simply smashed through them.

Will caught sight of something familiar. Although he couldn't hear what she was saying to Drake, Elliott was pointing at it. It was the tall boulder with the carving where Will had hidden one of the radio beacons, and where his father had leapt into Smoking Jean.

But for the life of him Will couldn't think what Drake was

intending to do next. The shots continued to rain on them from behind, so there was no way they could stop or go back.

They were almost at the void, and still Drake kept the vehicle moving at full throttle.

'Drake . . . what are you—? . . . DRAKE!' Will screamed at the top of his lungs as they careered past the tall boulder where the beacon was hidden. Will knew he was right about this because he could just make out the rash of clicks from the detector in Elliott's hand.

There was a crash as the roof of the digger caught the top of the opening on the side of Smoking Jean. But the digger simply crushed the rock.

Then they weren't on firm ground any longer.

They were tipping into the void.

Falling.

Drake killed the engine, leaving just the sound of rushing air as they gently turned over.

'Stay strapped in – in case we hit anything,' Drake advised.

A few loose stones floated around the cabin – even now the gravity was becoming less powerful.

And through the front windscreen Will caught glimpses of the red glow of lava veins on the sides of the void.

'You bloody *hooligan*!' Will said. 'I can't believe you just did that!' But he was laughing.

Chapter Twenty-three

As the Coprolite digger plunged downwards, it caught the tip of a fungal ledge protruding from the side of Smoking Jean, slamming straight through it. The obstruction caused the vehicle to flip end over end. Everyone was holding on tight, the motion making them feel more than a little disoriented, and increasingly ill.

Worse seemed to be in store for them.

The digger was rotating inexorably towards the side of the pore. They watched the intermittent view through the windscreen with bated breath, but the collision with the rock wall they were all dreading never came. Instead the temperature inside the cabin rocketed due to the proximity of the molten rock. Will was seriously asking himself if they'd all be barbecued where they sat when, luckily, the digger drifted away from the lava veins and back towards the centre of the pore. And as they continued, coming ever closer to the bottom of Smoking Jean, the digger settled down and was hardly spinning at all.

On several occasions a hammering echoed around the hull as they passed through bands of suspended rock debris, like a spaceship striking asteroid belts.

Then, with a last jarring impact, the digger came to a standstill. An unceasing groaning sound reverberated through the vehicle, but at least they were no longer on the move.

Drake unstrapped himself and floated towards the rear hatch. 'Everyone okay?' he asked, looking around. 'Someone wake Sparks up!' he exclaimed.

Unbuckling himself, Will swam over and nudged the big man.

'Are we there already?' Sweeney asked, yawning.

'You're unbelievable,' Will muttered. Then he joined Drake by the hatch, who swivelled the handle and pushed. The groaning was now deafening as it filled the interior. As Elliott, Sweeney and the Colonel joined them, all they could see were rounded boulders bobbing up and down like apples in a barrel of water.

Drake closed the hatch so it was easier to hear him. 'Right,' he said, 'We're going to rope ourselves together, then we might as well make a start across this zero-grav belt of yours, Will.'

'Um, there's two things about that,' the boy began nervously. 'First is that it's bloody humongous, and there's this thing my dad called the Crystal Belt across it. I really don't know if I'll able to find the way.'

Drake had the tracker in his hand. He let go of it, allowing it to spin several slow revolutions in the air before he caught it again.

'Trippy,' Sweeney said. 'Never been in space before.'

Drake moved the tracker around until it let out a burst of clicks and the needle twitched with the strong signal. It was pointing at the floor of the digger. 'That's the beacon you left by the Russian submarine,' he said.

'We landed upside down!' Elliott observed. The complete lack of gravity where they were in the Earth actually meant that this made no difference to them.

Then Drake pointed it in the opposite direction – at the roof of the digger. Although the reaction was far weaker, the tracker again registered a signal. 'And that'll be the beacon you planted in the opening on the other side of the belt, which is our way into the Colonel's inner world. What could be simpler?'

'Suppose,' Will sighed, still not convinced.

'And what was the second thing on your mind?' Drake asked.

'Can't we go across in this Coprolite machine?' Will proposed. 'It would be safer.'

'It's heavy and I want to conserve the propellants in the boosters,' Drake replied. 'Better if we travel light.'

With that they all got themselves ready for the crossing. As though they were survivors from a shipwreck, they were each linked by lengths of rope to a makeshift raft, which comprised the two nuclear devices and their other equipment, all lashed together.

When they exited from the digger, both Drake and Will had the boosters ready. As there was no way they could hear each other with all the noise from the Crystal Belt, Drake pointed at Will, who angled his booster and gave it the tiniest blip on the trigger.

The blue flame lanced from the funnel and they were off, but in completely the wrong direction. With several more attempts, Will was feeling more proficient at using the booster, and steered them around the loose aggregation of boulders where the digger had come to rest. Then they were on the way out of Smoking Jean, and rushing towards the huge emptiness, the far-off flicker of the lights from the Crystal Belt an unimaginable distance ahead of them.

Both Will and Drake took turns on the boosters, with Elliott continually checking the direction with the tracker.

Will intentionally gave the Crystal Belt a wide berth, just as he and Dr Burrows had when they'd made the same journey. The boosters were far more effective than using the recoil from the Sten gun. Will had no conception of how fast they were actually moving, but the wind in their faces was so strong it snatched their breath away.

And as the hours passed and they worked their way around the ethereal lights of the Crystal Belt, Will finally spotted the column of sunlight in the distance. He knew then that they were going to make it to the inner world.

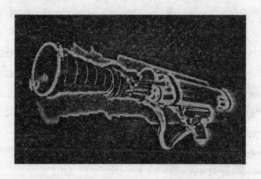

Chapter Twenty-four

Once they were out of the zero-gravity belt and moving into the cone-shaped opening, the rays of the second sun made everything shimmer as if they were under water. Will continued to blip his booster to maintain their speed while Elliott checked the readout from the tracker. There was no way that she could hear the clicking emanating from it, as the rumble from the zero-gravity belt continued to drown everything out.

It was half an hour before Drake signalled that they should head for the side of the void. As soon as they touched down, he and Sweeney detached themselves from the raft of nuclear weapons and equipment. Then they slid one of the bombs into position behind a large rock, securing it in place with a rope. Drake immediately opened a hatch in its side and began to prep it for detonation.

'We did it,' Elliott sighed wearily, as she lay down in the scree.

'Yep. Never ever thought we'd be here again,' Will said, slumping next to her. They shared a bar of chocolate, washing it down with water from a canteen. There was a loud gurgling noise, and Will looked away in embarrassment.

'Ohhhh,' he groaned. 'It's messed up my stomach again.'

'Mine too,' Elliott laughed. 'It's the low gravity, isn't it?'

Will didn't reply as he peered around in an attempt to find a feature he recognised from the last time they were there. He thought of the ledge where he, Elliott and Dr Burrows had landed, all of them immediately falling into a dead sleep because they were so thoroughly exhausted.

Will regarded the small Alpine plants around him – they were clinging onto the scree with trailing root systems like unravelled cotton, and there were also a number of the dwarf trees with tortured trunks. He could tell from the abundance of vegetation that they must have long since passed the ledge he'd been looking for. Realising it was futile to try to find anything familiar – the vast scale of the place made that highly unlikely – he shut his eyes.

'Are you thinking about the Doc?' Elliott asked gently.

'The Doc?' he said, blinking his eyes open again. It took him a moment to work out who Elliott was referring to. She was using her and Drake's nickname for his stepfather, Dr Burrows. 'I suppose that means you weren't,' Elliott decided after he failed to reply.

'No, I wasn't, and, you know . . . I don't think about him so much any more,' Will admitted. 'It's funny – but you've got your dad back now, and I sort of feel as though mine's gone. If all those years of Darklighting made him the way he was, then everything he did and said wasn't really *him* . . . and he doesn't seem so . . .' Will frowned, trying to come up with the right word. '*Important* . . . so important to me any longer,' he said eventually.

'He was still your father,' Elliott reminded him.

Drake finally closed the panel in the casing of the nuclear weapon, replacing the screws to secure it, then rejoined everyone. Sweeney and the Colonel had attached a harness around the remaining bomb so that it would be easier to carry it.

'Okey-doke,' Drake said, unhitching a radio detonator from his belt and pressing a sequence of buttons. Sweeney had an identical detonator in his hand. 'Check?' Drake asked.

'Check,' Sweeney confirmed.

'Good – that's one nuke ready to rock 'n' roll,' Drake announced.

'*Was ist das* rock 'n' roll?' the Colonel asked.

'Oh, sorry, I meant that it's primed,' Drake explained. 'I've also taken the precaution of installing an anti-tamper fuse on the inspection panel, and a trembler. So in the unlikely event that the Styx were to come all the way down here and stumble across our little surprise, it'll go off as they attempt to open or move it . . . and the job will be done. This opening will be one almighty mass of fused silica, and nothing will ever get through again.' He turned to look down at the darkness of the zero-gravity belt. 'Not that it's a viable route to the surface for them anyway.'

'And the second bomb?' Elliott asked.

'You and Colonel Bismarck know the terrain, so I want you to help me locate the Ancients' passage,' Drake replied. He squinted up at the sun. 'If we use both boosters on full power, we can really motor it as far as we can get to the top. Then we'll lug the device the rest of the way. And thank God for the low gravity.'

The boosters did help, but when the frequent bursts from them weren't enough to counter the increasing pull of gravity, everybody had to muck in. In pairs they took turns to haul the nuclear weapon up the forty-five-degree incline, and it was a good twelve hours before they arrived at the massive crater which marked the top of the void.

'Here are we,' Drake said, putting on a pair of sunglasses. 'Hope you all remembered to pack some sun block.'

They were covered in the red soil, and so exhausted and cramped from the climb that they could hardly stand.

Sweeney stretched his back with a groan. As he removed his hat to mop his forehead, the full force of the globe in the sky above hit him. 'Crikey!' he gasped. 'That's bright. It's worse than the bloomin' tropics.'

'Welcome to the Garden of the Second Sun,' Will said. 'Or, according to what my dad thought, *Eden*.'

'Pretty bloody far from my idea of Eden,' Sweeney complained, as he put his hat back on and surveyed the surrounding foothills, which were covered with patchy woodland.

'Try jumping,' the Colonel suggested to Drake and Sweeney.

The two men regarded him for a moment, then Sweeney crouched down and leapt into the air. He reached three or four times the height he'd have been able to achieve Topsoil. They heard him chortling as he came back to Earth. He immediately jumped again, using his powerful legs to drive himself even higher. When he landed, he had a look of schoolboy glee on his face.

'Maybe this place isn't so bad, after all,' he grinned.

Drake, Elliott and Colonel Bismarck left with the nuclear device, while Sweeney found somewhere he and Will could wait out. He chose a depression on the side of the nearest foothill. It didn't exactly give them much protection from the sun, but at least they weren't in full view if any Styx decided to come along.

Elliott didn't take long to locate the stream that would lead them to the waterfall and the entrance to the Ancients' passage. But as they emerged from the jungle, what the three of them saw stopped them dead in their tracks.

The waterfall shielding the entrance had been dammed, and there was no sign of the idyllic pool with the iridescent dragonflies that it had originally drained into.

But this wasn't what had brought them to a halt.

As far as the eye could see, the trees had been cut down and the jungle turned into fields of sun-hardened mud. And on these fields an unbelievable number of tanks, personnel carriers, large-bore guns and military aircraft had been assembled, all carefully arranged in ranks as if ready to bring into the tunnel at a moment's notice.

'My army,' was all Colonel Bismarck could murmur as he shook his head in disbelief.

'We didn't get here a moment too soon,' Drake said. 'When the Styx had finished widening the way through, this little lot would have found its way Topsoil . . . as toys for the Styx Warrior Class.' Drake was already scanning between the lines of equipment. 'And there are bound to be sentries dotted about – we need to get in and out as quickly as we can.'

As Elliott kept watch, Drake and the Colonel took the bomb into the passage. Once they'd rejoined Elliott, Drake again used his radio detonator to prime it, pressing the sequence of buttons.

'Rock 'n' roll?' Colonel Bismarck asked.

Drake nodded. 'All done. Let's get back to Will and Sparks

at the RV, then we can all go home again,' he said.

'I *am* home,' Colonel Bismarck pointed out.

Will and Sweeney had heard rumbles of distant thunder, but then there was a mighty peal, accompanied a moment later by a searing blue flash of lightning. It was visible even through the blinding sunlight.

'Whoa! What a buzz!' Sweeney said, clapping a hand to the side of his head. 'That gave the old capacitors a jolt.'

'So lightning affects you too?' Will asked.

'Only if it's a full-on electrical storm,' Sweeney replied.

'Well, you get plenty of those in this place,' Will told him. 'Are you going to be all r—'

'Hold on,' Sweeney interrupted him as he extracted his walkie-talkie from his pocket and read the small LCD. 'It's Drake. They're not far now. It's almost show time.'

'And we only just got here,' Will said, but as tired as he was, he couldn't have been happier that their mission was nearly over, and that they would soon be leaving the inner world.

He and Sweeney heaved their Bergens on. As they began towards the crater, the wind picked up and the sun was obscured by angry black clouds.

Sweeney spotted Drake and the others emerge from the tree line in the distance. And, as the two groups came together by the lip of the crater, they found themselves in the middle of a full-blown monsoon.

'Nice weather,' Drake joked, as soon as he was close enough to them. Taking his sunglasses off, he blinked the rain from his eyes.

'No problems with the locals?' Sweeney asked.

Drake quickly told him and Will about the huge amount

of New Germanian hardware they'd seen waiting to be transported to the outer surface. 'Sealing the route through should put a crimp in the Styx's plans, once and for all,' he said. 'And they won't be able to re-excavate the Ancients' passage for a good few decades because the rock will be too radioactive.'

The water was bucketing down around them, already forming large puddles on the ground. Not more than a couple of hundred of feet away, a blinding spike of electricity struck the earth with such power that it left a small sizzling crater.

'Jesus!' Sweeney shouted, slapping his forehead.

'Let's get down there, shall we?' Drake proposed, glancing over his shoulder at the crater, then back at Sweeney with concern.

'I'm not coming,' the Colonel announced abruptly. He was shouting to make himself heard over the sound of the wind and the torrential rain. 'This is my country. I want to try to salvage what I can.'

'But how are you going to do that, Colonel?' Drake asked. 'All by yourself?'

Colonel Bismarck indicated his Bergen. 'I have a Purger in there. Maybe I can deprogramme enough of my men to take on the Styx.'

Drake stepped over to him and shook his hand. 'Good luck.'

'Good luck to you,' Colonel Bismarck replied, looking at each of them in turn.

'There should be minimal radiation up here from the nukes,' Drake told Colonel Bismarck. 'But get yourself as far away as you can, just in case. You've got time, because I won't detonate them until we're well into the zero-grav belt. I'll—'

He never finished the sentence as a shot rang out. Colonel

Bismarck looked down at his chest, where blood from a gaping hole was mixing with the rainwater. It was a precise shot to the heart, and there was no question that he'd been fatally wounded.

As he dropped to the ground, everyone whipped around to see who was behind them.

'Nobody's going to detonate anything,' Rebecca One said.

'No!' Will gasped.

As if it wasn't enough that the Styx twin was standing there, beside her was Vane. It was the first time that Will or Elliott had seen a Styx woman for themselves. Their eyes widened at the sight of the woman's cheeks, puffed out by the three egg tubes wreathing in her mouth like snakes, and her limbs consisting of not much more than muscle and bone, while her abdomen was hugely distended.

She and Rebecca One were flanked on either side by a pair of Limiters, their weapons trained on Will and the others.

'Didn't see us sneaking up on you, did you?' Rebecca One said smarmily. 'Pretty sloppy for you, Drake.'

Will realised they must have approached around the inside lip of the crater. There was probably one of the odd-looking Drache Achgelis twin-rotor helicopters hidden in the jungle not far from where they were.

'Nice to finally meet you in the flesh,' Drake said tightly. He had his assault rifle slung over his shoulder and his hands in his pockets. Will couldn't believe that he appeared to be so relaxed, given the circumstances. 'How did you know we were here? Did you pick up the radio signals?' Drake asked.

Rebecca One shook her head.

'It was me,' Vane said, fluid spraying from her cracked black lips. 'I smelt another bitch on heat.' She was staring straight at Elliott. 'Why aren't you joining with us in the Phase?'

'Me?' Elliott mouthed wordlessly.

'Golly, gargoyle lady can talk!' Sweeney chimed in as he smiled at Vane.

Her face creasing with fury, Vane reared towards him, three pairs of insect limbs flailing out from her shoulders.

'That's new,' Will whispered as Elliott shot a glance at him.

'I . . . want . . . him,' Vane growled at Sweeney, one of the egg tubes poking from her mouth. 'I want to lay my babies in him.'

Sweeney chuckled mirthlessly. 'There's an offer I can't refuse.'

Vane's insect limbs threshed furiously at this impertinence.

Rebecca One placed a hand on the Styx woman's arm. 'All in good time, Vane,' she said. 'First, we're all professionals here, so I don't think you'll be wildly surprised that I want you to lay down your weapons. My men have you in their sights, so no funny stuff.'

Thinking that it was all over, Will and Elliott had begun to comply, when Drake spoke. He had slipped his hands from his pockets.

'No,' he said.

'Oh, please,' Rebecca One sighed wearily. 'Let's not prolong this. You can't escape – and I've got another detachment of men on the way. Take a look for yourselves if you don't believe me.'

Will and the others turned to see. Along the side of the crater there must have been forty or so New Germanian troops running in formation, a Limiter leading them. They were minutes away.

As the rain continued to beat down, Drake slowly raised his arms. 'No, I won't do what you say. In this hand I have the detonator,' he said coolly. 'One tiny-winey press and the nukes detonate and you're stranded in this world for ever. And if you think you might be able to stop me with a shot, then look at what Sparks is holding.'

Sweeney held up his identical detonator.

'If that isn't enough, I have something rather special from your Laboratories in my other hand,' Drake said. As he revealed it with a flourish, the blue flash of a lightning strike reflected from the small test tube.

He had Rebecca One's attention now. 'What's that?' she asked.

'I snitched it from the vaults in your Laboratories before I levelled the building. I'd heard rumours from the Scientists that you had something like it. You know how academics like to show off.' Drake agitated the test tube, the fluid inside spinning around. 'My immunologist friend says it's the most virulent pathogen he's ever encountered. He says the prospect of it getting out makes him shiver, because it's capable of killing just about every complex lifeform on the planet. Is that why the Scientists never deployed it, because it's indiscriminate? Because it kills Styx too?' Drake smiled. 'Is all this ringing a bell with you, Becky, dear?'

'Don't call me that,' she fumed, but her bluster had gone.

'And my friend Charlie tinkered with it. With a little bit of genetic manipulation, it's now not solely waterborne in its distribution, but airborne too. So it's spread by the wind, and it kills in a few hours. Very bloody nasty.' Drake raised his eyebrows. 'And have you had the vaccine for it? No? I didn't think so. Shame – all of us have.'

'You're bluffing,' Rebecca One said. She turned to Vane. 'He's bluffing. He won't use the virus because it might find its way to the surface. He's not going to take the risk.' She swung to Drake. 'I don't care what you say, because there's no way I'm backing off. So we've got ourselves a complete stalemate here.'

All of a sudden, a line in the ground seemed to burst open behind one of the pairs of Limiters. Will had the briefest glimpse of an extremely thin man with an unruly beard and the palest of faces. The man caught the first of the two Limiters completely unawares, slashing the Styx soldier's throat.

'Jiggs!' Drake exclaimed.

The second Limiter had more time to put up a fight; as he and Jiggs struggled with each other, they tipped over into the crater and out of sight.

Sweeney took full advantage of the distraction, covering the ground at superhuman speed. In a blur he'd disarmed the other two Limiters, quite literally tearing one of the soldier's heads from his torso using only his bare hands.

Although it all happened in not much than the blink of an eye, Will allowed himself to think they might be in the clear.

Until the Styx twin shouted at him.

'You're not getting out of this one, Will,' Rebecca One cried. 'Not this time.'

She'd drawn her handgun and was pointing it directly at him.

Will was frozen to the spot.

Rebecca One's finger tightened on the trigger.

In a heartbeat, Drake was on the move.

'Sparks!' he cried, flinging the test tube at him as he put himself in the way of the bullet meant for Will. It struck

Drake in the shoulder, but his momentum was enough to carry him forward. As Rebecca One went for a second shot, he swept her over into the crater with him.

Vane had joined the fray, but she'd set her sights on Elliott. The Styx woman pounced at the girl, knocking her to the ground. The egg tubes were out of her mouth and trying to insert themselves into Elliott's.

Will had his Sten up and was attempting to get a clear shot at the Styx woman. But Vane knew this, and kept rolling over, taking Elliott with her. Will dropped his Sten, instead trying to prise the woman off with his hands.

But, as if they had minds of their own, the pairs of insect limbs were lashing at him like animated lengths of barbed wire. As he came close to Vane, one of the limbs raked across his face, opening up a gash on his cheek.

An egg tube sank into Elliott's mouth. The girl was shouting with alarm, but it was garbled.

Will could see a pod squeezing down the tube.

'Come here, blondie,' Sweeney growled. He wrenched Vane from Elliott, the woman's insect limbs bunched together in one of his massive hands. The Styx woman could do nothing as she was lifted from the ground, her legs kicking ineffectually.

Sweeney turned to the approaching Styx Limiter and troop of New Germanians, Vane suspended high in the air. She was wailing like a banshee, liquid spraying everywhere. 'You make tracks right now, or I'll squash Ugly here under my foot!' he shouted.

The Limiter hesitated.

'Shove off, Sticky!' Sweeney shouted. He shook Vane threateningly. 'I'm not going to tell you again!'

The Limiter didn't have much idea of what had just happened, but in the absence of any other orders he couldn't put Vane's life at risk. So he and the New Germanian squad turned the way they'd come.

'Drake!' Elliott gasped, as she picked herself up. She and Will tore to the edge of the crater and peered in. Although they'd already fallen a long way, they could see that Drake and Rebecca One were still locked together as they struggled with each other.

Lower and lower they fell, spinning dizzyingly around. Drake's arm was broken at the shoulder and he couldn't move it. And although his hand was numb and his fingers unresponsive, he hadn't let go of the detonator. With his other arm he was trying to stop Rebecca One from taking a shot at him.

But he was losing blood and could feel himself succumbing to shock. Drawing on his last reserves of energy, he managed to wrestle the pistol from her grip. It went spinning off, but now she tried to gouge at his face and eyes with her nails.

He had a glimpse of the side of the void, a red blur as it flashed past him. He realised how far they'd fallen.

He knew he probably wasn't far from the nuclear device he'd planted.

But he didn't know if Sweeney would detonate it with him directly in the blast radius.

He couldn't take that risk.

At that moment, Drake knew he was likely to lose his life.

Rebecca One was preventing him from reaching the detonator with his good hand. But he had to reach it somehow.

That was when he remembered the booster attached to the side of his Bergen. He stopped shielding his face from the twin's vicious onslaught and managed to detach the booster and fire it up. The propellant mix was still on the maximum setting from when he'd last used the booster.

He and the Rebecca twin accelerated down the rest of the void, quickly reaching breakneck speed.

Drake angled the booster so that they went into a spin. His limp arm swung into his field of vision, and into his reach.

They were still moving at an incredible rate as he cut the booster and snatched the detonator from his numb fingers.

He and Rebecca One had almost reached the zero-gravity belt. Drake knew he was still far too close to the nuclear device.

But that didn't matter now.

He clicked the arming button.

The detonator in Sweeney's hand bleeped as it picked up the signal.

He glanced at it.

'BOMB!' Sweeney screamed at Will and Elliott. 'GET THE HELL OUT OF HERE!'

They weren't about to argue with him.

They sprinted away from the edge of the crater, the low gravity helping them as they fled.

'Nice knowing you, Becky,' Drake said to the Styx twin as they left the void and burst into the zero-gravity belt, still moving at phenomenal speed.

She saw he was smiling.

Then she saw his finger was poised over a button on the detonator.

Her lips began to form the word 'No,' but she never uttered it as Drake pressed down.

There was a blinding flash, as bright as a thousand suns.

Sweeney swung the struggling Styx woman in front of him. 'I can't get away in time.'

He moved Vane closer to him.

'The EMP will fry my circuits.'

He contemplated the Styx woman's wriggling egg tubes as they dripped liquid. He knew he should probably kill her, but at that moment life had become sacred to him. All life.

'Give us a last kiss, darl—' he whispered to her.

As the nuclear device went off down in the void, the electromagnetic pulse swept over him.

The grids on Sweeney's face instantly glowed white hot, the skin around them burning, and two small plumes of smoke issued from his ears.

Then as the circuitry in his head reached critical point, his head simply exploded. Like a massive felled tree, he toppled over, taking the Styx woman with him.

The earth shook, and a torrent of dust and debris shot from the crater. But this lasted for less than a second, as the bottom of the void closed in on itself.

As Vane tried to extricate herself from under the huge man, she was cackling to herself. Apart from a few broken ribs, she believed she'd escaped.

But in the aftershock of the bomb, she'd failed to hear the tiny tinkle of glass as Sweeney had hit the ground, crushing the test tube in his hip pocket.

By the time the Limiter General reached the scene half an hour later, Vane had lesions on her skin and was coughing up blood. When he tried to find out from her what had happened, she was too feverish and didn't make any sense.

He naturally assumed it was radiation sickness. That was until the Styx Limiter and the garrison of New Germanians, who'd been present at the crater, all began to show identical symptoms. But, in theory, they hadn't been close enough to the blast to be badly affected.

Within twelve hours, Vane and every one of the soldiers had died from the fever.

The Limiter General himself, having returned to the city of New Germania, collapsed and died shortly afterwards.

And, blown on the dry winds, the pathogen spread.

And spread.

Chapter Twenty-five

At the kitchen table Stephanie was browsing through a magazine she'd read more times than she cared to remember. As her grandfather entered, she looked up expectantly.

'Any news?' she asked.

'I got Parry, but I'm afraid he still hasn't heard anything,' Old Wilkie said, as he put the satphone on the dresser.

'Nothing? So we still don't know if Will's okay.'

Her grandfather shook his head. He opened his bag to extract two rabbits he'd just shot and laid them on the table. Stephanie wrinkled her nose in disgust.

'How's Chester doing?' Old Wilkie asked.

'Same old, same old. Just sitting there, like he always does,' she replied.

Old Wilkie nodded. 'What about those books I got for him? Parry says he enjoys reading.'

'He's, like, *whatever*. Can't say I blame him though. I started one of them called . . .' she groped for the title, '*The Highland Mole or something*.' She rolled her eyes as she stuck her tongue out. 'Talk about being, like, *completely* unrealistic.'

Shaking her head, she dropped her gaze to the magazine article she had, for the umpteenth time, been poring over with the title *X Factor – The Future of Britain's Talent*.

'He likes those types of books,' Old Wilkie countered. 'Just go and spend some time with him, will you? Try to get him to talk.'

Letting out a sigh, Stephanie slapped her magazine shut and rose from the table. As she reached the door, she pushed it open a fraction to peer into the adjoining room. Chester was simply staring through the window, at the sky above the sea.

As she went in, he quickly lifted the book in his lap. He didn't look at her, pretending to be immersed in the story.

Stephanie regarded him for a moment. He'd lost a lot of weight in the months they'd been in the cottage. And although there were some spectacular views from the cliffs where they were in Pembrokeshire, he never ventured out. The old Chester would have liked it there, probably going for long walks along the coastal paths.

But not now. He didn't want to talk to her or anyone else. There was no interest in anything any longer. He just wanted to be left alone with his grief.

Stephanie turned and went back into the kitchen where her grandfather was gutting the first of the rabbits.

On the very top of the pyramid, deep in the jungle, Will was facing where he knew the city of New Germania lay.

'I don't ever want to go back there. Never again,' he said. 'It was awful.'

Elliott stepped beside him. 'Don't say that – we might need to fetch some more supplies.'

But she too didn't sound very happy about the prospect of a second expedition to collect tinned foods and clothes from the silent shops. Together they'd walked the flyblown, deserted streets, the stench of the dead in their nostrils everywhere they went.

'We have all we need right here,' Will insisted, lowering his gaze to their old base in the giant tree, where they were living again.

A flock of bright blue parrots had gathered in the low branches beside it. They came every day, hoping for some scraps of food. Or maybe it was because not just all the humans and the Styx had been wiped out by the virus, but most of the mammalian species in the inner world too, and they were simply seeking the company of other living beings.

One of the parrots cawed noisily, as if it was complaining about having to wait for some leftovers.

'I saw one of the bushmen this morning,' Will said.

Elliott looked at him. With all the other predators eliminated from the inner world, the strange race of humanoids with their woody skin was the only thing that could pose a threat to them.

'It wasn't far from the spring. I was stepping over what I thought was a log on the ground, when I saw it had eyes. So it looks like they're all dead too.' Will sighed. 'It's just us, and the birds and the fish left.'

Elliott nodded. 'Talking of fish, guess what we're having for lunch.'

'Er . . . fish?' Will said, playing along with her.

'No. Mangoes,' she replied, laughing as he pulled a face. She fell silent for a moment. 'You were looking for the Doc again, weren't you?'

Will believed that the Limiters had dumped his father's body in the jungle somewhere close by, and was determined to find it. He and Elliott had already buried Colonel Bismarck and what was left of Sweeney's body beside the spring.

Without being aware he was doing it, Will turned to glance at the place on the top of the pyramid where his father had been gunned down by Rebecca Two.

'Yes, I was,' Will confessed. 'Even if Dad wasn't who I thought he was, he has a right to a proper burial. I owe him that.'

'And what about you?' Elliott asked suddenly. 'What if, all those years ago in Highfield, the Styx used their Dark Light on you, and turned you into someone else . . . someone that I fell in love with?'

'What?' Will said quickly, turning to her.

'You heard,' she said softly, putting her arms around him.

And he did the same, holding her tight.

Epilogue

'Emma, I'm sorry it didn't work out for you,' Rebecca Two said, as she held the door open for the long-limbed girl with tawny hair.

'So am I,' Emma replied, the regret evident in her eyes.

An hour earlier she'd been in the sauna with Hermione, the heat turned up as a Darklit human was thrown at her feet. It had been the masseur who had worked at the health farm, a choice specimen with his highly muscled body.

But, despite the proximity to Hermione, Emma hadn't changed. She'd experienced the shooting pains across her shoulders and the gagging sensation in her throat where her as-yet-undeveloped egg tube nestled, but that had been it.

She hadn't been induced because, quite simply, she wasn't ready for the Phase yet.

'Don't be a stranger,' Rebecca Two said as Emma made her way to the waiting car. The girl was crestfallen and didn't answer as she entered the vehicle. She'd go back to the elite girls' private school as if nothing had happened, and neither would her Topsoiler family be any the wiser about where she'd spent her Saturday.

As Rebecca Two remained outside in the chill of the late

afternoon, she watched the grey saucer of the sun as it slowly dipped towards the horizon. Without any warning, tears began to well up in her eyes.

As they'd returned Topsoil, it had been confirmed by a Limiter patrol that the passage into the inner world was impassable, sealed by what they thought had been a nuclear explosion. A second Limiter patrol had been tasked with the unpredictable journey through the zero-gravity belt, but hadn't yet reported back in. This might have been because they'd perished in the attempt, but Rebecca Two wasn't expecting good news anyway.

She'd had this feeling in her for weeks. It was as if part of her had suddenly been lopped off and, in its place, there was a dark shadow. Something had gone terribly wrong, and her twin sister was either in difficulty. Or dead.

She just knew it.

As she sniffed and wiped her eyes, the Old Styx appeared beside her. He gave her a lingering glance. It wasn't done for Styx to show such emotion, and he might have rebuked her if there hadn't been more pressing matters to attend to.

'You need to see this.'

He led her inside the building and up the steps to the viewing area at the end of the swimming pool.

As Rebecca Two peered down, she saw that the water was a murky brown from the blood and decay of the many corpses on the walkways around the pool. Plump Warrior larvae slithered along the tiles, while others had already gone into pupation, their chrysalis hanging from the walls.

'So? What am I looking at?' she asked curtly.

'There,' the Old Styx said.

She followed his gaze to a far corner of the pool. The water began to broil, then with a massive splash something burst from the surface and landed on the side.

As the filthy water drained from it, she could see a form the size of a man, but it was almost transparent, like a shrimp. Clear fluids pumped around its body as its gills fanned open, and it howled like nothing Rebecca Two had ever heard before.

'So it's not just a myth,' she whispered in awe. 'It's the Armagi'.

Acknowledgements

I would like to thank ...

My wife, Sophie, and my two sons. There wouldn't be anything without them.

Barry Cunningham, who is so much more than just my editor or publisher. Until we met up early in the summer of 2010, I had quite a different middle section planned for *Spiral*. Out of the blue, Barry asked me if the Styx were really human or not. As I do every time this question is bowled at me by readers, I tried to avoid giving him an answer, but he was insistent. Barry's like that. As I opened up a little to him and we continued to chat, it crystallised some radical ideas about the Styx women and changed the course of the book. So if you don't like the way the story turned out, you know who to speak to.

Catherine Pellegrino of Rogers, Coleridge & White – the best literary agent and hand-holder a writer could hope for.

Karen Everitt, who plays such a crucial part in the writing process as she corrects my countless mistakes using her encyclopaedic knowledge of the series.

Kirill Barybin, an exceptional young artist who got in contact through TunnelsDeeper.com, and who keeps me inspired with his work in those dark, lonely months of writing.

Andrew Douds for his invaluable advice. Any inaccuracies are entirely my own.

Rachel Hickman, Elinor Bagenal, Steve Wells and Nicki Marshall at Chicken House, and David Wyatt (cover artist extraordinaire), who together made this book what it is. And Siobhan McGowan at Scholastic in New York, who is always there for my pleas of help, no matter what time of night, and who is always so patient.

Simon and Jen Wilkie, and Craig Turner, who together with Karen Everitt run TunnelsDeeper.com, and have done so much for the series.

And a host of people I should have mentioned before now, because in various ways they've been so important in helping, supporting and influencing me as the series has progressed. They are: Mathew Horsman, Rosemary Gordon (my mother), Diana Harman (my sister), Patrick Robbins, Andrew Fusek Peters, Richard and Kathy Lynam, Chris and Sue White, Stuart Clarke, Simon and Miranda Grafftey-Smith, Ray Rough, Joel M. Guelzo, and Simon Finch.

Roderick Gordon 6 April 2011

ACKNOWLEDGEMENTS

Let's Panic Later, by Wire, from the album *154*, 1979.

The Book of Proliferation. English translation © 2000 Professor Grady Tripp, used with his kind permission.

The Son of God Goes Forth To War, 1812, Reginald Heber.

Time is on My Side, 1963, Jerry Ragovy, as later recorded by the Rolling Stones in 1964.

Every effort has been made to trace or contact all copyright holders. The publishers would be pleased to rectify any errors or omissions brought to their notice at the earliest opportunity.

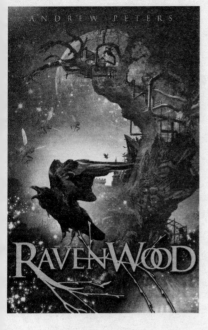